STRANGE ENGLAND

DOCTOR WHO – THE NEW ADVENTURES

Also available:

THE NEW

ADVENTURES

STRANGE ENGLAND

Simon Messingham

First published in Great Britain in 1994 by
Doctor Who Books
an imprint of Virgin Publishing Ltd
332 Ladbroke Grove
London W10 5AH

Cover illustration by Paul Campbell

ISBN 0 426 20419 0

Phototypeset by Intype, London
Printed and bound in Great Britain by
Cox & Wyman Ltd, Reading, Berks

for

my parents
Julie
and the Media Babies

special thanks to

Caz,
Mike and Simon Evans

Prologue

The woman in white was very old. She sat gracefully in the garden seat, pulling at the sun-hat which covered her grey hair.

Edith wondered how old the woman might be. She had a strange face, timeless despite the creases of age. It was like a mask.

The maid poured tea from the silver pot. The woman in white creaked forward in her chair and took a drink. Edith also accepted a cup. 'Thank you Marleen, that will be all,' she dismissed her servant. Marleen curtseyed and went away, back to the house. She was Belgian and for some reason disliked the heat of the occasional English summer day.

'Is Victoria still Queen?' asked the woman in white.

'Of course,' Edith replied stiffly. 'Have you been away?' She wondered whether this stranger was a foreigner.

A gleam came into the old woman's eye. 'On the contrary, I feel perfectly at home. I cannot think of a more idyllic setting than this. Of course, I have never travelled and am therefore ignorant of many important matters. Your lovely house, these woods, the grounds. What more could one wish for?'

Edith smiled. It was always pleasant to receive a compliment. There was a pause. The woman in white was looking around.

'Of course,' Edith said, 'we have had our share of troubles. The riots thirty years ago, about the farming machines.'

1

The woman was barely listening. Instead she seemed to answer an entirely different question: 'I knew a man once. A very great man. I was envious of his courage and integrity. He taught me many things. He claimed that perfection could only be found through endeavour and work. He was very moral. That did not make him popular with our contemporaries. I have not seen him for a very long time. One day I hoped I would match his goodness with an example of my own. Now I am dying. I hope I can live up to his great dreams.' She shook her head. 'Ah. Excellent tea, Lady Edith. Forgive an old woman's ramblings.'

Edith relaxed. Despite the woman's detached manner, she possessed an air of calm. She smiled at her. 'It's a lovely day and I don't receive much company out here. Please stay a little longer. Tell me about your life. I have little to do but listen.'

Again, the odd gleam came into the eyes of the woman in white. To Edith, it made her appear a little frightening. In her dry voice she spoke, 'My dear . . .'

Chapter 1

Mrs Irving had accompanied the girls into the grounds for lunch. She found the sun warm and pleasant. It was not too hot, just comfortable.

Charlotte sat on the woollen picnic blanket assembling various foods into strict alignment on her plate. Mrs Irving marvelled at how cool and composed the youngster looked as she picked her way through small squares of bread, plum jam, crystallized fruit and a large gleaming ham. It was only Charlotte's dark, inquisitive eyes that belied the fact that the girl was more than she seemed.

Mrs Irving lay back in the soft chair that Garvey, the butler, had brought out for her. She smiled, she was so comfortable.

'What is it?' asked Charlotte, who had clearly observed the involuntary action on her face.

'Nothing,' Mrs Irving sighed, opening her eyes and looking at the inquisitive girl. 'Where's Victoria?' She looked around from the House to the lake and back. The younger sister was nowhere to be seen, the grounds empty of anything except Alleyn's freshly cut grass.

'She went to the meadow,' replied Charlotte. 'She said she was looking for pirates. She's been reading about them.' A frown creased the girl's marble forehead. 'I told her there is no such thing in real life. But she went anyway.'

Mrs Irving laughed. The things that child dreamed up. 'Pirates,' she sighed good-naturedly and set about the serious task of dozing off.

Ted moved through the woods with all the skill and silent agility that befitted his role as gamekeeper at the House.

Abruptly he stopped and took in a deep sniff of the luxuriant, scented summer air. 'Hmm,' he muttered to himself. There was something in this smell, sure enough. He knew every inch of these woods including the smells but he couldn't put a name to this one. It was something very definitely apart from the sunshine and tall green trees around him. If Ted had been a suspicious man he would have said it felt like a storm. An omen.

Unable to shake the cobwebs of suspicion from his mind, he decided to plunge on to the little clearing about a hundred yards ahead. There the sun would be beaming confidently across that little circle of wild grass. He hoped he would feel better there.

He started to pick his way through the foliage. The hot weather had provided some of the plants with licence to grow to monstrous proportions. He'd never known them so big. Ferns with huge green and purple hands were spread out at the stumps of trees. Skeletal climbing mosses clambered in and out of one another. Even the trees themselves burned in the sun, burdened by the bright green leaves hanging like swollen fingers from their branches.

Ted shivered involuntarily and he felt goose-bumps streak down his arms. He wondered what was wrong with him. It would be nice and warm in that little clearing. It was as dark as 'night here. Uncomfortable. He laughed at himself, getting scared of a bit of darkness.

All the same, something did seem a bit odd. Something, someone staring at him. No, not staring. Eyes that burned into his back from behind. Ted whirled around, sure that someone was there. A man, lying down.

No one. He couldn't be mistaken. He'd been sure.

Breathing hard, Ted decided to press on towards the clearing. He was getting a headache. Tugging at his large handlebar moustache, he hoisted his stick up and began clearing a path to the glade.

4

Whatever it was, that odd tingling at the back of his neck, it just wouldn't shift.

Ted knew Garvey's likely reaction if he told him of his feelings. The butler would laugh, safe in the cellars of the House. It would be a different story if he was out here, if he could see those huge trunks towering over him, crowding and hounding him out of their woods. Because, if you thought about it, of course it wasn't his wood at all. It belonged to the trees. He was just a man, whatever that meant.

Ted looked about. These familiar woods didn't seem quite so well remembered now. He thought about how far away from the House he was. Too far. They could trap him here and even if he cried for help there was no one near enough to hear. He was on his own. He had walked straight into these trees without a second thought. Stupidly, like a child.

Sweat was running down his face. The woods were alive, he knew that through experience. But what if there was something more than the squirrels, the foxes, the birds? Something else, patient and waiting for just the right moment. Something in the trees.

He had to pull himself together. Trees didn't move. There was no creature waiting for him.

There was a noise in the undergrowth. Ted's nerve broke and, panting for breath, he ran for the clearing just ten yards away.

He'd never heard a noise like that before. Never. He couldn't tell what it might have been. Unless it was the trees laughing.

Suddenly, there was the clearing and he felt the sun beating away his fears. He was ashamed of his panic, even though no one had seen him. Ted took some deep breaths and felt better. His heart was pounding.

He managed a laugh. Ridiculous. He decided that it must have been a pheasant moving about in the dry bracken. He felt safe here in the clearing. In the sun. He would just stay here for a few minutes. He'd be better prepared to go back through the woods to the House. He needed some beer. He was dehydrated. The sun was getting to his brain, mixing it up.

He would go back in a minute. He couldn't go back now.

Ted gripped his stick until his knuckles whitened. He moaned. There was an unfamiliar tightness in his chest. He whirled around in pain, knowing that nothing could be happening. There was nothing staring coldly and dispassionately back at him, waiting and biding its time, ready to strike. No licking of wooden lips, in anticipation of the feast to come.

He tried to will his self-control back. It was no good. Something seemed to have taken control of his body. It was enjoying this new emotion it had created in him.

Ted made a huge effort of will and hauled himself away from the sunny glade towards the House. He had only taken two steps when he knew he was never going to make it. The black woods stared at him, inscrutable and impenetrable.

He stopped again. He tried to convince himself one last time. 'There is nothing there!' he screamed. His heartbeat was ragged and pounding inside him.

Something grabbed his ankle. It was a hand, growing from the ground. Ted tripped and fell against a tree that swallowed his right arm up to the elbow. It was stuck fast, buried in the trunk.

Frightened, Ted tried to pull himself free. It was as if his arm had become part of the tree. It had simply been sucked into the solid wood. 'Help me . . .' he whispered feebly, knowing he was beyond rescue. He was the only person who ever came into the woods.

The tree pulled again and he was sucked in further, up to the shoulder. Somewhere inside the trunk it was grinding his bones.

For a few seconds Ted thought that the hideous wheezing and screeching noise filling his ears was his own constricted breath. An immense pain blazed across his chest.

6

'Stop!' he shrieked just as the tree hauled the rest of his body into itself, crushing him. The pain was intense and total, and then life was extinguished.

The TARDIS appeared in the clearing. Needless to say, Ted did not witness the event. The tree had just enough time to revert to its normal shape by thoroughly pulverising and absorbing his body before Ace opened the door and poked her head out.

Bright sunshine. Lush woodland. A fresh breeze playing across her face. Ace sighed. This just had to be somewhere really dangerous.

She peered through the TARDIS doors with more than a degree of suspicion as she waited for the Doctor to climb into his cream linen jacket. 'You won't need that,' she called out to him. From the depths of the console room there came a low grunt.

Ace turned her attention back to the glade in front of her. It stared back, bathed in warm light. Despite the inevitable 'terrifying adventure' they were undoubtedly about to be embroiled in, she allowed herself a moment to relax and breathe in a lungful of the cool, scented air. It was so delicious that it almost curled up on her taste-buds.

Might as well enjoy the peace. It wouldn't last, not with the Doctor around. If there was one certainty in life with the TARDIS, it was the Time Lord's unique ability to attract trouble on a galactic scale. 'Wrong place wrong time' should have been emblazoned across the front of this so-called police box, warning the unfortunates it encountered.

The problem was, after three trips of rare tranquillity, Ace was getting trigger-happy. The Moscow City Carnival of 2219 had been dangerous and fun but it had lacked something. An edge.

She could tell that Bernice was feeling it too. The ex-archaeologist had started to wander the infinite corridors and rooms of the TARDIS, perhaps to find out what really made it tick. They had not seen her for a day or so, although the Doctor had sent a message for her now that they had landed. Trying to find that edge.

Ace struggled to define what she meant by an 'edge'. What was that she had heard in a dim and distant history lesson? A quote: 'There is no feeling like the feeling of being shot at and surviving.' Probably wrong. School was a million light-years away from Ace now.

As she stared out at the beautiful, exquisite woodland in front of her she realized with a sense of shock that she was missing the danger.

Bernice returned to the control room to find the Doctor sniffing the air, extracting scents like a wine-taster sampling a sumptuous bouquet. 'Lavender,' he whispered to himself. He stood half in and half out of his jacket. In his musing he missed Bernice's entrance, instead looking down at the control console as if puzzled by something. Bernice felt a warmth and affection for the troubled little man. 'Don't worry, it's not going anywhere,' she said.

The Doctor looked up at last to see that she was covered in grime. 'My dear Benny,' he replied, apparently amused by her appearance, 'you look in need of a particularly strong cup of tea.'

Bernice flopped into a chair, dust billowing from her jeans. She sighed, as if having completed a great effort of stamina and will. 'You know this machine goes on forever? I had entertained the rather misguided notion of exploring it fully. I would swear these rooms and corridors change their locations around just to irritate me. Can't you make them keep them still? In their proper place?'

The Doctor pulled a philosophical face. 'It's a universal law that I happen to like.'

'What is?'

'Change. Everything changes all the time. Either you enjoy the movement and uncertainty or you don't. Either way, everything moves on. Nothing can stay the same.'

Bernice sighed again. 'Never mind. Where are we?' She began to shake the white dust from her matted hair.

Ace shouted back from the door, 'It's a wood. Come on, hurry up. I'm getting bored hanging about here.'

The Doctor checked off a few items of data on the computer. 'Summer. High summer. And England, if I recall an oak tree correctly.' Bernice caught sight of a worried frown on his face. She shook her head. For all his fancy equipment the Doctor only seemed to care about that which he could see, hear or smell.

He walked to the doors and gazed round at the woodland in front of him. 'Shall we take a stroll?' he asked brightly.

It was just as idyllic as it seemed. The TARDIS had materialized in a roughly circular glade about twelve metres in diameter. Daisies sat mixed up in clumps with untended wild grass. The day was hot, bright and sunny. In the sky a pair of swallows chased each others' tails. Ace paced about on the grass, watching the Doctor emerge blinking from the TARDIS. He twirled his ever-present brolly.

'You won't need that,' said Ace. 'It's not going to rain.'

The Doctor looked hurt and then smiled. 'You're right. It's a ridiculous thing. I'll dispose of it immediately.' He seemed determined to enjoy himself in this beautiful weather, throwing the brolly back into the TARDIS.

'Ouch,' came an irate voice from inside. 'Thank you very much. I am hurrying.' The Doctor poked his head through the doors. 'Sorry Benny. Come on Ace, let's find a walking stick.' Ace grinned and they headed off into the woods.

Bernice finally fished the last of the accumulated filth from her hair and clothes. She stood up. 'Right,' she shouted to the outside. 'At last! I'm ready.'

She jogged to the door and looked out at an empty glade. There was no sign of the Doctor or Ace. 'Typical,' she said to herself. 'Why can that man not stay in one place for five minutes?'

Without a doubt the scenery was splendid. Ace felt curiously relaxed as she gave the immediate area a quick scan. She strolled through the woods with the Doctor, keeping her eyes open for information. The sky glowed with blue, the grass was healthy and lustrous and the temperature was hot but not unpleasant. All the time sweet air poured across them.

Surrounding the clearing had been tall, statuesque trees thick with ripe foliage. They must have arrived at the peak of summer, just prior to the leaves losing their green and embarking on the rapid descent into autumn.

'I love the summer,' remarked Ace. 'It reminds me of school holidays. On my own, for days.'

The Doctor doffed his recently donned jacket and slung it across his shoulders. He tilted his fedora to shade his face. 'Lemonade to drink and cucumber sandwiches to eat. A good solid game of village cricket.'

'Snob.'

'Normally I prefer the melancholy shades of autumn but just this once I'll agree with you. It is very pleasant.'

Ace stopped and laughed. 'You're agreeing with me? That's a first. What are you staring at?'

She observed the Doctor scrutinizing her clothing disapprovingly. 'Don't you think you'll get a bit hot in all that body armour and computerized mumbo-jumbo?'

Instinctively, Ace looked down at herself. She liked the way she dressed. She felt self-sufficient and ready for anything. In recent months that sort of criticism would have sparked off an argument. It pleased her to think they were getting on better now. She felt that the Doctor was perhaps testing the boundaries of her tolerance, and she was pleased to find that his remarks were charming rather than irritating. A sign of their new-found unity.

He looked around at the wood. 'It's odd that you say it's like the holidays you remember from your childhood.'

10

'What's odd about that?'

The Doctor remained elusive. 'Don't you feel it? It's almost unreal here. It's more the memory of a childhood summer than the reality of it. All the good bits. If you like.'

To Ace this was a clear indication that he was suspicious. She had uncomfortable memories of another time and place that was totally unreal. She sniffed, testing the air. 'You think it could be dangerous here?'

The Doctor shrugged and began to wander off. 'Let's keep an open mind,' he suggested. 'It's probably something far more strange.'

Ace followed, more out of habit than anything else.

'I say!' shouted Bernice, finally catching up with them. Ace stopped and waited for her. The older woman was flushed and panting. 'I thought you'd forgotten me,' she laughed breathlessly.

Ace nodded at the Time Lord's back, disappearing into the trees. 'It's him. He's off again.'

Bernice chuckled. 'I know what you mean. I could do with a drink.'

'Cider. In this weather it's got to be.'

'No, no, Ace. A glass of white wine, preferably German and light.'

Ace shrugged. 'Whatever you say. You're the cultured one. I just kill things.' She noticed the Doctor turn and stare disapprovingly at his companions.

'Hurry up!' he shouted, mock angry.

Ace and Bernice shared long-suffering glances. 'He's like a bloody scoutmaster,' Ace quipped.

'Out for a bracing walk in the country. All shorts and identifying roots,' Bernice replied. They linked arms and followed the Doctor's trail. 'Coming, Brown Owl!' Ace shouted.

'That's the Brownies, isn't it?'

'All right. How should I know? I used to blow them up, not go on walks with them.'

The three companions disappeared into the trees. Overhead the two swallows suddenly stiffened and plummeted, frozen solid, to the ground.

Victoria sat back onto the ruined, hollowed-out tree trunk. It lay, almost hidden, in the hip-length wild grass of the meadow.

Behind her, the edge of the woods dropped abruptly. The hill dipped rapidly to allow an almost aerial view of the House half a mile below.

As Victoria looked, she saw two tiny reclining figures. Mrs Irving and Charlotte were still lounging around by the picnic blanket.

Minutes earlier she had used this gargantuan fallen tree as a ship, dispatching hundreds of swarthy assailants from Barbary and the Orient, until coming to rest against its worn sides. It was funny, this tree. Victoria presumed it must have been a real tree once, growing out of the ground. She had only ever known it as this dark streak running through the grass like the spine of some huge, long-extinct dinosaur.

She would have to go back soon. Back to the grounds and Mrs Irving. Also Charlotte. It was strange how she and her sister could be so different. Charlotte had black hair and deep, deep eyes that contrasted sharply with Victoria's blonde hair and fair skin. Charlotte was always reading. Odd books, very dull. Science, botany and history. Victoria preferred books with stories. Pirates and dragons and especially things that happened far away.

An unfamiliar high-pitched humming interrupted her thoughts and she hauled open her heavy, drowsy eyelids, then pushed herself up from the broken tree and shoved the high grass to one side to gain a better view. The sound seemed to be emanating from somewhere in the woods.

She listened intently. It seemed to be an insistent, gentle ringing. Or humming. It permeated her whole body as if perfectly in tune with her bones and blood. The air around Victoria was scented and pungent. It felt thick and cloying.

Her eyes itched and she began to feel sleepy again, to an almost unbearable degree.

That noise. It was sweet, almost sickly, like a high-pitched choir singing in a whisper on one sustained note. It was beautiful, ethereal and almost ... yes, other-worldly. It was a voice but not human. A voice that spoke of faraway places and times. Something entirely other, far removed from the confines of the House, the grounds and the woods. Victoria felt she had been waiting all her life for such a sound.

She roused herself and collected her wits. It was the sound, it soothed but it took her away from herself, like bells in the distance. She would hardly have noticed it unless she had been listening. It seemed to tempt her. Tempt her to ... to ...

She had to find out what made the sound. There was nothing more important than a mystery to be solved. Solved and discussed with her sister. Charlotte would want to know.

Victoria gathered up her skirts, ready to discover the source of the noise. She stumbled through the grass, up the slope and into the woods.

Bernice saw the Doctor breathe in some of the thick air and glance around. Shafts of light streamed down between the trees in this dense and overgrown wood.

The two companions finally reached him. Ace looked sweaty and the body armour was clearly weighing her down. Bernice was flushed but composed, enjoying the walk. After what seemed like forever wandering the disor-ientating corridors of the TARDIS it was nice to get out in the open air again. She prided herself on being the outdoors type and longed all of a sudden for the open space of Heaven, just before ... well that was best left in the past.

She perched herself on a log. 'I must say,' she sighed. 'I'm glad I don't suffer from hay fever. The air is thick with – '

'Something's wrong.' Ace suddenly looked on full alert. She clutched the Doctor's arm with a gauntleted hand. Bernice turned to follow Ace's gaze. She perceived nothing but trees and the silken breeze. 'What is it?' she whispered. For all its occasional lack of subtlety, she had come to rely on Ace's instinct for danger.

Ace was struggling for the right words. Even the Doctor seemed caught up in the tension. He looked about warily. 'What's the matter?'

'Listen,' said Ace.

The Doctor and Bernice did so.

'There's no bird-song,' she stated. 'It's completely silent.' Ace's urgent words tailed off and Bernice saw the Doctor sighing. He straightened himself up and relaxed his knotted shoulders. Despite their new-found bonds of friendship with each other, at times he still liked playing the pompous headmaster.

'What?' Ace asked, clearly deflated and resentful that he had been so utterly dismissive of her observations.

The Doctor was impassive, superior.

'All right,' said Ace wearily, 'what have I got wrong now?'

He strode off into the trees, as if knowing Ace would follow. She did so. Bernice decided to join the couple, to give her some moral support. Ace seemed to find the Doctor's affectations less amusing than Bernice, perhaps because of the past differences they had tried so hard to overcome. Anyway, she was interested in the explanation.

The Doctor took on his familiar air of the sage imparting great knowledge to the aspiring novice. Bernice wondered how much of these moods was self-mockery and how much he actually believed the sound of his own voice. He stared out at the wood. 'Birds,' he stated loftily, 'in England are especially silent in August. The thrush, swallow, wren and blackbird become shy. Gilbert White called August "the most mute month" because of this.'

'Gilbert who?'

'Then again, I did give him the phrase so I am entitled

14

to the presumption of using it myself. Superb naturalist, Gilbert, but could barely string two sentences together. Used to preserve his subjects in brandy. Always found that a bit excessive for keeping things in stasis. Waste of good brandy too.'

Ace was stifling a yawn when the Doctor stopped suddenly next to a large and venerable oak. 'What now?' she asked disinterestedly. She began to kick at the heads of a clump of stinging nettles.

'Can you hear something?' enquired the Doctor, seemingly preoccupied with listening.

Bernice decided to get involved again. 'What is it?'

'Shh. Listen.'

'Thank you very much.'

Ace inclined her head. After some seconds she came to a decision. 'Can't hear a thing.'

Bernice couldn't resist a jibe. 'August is the most mute month, is it not.'

The Doctor ignored her. Ace tried again. 'What is it? Answer me.'

He turned to her in distracted irritation. 'If I knew I wouldn't be asking you, would I?'

'Well I don't know, do I?'

Bernice was confused. 'You don't know what?'

'What?' Now Ace was confused.

'Look,' the Doctor said with an enforced patience, 'I'm just saying I thought I heard something.'

Ace was clearly restraining herself from thumping him. 'I know. I'm asking what the sound sounded like.'

Bernice misheard, trying to listen for the noise. 'What the sound sounded like?'

'Just tell me!'

The Doctor put a finger to his lips. 'Quiet. I'm listening.'

Silence.

'Doctor,' said Bernice, as reasonably as she could manage. 'There is no sound.'

All at once a faint, high-pitched humming, like singing, permeated the warm, still air of the wood.

Mrs Irving flinched suddenly. It was as if an icy wind had whipped itself quickly and thoroughly through her, fleecing her bones. Goose-pimples erupted on her arms and legs despite the heat of the sun.

For a split second, almost imperceptibly, she seemed to see the figure of a woman standing up there on the slope, in the meadow with the fallen tree. Almost as if she had been standing up there herself. Strange. Mrs Irving hadn't even been looking in that direction.

What was also strange was that she could still see the woman now, tiny and distant, a mile away in the meadow. She could distinctly see her smile. The woman was like a dark smudge against the sun-drenched grass on the hill. The smile contained no warmth. It seemed to penetrate everything: clothes, skin, blood, bones. It was a smile that could stop a heart. Mrs Irving groaned at a sudden constriction in her chest.

'Are you all right?' asked a voice from somewhere beyond that terrible grin. Charlotte.

It brought Mrs Irving back to life. She hauled herself out of her garden chair. She felt dizzy, sick. She could not bear to recall that smile. It was death, and that was unheard of here. Charlotte was immediately at her side, small arms wrapping around her for support.

'I feel ill,' Mrs Irving managed, not wanting to alarm the child without really knowing what that meant. Something, a dark cloud, burrowed into her mind. It held back any further words. Charlotte stared at her with fierce eyes.

Mrs Irving was hot, for once too hot, and the air was thick with dust and pollen. Grains like boulders that could enter the lungs and choke her.

Charlotte looked puzzled. Mrs Irving struggled to come to terms with these new, confusing feelings.

There was a brief moment of bewilderment. Then it all came clear.

Victoria!

She began to run towards the meadow. She was vaguely

16

aware that Charlotte was following. Panic flooded her mind and she ran faster.

Not for the first time in her adventures, Victoria cursed the heavy crinolines that weighed her down as she trudged through the bright wood. She hoisted up the various layers of white lace and cloth and pushed her way through some particularly bloated ferns. Beneath them somewhere came the sound of trickling water. The plants were heavily scented and the hot weather seemed to capture that scent and leave it hanging in the air. Coupled with this odour, the ferns were doubly hard to break through.

The sound did not help matters. It was still there, leading Victoria on in its clear, ringing way. Although pleasant, she was beginning to find the noise a little too insistent and piercing. It was the musical equivalent of having sugar rubbed into the teeth. One could have too much of a good thing. Still, she was determined to locate its source, somewhere under this fleshy plantlife that obscured the ground beneath it.

Cocking her head slightly, Victoria tried to gain a precise direction for the origin of the humming. Now she had halted in her tracks she realized she was perspiring heavily under her summer dress.

At last, she seemed to have detected the source of the noise: a large clump of bluebells under an oak tree. The sweet, sickly ringing emanated from the centre of those flowers, as if the petals themselves were sounding. Unnervingly, the tree they were crowding round was so thick with leaves that it cast the clump into dark shadow. This shadow was made even thicker by the contrast with the bright sunlight all around it. It was as if the tree had formed a dark canopy over the bluebells to deliberately keep the light at bay.

Victoria pushed her way impetuously through the swollen purple flowers. They seemed almost unnaturally healthy, their heads bursting with colour as if straining to uproot and break themselves free from their earthly bonds. They packed themselves tightly together like spectators attempting to gain a better view of Victoria as she battled her way to the centre. She fancied they were chattering to each other about this colourless stranger that had entered their midst. Their smell was pungent and tart, reminiscent somehow of the persistent shrill of that humming.

Victoria wondered where the sound was coming from. Surely the flowers couldn't be making that noise, their domed heads acting as bizarre phonograph horns?

She spotted a sudden flurry of wings. Not bird's wings, there was no flapping. A buzz of incredible motion like a bee's except much larger and faster than the eye could follow.

Victoria gasped. It was an insect. A creature about as big as a trout but thin, slender. Its wings were large, delicate sheets of gossamer that pounded with a fierce energy. It was like an enlarged, fairy-tale dragonfly.

Bending closer to it, Victoria marvelled at its incredibly thin, segmented body. Thorax and abdomen were struck through with shining blue and green colours that seemed to shimmer like oil. Its legs were spindly and short. The whole creature looked as if it had been fashioned from glass by the hand of some master craftsman. Beautiful but capable of shattering under the slightest pressure.

The most striking, wondrous feature of the insect, however, was its head. Again, it was tiny and could have been sculpted by patient, precise hands. And the eyes. To Victoria they looked almost melancholy, human. There was a slight spiny black crest at the back of the fragile head with barbs that seemed as soft as down.

A long, thin, reed-like proboscis protruded from beneath the eyes. It was from here that the high-pitched mournful humming was being generated. The insect must have possessed an incredible set of lungs to produce a sound that was so penetrating in volume and intensity.

Almost as if noticing Victoria, the insect ceased its furious flapping and the transparent, membranous wings folded back on themselves. It became still, but the sound continued.

'You're beautiful,' she whispered, awestruck.

The creature started suddenly as if in reaction to the sound of her voice and it cease its singing. The silence was odd after the minutes of steady, unbroken noise.

Victoria knelt down even closer to the insect, completely taken in by its exotic delicacy and beauty. The bluebells surrounding her smothered her with their pungent pollen, fanning thick scented air into her face. Time was absolutely still as she sat transfixed by the creature.

The insect turned itself elegantly around on its needle-thin legs and faced Victoria. Its eyes were pools of rich, velvet darkness which held her in a penetrating stare. The downy abdomen pulsed once like a dog shaking water away and the chilling, silver humming began again. It surrounded and smothered Victoria with its subtle tones.

She felt herself drifting off into visions of hot, far-away Eastern realms, with the heavy tang of spice clinging to the air. Warm, bright blue oceans were filled with yellow-sailed ships pounding through surf. In the music she saw vast expanses of desert with dusty, ancient pyramids visible in the heat haze. Jungles cloaked green with mystery, boiling swamps steaming with heat . . .

The insect unfolded its wings and flicked into motion. The head lifted first, followed by the rest of its thin body. It rose from the ground and hovered in front of Victoria's face. She stared at it in the fixated, hypnotized way a snake stares at its charmer.

The spell broke for a second and Victoria came to her senses. She clapped her hands in delight. 'So you can fly!' she laughed.

The insect, in one quick, smooth motion, flew into her mouth.

Victoria felt the warm, furry body dart between her lips. The tiny legs scurried past her teeth and it hoisted itself into her throat.

Instinctively, Victoria attempted to retch, her neck constricting. However, the blockage in her windpipe forced the movement back again. She felt like she was drowning. It was moving about inside, trying to gain a purchase and this irritated her throat even more. She felt her head might burst.

Victoria thrashed about on the heap of flowers as the insect continued to burrow its way into her lungs. She leapt up and staggered through the bluebells, only to fall again before she could break free.

Then it stung her in the vocal chords. She felt a clean incision as if with an extremely sharp needle.

Victoria's last sensation before fainting was that she had started to sing.

All of a sudden, the sound that Ace and the others had been straining to follow stopped. She halted, confused. There was a pause for about thirty seconds and it started up again, only now considerably louder and more powerful.

Ace shuddered. The sound, although undeniably gorgeous in its purity, was not a warm sound. It was not quite a human voice but of sufficient approximation to put the wind up her. In her mind she conjured up the image of a Cyberman trying to sing. A choir of them, all standing in a row with hymn-books. With this mental picture firmly in her mind she was less apprehensive about finding the source, whatever it might be, of that hideous song.

They moved through the woods, more cautious now.

The Doctor was on full Time Lord alert. Ace could see his ears were cocked and his head was darting from side to side, all senses attuned to every scrap of data. He was clearly worried. 'I don't think Gilbert White noted anything like this,' he whispered.

Ace realized that was supposed to be a joke. The Doctor really was worried. It looked like they were going to have their terrifying adventure after all.

Bernice turned her head to him, she had noticed it too.

'What on earth is that noise?' she asked, her body tense. 'It's coming from over there. Those flowers.'

The bluebells were rich, dark and heavy as if bloated with purple ink. They were pressed tightly together and wrapped around the dark oak that loomed over them. For some reason, the flushed petals reminded Ace of some poisoned, stagnant pond thick and dense with weeds, undisturbed for months. Its scent sent her mind reeling. Rich and ripe.

'Flowers. Waving gently in the summer breeze,' the Doctor remarked wistfully, eyebrows knotted as he peered into the clump.

'What d'you...? I get it, no breeze any more.' Ace answered her own question.

The Doctor smiled a troubled smile. 'You're learning,' he said pensively.

The song, very loud now, seemed to be emanating from the middle of the patch of bluebells.

'Strange,' the Doctor whispered to himself. 'A strange England indeed.'

A girl suddenly leapt up from the flowers, leaving thick sandy globules of pollen in her wake. She seemed to be performing some bizarre dance of panic, arms and legs frantically flailing around.

'The song. It's coming from her!' shouted the Doctor.

Ace had to agree; the chilling choir sound was booming, if a sound so sugary could boom, from the girl's vibrating mouth.

She was dressed, and Ace was thinking that she must be well hot in them, in layer upon layer of lace and crinoline. She desperately thrashed about. Her face was beetroot-red, contrasting with the frame of strawberry-blonde hair. She was choking.

'Goodness!' the Doctor cried out in shock. The persistent ringing continued unabated.

As Ace stood rigid with surprise, the girl collapsed back out of sight into the velvet arms of the iridescent bluebells. Instantly, Ace reacted and dived into the flower bed, snap-

21

ping and crushing their rich heads. Somewhat more cautiously, Bernice and the Doctor followed.

When Ace reached the struggling girl she stopped. There was an innocence in those sky-blue eyes that pierced the thickest of body-armoured skins. The girl couldn't have been more than sixteen. She had a face that looked as if time had left it alone. There was not a blemish or imperfection on it. Tears sprang to Ace's own eyes. She brushed them away. They were two opposites meeting, innocence and hard, hard experience. Just for a second the two women connected, then the innocent's eyes bulged and she began to panic again.

There was something in her mouth. At first, Ace thought it was a sock or something similar that had maybe been used to gag her. Then it moved.

The Doctor reached the girl and jumped back, aghast. A second passed and the scientific detachment appeared to click in. 'What on earth is that?' he said to Ace. Bernice peered over his shoulder and screwed up her face in disgust. Ace tried to hold the girl's head still.

'Right,' Bernice said to the Doctor, 'what do we do about this?'

Ace marvelled at her friend's composure in spite of the irritating sound. It was disrupting her concentration, preventing her brain from functioning in an ordered way. It was coming from the child's mouth but was clearly beyond the range of any human voice.

'Doctor!' Ace insisted. The Time Lord seemed to be particularly affected by the sound. She noted that perhaps it wasn't always an advantage to have super space hearing abilities. He looked as if he was trying to put himself into one of those self-induced trances his species was capable of. Ace wished she had that ability. Anything to get that damn noise out of her head.

Bernice had clearly decided to act. She reached for the girl's mouth to drag the furry, buzzing thing from it.

'No!' The Doctor pulled her away. 'You'll kill her.'

'How do we get it out?' she asked.

22

'Quiet,' the Doctor snapped. 'I'm thinking.'

'And she's suffocating.'

The girl spasmed once and went limp, her eyes closing. The sound dropped for an instant and then started up again. Her throat pulsed and shifted as the insect manoeuvred itself into a more comfortable position.

'She's dead,' said Ace, despairing but still cradling the girl's head. She had failed. They had just stood there and watched.

The Doctor knelt down beside the girl and with a sense of urgency his hands pressed onto her chest. 'She's still breathing, just. We've got to get her out of here. The insect seems to have attached itself to her throat. She must be receiving oxygen from somewhere, perhaps filtered through the body of the parasite.'

Ace relaxed slightly; at least the girl was still alive. 'Why can't we just pull the thing out?'

'We don't know how it's fixed itself to her, we might drag her lungs out with it.'

Bernice sighed, revealing some of the frustration behind the composure. 'Well, we can't just leave her lying here.'

'I know,' said the Doctor abruptly. 'What do you think I'm trying to do? Put her in the school choir?'

Ace took command, for once feeling the most level-headed person around. 'Shut up! Both of you. We need to get this sorted!'

Bernice turned away. She kicked at the heads of the bloated flowers.

'I'm sorry,' said the Doctor. 'It's this sound, it's driving me mad.'

'It's all right,' muttered Bernice, 'I just feel so helpless.'

Ace reminded them of the urgency of the situation. 'Look, this is no time for self bloody pity. Think of something.'

The Doctor grinned and reached into his trouser pocket. He pulled out a small battered-looking box constructed of cardboard.

'What's that?' asked Ace. 'Drugs? A medi-pack?'

23

The Doctor shook his head and opened the lid of the box. 'Even better,' he said. 'Wax ear-plugs. I can't think with all this racket.'

He lifted one brown blob and inserted it into an ear. He then repeated the process with the other. 'That's better!' he shouted.

Ace looked at the girl lying still and unconscious on the bed of bluebells. She was so pale compared to the overripe blooms. She looked like some beautiful, mournful, marble statue. It was easy to believe that she was dead.

The Doctor placed his long fingers around the girl's throat, careful not to excite the insect too much. Calmly he probed the jaw of the unconscious, placid child. Ace watched him work. There was no exterior damage. The insect had stuck to its job. He pressed the throat softly.

'Can you get it out?' asked Ace.

'Eh?' shouted the Doctor.

Ace pulled one of the plugs from his ear. 'Can you get it out?' she repeated.

The Doctor shook his head. 'Unsurprisingly, it seems to have a grip on something inside the girl. It's stuck fast.' He snatched the plug back and replaced it. He took a deep breath and shouted, 'This is not going to be easy.'

Ace turned away; she could not look any more. The child's eyes had opened slightly, either through the Doctor's examinations or some unconscious reflex. They seemed to be staring in fear at her. Tears pricked Ace's face and the sound hammered at her brain, shrill and persistent. She had a considerable headache. Help was obviously required. They had no idea where they were or in what direction they might find civilization. The Doctor was preoccupied with the insect. She had to make a decision. Starting to run, she headed up the slope and into the woods.

'Ace!' shouted Bernice.

'I'm going to see if I can fetch help,' Ace bellowed back and disappeared into the trees.

The Doctor apparently neither saw nor heard her leave. Bernice looked about, not knowing what action to take. Lost in her thoughts, she failed to hear a second tiny voice join in the song, a few metres away in the flowers.

Bernice looked up the hill once more, in case Ace was coming back. She sighed. The only thing she could think of to do was help the Doctor. There was no sense in both of them wandering off and getting lost. She knelt down by the girl.

Examining her mouth, she could just see slight barbs attached to the abdomen of the insect. Doubtless the creature would be covered in such spines in order to prevent the very task that the Doctor needed to perform. Something else was happening too. The girl's skin was becoming coarsened and white. Blue veins were beginning to protrude from her arms. Something vital was being drained from the child.

She was dying. The song was getting louder and louder as the insect gained strength. How much time was left to her was anyone's guess. The sound looked as if it was penetrating even the Doctor's ear-plugs. He winced in annoyance.

'Any ideas?' she shouted into his ear as much to distract him from the sound as to get an answer.

The Doctor shook his head, continuing to feel the girl's throat. 'Keep talking to me,' he said. 'It helps me concentrate.'

Bernice racked her brains to think of something to say. 'What sort of insect is it?' she asked, to spark off some sort of reaction.

'I can't get it out of my head the feeling that this insect is intelligent,' he replied. 'An evil, malign intelligence. It knows what I'm trying to do.'

Bernice thought for a minute. 'Doctor,' she countered, 'how can a creature like this be evil or malign? At this level of intelligence it's working on instinct. Millions of years of evolutionary programming. How can it be capable of making moral decisions?'

The Doctor sat up and stared at the still child. He looked sleepy, tired all of a sudden. He seemed to be trying to concentrate on something out of his vision. She felt it too. Her mind was wandering, her thoughts becoming fixed on their debate. It was like being drunk. Aware and not aware, the brain refusing to be budged off its subject.

'You may find it odd, Benny,' he said slowly, 'but I have always believed in evil as a force.' Bernice felt weird. Drugged. So did the Doctor, apparently. She tried to follow his pattern of thoughts. She found his words soothing, reassuring. He laughed. 'I made a bit of a name for myself on Gallifrey, back in the old days. Most of my contemporaries considered notions like good and evil to be outdated, archaic and redundant and found my preoccupation with such morality to be incomprehensible.' He slowly raised a wagging, unco-ordinated finger. 'Then again, they didn't steal a TARDIS did they? Didn't go round the universe to discover evil for themselves.'

Bernice struggled to comprehend. Was the Doctor actually opening up about his past? That was a first. Or was it just another one of his elaborate stories, designed to conceal what his real motivations were. Or was it a double bluff? You could go round in circles thinking about this. Round and round and round . . .

She watched through some kind of haze as the Doctor started awake. She wondered what was happening, trying to pull herself out of the daze. It was as if she'd been in a trance, lost in his words. She looked at the Doctor. His eyes were heavy, thick with sleep. It took a supreme effort of will to stay conscious.

As Bernice watched the Doctor shake his head to clear his thoughts, the second insect jumped for his throat. It was because of this shaking that it missed. A blur of frenzied, gossamered, furry wings slapped his face. He fell backwards and the insect sped towards him again.

Somehow he snapped his hands together just as the creature attacked. Bernice saw a thin, needle-like tongue burst from the vibrating mouth of the insect and snake toward the Doctor's face. He threw his head backwards. Grasping the barbed body, he cried out as the spines dug into his hands. It attempted to wriggle out of his grip and his blood soaked into its abdomen. It was clearly not as delicate as it looked. It seemed to take all of the Doctor's strength to keep hold of the thing.

Bernice tried to move to help him but the song, that hypnotic sound, kept her immobile. She watched the Doctor's struggles as if in a dream.

He swung himself over onto his knees in an attempt to pin the insect to the ground. The pain in his hands was clearly increasing. It twisted itself almost deliberately, in order to rake its spines across his raw palms. Crying out, the Doctor looked as if he was going to have to let go. Bernice willed herself to wake up. She leapt to her feet and felt her mind burst free. She breathed in and coughed.

'Benny!' shouted the Doctor, teeth gritted in agony. He rolled around, blood streaming like ribbons from his hands.

Bernice looked around and saw his walking stick lying a metre away in the flowers. She dived across the knoll. 'Let go of it!' she shouted, brandishing the stick.

Moaning, the Doctor pinned the insect down, trying to crush it into the foliage. He let go and was up in an instant, heading for Bernice, blood pouring from his hands. It shot up from the flowers and darted towards him. The sweet sound burst out loud on his tail and there was a flutter of ferocious wings. 'Duck!' cried Bernice.

He dived to the ground. The insect flew past him and changed its target to Bernice with frightening acceleration. In one swift movement she whirled the stick round at the approaching blur of blue and silver. The insect separated, neatly bisected, and fell lightly into the bluebells.

The Doctor began bandaging his ruined hands. Bernice was looking down at the body of the insect. It lay in two halves on the ground in front of them. 'Obviously that

27

damned sound has a way of diverting your thoughts and lulling you into a semi-comatose state,' she deduced.

The Doctor grunted. 'A low-grade hypnotism. Perhaps the sound is a defence mechanism to disrupt and drug the concentration of would-be predators.'

'Or prey,' Bernice offered grimly.

'Yes. Victims would be attracted, like us, to investigate the source of the sound, follow it and become ensnared. It was only good fortune that prevented us from ending up like this unfortunate girl.'

Bernice nodded in agreement. 'This begs other questions,' she said. 'What is this insect? Where does it come from and what is it doing in nineteenth-century England?'

The Doctor looked thoughtful for a moment. 'As far as I know no such creature is native to Earth in this time period. Anyway, we have other matters that concern us.' He was staring down at the girl.

Bernice looked at the child. It was obvious that she was going to die. Her skin was waferlike and colourless. Something was still being drained out of her. Bernice bit her lip. She looked up at the Doctor. 'We have to remove this thing as quickly as possible,' she said. 'But how?' At present, there seemed only one option and that was a very unpleasant one.

The Doctor seemed to be reading her mind again. 'Surgery. That's the only way as far as I can see,' he said, his tone revealing the reticence he felt for the idea.

'What about your hands?' Bernice asked.

He held up his palms, bandages stained with blood. 'What choice do we have?' he replied. 'We must do whatever we can.'

The Doctor's ruminations were broken up by a shout. Bernice looked up to see another young girl racing towards them, this one with black hair, with a red-faced, matronly woman panting along behind.

The woman collapsed down near the child lying in the flowers and stared incredulously at the thing lodged in her throat. She looked up at the Doctor in confusion. 'Victoria! I knew something was happening. What is it?'

The Doctor pressed the old woman's arm gently, 'She needs help,' he said kindly, 'urgently. Is there anywhere to take her?'

The woman stared at him. 'Are you a doctor?' she asked.

The young girl with black hair was some distance from the injured child, wary but interested. With amazing detachment she asked, 'What is that in her mouth?'

The Doctor ushered her away. 'Keep back. There are more of those insects around here.'

Bernice stared at the new arrivals. 'Please,' she said to the older woman. 'She needs help now. We must get her out of here.'

With the Doctor's help, she lifted up the limp body of the dying girl. Victoria. If that was her name.

The older woman seemed lost in a world of her own. Her blotchy red face stared around blindly. She tried to form words. 'That sound . . . it's beautiful . . .'

'It's coming from Victoria,' stated the dark-haired girl. She looked enquiringly at the Doctor.

'I know,' he replied. 'We must carry her. Now. Come on Benny.'

Spurred on, Bernice shouldered the girl and together they carried her out of the nest of flowers.

Mrs Irving fussed around Victoria whilst Charlotte led the way, guiding them. They moved out of the woods and away from the knoll. Bernice felt her head clear. That sound, coupled with the scent from those flowers had been enough to drive anyone mad.

They emerged from the trees and she found herself staring down a steep-sided meadow at a large mansion house. It lay in a valley about half a mile below them. There were neat, well ordered lawns surrounding it and a lake that glittered at the foot of the hill opposite. All in all a very inviting and civilized place. The mansion seemed to be built primarily of brown sandstone and was a mixture of Gothic ramparts and baroque decorative balconies. Despite the intricate construction there was a pleasing symmetry about the building that appeared relaxing and exciting at the same time. Bernice mentally applauded the architect's talent and taste.

Suddenly her attention was drawn to the lake. Squinting, she could just make out the figure of a man standing by the water, or even in it. Strangely, there seemed to be smoke coming out of him.

'Come on Benny,' said a puffing Doctor, 'this is no time for day-dreaming.'

Bernice frowned, puzzled by the vision. She shrugged and followed Charlotte down through the long grass of the meadow. All the while the sun burned brightly and not a bird sang.

Chapter 2

The small door stuck sligthly, then creaked open. Garvey poked his long, thin head through the gap and looked into the labyrinthine wine cellar.

The place resembled a vast, dry, underground dungeon stacked not with prisoners but with row upon row of dust-whitened glass bottles. The rickety wooden racks stretched off into the darkness, containing vintages from untold past pressings. Garvey took a pride in knowing the location of every type, colour and flavour of wine in the cellar.

As he often told Ted on their numerous evenings spent down here, he looked upon this room as his hobby. Granted, it was included in his duties as the butler to oversee this part of the house as much as any other but it was this cellar that took the greater part of his attention. And love, he would add if pressed.

There was a pleasant feeling of security here. Garvey would sit in his chipped but sturdy oaken chair at the end of the day, pour himself a moderate glass of Ted's ale and relax, content that everything was running smoothly, as it always did. This was his library. Everything was noted, ordered and comfortable. It was snug and quiet like some faithful, slothful pet. Sometimes he fancied he could hear the House singing to him. A low murmuring voice composed of millions of creaks and echoes twisting their way down into the roots of the building.

However, as he pushed the door open more fully, Garvey sensed that something had changed. He had the distinct impression that just as he had peeped his head through the doorway someone had leapt agilely out of his vision.

Of course, that was impossible because he had the only key. However, he still felt a blurred after-image upon his eyes that he could not attribute to anything but movement just out of the centre of his focus. Suddenly, the enthusiasm for choosing the night's wine had gone. There seemed to be an extra weight down here. For the first time Garvey felt claustrophobic. The rafters propping up the roof looked, in the gloom, like the roots of gnarled, evil old trees for all their man-made regularity.

He forced himself to go on with his daily routine and wandered off down one of the aisles looking, without vigour, for a suitable bottle.

Perhaps he required company. It was a demanding enough job running this house for the young ladies and organizing the domestics. He would invite old Ted down here tonight and they would laugh at his fears. Ted would tell him how the grounds and the woods were coming along. They suited each other well. They were like magnets, equal but opposite. No pressure, just two professionals chatting of an evening about each other's work.

'Garvey,' whispered a voice in the darkness.

The butler froze. He leaned his bony frame against the rack. The whisper had been so faint as to be almost imperceptible. Perhaps he had imagined it.

His old heart was doing something unfamiliar. It was thumping in his chest. He did not understand why his scalp felt tight, why he was short of breath.

Quickly, Garvey pulled a bottle from its shelf and, without looking at the label, he hurried back down the aisle.

He reached the end of the racks and stopped, puzzled. Stretching ahead of him was another row of shelves. Surely he should be at the door. He hadn't gone that far into the cellar.

He stopped to think. After a minute he began to stride onwards along the second aisle. It was too dark to see the door on the far wall. It still had to be there.

32

He reached the end of the aisle. Another one stretched away ahead of him.

Confused now, Garvey felt a sense of disorientation. He might have forgotten passing one aisle but surely not two. The wooden shelves blurred and shifted in front of his eyes as he tried to understand the unfamiliar emotion coursing through his body.

He just had to keep going.

As he walked, Garvey heard someone move in the aisle parallel to his. He creaked his tired head round and something ducked out of view. Dust, cobwebs and bottles obscured a clear vision but someone was there, totally still. Just to trick his sight. He squinted harder.

There was someone there. He could sense it. Another presence. Something new and untapped in his brain shrieked. For the first time in his existence, Garvey registered fear.

He ran, not knowing why. Behind him, something big crashed through bottles and wood. He did not look back. The darkness threw itself up like a curtain in front of him.

Whatever was behind him was closing. He summoned up every last drop of strength and plunged on, knees cracking like pistol shots. He let loose the bottle of wine in his hand.

Just as he thought the thing behind him had him in its grip he collided with the open door. It knocked him flat.

The presence ceased to be there. All was quiet again. Garvey looked around and saw the comfortable, yet changed, surroundings of the wine cellar. A few yards along the aisle, a single bottle lay shattered on the ground, its contents bleeding into the floor.

He wondered what had happened to him.

Hauling himself into his chair, he waited for his heart to settle down. It was not like him to behave like that in the dark. It must be that loneliness he'd been thinking about. Get Ted down for a drink. That was what he needed.

Garvey selected a bottle at random from the shelf and

hurried through the door, unaware that every drop of wine in the cellar had soured to vinegar inside its glass.

Bernice gave a low whistle as they bundled Victoria through the large open doors of the House and into a porticoed hall.

Inside, it was a work of art. Intricate, detailed and statuesque, from the coloured crystalline windows to the ornate sculptured brickwork. Flowers decorated the stone in the large entrance hall. Lining the walls, tucked away in cornices, white marble statues stared at them, draped with garlands.

Bernice had helped the Doctor and Charlotte carry Victoria down from the steep meadow. The insect's sinister song had scraped at her ears. It had been a nightmare. Mrs Irving had flapped around them, panicking and getting in the way of constructive help.

All the while, something about the behaviour of the two women was bothering Bernice. She couldn't put her finger on it yet but there was definitely something skew-whiff about them. It wasn't that their concern and panic wasn't sincere. In fact, the opposite was true, they were too sincere, as if they'd never experienced these emotions before.

Charlotte was a cool one. Carefully controlling her worry, she had acted sensibly and logically about helping her sister out. Bernice liked her, she had a strength, even if she did not yet know it herself.

Bernice bore the weight of Victoria's tiny shoulders with determination. Their heavy steps echoed through the hall as they hefted the weight of the barely breathing girl. The insect's song, with Victoria's voice, bored into their ears like some sugar-coated worm. The booming acoustics of the hall made the sound even more penetrating and unbearable. In the girl's throat she could see tiny, rippling movements betraying the presence of the delicate monster. What really got to her was that sound, now the worst it had ever been. It reminded her of bubbleshake, the sweet but fatal drug she'd been addicted to. It seemed to symbolize the life being drained out of the girl. Victoria was appallingly pale and her breathing barely perceptible.

They laid the girl down onto the cold marble slabs of the floor. The four of them stepped back to try and gain a clearer picture of what to do next.

The Doctor looked worried. Bernice wondered what they were going to do. If it was going to be surgery it would have to be quick. She cast her mind back over the various field dressings and impromptu operations she had had to perform over the years. This wouldn't be the most difficult, just the most fiddly. No room for error. 'Doctor,' she gently cajoled, 'she's dying.'

Victoria was now nothing but a bag of bones wrapped tightly in skin as white as the marble floor.

'Keep her still,' replied the Doctor pensively. 'It may lessen the damage.' He seemed to be thinking furiously, trying to work out a way to gain time.

The singing took on a different timbre here. It bounced around the pillars, drilled through the ears of the unwilling audience and ended up high in the decorated ceiling as if trying to escape.

'What can we do? What can we do?' cried Mrs Irving, looking for hope in the worried faces around her.

'Oh, give it a rest!' Bernice snapped. She never liked people panicking around her. Losing your grip was the worst thing anyone could do in a crisis. It had a habit of being infectious and that noise was getting too much to bear without any other bother. The Doctor was clearly steaming through his brain to find a solution. The best thing would be to give the woman something to do. Take her mind off the problem. Get her out of the way. 'Mrs Irving,' she asked politely, 'would you fetch a blanket for Victoria, please?'

Bernice was relieved to see her plan work. Gladly, the distraught woman rushed off through one of the doors leading from the hall.

Charlotte peered into Victoria's face. 'She looks pale. What's it doing to her?'

Bernice was impressed with the girl's composure but found her detachment disturbing. 'That's your sister, isn't it?' she asked.

Charlotte nodded. 'How can you help her?'

Bernice decided it was better not to tell her too much about their plans. As far as she knew medical knowledge was very primitive in the nineteenth century and they would have to be careful. The Doctor was hot on not slipping anachronisms into the wrong time period. Well, in this instance Bernice disagreed. As far as she was concerned anything that would help would have to do. 'Don't worry, the Doctor knows what he's doing.'

Charlotte looked confused. Again, something about her worried Bernice. She was too analytical.

The Doctor examined Victoria for the umpteenth time. He rubbed his chin with his hand. He seemed to be thinking aloud. 'There simply isn't time for anything but the most drastic action. Keep calm and think. There has to be another way. There always is. I'm the Doctor, aren't I?'

Victoria coughed. It sounded like a large, dirty belch. The singing halted and started up again.

Charlotte knelt down, taking her sister's ice-cold hand in her own. The Doctor dropped his gaze and stared at the floor as if in utter despair. Bernice could see the girl only had a short time left to her. It was the moment to get the Doctor to turn his Time Lord brain off and act instinctively. Rarely had she seen him so paralysed with indecision. She placed a gentle arm on his shoulder. 'Come on Doctor. There's no choice. Let's do it.'

Abruptly the Doctor whipped his head up and stared at his companion. For a second Bernice thought he was going to snap at her. Instead he nodded wearily and said, 'Of course, you're right. Thank you Benny. We haven't much time. Charlotte, find Mrs Irving and tell her to get some hot water, bandages and towels.'

Charlotte nodded, unclear as to what the Doctor was going to do.

'Go!' shouted Bernice, desperate to get on and save the girl. Charlotte ran off, footsteps echoing on the stone.

Slowly, the Doctor produced a leather bag from his voluminous pockets. He unclipped the bag and unrolled the creased leather. 'You're going to have to keep her breathing. Hold her throat open while I ... do it.'

Inside the bag, lying in a neat row, were six glinting surgical blades. The Doctor looked at them as if hypnotized. Bernice placed her hand on his shoulder again. 'Come on Doctor. You've got to save her.'

Grimly, the Doctor selected one of the scalpels and pulled it from its docket. It hissed as the metal brushed against leather.

'No!' shouted the returning Mrs Irving, weighed down with the equipment. The Doctor closed his eyes as if in pain.

Bernice pushed down hard onto Victoria's chest. The insect's song was boosted briefly with the expulsion of breath. The Doctor raised the scalpel and held it to the throat.

Charlotte arrived in the hall and managed to hold Mrs Irving back from rushing in to interfere. 'Leave them!' she commanded.

Talking quickly through gritted teeth, the Doctor gave instructions to Bernice. She suspected they were for his own sake as much as hers. 'I'll make one quick incision vertically down the neck, avoiding the jugular. You ... you'll have to get the throat closed the instant I've pulled the insect out. Then it's stitching and sterilizing.' He closed his eyes, 'Ready?'

Bernice nodded. 'Don't worry,' she said. 'It'll work.' They both paused.

'Do it! Do it now!' shouted Charlotte.

The Doctor checked the precise area for incision.

'Wait,' said Bernice suddenly. An expression of frustration appeared in her eyes. She fought it off and her

37

fingers raced to find a pulse. She looked up at the Doctor. 'She . . . she's stopped breathing.'

The Time Lord froze, scalpel poised.

'She's dead,' Bernice said without any intonation at all.

For the first time, a chill wind blew through the House. They all felt it, from Garvey, now rushing through corridors to the entrance hall, to the two kitchen maids preparing the pastry for the evening meal.

The icy air made its way along the wide, luxurious carpets of the ground floor, up the lush staircases with their carved banister rails and into the crisp, lightly furnished bedrooms.

Tillie the maid felt the wind as it crept under the door and into the girls' rooms. Peter felt it as he carried two pairs of shoes for cleaning downstairs. Even the obese Mrs Chamberlain felt this new phenomenon as she cleaned the scullery.

The only person who did not feel the wind was Alleyn and that was because he was lying in his greenhouse, strands of thorny rose branches twisted round his neck and stuffed into his mouth. He had been dead since morning, just after Ted had gone walking into the woods. Alleyn had arrived to do his regular morning's watering to discover his carefully cultivated plants waiting for him.

Though nobody was consciously aware of it, this chilly gust of wind was enough to make them feel distinctly uneasy. This was a house where nothing changed, nothing ever disrupted the status quo and where there were never any surprises.

However, to even the most limited of minds here it was clear something was about to happen. The long summer was finally ending.

Garvey rushed along the hall, trying to drive from his mind the disturbing vision he'd experienced in the cellar. He was following a strange sound that seemed to be emanating from the portico hall.

He emerged from one of the corridors and stood, stock still. There were people here. People he didn't know. A small funny-looking little man in a white linen suit and a strange woman in tight, unfamiliar blue clothes. Garvey felt almost as shocked as he had in the cellar.

Lying on the floor, asleep or something, was Miss Victoria. Miss Charlotte and Mrs Irving were standing round her. The little man knelt by her side whilst the woman paced about the marble floor.

As Garvey watched, the man slipped a scalpel into a small leather pouch. His eyes were strange and his body moved with a heaviness unfamiliar to Garvey. The woman, noting his entrance, stomped around the hall, staring down the impassive statues that eyed her dispassionately from their cornices. The sound, so loud and piercing a minute ago, stopped and the hall became silent. Garvey saw something monstrous lodged in Miss Victoria's throat, something that pulsed gently. He turned his eyes away. For a minute the echo of the song remained in the ears of the listeners.

Garvey stood up straight and cast his seamed head round to the various people in the hall. They stared back in a funny, uncomfortable manner. Finally, his gaze again found a resting place on Victoria. 'What is going on here?' he asked sternly.

No one seemed in a fit state to answer until the oddly dressed woman took the initiative. 'We did our best,' she said with an unfamiliar, sensitive tone. Garvey tried to understand what she meant. She was hinting at something he didn't comprehend. He had never heard anyone talk like that.

Mrs Irving suddenly rushed from the hall, clutching her head. Garvey wondered why she had done that. He stared at the two strangers as if he had never seen another living person before. Icily he asked, 'And just who are you?'

The woman turned abruptly, seemingly amazed at his manner. She seemed to be about to say something when she changed her mind, slapping her hand against a pillar.

Garvey frowned, unclear as to how to react. Eventually he decided that introducing himself might bring about an explanation. 'I am the manservant of the House. My name is Garvey. I repeat my question. Who are you?'

The woman opened her mouth again when the little man stood up and spoke first. 'Not now Benny. My good fellow, I am the Doctor and this is my normally even-tempered friend Professor Bernice Summerfield. We have had a long day and I for one am in no mood for the customary interrogation.'

This served to confuse Garvey, who stared curiously at them. He looked down at Victoria. 'Why is Miss Victoria lying on the floor?'

The man who called himself the Doctor looked at him with an unfamiliar expression. He coughed. 'We had better get a sheet to cover her with,' he said sadly.

Garvey stared at Charlotte, puzzled and hoping the mistress might enlighten him.

'Come on. Chop chop,' the Doctor chided them.

'Why?' asked Charlotte.

'Well . . .' He seemed to struggle to find the right words. 'We can't just leave her here.'

'Why not?'

Bernice and the Doctor exchanged looks. Bernice walked to them, apparently tongue-tied. 'Well . . . because she's dead.'

Garvey walked a few paces towards the body, knees clicking. Victoria lay there pale and inert. Again, he felt as if he had missed out on something. 'Dead?' he asked.

Charlotte knelt by her sister and held her hand gently. She looked up at the Doctor, a strand of black hair falling across her face. Garvey noticed a reaction on the man's face, like a shock of icy water. The Doctor looked more closely at Charlotte. 'Do I know you from somewhere?' he asked.

Her eyes were inquisitive and there was some sort of moisture in them. This was all getting too much for Garvey.

Charlotte either did not hear, or ignored the Doctor's

question, instead asking, 'Is this "dead"? I seem to know of it. Perhaps I read about it. I am aware of its meaning but I've never seen it before.' Her eyes stared unflinchingly into the Doctor's.

Garvey jumped as the woman called Bernice uttered a gasp of surprise. She seemed about to say something when the Doctor shook his head, implying 'save it for later'. 'Charlotte,' he asked gently, 'what year is this?'

The girl looked at Garvey. He gazed blankly back. She frowned. 'I'm afraid I don't know what that means either.'

The Doctor continued, 'Well, do you know where we are? This estate, its location?'

Charlotte produced a blank smile. 'Of course. This is the House.'

'Which house?'

'The House. I don't know what you want me to say.'

Bernice raised her voice: 'He's asking you where we are. What town. County. At least tell us that this is England!'

Charlotte remained silent.

'Well, are we on Earth?' Bernice snapped.

Garvey interrupted, kindly but firmly: 'Excuse me, Miss, but shouting at Miss Charlotte will not empower her to answer the questions you ask.'

Bernice shrugged, an expression of incredulity on her face. 'I give up,' she sighed.

Charlotte looked around, apparently trying to answer Bernice's questions but, like Garvey, having no inkling as to what to say. At last some form of inspiration seemed to come to her. 'England. That is familiar, but I can't say how or why.'

Garvey watched as the Doctor and Bernice stood together and conferred. He tried unsuccessfully to follow their dialogue.

'I don't believe this,' said Bernice.

'Things are clearly not what they seem,' replied the Doctor. 'An apparent lack of awareness about death of any kind. Yet they are capable of expressing the emotions related to the phenomenon. I think we rushed to conclusions assuming this was nineteenth-century England. I thought the TARDIS instruments were giving out odd readings.'

'I saw you looking at them. I wondered what was up. Has it gone wrong again?'

The Doctor shook his head, 'No, no. They read England correctly, and the time period. It was just . . .'

'Just what?'

The Doctor frowned, 'Just that the TARDIS took a long time giving me the information. As if . . . as if it wasn't sure.'

Garvey was fascinated by their presence, by the way they acted, despite his surprise at having encountered them and the disruption it had caused.

Bernice seemed to think of something else. 'Charlotte. You seemed to know her. Have you met her before?'

The Doctor smiled mysteriously. 'Later, Benny.'

Charlotte spoke again, interrupting the conversation. Her dark eyes were shadowed and her lips pursed. She seemed to be struggling with a previously unknown emotion. 'It isn't clear. I am trying to remember. Dead. I feel . . . sad and a sense of loss but it feels like a dream I've forgotten. I can't remember anything. Why do I feel like this? Victoria . . . is gone.'

Something was dawning in Garvey's mind too. He did know what death was. If he looked at Victoria, white and still on the floor, it occurred to him that it did make sense. It was right. No, he thought, that must not be. He must only think about the familiar, the known.

The Doctor clutched Bernice's arm. 'Have a look round the house,' he whispered. 'See if you can find any clues. I'll sort things out here.'

The butler noticed Bernice's look of . . . something he didn't understand. 'What about Ace? She's probably half-way up a mountain by now.'

'No mountains here, Benny. This is England, apparently. I know Ace has probably got herself into terrible danger and I'm just as concerned as you are. I'll go and look for her once we've sorted this out. Please, do what I asked you.'

Again Bernice was twisting her face into an expression that Garvey failed to recognize. 'You wouldn't be trying to get me out of the way, would you?' she said.

The Doctor flashed his most innocent smile. Garvey recognized that expression, smiles were common here. He warmed to the little man. 'Benny, of course not. I just need more to go on.'

Bernice kept a lowered gaze on the Doctor. 'All right,' she said slowly and strolled off into one of the corridors. 'But I'm suspicious,' her voice echoed back into the hall.

Charlotte watched her go and then turned to the Doctor. She seemed to need to be told what to do. He smiled wickedly. 'Go on then,' he said mischievously. 'Get after her. You'll learn something.'

Charlotte nodded and scurried out.

'We've all got to learn,' the Time Lord whispered to himself as he stared down at Victoria's pale, perfect corpse. He rubbed his hands. 'Right, Mr Garvey, let's get this sorted out shall we? You haven't seen Ace, have you? Tall girl, stocky, prone to acts of random violence.'

Garvey ignored this stream of verbal nonsense. He had found a way of coping with the extraordinary situation: normality. 'Dinner is nearly ready, Doctor,' he said officiously. 'Shall I allow you ten minutes to change and wash?'

The butler stood there, calm and unruffled, as if nothing of any consequence had occurred. The Doctor sighed. Garvey was surprised, he had not expected a reaction like that. He thought the man would have been pleased to get back into the routine.

A breeze had sprung up and was blowing freely through the open doors from outside.

'It's cold,' said the Doctor. Garvey, typically, knew nothing of the meaning of the word.

Charlotte followed Bernice's footsteps through the maze-like corridors of the ground floor. Huge oil paintings hung from the walls. They were portraits of people she had no knowledge of. They must be dead too. For some reason their staring faces had become disturbing. Charlotte felt they were looking at her.

She followed the sound of footsteps to a narrow but high set of stone steps leading up to the first floor. She caught a glimpse of Bernice closing the door at the top of the stairs. Charlotte started climbing.

Her head was a mass of confusions. She had felt a new sensation upon seeing Victoria lying still on the floor but as yet was unable to grasp what it might mean.

What Charlotte did understand was that it was the arrival of these strangers that had altered everything here. Even the knowledge of what strangers were had only just come to her, nothing even remotely similar had ever existed in her life before.

She watched Bernice go through a set of glass doors onto a balcony. She was kicking out at the white gravel on the ground. A large red sun was sinking behind the hills. The woods covering them were black silhouettes, smudges in the distance.

Charlotte hesitated behind the wooden framed door that led to the balcony. This strange woman was so different to the people of the House. They were crystal clear, always calm and unhurried. Yes, they had their characters: Victoria with her fantasies and dreams of other places; Mrs Irving and her fussing; Garvey with his rigid devotion to the House; but they were all obvious. They never changed or did anything out of the ordinary. The woman Bernice was a mass of contradictions. Charlotte had to find out more, she burned with curiosity.

She shifted her position slightly and knocked against the open door. Bernice whirled round and squinted into the darkness. 'Come out,' she ordered.

Charlotte walked sheepishly onto the balcony. She shivered. It was ... another new word ... cold! She wrapped her arms around herself and rubbed.

'Bernice?' she asked timidly, unsure of what to say. The older woman looked mysterious and beautiful in the evening light. Bernice prevented her from speaking further. 'Yes, look, I'm sorry. It's just that I . . .'

'I know.' Charlotte was quick to smooth any feathers that had become ruffled. 'I have to talk to you. Please.'

The girl warmed to Bernice. She could see nothing but compassion in her eyes. Compassion and something else, something reassuring as she spoke: 'I'm worried about my friend Ace. She ran off into the woods and I haven't seen her since.' She relaxed and laughed. 'You still haven't explained where the hell this place is.'

Charlotte smiled. The barrier had come down. 'I cannot answer your question, please don't get annoyed with me. I don't know what to say. Thoughts like that have never been with me before. I don't know why.'

Bernice shrugged. 'You and me both. There's something distinctly odd going on here. It's like you've all lost your memories or something. You're not aliens disguised as humans are you? I've seen that one before.'

Charlotte frowned, concerned again. 'I do not think so. If I am I'm not aware of it.'

Bernice turned to look out at the sunset. 'This place, it's like a dream. It's all so perfect. Like a kid's book. You, the little Victorian madam, that butler just what a butler should be and that fussy little housekeeper. You're all exactly how you're supposed to be.'

Charlotte sat down on the stone balustrade at the edge of the balcony. She looked at Bernice. 'You know,' she said, 'I'm always supposed to have been the curious one yet I have never even walked over those hills to see what is there.'

'Not even when you were a child?'

Charlotte stared out. The sun had nearly disappeared. All that remained were red fingers stretching up into the darkening sky. She laughed mournfully. 'A child? I am a child now, apparently. Again you use words in a way I don't understand.'

Bernice struggled to deal with Charlotte's incredible ignorance. 'A child. A young adult. You must have been a kid. Young, growing up and all that.'

Charlotte shook her head. 'I have never changed, nor has anything here. It doesn't. I have always been as I am now. So has everyone else. I thought everything was like that.'

Bernice seemed just as confused as Charlotte. 'You must have been a kid. Been born. You must have come from somewhere.'

'I'm sorry. I can't tell you. I don't know.'

Bernice sat down on the gravel. 'How can someone never have been born? Someone that looks and acts like a person?'

Charlotte was silent, not knowing what to say. Bernice sighed and spoke again, 'Something else bothers me. This isn't some mystical alien planet, this is Earth, England. It has to be. Every planet has a different feel to it and I know enough about Earth to be sure. What's the big mystery?'

She shook her head and stared at the nearest of the bushes lining the balcony. 'Evening,' it said in a voice like black ice.

Charlotte caught a glimpse of thorns and teeth fashioned from twisted wood, and behind them a pair of sickly yellow eyes.

Before Bernice could react it spewed out from the hedge in a mass of leaves and twigs. It tried to wrap itself around Charlotte. The girl screamed and was knocked to the floor by the creature. All that she could see was a blur of flying razor-sharp talons and dense oily smoke.

'Charlotte!' cried Bernice and plunged, hands across her face, into the mêlée. Charlotte felt stinging spikes raking her as Bernice grabbed at her parcelled body and began tugging wildly at the living wood that held her fast.

As she instinctively snapped and broke the creature apart, Charlotte watched as thicker strands of the hedge encircled Bernice's legs and tightened. She dug her heels into the gravel and continued to break Charlotte free. The hedge was trying to overbalance them both.

At last Charlotte found a handhold on the balustrade and used its purchase to lever herself into a more stable position. Without realizing she had done it she had launched herself forward and torn free. She threw herself back at the door and into the House.

Bernice, meanwhile, was getting ever more tangled up. Charlotte turned to see thorns ripping the woman's skin and one of the branches worming its way around her neck. Bernice stopped fighting and attempted to prevent it from choking her. As Charlotte watched, a blurred, manic face suddenly loomed up through the leaves at Bernice. It seemed to consist of smoke and twigs. 'Going down,' it laughed and tipped her over the balcony.

'Bernice!' screamed Charlotte from the door.

Bernice used the hedge to stop herself falling. Despite its squirming violence it was all that prevented her from dropping fifty feet to the ground. Thorns exploded into her hands and she almost let go.

Charlotte couldn't stand and watch. A new part of her mind, one that had never been tested before, refused to let Bernice die. She was going to change the course of events. She ran for the balcony.

'Let go of her! Let go!' Charlotte shouted as she grabbed Bernice's denim jacket and pulled. Bernice used her feet to scrabble back over the stone and onto the balcony again. The hedge seemed to be preparing itself for another onslaught.

'Thanks. Run!' Bernice screamed and they both half scrambled, half dived for the open door.

Quick as lightning one of the branches shot forward and clutched Charlotte's leg. She felt Bernice grab her with bleeding hands and drag her through the doorway, then slam it shut, trapping the snaking wood. It dug itself into Charlotte's ankle, causing her to cry out in pain. Through the glass in the door she saw the hedge blast

towards her in a battering ram of black wood and leaves.
'Get down!' shouted Bernice and ducked.

Glass disintegrated over Charlotte. 'It's got me!' she
cried, almost passing out from the crushing pain in her
leg.

Again, Bernice was there to help, pulling away at the
wood. The sound of tearing, scratching and snapping filled
the air. Somehow, Charlotte managed to rip herself free.
White weals stained her leg in the outline of the branch.

All at once, the hedge flew backwards and shrank back
to its normal, placid size around the balcony. 'Shame . . .'
the two heard as a faint whisper from outside.

For a few moments they lay there covered in glass and
twigs. Their clothes were shredded and bloody from a
hundred small cuts. Neither could speak, a mixture of
shock and relief that they had survived something
unspeakable.

At last, Charlotte saw Bernice lift her bruised and
bloodied head. Torn and wrenched hair spilled over her
brow. She grinned at the shivering, unbelieving face of
Charlotte. 'You know something,' she said, 'you look like
you've just been dragged through a hedge backwards.'

The Doctor found Mrs Irving wandering around the corridors on the ground floor. She had the dazed and confused
expression on her face that he was getting used to here.

Together they carefully carried Victoria up a large, wide
flight of golden-carpeted stairs to a small bedroom. There,
they lowered her onto an ornate four-poster bed. The
insect had become restless again and squirmed
unpleasantly inside the dead girl's throat. The Doctor was
careful not to disturb the creature for fear of triggering
some new development with it. The last thing he wanted
was that thing darting about looking for a new victim. He
had Mrs Irving dig out a large, brass-rimmed bell-jar ready
for any emergence by the creature. It was placed on a
small table by the bed.

The Doctor had still not asked Mrs Irving the questions

he was burning to find answers to. Anyway he doubted whether the woman would be able to give him any coherent explanation. Somehow, their minds were incomplete, memories lost, self-awareness limited.

'She was so young, Doctor,' Mrs Irving said wistfully, looking down at Victoria, pale and sad on the bed.

He had to have more data. 'How are you feeling?' he asked innocently.

She stared up at him. The Doctor tried to read her eyes but they were just empty. 'I'm not entirely myself sir, if that's what you mean,' came her cryptic reply. She appeared to be trying to come to some sort of major decision. He nodded, implying that she should speak her mind. After a pause she spoke: 'I've never felt like this before. I don't understand what's going on.'

'That makes two of us, Mrs Irving.'

'If you don't mind sir, I'd like to find Miss Charlotte, being as how she's my responsibility as well.'

The Doctor looked at the body on the bed. 'You still haven't grasped it yet, have you?'

Mrs Irving turned from Victoria, put her finger to her mouth as if she had forgotten something and walked calmly from the room. The Doctor sank into a chair muttering, 'Odd. Exceedingly odd all round. I wonder where Ace has got to.'

He sat staring at his reflection in the glass bell-jar. The reflection looked as confused as he did.

Her head boiling with unusual and disturbing thoughts and emotions, Mrs Irving wandered through the corridors again. Her face was a picture of distraction. Strange and unwelcome ideas kept pushing their way into her mind. Thoughts of a girl she had known forever but now no longer with her.

All at once she had needed the reassurance of her sole remaining charge. She had to find Charlotte. She would know the answers. She read books. This Doctor and his friend, they were, well, intrusions into a routine that had lasted as long as anyone could remember. They did not belong here. Strangers were unknown.

Like Garvey, what kept Mrs Irving going was her sense of duty. It allowed her to blank out those emotions that threatened to undermine the placid security of the House. If there was something to sort out, then that was Garvey's job. Hers was to look after the children.

What stopped her in her tracks was remembering the vision she had seen on the meadow. The dark woman with the eyes of a corpse.

Mrs Irving gasped and fell against the corridor wall, paralysed with fear. It was as if the eyes were still there, had always been up there, on that hill. There had been something familiar about them, that had been the worst part. As if she'd been looking into herself. They were part of her, a part of her mind that had kept black thoughts hidden at bay. She had veiled them well behind the curtain of routine and security but they had always been there. She wondered briefly why it was only now that they had wormed their way into the open.

Things were changing here forever, that was obvious, and Mrs Irving, for the first time in her life, was forced to face up to that prospect.

Bernice was carrying Charlotte away from the smashed door of the balcony. They both shivered in shock and pain from the many lacerations and cuts caused by the hedge. They bumped into Mrs Irving as they reached the foot of the stairs. Bernice stopped, 'We've had some hassle with a hedge,' she muttered dryly. She was totally unprepared for Mrs Irving's look of absolute shock and horror. The woman appeared about to have a heart attack or something. 'It's all right,' Bernice said, puzzled. 'We don't look that bad do we?'

Mrs Irving stepped back, almost toppling to the floor and stretched out a finger to point at Charlotte.

'What is the matter with you?' Bernice demanded,

taken aback by this extreme reaction. Charlotte seemed equally puzzled. 'Mrs Irving? Is something wrong?'

The housekeeper gasped for breath, beside herself with shock. At last she managed to speak. Hoarsely, she whispered, 'Charlotte, your face.'

Bernice turned to look at Charlotte's frowning features and could not contain a gasp of her own.

'What? What is it?' moaned Charlotte, looking uneasy.

'There's a mirror on the wall there,' said Bernice gravely. 'I think you'd better take a look.'

They ran past Mrs Irving, leaving her to fall dazedly onto the stairs. Bernice pulled Charlotte in front of a large, gilt-edged mirror. 'Look,' she whispered.

Charlotte stared in wonder at the mirror. In the glass a twenty-year-old Charlotte stared back at her.

For the first time since Victoria's death, the Doctor was enjoying himself. He had made an attempt to find Ace, wandering across the grounds towards the meadow on the steep hill. The air had been very warm still and he had watched the red sun sink into the distance.

Something about being outside had bothered him. He couldn't place the unease but eventually had pinned it down to a feeling of claustrophobia. Why he should have felt like this when he was outside he did not know.

What disturbed him more was that there had been an absence of the telepathic itch that he felt when Ace was in the vicinity. It was always there, a subconscious contact with his companions, beyond even Time Lord comprehension. Now that feeling was gone. She couldn't have died, surely he would have felt that. It was as if she had been lifted clean away from the planet.

He had realized that someone was watching him. Up in the dark, inscrutable hills, eyes had burned into him. Something about the gaze had made him turn back to the House. They were powerful eyes, unsettling and intrusive. He had known then that he was not going to be allowed to find Ace.

Returning, he had been directed by Garvey to a large study. The butler had invited him to change.

Now he was here, the Doctor decided to make a more thorough investigation. The study was filled with strange and wonderful pieces of bric-a-brac. In the corner squatted a large brown globe, the countries of the world engraved on it. If it wasn't Earth then someone had made an excellent job of copying it.

He looked at the bookshelf behind the large mahogany desk. It was full of leather-bound volumes. 'The good old Encyclopaedia Britannica,' he laughed. 'So they did get it off the ground. I was wrong.'

He pulled out one book from the shelf and opened it. The pages were yellowed and well thumbed but completely blank. 'The expurgated version?'

Moving around the room the Doctor found that Garvey, or somebody, had left a suit, bow-tie and tails, draped across a sumptuous chaise longue. 'Hmm ...' he pondered. 'Will the suit suit?'

Normally reticent about changing out of his linen suit and brogues, the Time Lord was so impressed by the cut of the cloth that he decided to give it a go. He looked down at his hands. They were sore but seemed to be healing nicely.

Minutes later, standing in front of a mirror which was slightly dusty through lack of use, he was impressed. 'Not bad. I'm pleasantly surprised.' He turned around to get a look from the other side. 'Hmm. Quite the dandy. I could get used to this type of clobber again.'

Unfortunately, thinking about one of his previous incarnations conjured up in his mind's eye the figure of a tall, dashing silver-haired man dressed in a frilly shirt and a smart velvet suit. He felt this previous self stare in disapproval.

'You don't think it's quite me then?' he asked himself, pulling a sour face at the mirror. In his mind the other Doctor put his finger to his not inconsiderable nose, shook his head and said, 'My dear chap, you look like a lumpy penguin. It won't do, y'know.'

The Doctor dismissed the vision from his mind. 'Oh, get lost. What did you ever know about fashion?'

Still, perhaps the fellow had been right. He held a lot of respect for his own opinions. He decided to play safe and change back. Plain and simple, the old linen suit. Unostentatious. Better to play safe. You knew who you were then.

Now Bernice looked clearly, yes, it was obvious. Somehow, in the last half hour, Charlotte had aged four years. Her face had more character, was less childlike. The hair and figure were slightly fuller and the impressions of lines were shadowed across her brow. She even seemed to have grown an inch or two.

Charlotte stared down at herself. Again, she seemed a little detached from the situation, as if observing from a distance. However, if you looked in her eyes Bernice thought she could detect panic being held back. 'What's happening to me?' the woman asked of her own body. 'I'm different.'

'You're older,' stated Bernice.

Charlotte seemed puzzled. 'You're confusing me. Older? Something else I don't understand.'

Bernice thought about taking the point up but thought better of it. 'The Doctor will explain,' came her universal reply. She looked up the stairs at Mrs Irving. The housekeeper seemed shocked rigid by Charlotte's change.

Bernice supposed it was because she had been with the girl the whole time that she hadn't noticed the ageing. It must have happened too slowly to have registered. It was only because Mrs Irving had been away from her charge for half an hour that the difference had become apparent. Poor old woman, she looked as if her ticker was not going to stand much more of this kind of behaviour.

Grabbing Charlotte, Bernice headed back along the corridor to find the Doctor. He would know what was going on, he always did. His infuriating habit of always knowing everything in advance would come in useful for once.

'Bernice,' said Charlotte, breaking into her thoughts.

Bernice stopped. 'What?'

'Look. I'm frightened. I'm confused.'

'You're confused? You live here. I haven't got a clue what's going on. If anybody has the right to be confused it's me.'

Charlotte stared at her hands. 'I can feel myself changing. I can almost see it happening.'

Bernice placed a hand on her shoulder. 'Come to the Doctor with me. He can help.'

Charlotte seemed lost and only half listening. Distractedly she murmured, 'I need time. I need to think.'

Bernice thought briefly of dragging Charlotte bodily off to the Doctor and decided against it. She had no right to be telling people what they should and shouldn't be doing when she was so confused herself. 'Of course, you must have a lot to deal with right now. But you must come to the Doctor soon. He really is rather good at helping people out.'

Charlotte hesitated, then walked away through a door to some downward-leading steps. Bernice shook her head. She tried to think of what to do next. She could go and see if she could help Mrs Irving. She would do that.

However, when she reached the staircase there was no sign of the housekeeper. She shrugged her shoulders, stumped. She supposed there was always one person with whom you could guarantee a conversation, even if most of it was one way. Having reached her decision, Bernice headed back to find the Doctor.

'Answers, Benny?' The Doctor was still admiring himself in the mirror, now wearing his regular outfit. 'Not yet, not by a long chalk.'

At last, the Time Lord seemed to tire of his own reflection and flopped down into the red leather swivel chair behind the desk. It made a dwarf of him. Still with one eye on the mirror, he tilted his fedora theatrically over his forehead.

Bernice twisted the chair round to face her. 'But you always know the answer. Half the time you know it before it's even happened, the other half you've started it yourself.'

A grin appeared from beneath the hat. 'How are Charlotte and Mrs Irving?'

Bernice paced around the room staring up at the blank books. 'Confused, frustrated, scared. A bit like me really. Are you sure you don't know what's going on?'

The Doctor shook his head sadly. 'My dear Benny, you have such a suspicious mind. No, I promise I haven't a clue.'

Bernice relaxed. Upon occasion you just had to trust the Doctor, even if you only half believed him. She asked, 'Well, ideas then? How can these things happen in nineteenth-century England? Where I know we are not, by the way.'

The Doctor stared out of the bay window at the pale blue twilight settling in outside. 'About half past nine,' he said, apparently to himself. 'All right,' he announced. 'Ideas.' He paused for a second and then continued: 'You were right about Charlotte's ageing. You didn't notice it because it has been happening too slowly for you to perceive – by the way I would like to see her – yet it still happened, frighteningly quickly. You know what that reminds me of?'

Bernice already had the answer to that one. 'The minute hand on a clock.'

'Exactly. Have you ever noticed your hair growing, or your nails?'

Bernice was thinking aloud. 'Some kind of time distortion or something? A localised field?'

Smiling, the Doctor waggled a finger at her. 'Naughty naughty Benny. Don't find the cure until you know the illness. Sixteen years old, then half an hour later at least twenty. You know, I get the impression that this whole place is a bit like a broken clock.'

Bernice moved over to the globe, needing something to do whilst concentrating her thoughts. She spun it slowly. Something clicked in her mind, 'Ace! Where is she? We'd better go and find her.'

The Doctor shook his head. 'Ace is wherever she is. Looking for her will do no good. If she was coming then she would be here by now.'

'She might be hurt.'

'Probably, but Ace spends her whole life hurt and she always comes through it. We must trust her, that usually works.'

The Doctor giggled and Bernice wondered if this House had affected his brain too. 'I don't like it. I want to go out and look for her.' She was insistent.

What stopped her in her tracks was the Doctor's look of absolute seriousness. A chill trickled down her spine. 'You're not to go out there, Benny, whatever you might want to do,' he said, and there was no way Bernice was going to disobey.

The moment of unease lasted for a few seconds and then the Doctor looked away again. A smile jumped back onto his face. 'If I may continue with my explanation,' he said, 'think of it like this. I get the feeling that nothing has moved her for some considerable time. If I can re-use my own simile, the clock had wound too far down and had stopped. Nothing could happen until somebody found the key and wound it back up again.'

'Somebody like us, you mean.' Bernice sighed. She wondered if he'd been using some of that hypnotism on her. She felt the beginnings of a headache. 'Trust us to jump right into the middle of it. It is something to do with time, then?'

The Doctor stared out of the window once more. Bernice wondered whether he was peering up at the woods where the TARDIS stood waiting for them.

'Of course it's to do with time. It always is,' he finally

answered. 'The question is "what?" I can't quite fit the pieces together. But we shall soldier on. I have a feeling that now it's all started up, events will proceed at a goodly pace. You know, at first I thought it was a Timescoop again.'

'Again?'

'However, I am now sure that it isn't. These people haven't lost their memories, they never had any in the first place. Anyway, where we are is not what's worrying me at the moment.'

He pushed the fedora up off his forehead and turned to face Bernice who stopped spinning the globe. Furrowing her eyebrows she asked, 'Well, it's worrying me. What's worrying you?'

'The other possibility about the cause of everything here. If we didn't wind up the clock, who did?'

Mrs Irving looked wistfully down at Victoria's body as it lay, placid and still on the four-poster bed. The bell-jar sat obediently on the table next to her. Outside it was fully dark now. The last beams of light had disappeared over the hill, the last remnants of daylight.

Mrs Irving reached across for the heavy velvet curtains at the window and pulled them closed. She did not suppose it made much difference to Victoria but it was reassuring to be thorough.

She had come up here again with the feeling that she had lost both of the girls. Charlotte was as different now as Victoria and just as remote. Victoria at least still looked the same. Charlotte seemed to be a different person entirely.

She lit up a candle and turned back to the body. The insect, quiet and still up to now, was gently easing itself out of Victoria's mouth. The girl's jaw was moving up and down in a parody of speech.

The creature was slow, fat and bloated. Its fur was damp with some sticky fluid, like honey. To Mrs Irving it looked drunk or sleepy. The Doctor wanted to examine it, that was what he had said. She was sure he had said that. She wondered whether she should go and fetch him.

No.

A new and ugly thought was growing in her mind. Her brain, having never experienced anger before, was drowned in a red, blazing fury.

The Doctor, whoever he was, would want to keep it alive for study. This . . . thing that had sucked the life from this girl and from Mrs Irving's world, why should it live?

She looked around and found a brass candlestick. Sweating and shaking with the force of this new emotion, she raised it high over her head.

On the bed, the insect swayed slowly across Victoria's face, leaving a glutinous trail in its wake. It plopped onto the pillow.

With surprising speed for one so plump and unused to physical activity, Mrs Irving brought the candlestick down and across the creature's back. There was a wet crunch and she hoisted the weapon up again, strings of resin hanging from its stem. The creature tried feebly to haul itself across the heavy bedspread. As the housekeeper watched, it flopped onto the floor, legs thrashing wildly.

'Filthy thing!' she shouted and knelt to hit it harder. She watched the monster try to flex its ruined, dripping gossamer wings.

In a rage she pounded the candlestick onto the insect again and again, sending booming thuds out of the room to the corridor. Tears streamed down her face. Her hands were covered with pulp when she had finished. Shocked, she let go of the stick. It clanged to the floor.

She could not remember how long she knelt there in its remains, feeling the grief and anger drain out of her. It was a voice that awoke her from her trance. It came lifeless, from the bed: 'I'm hungry.'

Despite the fact that it was nothing but a whisper Mrs Irving recognized the voice instantly. 'Victoria!' she exclaimed.

Relief coursed through her heart. The Doctor had been wrong. Everything was going to be all right after all.

'I can't see,' said the voice.

Mrs Irving lifted herself up onto the bed, knees cracking as she did so. Victoria lay there, pale and cold. Her eyes were closed. 'My dear,' the housekeeper cried with joy.

The eyes opened but wandered in their sockets as if unseeing. They held as little humanity as the voice. 'I'm hungry. Help me.'

Mrs Irving, even in her euphoric state, knew something was not right. She thought, and she knew she was lying to herself, that the reason the girl was so strange was because the insect had poisoned and disorientated her. She selectively ignored the fact that the girl's chest was still, she was not breathing. 'What can I do?' the house-keeper whispered.

The body did not move but the eyes jumped before slowly coming to rest on Mrs Irving. They were the eyes of the woman in the field. Mrs Irving stared at her own death. The mouth produced an imitation of a grin. 'Come closer, Mrs Irving. I want to give you a kiss.'

Despite the knowledge that it was the end, Mrs Irving obeyed. It was easier that way. At last her life made sense again.

Chapter 3

Ace cleared the woods. She reached the top of the slope and the trees thinned out around her. Looking down into the valley she saw a lake shining in the sun's light. The water appeared serene and inviting. Ducks skimmed across its silver surface. Ace reckoned it was about a mile away.

Between her and the bright water was a field of shoulder-high wheat. Pollen and dust hung lazily in the air. She thought getting through it would be a struggle but she'd manage it quickly enough.

Beyond the lake was what was important. Some perfectly manicured lawns framed a large old mansion house and rising up behind that was another hill, again crested with a deep wood.

Ace disliked these fiddly, non-techno problems. She longed for good old Daleks. You saw them, you blew them up. Even cracking the ice on some sophisticated security system was better than an insect in a throat. It would have been nice to have inserted a frag grenade up that beastie's backside. That would have sorted it out.

Ace scanned the wheatfield again. She'd be through it in fifteen minutes.

As she scampered down the hill she caught sight of four figures on the opposite side of the valley. They were a long way away but by squinting through the sweat in her eyes she could make out some detail. The people were carrying something through a meadow. Something like a white sheet.

Christ. One of them looked like the Doctor.

How could that be? She'd just left him and Benny half a mile behind her.

Something cracked at Ace's ankle. Correction. It was the armour that cocooned and protected the ankle. Looking down, she gasped. The indestructible armour had split up the shin to the knee. The useless fabric hung open like a flap of torn skin.

Ace was shocked. Armour didn't do that. It was built to withstand direct hits from blaster fire. There came another crack and another, this time across her chest. It split and a gash of about twenty centimetres billowed open. Ace looked about wildly. She wondered if she was under attack.

Nothing. It was as if the suit had contracted leprosy.

She tried the wrist computer to obtain a diagnostic. It emitted a single bleep, came on, coughed and passed peacefully away.

Wonderful, thought Ace, now what do I do?

She felt like Worzel Gummidge, standing there in a suit of heavy rags. Get rid of it. The girl in the woods still needed help. Forget your stupid armour. Worry about it later.

Stepping out of the bones of the suit, Ace looked down at her body, clad in black tee-shirt and shorts. It seemed like the first time in months she'd seen herself. She lifted her sunglasses for a better look. She was pale. Too long in space. She felt she could do with some serious sunbathing.

Snapping herself back into action, Ace ran down the slope and into the wheatfield, leaving the armour behind.

Behind her, the clothes waited peacefully in the warm afternoon. Minutes passed.

Small mounds of earth were pushed up in a ring, encircling the suit. Thin, fibrous roots emerged from the mounds and felt their way to the armour. Within seconds it was covered in the spidery fingers. Gripping tightly, they pulled the rotten material back into the ground with them.

* * *

Covering her mouth and nostrils with her hand to protect herself, Ace fought her way through the stalks of wheat. She kicked up clouds of dust as she walked. This was tougher than she had thought. And hot. Like all the vegetation in this place the wheat was ripe to the point of bursting.

Something moved about ten metres in front of her. There was a hiss of steam, like some sort of engine.

Ace stood still for five minutes, all senses fully alert. She heard no repetition of the sound. 'What is this?' she whispered.

She started to move. Again the noise. Ace stopped dead. This time it had come from her left. Metal against metal. An old iron sound, not high-tech at all. She thought she saw smoke rising somewhere ahead. She couldn't see anything properly through the dust and muck. She realized how vulnerable she was. No weaponry, no armour and no manoeuvrability. If something big came to get her it wouldn't have much trouble. Better to butch it out.

'Who's there?' she shouted, trying to sound as hard as possible. She softened her tone. 'Someone's been injured. I need help.'

Nothing.

Ace turned in a slow circle, trying to get some sort of reading on the situation. There was a jungle heat in this field and the dust was clogging her sinuses. Her eyes streamed with irritation.

Still nothing. Ace clenched her fists tightly. She would have to keep moving in whatever direction she thought best. Sweat soaked her thin clothes. She had to get away.

Then she heard a voice. A man's voice, some way away. There was a strong tang of the West Country to it. 'Ello?' it shouted. 'Who's that then?'

It came from somewhere off to Ace's right. She decided any accent that stupid had to be friendly. 'Over here!' she cried out. 'Oy mate! Come and get us.' Ace supposed there were worse things in life than being rescued by one of the Wurzels.

The long stalks of wheat were brushed aside as a tall, fair-haired man strode into view. He was tanned, fit and dressed in off-white clothing that looked freshly laundered. The face was pleasant, ruddy and handsome. He was very masculine but Ace detected a softness there. He hadn't seen much action. Another innocent.

As if startled, his blue eyes gazed at her in wonder. His jaw very nearly dropped open. Ace presumed he was startled by her very un-Victorian clothing. She took the initiative: 'Hi. I'm Ace. Who are you?'

The man continued to stare at her before a big grin covered his face. 'Err,' he said, 'Arthur, miss. My name is Arthur. I mean, that's my name.'

'Right, Arthur. There's an injured girl up the hill and she needs help badly. Where's the nearest doctor.'

'I don't know,' came his reply.

Ace took in a deep breath: she had to stay in control. He would help in the end. 'Look,' she tried again, 'Can you get me to that house over there? This girl, she's going to die.'

Still Arthur seemed totally bewildered. 'Die?'

All right, Ace thought, back even further. He would just have to be forced. 'Take me to the house. Now!'

At last, she thought, light at the end of the tunnel. Something in his brain made a connection. He pondered and pursed his lips for a second before saying. 'This way. I'll take you to Garvey. He'll know.'

He turned and led the way through the wheat. Ace relaxed.

'I often bring the girls here,' Arthur chatted as he followed some mystifying trail. 'I just tend to the fields. Workin' in 'em, the wheat and the hops. The girls like to come here and see how they're growin'.'

Ace felt frustrated and impatient. She wondered if this man really knew what he was doing. 'How long before we get there?' she asked brusquely.

'Not long miss, just as soon as we get out of this field.'

As they walked, Ace snapped off one of the ears of

wheat and inspected it. That was what the Doctor would have done, look for clues. The grains were ripe and healthy, ready for the chop. 'Going to be a good harvest this year, I'd say,' she commented.

'Harvest?' Arthur asked mildly, still forcing his burly frame through the crop. 'What's that then?'

'Well, when you cut all this lot down or whatever.'

Arthur stopped and looked at Ace. 'Cut it down? Why would I do that?' He seemed genuinely puzzled, as was Ace. 'You must know . . .' she started. 'Oh, forget it.'

The noise came again, steam and grinding metal. It was ahead of them. It was like a belch of evil black smoke. Arthur did not seem to have noticed anything.

'Wait,' Ace grabbed the back of his shirt.

'What's the matter?' Arthur asked cheerfully. 'I've got to say miss, you've . . .'

'Shut up.'

The sound came again. And more. Clear now, clanking iron gears thumping the ground like some mechanical tiger circling its prey. There was breathing, a harsh rattle produced from engine lungs. Still Ace could see nothing.

Ahead the ground boomed as something big and heavy approached fast. Arthur seemed unafraid and oblivious to danger.

'You know what's making that sound?' Ace asked. She looked hopefully about for a weapon.

'Never heard anything like it,' he replied neutrally. Ace could see he was listening for something. Abruptly his expression changed as the sound grew stronger.

'What is it?' he whispered anxiously. Ace put a finger to his lips. She scanned the crops in front of her. The noise was getting closer. 'I think it's big and after us. It knows exactly where we are. Let's get the hell out of this field. Now!'

'This way,' said Arthur and they began to move quickly, back the way they had come. His eyes darted from side to side.

The sound disappeared and then started up in front of them.

'How can it move that quickly?' Ace asked herself, amazed.

She wondered what they could do. She'd got out of worse holes than this. Why didn't it just attack them? Why was it playing games?

As if on cue there was a huge bellow and something black and metallic, half glimpsed through the wheat, came roaring towards them. Ace caught sight of stinking black smoke. It was hurtling at them like an express train. 'Run! Arthur, run!'

Ace pulled him back round and smashed her way through the undergrowth. The hard, unyielding wheat scratched and scraped at her arms and face, drawing blood. Dust filled her lungs and she could barely see through tears.

An intense heat burned at her back. Whatever it was, it was gaining. Through the red pounding in her ears she discerned a coughing, mechanical laughter. Arthur was beside her, terrified and lost. He seemed in shock.

Sprinting and stumbling, she crashed blindly onwards, no thought in her head except escape and the certain knowledge that she was not going to. The roaring of the thing pursuing them seemed to flatten the wheat in front of it and began to deafen Ace. Blood pounded in her head.

She dived up at a particularly thick clump of vegetation and caught her booted foot. She tripped and plummeted head-first through the stalks, snapping them as they whipped her face. She fell down a small rise in the ground and her head slammed against hard, dry earth, knocking her sight haywire for a second.

Something flew over her in a blast of orange flame: something that was a bolted-together iron hybrid of a locomotive and a segmented worm. The thing slid through the wheat, braking hard. It left a trail of ruined, blackened crops in its wake. With a grinding shriek, it scrabbled to turn itself around and launch back at her.

'Arthur,' Ace moaned, half dead with exhaustion and heat. Through crisped eyelids she turned and saw the man. He was buried up to his waist in earth, a disbelieving look on his face. 'It's pulling me . . .' he shouted.

Body aching, Ace crawled to him. Somewhere in the distance a mechanical creature was revving up to attack. She grabbed his arm. 'Hold on,' she said, 'I'll get you out.'

'What's goin' on?' Arthur asked, wide-eyed.

The creature bellowed again and began its run towards them. Ace tried to ignore the sound. She pulled at Arthur.

'No good,' he said. 'I'm going.'

'Shut up,' Ace cursed through clenched teeth. This was proving impossible. She wasn't going to be able to get him out. Not before that thing smashed into them.

The ground gave way beneath Ace. It sucked her down like quicksand.

There was a drowning noise in her ears but she could not tell if it was due to exhaustion, the creature or the ground eating her. She passed out.

Water. Drops of the stuff tapping her face.

After the comfort of unconsciousness Ace became aware of an interesting combination of pains arching across her body. She felt like she'd been microwaved and then dropped into a washing machine. Every limb, every extremity cried out in agony. It would have been nice to lie here in this wet mud and sleep a lot longer. Nice.

Hauling her complaining eyelids open, Ace forced herself back to combat readiness. She had to stay alert.

She was lying in a puddle, in a field, in the rain. It was cold and unpleasant, wet and miserable. Sad trees lined the fences around the field, partially obscured by mist and a thin blanket of drizzle.

'Where the hell?' Ace sat up and looked around. Grim. Grim and cold. It had to be the English countryside: one that she remembered as real. 'Feels like a camping holiday,' she muttered.

Expecting the worst, she tentatively lowered her eyes to check herself out. It was as bad as she'd thought. Somewhere underneath the mud, damp matted hair and bruises was a woman. Her tee-shirt and shorts were singed, bloody and caked with filth. 'Ace,' she whispered ironically. At least her shades were intact.

There was a moan from behind her. She turned to see Arthur lying buried in the same mud as herself. He was bruised, bleeding and still semi-conscious. Ace pulled herself out of the puddle and stood up. She felt all right. The damage looked worse than it was.

This was a different countryside to that other one, like a flip-side to it, and it looked like she was stuck here without equipment or technology, fried and soaked. Not the best start to an adventure she'd ever had.

'Arthur?' She knelt down by him.

Arthur rolled over, apparently hurt. His long blond locks straggled over his face. He managed a weak smile. 'I feel strange,' he whispered.

'Are you injured?' Ace asked. 'Wounded?' She ran her hands over his body to check for breaks or sprains.

He laughed weakly. 'You use them words I don't understand.'

'Are you hurt?' She tried to make things clear for him. 'Any pain or bleeding?'

Arthur shook his head; he seemed almost delirious. 'I feel . . . different.' His West-Country burr sounded even stronger. 'Not myself.'

'Come on,' she said and hauled Arthur up to his feet. He fell weakly onto her, almost sending them both back into the mud.

'Something is happening here,' he gasped.

'You're not kidding mate,' Ace replied, taking his weight. 'You've got some explaining to do.'

Together, like crippled children, they staggered to the

five-bar gate at the far end of the field. The drizzle, almost deliberately, began to drum down even harder.

Bert Robbins, landlord of the Wychborn Arms for nearly ten years, led the young gentleman up to the best room in the inn. Struggling with a large trunk, he finally reached the landing. The gentleman followed him up the stairs. 'Not too heavy is it?' he asked Bert, noting the older man's sweating face.

Bert shook his head. 'I'm fine, Mr Aickland. Been doin' this all me life.'

This seemed to appease the young man, who smiled. 'Good, good. Wouldn't like to impose, y'know.' Bert contained a grin. Round here posh accents were rare enough to be a novelty. He wiped his hands on his apron before smoothing down his silver sideburns. 'From London are you sir?' he asked.

The young man looked slightly embarrassed, his thin face glowing pink. On his head sat a mop of unruly brown hair and his sharp nose seemed to require the decoration of spectacles. 'Camberwell actually. I left Waterloo yesterday and spent last night in Exeter.'

'Aye.' Bert nodded, not really knowing what to say. Didn't often get wealthy-looking gentlemen in Wychborn. This one didn't look more than a boy. He'd better watch himself in this village. Bert hoisted the trunk up again. 'This is the room, sir. I hope you'll find it suitable.'

He struggled over to the door of the guest room, opened it and staggered in, almost dropping the heavy trunk onto the floor. 'What the hell you got in 'ere?' he gasped, forgetting his manners.

'Just books . . . and things,' Aickland replied. 'Why? Do you think I've brought too much?'

'Not for me to say, is it sir.'

Aickland walked around, apparently inspecting the furniture. A small single bed sat in the centre of the room. Heavy rain drummed against the window.

'T'ain't much, I know sir,' Bert said. 'Never 'ad a gentleman staying here before.'

Aickland seemed delighted. He moved about on the spot as if unable to contain himself. 'No, no. It's wonderful. It's my first time out of London, you know.'

Bert nodded. He wondered whether to warn Aickland. Did the man know what went on here? Best not to make a fuss, perhaps he would only stay a few days.

Aickland appeared concerned about something. At last he plucked up courage and asked, 'Is it possible I might have some food? It's been rather a long day.'

'Aye, I'll get the wife onto it. Nothin' fancy I'm afraid sir.'

'Anything at all.'

Bert nodded again and left the room. He heard Aickland close the door behind him.

Going downstairs, Bert rushed across the bar and into the kitchen where his wife was preparing a rabbit. They made a good couple, Bert and Madge Robbins, both stout, ruddy and grey-haired.

'Got him upstairs then?' she asked, not taking her eyes from her work. Bert looked up at the ceiling, as if seeing through it and into the room. 'Aye. Wonder what he's come here for? I don't like it.'

'What's there to like? He's a gentleman out on his travels. You know.'

'No I don't. What's 'e want to come from London for? Why Wychborn?'

Madge looked up from the rabbit. 'You never said nothin', did you?'

Bert looked away. 'Course not.'

'We should warn him.'

'Don't be daft. And 'ave all that trouble down on our heads? We keep ourselves to ourselves and don't forget it. Still . . .' Bert faltered and glanced up at the ceiling again. His wife frowned. 'What?'

Bert shook his head. 'Nothing. That trunk of his.

Weighed a bloody ton. I don't think he knew what he was supposed to bring on a journey.'

The front door rattled on its hinges. Bert ran into the bar to see two capped and overcoated men come inside. For a second he failed to recognize them. They pulled their soaking collars down and shook off drops of rain.

Archie and Thorold Lewis. Brothers that worked up at the Rix farm. Big men from the village. The third brother, Stan, had drowned somewhere foreign while in the Navy.

Bert instinctively picked up a cloth and wiped the counter. The brothers made him nervous. They were decent enough but it was well known they had a vicious streak. Thos liked to break poachers' fingers when Rix let him, and there were stories about Archie and that little wife of his, Joanna. Bert had seen the bruises himself. You learned a lot as a landlord in a village pub, things you didn't always want to learn. You knew but you never took sides.

Bert wiped some tankards clean. 'Early today, lads. Trouble?'

Archie, the smaller and swarthier brother, laughed. 'Nay. In the middle of trapping ain't we? Pissin' it down so Rix give us the afternoon off.'

Trapping. Mantraps to stop pheasant poaching in Rix's woods. Thos nodded and settled his heavy frame onto a wooden stool. 'No bloody poachers on a day like this,' he said slowly. 'Too scared, too much noise.'

Bert laughed but he was remembering the state of the last poacher the brothers had caught. They'd been happy that night.

The beer was pulled and Bert scraped the foam from the tops of the tankards.

'That's what we want,' said Archie. 'Nothing to beat ale on a day like this.' Thos just nodded.

'Food?' asked Bert, hoping they would say no.

'Later, Bert.'

'I'll just go and get started in the kitchen then. You'll be all right boys?' He scratched at his balding scalp.

Thos grinned. He looked like an ox. 'Don't you worry, Bert. You go do your cooking.'

If that was meant to be an insult then Bert ignored it. Best with Thos not to make any comment at all unless invited.

The journey through the muddy, rain-soaked tracks had taken hours. Carrying Arthur was no joke, he weighed a ton. By now they were both soaked in mud, freezing and on the verge of exhaustion. Ace knew they were going to have to find shelter soon. It was starting to get dark.

Blinking rain out of her eyes, she became aware that she was looking at lights. Not natural light but the flickering glow of lamplight through small windows. The road had widened out and she realized that without noticing she had walked straight into the middle of a village. Primitive, tired-looking cottages lined the road and somewhere rain poured out of a roof-gutter and into a trough. There were no people about.

Hoisting Arthur up again, Ace carried him towards the nearest building.

Now evening was here, the Wychborn Arms had livened up. The regulars had arrived out of the rain for their beer and food. Bert felt better, this was the routine. As his wife prepared meals in the kitchen, he worked the bar, serving customers.

The front door opened, sending a blast of icy wind through the room. The seven drinkers turned their heads to see which of their mates had dared the rain to get here. 'Bloody hell,' shouted Old Skinner, who was right next to the door. 'Come in and shut the bloody thing.'

Two figures literally fell into the inn. Bert gasped.

One of them might have been a young woman under all the filth. She wore odd black spectacles across her eyes but yes, definitely a woman. Half dressed and the few clothes she was wearing were both strange and torn. She

71

was carrying someone. 'Help me then,' she snapped. Bert didn't recognize the accent.

She undraped the large, equally filthy man from her shoulders and gracefully laid him across a table. She had muscles, Bert could see that.

The young woman stumbled to her knees and stared at the fire, clearly exhausted. Her long hair hung in knots across her face. Bert saw she was breathing heavily.

'Heaven's sake, Bert,' shouted Madge from behind him. 'She's freezing. Fetch a blanket.'

The man on the table was still and quiet. Big bloke but somehow . . . soft. Different. It made Bert uncomfortable.

'Bert!' shouted his wife.

The landlord turned and walked past his wife to grab a woollen blanket hanging up in the kitchen. So far, none of the other customers had moved.

The young woman managed to catch her breath but had started to shiver. 'Hello,' she stammered, 'I'm Ace. This is my friend Arthur.'

Old Skinner, motivated to action at last, got up and slammed the door shut.

After a bowl of hot soup Ace was feeling more like a human being and less like a wet rag. She sat gracefully in front of the roaring fire.

She looked at Arthur's body on the table. It was clear to her that he was ill. His large frame seemed to shrink under the blanket and despite the warmth of the room he was shivering and pale. A man, presumably the landlord, was sitting next to him, trying to feed him some soup.

Finding her strength again, Ace stood up. Watched by the suspicious, silent drinkers, she walked over to Arthur. 'You okay, mate?' she asked cautiously.

Watery eyes flicked open and stared at her. 'Hello Ace,' he said. 'What's happening to me? I don't like it.'

Ace knelt next to him, stroking his head. 'You're weird. I wish I knew what to do.'

He smiled, handsome despite the illness. 'Me too. I've got a strange tingling in me body. Like something wants to get out.'

Bert spooned some soup into his mouth. 'Quiet, lad. Keep drinking the broth, it'll stop the cold.'

Ace started to become aware that the blurred faces around her were in fact people. Rough and ready but still people.

'You got a doctor here?' she asked Bert who despite his dandy sideburns seemed a decent-looking bloke. She was surprised to see him shudder and turn to his wife. She shook her head, very economically.

'Well?' This was no time for conspiracies. 'Yes or no?'

One of the men in the inn, a large mean one, muttered from his beer. 'Bert? Perhaps Doctor Rix would like to hear about this.' It sounded like a threat.

Bert was quick to answer. Ace spotted his nervousness. 'Now, Thos. Lad's got a bit o'cold on him. He just needs some sleep and a warm bed. He'll be all right.'

Ace watched as the big man stood up from his stool. His companion, who looked like a leaner and wirier version of him, did the same. She sized them up. Tough enough. Big and brutal and able to soak up damage, but no technique. If you hit them quick and hard they'd be no trouble.

'What d'you say, Bert?' asked Thos, a grin appearing on his face. 'Didn't quite catch it.'

Ace decided to intervene. They had other things to worry about than this. The two creeps looked mean and vicious, used to getting their own way. 'Listen you two,' she said calmly, 'this man is ill. If you know a doctor go and get him. Otherwise leave us to it.'

The wiry man's eyes lit up. 'Lady likes to take charge does she? Perhaps she needs larnin'. Running about half dressed, ain't decent.'

Ace could have screamed. On top of everything, two dickheads out for some nasty fun. She'd better get ready for trouble.

73

'Lads,' said Bert in a quavering voice, 'come on. The boy's hurt here.'

Archie raised a warning finger, 'Careful, Bert. Or we might have to teach you too.'

Bert's customers clearly knew the brothers' habits. Old Skinner was up and out of the door. The others quickly followed him. Mrs Robbins emerged from the kitchen with a broom. 'You two! Out!' She began pushing at Archie and Thos. 'We don't have no trouble in this house.'

Quick as lightning, Archie whipped his hand up and slapped her hard across the face, knocking her over. He seemed to be enjoying himself.

Ace decided it was time for a little rest and relaxation. It would make a change. She dropped into a fighting stance. Archie and Thos looked warily at her. 'Okay boys, let the good times roll.'

It was all over in five seconds. Bert couldn't believe his eyes. She had moved so quickly, with such precision. Archie was crawling on the floor clutching his crushed genitalia, half unconscious from the roundhouse kick that had sent him flying over the bar. Of Thos there was no sign except a few teeth and a trail of blood out of the door where he had been thrown head-first.

'Time gentlemen please,' Ace commented, dusting herself down. Bert helped his wife to her feet. He tried to speak, 'How did you . . .?'

Ace gave him a wink. 'I do aerobics.' She walked over to Archie and grabbed his compliant neck. While he moaned she dragged him, muscles bulging, over to the door. 'You're barred, pal,' she laughed and kicked him outside into the mud.

He turned back, spittle hanging from his mouth. 'You bitch,' he managed. 'Rix'll fix you. We'll be back.' With that he limped to his feet and staggered off cursing into the dark.

'Any time,' Ace bellowed after him.

Bert sat his wife down and steeled himself to ask some questions. 'Just who are you, miss?'

A wicked smile broke across her face, 'Me? I'm Ace!' With that, she fell back into a chair. 'Must be tired, I let them live.'

Clutching her bruised face, Mrs Robbins warned, 'They will come back, you know. And there'll be more of them.'

Ace shrugged. 'Let them come. I'm out of here anyway.'

Bert was looking at Arthur again. Turning, he spoke softly. 'I dunno 'bout that, miss. He's worse.'

They crowded round the silent man. He did look worse. Somehow, he seemed transparent, insubstantial. Bert watched as Ace touched the man's face. 'Christ,' she exclaimed, 'he's feverish.'

Arthur opened his eyes once more. He seemed unaware of the three faces looking down at him. Blond hair, washed pale by the rain, stuck up from his head. The mud caking him was flaking off, deserting him. Bert could see an odd golden glint in his eye that seemed more than just a reflection of the fireside glow. 'This is new,' Arthur whispered, slightly afraid. 'Help me.'

Bert was horrified. 'He's bewitched, that's what it is.'

His wife thumped him. 'Don't be daft. He's sick, that's all.' All the same, Bert saw fear in her face.

Ace leaned over Arthur, perhaps to detect his breath. 'I think he's dying.' She grabbed his hand and squeezed. 'Stay with me, Arthur. I'll help you.'

Arthur smiled. Bert thought his features seemed to be less defined, as if he was smoothing out. 'I'm full up,' whispered the man. 'I can't keep it in.'

A door opened behind them: the door to the stairs. Bert turned, expecting trouble. The gentleman from London stood in the doorway. 'What the devil is all this racket?' he asked imperiously.

Bert rushed over, desperate to get him out of the way. 'It's nothing Mr Aickland,' he gabbled, 'nothing for you to worry about. I'll have your tea sent up in a minute.'

Aickland was clearly not put off by Bert's evasions. 'Wait. You two.' He looked at Ace and Arthur, and his

75

tone changed to one of worry: 'You look awfully tired. Could I offer you tea and a bath?'

Bert was surprised to hear Ace laugh. 'All right,' she said, 'you've made my day.'

Richard Aickland, on his first trip away from his aunts in London, was amazed at his own recklessness. 'I do not normally indulge young women in this manner,' he said. 'However you two did seem in particular need.' He paced the room uncomfortably.

Ace finished drying her hair by the fire. She chewed on a piece of tough rabbit. 'This is as bad as the rations they dish out to the Auxies.'

'The who?'

Ace smiled and for the first time Aickland became aware of her femininity. As usual on these situations, he blushed. 'Never mind,' she said cryptically. 'I'm sorry, I don't know your name.'

Mortified by his lack of etiquette, Aickland proffered a hand. 'I'm terribly sorry. Richard Aickland. From Camberwell. That's in London.'

'I know. I'm from Perivale.'

'The village in Middlesex?'

Ace nodded. Aickland detected a reluctance on her part to tell him too much. 'What are you doing here?' she asked. 'Wherever here is.'

Aickland frowned. Clearly, they had got themselves lost on the road. 'This is the village of Wychborn, in Devon,' he said. 'Were you travelling to Plymouth?'

'Sort of. If you're from Camberwell, how come you ended up here?'

Aickland laughed. That question. 'Where do I begin? I am twenty-two years of age. I have never travelled. I live with my aunts and am the recipient of a very large inheritance from my father. He was in the army and died a long time ago.' He stopped and looked at Ace. 'I'm not being tedious, am I?'

Ace shook her head. She pushed the remains of her

meal away. 'Course not. I'm used to it. Certain people telling long involved stories. Carry on Doctor.' She glanced at the bed where Arthur lay wrapped up and asleep.

Unsure of what Ace meant, Aickland continued: 'I have not seen much of life. Kindly as my aunts are, they have not encourage me to travel. They worry I might fall ill, since I was a somewhat sickly infant. Anyway, in recent years I have become ... restless. I became very bored with society life. One of the disadvantages of being rich and having a minor title is that one becomes prey to every eligible young lady in London. And their overbearing families. I have no desire for anything except my liberty.'

'I can understand that.'

'The upshot of the story is that I became interested in certain ... occurrences. Unusual occurrences, you might say.'

Aickland sat down in the chair next to Ace. He wondered why he was telling her so much about himself. Was it because she was different? She had none of the stifling obsessions with manners that afflicted so many women.

'What sort of occurrences?' Ace asked.

'You'll laugh. How is your friend?'

She walked over to the bed. As if detecting her, Arthur moved and moaned. Aickland watched as Ace bent down to his face. 'Arthur?' she whispered.

'Ace?' said Arthur. 'I can't see you. Only grey things.' Interested, Aickland went to the other side of the bed. He saw Ace frown with confusion. 'Grey things?' he asked Arthur.

Arthur answered as best he could: 'I dunno, I ain't never seen 'em before.' He slipped back into unconsciousness. Ace bit her lip. 'I wish I knew what was wrong with him. He's been like this ever since ...' Her voice tailed off as she realized Aickland was looking at her.

Her eyes flicked over to some of Aickland's clothes

lying neatly on the bed: a white shirt and plain suit. 'You need them?' she asked.

Aickland was puzzled, 'I beg your . . . Oh yes, I mean no. I don't.' He realized what he was saying. 'But they are clothes for men.'

Ace grinned at him. 'Don't worry, I've done this before too.'

Arthur appeared to be sound asleep. Aickland scratched his head, trying to avert his gaze from Ace as she climbed into his spare suit. 'Chap's gone bonkers,' was his diagnosis of Arthur's condition.

'I don't know,' Ace replied, pulling on the breeches. 'I might as well tell you. He's been like this since we left the field.'

'Field?'

Ace sighed. 'We were in this field, only it was the middle of summer. Somehow we fell into a hole and landed up here. Like Alice.'

'Alice?'

'Never mind. That's it.'

Aickland was confused but not immediately disbelieving. Ace seemed sincere enough. He thought for a moment and then said, 'Well. I'll try to assume you are telling the truth and you're not actually mad. You came from the summer, fell down a hole and ended up here in Wychborn.'

'You think I am mad, don't you?'

Aickland laughed. 'I can think of worse things to be. Actually, that's what I came here for: the occurrences I mentioned earlier. Strange happenings are my forte. The supernatural. You see, that is what I've been studying for the last three years. I have theories. It is my belief that what we term "the supernatural" is actually a world parallel to our own. Sometimes they cross each other and an event occurs in one or the other. Like seeing a ghost or hearing a spectral sound.'

He sighed, deflated. 'Actually, I've never told anyone that before. I suppose I am a bit of a bore on the subject.

Perhaps you're not as mad as you think. Anyway, that is why I have come here, to Wychborn. I suppose you could say I am a ghost hunter.'

'Why here?'

He looked down, shamefaced. 'I decided to see if I could find any evidence for my theories. There's a house. I mean, you had to come from somewhere. You look like you're from another place, that's certain.'

Ace smiled but Aickland detected no mockery in it. She really was a mystery.

'Well,' he said firmly, 'no doubt I am wrong. Life never really has anything interesting in it. The real explanations are always dull. No doubt there is a perfectly rational reason for you being here.'

This time Ace laughed out aloud. 'Well, Richard, I think you're in for a treat.'

There was a knock at the door. It was Bert. 'Just come to take your plates,' he muttered. He took a nervous look at Arthur, picked up the remains of the meal and disappeared out of the room.

Aickland inspected Arthur again. He was no doctor but it was clear that the man was very sick. This was no cold he was suffering, it was something else altogether.

After all his research on Wychborn House, Aickland had been certain he would encounter something odd here. He knew it was an unusual place. However, he had not expected the strangeness to begin before he even got there. He wondered whether Ace and Arthur had some sort of connection with the House. He felt he should at least mention it.

He turned and looked. Ace was fast asleep in the chair. 'Oh well,' said Aickland to himself. 'It can wait.'

There was a loud knocking at the door. For a moment Aickland wondered where he was.

'Open up!' shouted Bert.

Aickland opened his eyes. Ace was snoring in her chair by the fire. Arthur lay glowing in the bed. He was asleep

79

but his body was surrounded by a slight haze of golden light. Aickland took a closer look. This was no reflection from the fire, this was him. Arthur's body was less substantial than ever, he could see through it to the cushion under his head. It was as if his innards were being drained and converted into the light that surrounded him.

Again there was a fierce hammering at the door. Ace stirred in her chair and woke up. 'Have I been asleep?' she asked blearily.

'Open up!' Bert shouted again.

Aickland snapped back, 'In a minute! Ace, look at him. He's changed even more.'

Ace was up in an instant and staring at the new, wide-eyed Arthur. 'What the hell?'

There came more hammering at the door. Ace went to unlatch it. She kept her gaze on Arthur, not wanting him out of her sight. 'He's turning into something.'

The door burst open. Aickland turned to see an iron bar heading for Ace's skull. She dodged and the bar caught her across the neck. There was a crunch and she dropped like a stone.

A gang of men piled into the room. They included the injured Archie and Thos Lewis. Aickland recognized them from Ace's description. Bert was dragged in, a cut on his forehead. 'I'm sorry Mr Aickland, they . . .'

'Quiet, Bert.' Thos gave the landlord a punch to the head and threw him out.

Aickland stepped back, terrified by the intrusion. 'Wh-what do you want?'

Archie looked down at the motionless body of Ace and chuckled. 'Told you I'd be back, din' I?'

Feeling more like he ought to do something brave rather than wanting to, Aickland jumped at the man that had felled Ace. He was caught and held by a burly youth who had followed the brothers into the room.

'Sright Billy,' said Archie, 'you're larnin' fast.'

Two other men poked their heads through the door.

Archie barked orders at them. 'Frankie, Gray, in here. Billy, you hold the gentleman.'

Aickland nodded at Ace. He had gone white and tried hard not to show his fear. 'What about her?'

Archie gave the body a cursory glance. He did not bother to reply. Frankie and Gray, the two older men at the door, shouldered their way in and began ransacking Aickland's belongings. They hauled open wardrobes, drawers and his wallet.

'What shall I do with this one?' asked Billy, excited and full of blood-lust.

Thos smiled revealing a set of broken and missing teeth. 'Hold him tight. I've always wanted to give a gentleman a going-over.'

He spat bloody phlegm and rubbed his hands. Aickland closed his eyes. When Thos punched him it was like being hit by a steam hammer. It landed in his stomach and felt as if it had caved through his ribs. Bile shot from Aickland's mouth. He couldn't breathe, his guts were on fire. Another blow landed, this time pounding into his face.

'You like that sir?' asked Thos politely. Billy let go and Aickland fell to the floor, head ringing, unaware of anything except pain. He had felt cartilage crunch in his nose and he hoped desperately it wasn't broken. There was blood on his face. 'Ace,' he moaned weakly, vaguely seeing a tear-blurred figure next to him. Sounds and voices swam about in his ears.

'You hit her too hard Archie,' said somebody. 'Near killed her.'

'You should worry, she had it coming.'

'But she's . . .'

'Shut up. It's that one Rix wants, lift him up.'

There came a flash of golden light. Aickland lifted his head to see Frankie and Gray backing away in horror from something. Aickland struggled to clear his senses.

'I'm burning!' Arthur cried out. Aickland forced his eyes to focus. Voices still assailed his ears. 'Holy God!'

'Get back! Get back!'

At last Aickland saw what was going on around him. Arthur was somehow floating in the air, a foot above the sofa. The glow burst out from him. He was suffused with light. It pulsed, turning his body translucent. Two golden eyes gleamed out at them all.

'Ace, wake up,' whimpered Aickland, unable to look at the light. His lungs felt crushed, his breathing hoarse and laboured.

Ace remained still, blood trickling from her left ear. Aickland crawled to her and felt her chest. Her breathing was shallow and slowing down. Eyes stared up sightlessly and the head lolled at the wrong angle. 'You've broken her neck,' breathed Aickland.

The men, silhouetted against the light, backed off from the glowing creature. Billy simply bolted from the room. Aickland could only watch as Thos bellowed at the gang: 'Frankie, Gray, grab the bastard.'

Frankie, a thin white-haired man, fell backwards over the chair Aickland had slept in. Gray, the ginger-headed one, dropped to his knees in fear, murmuring, ''Tis an angel, Thos, an angel . . .'

Thos snatched the iron bar from his stupefied brother and brandished it at the two men. 'Get him! Or I'll get you with this!'

Finding a strength from somewhere, Aickland suddenly leapt up, pain gone in the face of unremitting rage. He threw himself at Thos screaming, 'She's dead!'

Thos felled him with a single blow. Aickland slumped to the floor, looking up to see the burly man order Frankie and Gray to grab Arthur.

Nervously Gray placed a hand on the figure's arm. There was a bright spark, like lightning, and he flew back, smashing into a cabinet. He slumped to the ground without a word.

Arthur sat up. His eyes were gold, no trace of humanity in them. The men scrambled to the walls to avoid the all-enveloping glow. 'Ace,' came Arthur's voice in Aickland's head. 'Ace, you are hurt.'

The figure began to move slowly. It floated over Aickland and hung above Ace, golden eyes staring at her body. Aickland felt disorientated from the blow. He stared up at Arthur's inhuman face. There was a strange electrical charge in the air, an ozone tension.

Slowly, the vision descended on Ace. Arthur lowered an arm and touched her lolling head. 'Ace,' came the powerful voice again.

Light pulsed through the arm and melted into Ace's head. It flickered and then disappeared into her neck. As Aickland watched in disbelief, bones adjusted and twisted until her head was back in position. Her breathing grew stronger and a healthy flush came back into her cheeks.

The glow of the creature diminished and suddenly Arthur dropped with a thud to the ground. He still glowed but had regained human form.

Aickland found the strength to reach him. He seemed to be breathing normally.

'Wha?' came a gruff but feminine voice from beside him. He turned and felt Ace's neck. It was totally undamaged.

'Where am I?' she growled, clearly ready to commit an act of violence on somebody. Aickland decided to act quickly before the victim became him. 'Ace!' he shouted. 'You're all right again!'

'Am I?' came a groggy reply. 'I am glad.' She opened her eyes and looked at him. 'Christ,' she said, 'you look rough.'

Reminded of his injuries, Aickland realized how much pain he was in. Blood poured from his nose and he could feel bruises swelling on his stomach. He hoped nothing had been ruptured. Shame Arthur couldn't have put some of that light into him.

Without warning, Archie kicked Aickland in the head and he fell to one side, moaning. He rolled over and stared up into his attacker's face.

Archie looked scared and more dangerous than ever. Turning his attention to Ace, he sneered, 'Get up or I'll crack you again. This time there'll be no fairy to save you.'

He pulled Ace to her feet and threw her at Thos. 'Hold her,' he ordered. His brother, looking dazed, obeyed.

Gray and Frankie were still cowering on the floor in the far corners of the room. Archie glared at them. 'Pick him up,' he commanded, indicating Arthur. 'He looks harmless enough now.'

They remained kneeling, apparently too frightened to react.

'Do it!' Archie shouted.

Shaking, the two men obeyed. This time there were no shocks. They hauled Arthur to his feet.

Thos was holding Ace up by the hair. She appeared too shaken to know where she was. Thos nodded. 'I'll take this one. It's my turn with her.'

Archie smiled and looked around. The room was a mess. Smashed furniture and crockery were everywhere and the air was tainted with a smell of charring. Frankie and Gray held Arthur between them.

Archie seemed to come to a decision. 'Get some rope,' he said. 'We'll tie 'em up and drag 'em to Rix's in case they start up again. All of 'em. Tie 'em all up!' Aickland saw the men react to the hysteria in his voice.

Archie turned and saw Billy skulking back through the door. He grinned and slapped the boy in the face. 'Come on. It's all over,' he laughed. It was clear no one was going to disobey.

Bert and his wife watched sullenly as Rix's thugs came down the stairs.

Archie led the way, once more clutching his iron bar. He was followed by Thos, who held the semi-conscious Ace in a crushing grip. After them came Billy, holding a still bleeding Aickland in a neck-lock. Finally, Frankie and Gray gingerly dragged Arthur down the stairs. They looked uncomfortable and scared, endeavouring to have as little contact with the man as possible.

Bert was furious. Who the hell did Rix think he was? Those three had done nothing to merit this sort of treatment from Rix's paid bullies. The villagers lived in fear of Rix and Bert knew no one would lift a finger to help. Well, he'd had enough. He could be neutral no longer.

'You'd better clear up in there, Bert,' Archie shouted at him. 'It's a right bloody mess.'

The man laughed as he opened the door onto the drizzling dawn. A faint blue morning light took the edge off the darkness. It seemed odd but Bert could have sworn that Arthur was... well, glowing. Archie gave the slumped man a kick as he was carried out of the Wychborn Arms.

Just you wait, Archibald Lewis, vowed Bert.

The men dragged their three prisoners into the muddy street. What few passers-by there were obviously knew better than to question the Lewis brothers.

'Keep them ropes tight, boys,' ordered Archie. 'We'll drag 'em through the mud.'

Ace felt thick hemp ropes wrapped round her body. She was beginning to make sense of the situation after what had seemed like hours of darkness and confusion. The last thing she remembered clearly was opening the door to the room and feeling something hit her. Strange that she now felt no pain at all. In fact, she felt energized and full of life.

Squinting into the morning light, she saw Richard Aickland, ugly bruises welling up on his face, kneeling in a puddle. He was draped with ropes similar to those which bound her. Poor sod. He looked half dead. She was surprised to feel an almost motherly concern for him.

A snap on the rope pulled Ace over into the road. It was Thos, grinning at her through his broken mouth. The three prisoners were dragged through the wet streets of Wychborn as a weak sun came up over the horizon. Thos had bound Ace's legs so that she was only able to hobble along, constantly being pulled off balance. The journey was clearly designed to humiliate and exhaust them. Ace realized that she had to keep her new-found energy a secret. It might prove a vital advantage at a later stage. She could handle the journey as long as she didn't get drowned in mud or scoured on the stony ground.

She cursed as she fell again and was dragged a few metres before she managed to scramble back to her feet. She mentally apologized to Richard for ruining his expensive clothes.

Thos was pulling her on his own, she noted, whereas it took both Archie and Billy to drag Aickland, while Frankie and Gray carted the semi-conscious Arthur between them. So, although her progress was slower and more painful than the others, her captor would tire more quickly.

Ace tried to reach him but a jerk on the rope showed that Thos was still strong enough to resist her. Deciding to save her energy for later, she concentrated on staying upright.

The prisoners were led out of the village and up a steep wooded hill. The road was winding and narrow, and Ace found it impossible to guess where they were being led. There were frequent stops for rest but the gang was too alert and the captives too exhausted for there to be any hope of escape.

Ace used the journey to review the events of the last few hours. She realized she couldn't even remember the location of the field where she and Arthur had landed. Feeling more trapped than ever, she stumbled slowly up the hill in the rain.

Richard Aickland was exhausted. Archie and Billy seemed to have taken a particular delight in dragging him across the worst of the mud and stones. His wounds were killing him and the blood would not stop running. He had tried to keep an eye on Ace and Arthur but his own predicament had kept him from helping them.

Aickland was most worried about Archie. For all his

apparent air of command, it was obvious that the swarthy man was losing his grip.

'Rix'll know what to do ... he rewards loyalty, he told me. He'll sort everything out ...' Aickland heard Archie muttering. Even Billy looked worried, casting nervous glances at his leader. The words continued without stopping: 'Just get up to the farm. Rix'll know what to do. Everything'll be all right.'

Aickland groaned and fell into the mud again.

At last they came over a rise in sight of a large, comfortable farmhouse. A welcome yellow light from the kitchen revealed an occupant within.

They reached a stone path leading to a hinged wooden door at the front of the building. The door opened and a short, ruddy-faced old man stood looking at them. 'My, my,' he said in a gentle Scots accent. 'What have we here?'

Aickland looked at Archie. The man seemed so tired that he could think of nothing to say. After a minute, he had clearly recovered some of his energy. He took a deep breath and waved an arm back at Aickland. Wearily, he spoke: 'Doctor Rix. Thank God.'

Chapter 4

At ten o'clock, Bernice made her way to the dining-room. She found the Doctor and Garvey waiting for her. Garvey opened an ornate set of double doors and ushered them inside. The large room was entirely lit by candles. They were everywhere, covering every available space, tables, sideboards and on brackets in the walls.

The Doctor was clearly delighted at the sumptuous decor. 'You shouldn't have,' he exclaimed.

'Nonsense, Doctor,' Garvey acquiesced. 'This is what we always do. Every evening.'

Bernice watched him limp away towards the food. Covered trays were laid out on a large mahogany dining table. The butler glowed in the flickering light from the candles. He stopped and held his chin, as if pondering some important matter. He turned back to the Doctor and Bernice. 'I believe that to arrange matters correctly is . . . a pleasure.' He seemed satisfied that he had found another new word and began lifting the lids from the trays. He examined the contents and replaced the lids again.

Bernice noticed the Doctor looking at her jeans and jacket. 'You could have dressed for the occasion,' he said grumpily.

Bernice laughed and stared back. 'You can talk, you old tramp. Anyway, one of the maids did offer me a frock. Not really what you want to be caught in when the bad guys arrive.'

The Doctor tapped his nose. 'Tut tut Benny, you are too suspicious. It'll be your undoing.'

Garvey pulled a chair back, standing over it like a silver-maned bloodhound. 'Professor Summerfield,' he requested. 'If you please.'

Bernice gave a little demure smile. 'Thank you Mr Garvey, I would be delighted.' She sat down, noticing that four places had been laid for dinner: herself, the Doctor, possibly Charlotte and one other. 'Expecting more guests, Mr Garvey?' she asked politely, as the old man pulled out a chair for the Doctor.

Garvey frowned for a moment as if something was bothering him. Slowly he said, 'No, Professor. Just you, the Doctor here, Miss Charlotte and . . . and Miss Victoria.' Again the frown, as if he had a headache.

'Of course,' the Doctor replied, seating himself. 'You know, I am rather famished.'

The two maids, Mary and Jane, stood silently by the main double doors. Bernice leaned forward to whisper to the Doctor: 'Do they have to stand there? It unsettles me.'

The Doctor looked at the two women. One was plump and ginger, the other thin as a rake with long, black hair bulging under a tight hat.

Bernice scowled. 'I hate the idea of servants. I get edgy when waiters try to serve me in restaurants. I am perfectly capable of preparing my own food.'

The Doctor sighed. 'Sometimes Benny, you can be too much of a martyr. Just drink the wine. It's a white and I think you'll like it.'

Garvey returned to the Doctor's side, red-faced and full of apology. 'I'm sorry Doctor, Professor,' he said. 'The wine has been opened some time. I . . . I was unable to procure a new one from the cellar this morning.' Again, the butler seemed distracted.

Bernice pinged her glass with a knife. 'Don't worry old chap, I'm sure it'll be delicious.'

Garvey and the maids, with a strict military flair, uncovered the food. Lifting the lids from the platters, they revealed what to Bernice was a veritable feast. Pork and chicken had been roasted and expertly carved. Fresh vegetables steamed in their bowls surrounded by a host of garnishes. Everything was perfectly arranged on the silver dishes.

Bernice was impressed, despite wondering how her friends in the largely vegetarian twenty-fifth century would have reacted to such a spread. She prepared herself to tuck in but caught a disapproving glance from the Doctor. 'I think we should wait for the rest of the guests to arrive,' he murmured.

Abruptly, he picked up a pair of silver spoons and began playing them on his knee. 'A little entertainment to take your mind off food?'

Bernice put her head in her hands. 'Don't start.'

'Good evening,' came a voice from the door. Bernice turned to see a beautiful woman glide into the dining room. She was dressed in a simple silk dress of white and gold. Around her neck a choker of diamonds glinted in the candle light. Her black hair was swept high off her forehead and her dark eyes flickered in the soft flame of the room.

'Ch-Charlotte?' whispered Bernice, feeling distinctly under-dressed. The woman looked unbelievable, stunning.

Charlotte stopped at her place at the table. She looked at the fourth setting and sighed. 'Garvey,' and there was a concealed sadness in her voice, 'Victoria has gone. She will not require dinner, she is dead.'

To Bernice, Charlotte's voice sounded different. It was deeper, more . . . more experienced. She attempted to get a better look at that perfect, oval face. It was difficult to see in the red and yellow light. She gasped and immediately covered her mouth with a napkin. Charlotte now appeared to be the same age as her.

'Yes,' remarked the woman, 'the change continues.'

She smiled at Garvey who bowed and held out a chair for her. She sat gracefully down, to Bernice every inch the mannered lady. Next to her, she felt like a clod-hopping incompetent. Charlotte turned to her and the Doctor sitting opposite and said, 'I apologize for being late. I trust you understand. I have much on my mind at present. Soup please, Garvey.'

The butler clapped his hands and the two maids came to the table and began to serve. Bernice glanced at the Doctor, hoping for some comment on the vision at the table with them. She was surprised to see him tensed up in his chair, eyes wide and staring at Charlotte. 'What is it?' she asked.

The Doctor took his glass in his hand and gulped down the entire contents. This seemed to break him out of his trance. He beamed a relaxed smile and leaned forward. 'Excuse me,' he asked Charlotte politely. 'I have the overwhelming impression that I have met you somewhere, some time before. A very, very long time ago.'

Charlotte, this new mature Charlotte, appeared unruffled, although Bernice detected a nervous quality in her body language. It was too mannered, too refined. 'Doctor,' the woman replied, 'we may well have met before. Alas, I am unaware of this, as I seem to be unaware of so many things these days.'

This silenced the Doctor who began thoughtfully tucking in to his hot soup. Bernice watched him eat. It was unlike the Time Lord to be so thrown by events.

'How are your investigations proceeding, Doctor?' asked Charlotte, apparently making polite conversation.

There was a pause before the Doctor answered: 'Excellent soup, Charlotte. Game, is it not?'

'Game for anything, I'll wager.'

'Thank you Professor Summerfield.'

Charlotte smiled again, clearly not understanding the joke, if indeed there had been one.

'I am worried,' the Doctor finally admitted. Somehow he had managed to spill three dollops of soup onto his jumper. 'Events are occurring too quickly. Accelerating out of control. I'm worried that by the time I've worked it out it'll all be over.'

Charlotte nodded, pushing her soup bowl away. She spoke: 'We must find out. Nothing has ever altered here. Ever. Now the pattern of our lives is disrupted. It may never be the same again. For the first time we in the House may be forced to . . .' She searched for the words.

The Doctor supplied them: 'Adapt. Change.'

Charlotte nodded again. 'If you like. What practical steps can be taken?'

The Doctor seemed to think for a minute. He dipped his fingers into his wine and attempted to use the liquid to wipe the stains from his jumper. As he did so he said, 'Firstly, I must know exactly who lives here. How many people do you actually know?'

Bernice watched in disgust as the Doctor smeared the stains more deeply into the wool until they were thoroughly absorbed. 'Stop that,' she complained. 'You're making it worse. Leave it alone.'

'But it's stained now.'

'You'll just have to leave it. Wash it later, or better still get rid of it altogether.'

Charlotte waited until the Doctor had finished spluttering at Bernice's remarks. 'There are twelve here, Doctor,' she said. A frown creased her flawless forehead. 'Eleven now.'

The Doctor pulled a notebook and stubby pencil from his pocket. He licked the tip of the pencil. 'And they are?'

Charlotte counted on her fingers. 'Victoria has gone of course. Myself, Mr Garvey, Mary, Jane, Mrs Chamberlain the cook, Mrs Irving, Tillie the chambermaid, and Peter. They are the staff for the House. For the grounds, Ted the gamekeeper, Mr Alleyn the gardener . . . oh, and Arthur who works in the fields. That is twelve, I think.'

The Doctor hurriedly wrote down the names and looked up. 'And how many have been seen today?'

Charlotte shrugged. 'I don't know. Everyone except Ted, Mr Alleyn and Arthur. What about you, Garvey?'

Garvey's face was hidden in shadow. He looked at his

feet. 'Well miss,' he said slowly, 'I saw Alleyn go to the Camellia House this morning. I have not seen him since.'

Straight away, Bernice realized that he wasn't telling the full story. Suddenly she was reminded of something. 'I think I saw someone,' she announced. 'When I was coming down the hill in the afternoon. A man, down by that lake. He was a long way away but I think he was dressed in a black suit.'

Charlotte and Garvey exchanged puzzled glances. They both shook their heads. Charlotte seemed confused. 'I do not know of anyone in a black suit apart from Mr Garvey and I am sure he would not be at the lake in the afternoon.'

'I was not, miss.'

Bernice shrugged. 'I'm sure I... Oh well, must have been mistaken,' she said, unconvinced.

The Doctor looked up again from his list. 'Mrs Irving. Where is she now?'

Charlotte looked around confidently and then paused. She seemed surprised. 'She... I don't know. I haven't seen her for hours.'

The Doctor shut his book and put it in his pocket. His lips tightened as if thinking about what to say next. 'I think,' he said gravely, 'we should find everyone and get them all together. To be sure they are warned about the changes going on here. Although, and I don't wish to be alarmist, I am certain that the little we have seen has certainly occurred elsewhere.'

There was a pause. Bernice sniffed and sniffed again. 'What on earth is that appalling smell?'

There was an unpleasant odour in the air. A smell of decay, pungent and rotten. Bernice looked and saw that it came from the table in front of them.

'The food!' gasped Charlotte.

The meat was going bad, drying and turning yellow.

'It's like stop-motion photography,' observed the Doctor, obviously fascinated.

The edges of the pork curled up and flaked apart. It

began to melt and bubble. The carrots softened and pulped, the potatoes blackened and sprouted sickly white shoots. The stench grew and permeated.

'Oh my God,' retched Bernice who stood up and backed away. She felt sick and wondered about the state of the soup in her belly.

Tiny white maggots hatched and grew, then devoured the heaps of rot that lay neatly arranged on the table. Charlotte simply sat and stared, perhaps becoming accustomed to absurd occurrences in the House. Garvey made a move towards the heaps on the platters.

'Leave it!' shouted the Doctor. 'Stay well back.' He shivered. 'I'll open the windows.' He went to the plush red velvet curtains and hauled them open, revealing a panoramic view of the night-dark hills surrounding them. A sudden gust of air extinguished half the candles in the room.

'Doctor,' asked Bernice, frightened now, 'what's happening? Where did that wind come from?'

'Quiet Benny. I'll get the window open so we can breathe. Get rid of this stench.'

Bernice turned, holding her nose, to see Charlotte moving slowly away from the table. The woman was marvellously calm.

The process of decay had almost run its course. Soon there was nothing on the platters but dry dust. The Doctor unlatched a large window and pulled it open. A fresh breeze lifted the smell and washed it from the room.

'May I clear up now, Doctor?' asked Garvey, as if nothing unusual had happened. Glancing at the table, the Doctor nodded. 'All right, but be careful.'

The room became quiet except for the ticking of a grandfather clock in the corner. Garvey and the maids rushed over to clear away the ruined remains of the meal.

'I must apologize again Doctor,' Charlotte remarked, looking shaken but composed. 'This is dreadfully embarrassing.'

The Doctor smiled wryly back. 'Don't worry, I think it's all over now.'

From the woods on the hills outside came a deafening, thunderous rustling. The Doctor's shoulders sagged and he looked shamefacedly at Bernice. 'Me and my big mouth.'

On the hills, the trees were moving. They rippled and swayed with lively animation. The darkness made it difficult to see properly so Bernice could only gain an impression. It was like a great invisible wave crashing over the woods. The trees cracked and spat like a fire. 'What the hell is that?' she mouthed.

'It's the leaves,' said the Doctor wonderingly. 'Billions of them. All of them, dying at once.'

Charlotte, hand to her mouth, dashed to the open window. She seemed overwhelmed by fear and frustration, unable to maintain her composure. 'Stop it! Stop the noise!' She clapped her hands over her ears.

One word echoed in Bernice's mind. Her brain struggled to make sense of it. She turned to the Doctor. 'Leaves? What do you mean?'

He was detached, observing the phenomenon, analysing it. He grinned. 'Leaves. Falling from the trees. All at once.'

Charlotte was breathing heavily. Strands of hair fell across her face, giving her a dishevelled, unearthly look. 'I don't understand.'

The Doctor stepped back, seemingly exhilarated by the event. His mischievous face was alight, his eyes shining. 'You know what it is? It's autumn!'

Charlotte staggered back to a chair and fell into it. The Doctor ignored her and, arms swinging, declaimed, 'They're coming off the trees. Can't you feel the temperature drop? Autumn in thirty seconds. I've never seen anything like it.'

Bernice was peering out into the blackness. 'How can you tell? I can't see a thing. You've had too much wine.' Her voice altered abruptly. 'My God! I think you're right.'

As she watched, another wave passed over the dark

wood. As it travelled, every tree in its wake shed its leaves and sat there stark and bare. Within seconds, the hills became cemeteries of dark, spidery trunks growing from beds of grey leaves.

'This is going to look fabulous in the morning,' Bernice joked nervously. She felt herself perspiring. She could have done with a drink but the wine was probably pickled.

Charlotte had recovered her composure and stood, pale and beautiful, staring out into the night. To Bernice she looked like a ghost, out of time.

There came a different noise from the hills. Bernice heard it as a faint crying in the distance, gaining in volume and momentum. It was not a pleasant sound, reminding her of the insect. 'What now?' she asked.

The sound became many sounds, lots of voices far away. They were shrieks and wails from the mouths of unimaginable creatures.

'There's something in the woods,' Bernice whispered to the Doctor. 'Something alive. But not human.'

'Something less than human,' he replied grimly.

A fire blazed up at the top of the hill straight ahead of them. Orange flames silhouetted the skeletal trees. Another one, to its left, also started up. Plumes of smoke billowed up into the night sky.

'Someone's burning the woods,' said Charlotte mournfully.

The Doctor was watching the fires. 'The flames are coming from quite specific places. Man-made. Bonfires. Regular and controlled.'

A third fire, a quarter of a mile to the right of the first one, was lit. All three were right at the top of the hills. All burned fiercely, like beacons.

'I think somebody wants to make a point,' stated Bernice, beginning to climb through the window. 'I'm going to find out who they are and what they want.'

The Doctor pulled her back inside. 'It's too dangerous,' he said quietly.

Bernice breathed a sigh of relief. 'I was hoping you were going to say that.'

The Doctor had an expression on his face that told her that this was not the time for jokes. The glow from the candles highlighted the lines etched into his face. He looked very old. He seemed alien, inhuman, which of course he was. Bernice realized how little she really knew him. 'That's twice you've held me back,' she said. 'Someone has to investigate.'

His eyes glinted, mysterious and striking. He did not blink. His voice was soft but devastatingly sincere: 'I'm telling you, it's too dangerous.'

The spell broke and he paced back into the room. 'Go to bed,' he ordered. 'Go to bed, all of you. I'll stay up and watch out for you. I have a feeling it will be your last sleep for some time. I need to think.'

He sat at the dining table and stared out of the window. Nobody disobeyed him. Silently, Charlotte and the others left the room. Bernice turned back for a final glance and then hurried off after them.

The clock chimed midnight. The fires outside continued burning. The sounds and whatever creatures made them also continued. All was still in the dining room. Bernice and the others had gone hours ago. The Doctor sat still, at the table, staring out of the window.

It had been a long day. For all of them. It would be nice to rest his head on the table, if only there had not been work to do. Just for a second, just to rest his head on the table. Relax and let the brain take care of itself. It might produce some results.

Of course, he would not do it. He would not actually fall asleep. Not now. It was dreadfully important not to. Not even for a minute.

The Doctor dreamed.

Strange to dream of Jo. Jo Grant. Little, fragile UNIT Jo. 'Come on Doctor,' she said, 'we've a long way to go.'

97

He was standing in a desert. All around, dunes blazed in the afternoon sun. Jo was there, eager to get going.

Of course, the Story of the Rock. Why would he want to dream that? Was it important?

There it was, the rock, a hundred yards ahead in the heat haze. Red stone, a gigantic cube.

'It's like a tiny Ayers Rock.' Jo laughed. 'It's been quite a journey getting here.'

'The man,' warned the Doctor. 'The chained man.'

They walked. There was no sound but the rushing noise in his head. It was like walking through mud. As they approached, Jo ran on ahead.

'Stop,' he wanted to shout. 'The chained man,' but he couldn't speak and lethargy held him back.

At last they reached the rock. The chained man was there, starved and thin. The chains that bound him to the rock were long and heavy. The bolts that secured him to the stone were rusty but secure. His eyes gleamed as red as the rock. He was speaking to Jo but the Doctor could not hear the words. He didn't need to. He knew what they were without hearing them.

'Come and look,' he would be saying. His teeth were yellowed and pointed. His hair grew long around his pitiful, wasted frame. He glared at the Doctor. 'Come and look behind the rock.' He beckoned to where the rock turned on its corner, a long way ahead. 'Come and look at what's there.'

Jo, excited, turned to the Doctor for permission. Smiling, she asked, 'Doctor?'

But the Doctor had seen the hungry look in the man's eye. 'No Jo, I won't allow it.'

'Come and look,' asked the chained man.

It was hot and the Doctor couldn't think.

'Doctor?' Sarah asked again. 'I'm an investigative journalist. It's my job.'

Sarah? But hadn't she been...? 'No,' the Doctor repeated.

'Come and look behind the rock.'

'Sarah!'

She shook her brown hair and half-turned to the man. The Doctor knew she would go.

'Come and look at what's there.' The chained man breathed foul air into the Doctor's face. It was the third time of asking.

Suddenly the Doctor was tired. Sarah was becoming more determined. 'I'm going.'

He fell to his knees with fatigue. She would go and look. It was in the story.

The chained man was so delighted he danced a little jig, sending ripples down the chains. He proffered his hands theatrically in the direction of the rock's edge. The Doctor heard a quiet, stertorous breathing somewhere out of sight. No, he tried to cry, but Sarah could not hear him. She half-turned to nervously look at him, then went round the rock and out of sight. She was gone.

For a week, the Doctor waited, kneeling in the burning sand. All the while the chained man pleaded and begged him to follow Sarah. The Doctor refused to move. Following was not in the story.

His lips cracked with dehydration. His face burned despite the protection of his fedora. His clothes dried and ripped. The chained man laughed and taunted, pleading for him to go. He would not.

Of course, in the end, he agreed. He had to. Pulling himself up, his legs cramping with neglect, he fell against the rock and limped towards the edge.

'Come and look!' the chained man squealed, delirious with happiness. The Doctor turned to see him fall over onto the sand, grinding himself into the ground with joy.

Hand after burning hand, he dragged himself along. The corner approached. Fear gnawed at his mind, fear of the unknown. He must keep going, find out what happened to Sarah. The corner neared and he heard the heavy, evil breathing. Keep going.

He was there, the edge. He must not stop, he must turn the corner. Do it!

With the last of his energy, the Doctor hauled himself round the corner and met what was there waiting for him.

He leapt up from the chair, barking his knees on the dining table. He was half-way across the room before he realized he was awake. 'The Story of the Rock,' he moaned, breath coming in short gasps. 'Why?'

And why had the ending changed?

The Doctor felt his normal composure return to him. The Story of the Rock, that old fairy-tale meant to frighten children, to stop them doing . . .

The second traveller didn't go round the rock. That was the whole point of the story. A nasty little story to stop nice little Time Lords poking their noses into things, to stem the sort of curiosity he had always been replete with. Why that?

Deciding that he was still shocked, he decided to visit the kitchen and obtain a glass of water.

The clock in the hall chimed half past three.

There was a knocking at Bernice's door. She was surprised to find out that she had been asleep. 'I'm coming,' she shouted.

She pulled back the sheets of the large four-poster bed. She had slept in her clothes. The strange cries from outside could be heard through the small closed window and heavy curtains.

Bernice stumbled out of bed and knocked over a chamber-pot full of water. The liquid soaked into the carpet. 'Damn.'

The knocking came again.

'All right, all right,' she grumbled, stumbling over to the door. She unlatched it. Standing in the corridor, dressed in a white gown and holding a candle, was Charlotte.

'What's up?' Bernice asked, shivering. It was cold out here.

Charlotte's face was flushed, excited and not a little scared. 'Victoria's gone. I was trying to find Mrs Irving. I

100

went to the room she was in. It was empty. All I found was a bell-jar and a candlestick on the floor. Oh yes, and a squashed insect. Nothing else.'

'Eh?'

'She's gone. The window was open.' She grabbed Bernice's arm and pulled her along the corridor. 'I didn't know what to do.'

The candle was throwing up some rather nasty shadows and Bernice felt the hairs stiffen on her arm. She bumped into Charlotte's back as the woman stopped abruptly. 'What now?' she sighed.

Charlotte turned, dark eyes widened. She inclined her head down the corridor. 'There's someone standing outside my room. There.'

Bernice squinted into the gloom. She could not tell whether a shape was there or not. The candle was useless, it just made the shadows jump around. If there was someone there they were staying very still.

'Come on,' hissed Charlotte.

'Who's there?' demanded Bernice, sick of skulking about.

'It's me,' came a young man's voice. Charlotte breathed a sigh of relief. 'It's Peter,' she gasped, ready to rush to the dark shape. Bernice held her back.

She took the candle and edged forward. 'Show yourself' she ordered, trying to conceal any panic or fear.

The shape approached. Into the small circle of light entered a young, smart-looking boy of about seventeen. He was dressed in what looked to Bernice like a bellboy's uniform, complete with round hat and shiny buttons.

'Peter,' asked Charlotte, 'what are you doing up?'

He looked excited and had the same innocent expression common to all the occupants of the House. He pointed to the open door of Charlotte's room. 'I heard somebody walking about up here. I thought Miss Charlotte might be wanting something.'

'Why?' Bernice was suspicious.

The boy looked puzzled. He struggled to find the words. 'It's my job.'

Charlotte nodded.

'What's going on?' asked Peter, evidently enjoying the mystery. Bernice thrust the candlestick into his hand.

'You're the man in this movie,' she told him, 'you carry the candle. Where's this room?'

Charlotte pointed to a door at the top of a small flight of stairs. Bernice nodded.

Peter led the way to the door. He was about to open it when Bernice pulled him back. 'Wait,' she ordered. 'Leave it to me. I have experience in these matters.'

Charlotte and Peter glanced at each other, clearly failing to catch the irony in her voice. Bernice grasped the door handle. 'Here goes. Wish me luck.'

She turned the handle and pushed the door open, giving her two followers a glib smile.

The door opened and Bernice slowly entered the room. Bright moonlight flooded the scene: empty bed, upturned bell-jar and crushed creature. A sticky trail gleamed across the covers of the four-poster bed. A candlestick lay discarded on the floor next to the insect. There was a faint orange glow from the distant fires and a fresh breeze carried the sound of the cries into the room.

'Nothing,' said Bernice confidently, hiding her relief. 'May I go back to bed now?'

Charlotte looked about. She seemed tired, unable to think. 'But where have they gone?' she asked.

'I don't know but I am not prowling around this house in the middle of the night looking for a corpse.'

Bernice caught Charlotte's gaze. The woman was scared. 'Look,' she said to her, 'we'll go investigating in the morning. Mrs Irving is probably in bed somewhere. And Victoria didn't get up and walk off on her own, did she? Come on. Bed.'

Charlotte nodded reluctantly.

Bernice strode past Peter. He was waving the candle around in the doorway, apparently looking for any place where missing people might be hiding. He looked up with a big smile on his face. 'This is exciting, isn't it?' he beamed. 'I've never done anything like this before.'

Bernice stopped. She said flatly, 'Peter, it is four o'clock in the morning. Go to bed.'

They moved out of the room. Charlotte gently closed the door and followed the others up the corridor.

Still fighting the effects of the dream, the Doctor strolled through the ground floor of the House, looking for the kitchen. He found steps leading down to some sort of cellar. They were dusty with disuse. He peered down into the darkness. 'I don't think so,' he muttered. 'Not tonight.'

He held no light but trusted his superior vision and instincts to keep him on the right track. He presumed the kitchen would not be far from the dining room. Following the long corridor, he passed various doors. Opening them, he discovered a series of drawing rooms, studies, a library and a billiard room.

At last the corridor ended in a stone-flagged floor and a rather worn door. A sack of potatoes lay propped up next to it. 'Ah,' he said to himself, 'promising.'

He walked forward and tried the door handle. It was unlocked. He turned the handle and pushed the door open.

It was the kitchen. Somewhere in there water was dripping. Two large windows glowed with moonlight. One was open and swinging. Through them, the Doctor saw a small kitchen garden and a conservatory.

The room itself was huge. A black range stretched across the far wall beneath the windows. The air was pungent with the smell of flour and cooking. There was a large table in the middle of the room. A whole heap of foods, presumably the breakfast for the morning, lay on it, partially concealed by a white sheet. Herbs and spices were carefully labelled and racked on shelves around the walls. Cooking implements hung from hooks.

From the cavernous sink, water dripped from a tap. The

Doctor walked in and turned the tap fully off. 'That's better.'

The dripping continued. Frowning, the Doctor checked the tap. The sound was coming from elsewhere.

He turned to investigate. It seemed to emanate from the table of food he had seen earlier. 'Oh no,' he whispered, 'I'm not going to like this.'

He walked to the sheet. Closer up he could see that it was stained with a dark liquid that seeped through the cloth and onto the floor. There was a familiar tart odour in the air. Gingerly holding the sheet, he lifted it up.

The open window suddenly banged shut, startling him. Again, he looked.

It must have been the cook. A woman, middle-aged and fat. She had been eaten.

Garvey drank another mouthful of wine. Despite its sour taste it was welcome enough.

He sat, candle burning, in the wine cellar. In his lap rested a large black iron poker.

All day, the incident in this cellar had haunted him. He was a practical man, unused to disruption and danger, but it was clear to him what he had to do. His House had become infected. It was his duty to clean it out.

For the first time, Garvey was aware of how frail and inefficient his body was. He could not work as quickly or as well as the others in the House. Was this what the Doctor had meant by 'old'?

So many new words. 'Old', 'cold', 'fear'. Why did he understand them when they were said to him, but not before?

Despite the feeble state of his limbs, Garvey knew his mind was alert. He had his duty, his routine. They defined him. Now he would fight for these things. This was all he could think of, to sit in the cellar and wait for Ted to come back. It was a problem he could deal with simply and directly away from the confusing influence of the

Doctor and Professor Summerfield. It was all that was left to do.

He realized he enjoyed his life here. He would not allow it to go away, he would not allow change.

Garvey stared at the shadowed racks of wine. The perspective seemed to make the beams of the roof merge with the wooden shelves in the distance. The bottles sat in their homes like sleeping children, silent.

He would wait. Wait and see what happened.

Bernice was woken up again by a knocking at her door. She turned over and moaned. It took some seconds for her to realize what was happening. 'For God's sake!' she shouted. 'Go to sleep!'

A timid voice came from the other side of the door: 'It's me, Peter. I heard a cry.'

'That was me! I was asleep. Dreaming.'

The voice paused, then said, 'It was from Miss Charlotte's room. I think there's somebody in there with her.'

Wearily, Bernice pulled herself out of bed again and staggered over to the door. She hauled it open. Peter stood there, just as excited as before. 'Come on then,' she snapped. 'Let's get it over with.'

Grabbing the candlestick off the boy, she stomped off down the corridor. Peter followed brightly.

When Bernice reached the door to Charlotte's room she rapped on it three times. 'Charlotte?' she bellowed, 'are you all right?'

Silence.

Bernice turned haughtily to Peter. 'Charlotte is asleep. You should be asleep. I wish to be asleep. Can we go?'

Peter tugged at her sleeve. He rested his head against the door to listen. 'I heard something. Talking.'

Bernice realized they had to check it out. Peter might be right. 'Fair enough,' she whispered. 'But keep quiet, in case she is asleep.'

Peter nodded excitedly. Bernice stopped him as he was about to open the door. 'Peter, please.'

'Yes?'

'Don't be so enthusiastic. It's a trifle wearing.'

'All right. Shall we go?' He was almost out of breath.

Bernice sighed. 'Come on then.'

He opened the door slowly and Bernice thrust the candle out into the gloom. The room was dark and quiet. The bed was empty.

'Charlotte?' Bernice whispered.

There was a flash of movement from the window. Bernice caught the sight of a shape, large, dark and bulky, moving out of her vision. From outside. Charlotte was lying on the floor by the frame. She appeared to have fainted. Bernice rushed straight over to her, worried.

Peter looked about. 'What's wrong with her?'

'I don't know,' Bernice replied, kneeling down to check Charlotte's pulse. It was strong and regular. She sighed with relief. 'Charlotte,' she hissed. 'Wake up!'

Charlotte gave a moan and stirred. She blinked and came to consciousness. For a second she looked dazed, then she grabbed Bernice's hand, an expression of alarm on her face. 'It was Victoria,' she whispered. 'Outside my window.'

Bernice looked at the glass and remembered the half-glimpsed shape. It had not been the shape of a little girl.

'Outside?' asked Peter and went to the window.

'Stay back,' ordered Bernice. She squeezed Charlotte's hand. 'You were dreaming. She couldn't be out there. She . . . she's dead.'

Charlotte threw Bernice off and stood up. She pushed hair from her face. Calmly she restated, 'It was Victoria. I heard her voice. I saw her face.'

Picking the candle up from the floor, Bernice decided to take a look. She pressed her face up against the window, hoping nothing hideous would come crashing through it.

She looked out. There was nothing but moonlight and the fires in the distance. She looked down to the ground. Far below, white flagstones gleamed in the moon's rays.

'Nothing,' she said. 'There's nobody outside. How could she climb the wall anyway? She'd fall off, wouldn't she?'

Charlotte sat back onto the bed. 'I'm sure I . . .' she nodded. 'No, you're right. I couldn't have, could I?'

Bernice sat down next to her. 'Don't worry,' she said to her. 'It happens. Especially when you're frightened.'

'Charlotte,' came a voice from the window.

Bernice froze, viscera turning to ice. It spoke again: 'Charlotte.'

Bernice recognized Victoria's voice. On the surface. However, there was not a trace of humanity in it. It was a black, dead voice.

Peter stepped back from the window, shaking. He looked to Bernice for guidance. She stood up. 'Stay there Charlotte.'

She walked to the window, holding the candle out in front of her.

For the second time, Bernice stared out into the night. She saw nothing, like before. She held her breath. The voice had to have come from somewhere. It didn't make sense. 'Victoria?' she whispered, about to turn and tell Charlotte to get out of the room.

A black shape dropped down onto the pane. It slapped against the glass and somehow stuck there. Bernice leapt back, catching a glimpse of a pale, vulpine face. Scaly, furry limbs scrabbled at the window. The candle fell from Bernice's grasp and died on the carpet. She saw a large, misshapen silhouette against the moonlight.

Something with Victoria's face and glowing eyes hissed at them. Fluid seeped from a mouth full of sharp teeth. 'Charlotte,' it said, 'I'm hungry.'

Ashen-faced, Bernice walked backwards into Peter. Charlotte made a move for the spent candle.

'Leave it!' shouted Bernice and lunged forward. The window burst inwards, covering her with glass.

A shape crawled in through the smashed frame. In the dark all Bernice could see was something part crab, part spider and part Victoria. Large, fibrous legs clung and thrashed.

'Move!' she shouted, not wanting to look any more.

Dead eyes stared at Charlotte. A mouth twisted into the parody of affection. 'Come here Charlotte,' it rasped. 'It's your sister.'

Charlotte crawled away from the thing. It jerked its head about, as if trying to focus. She looked at it, tears streaming down her face. To Bernice, she seemed hypnotized.

'That's not your sister,' cried Bernice, backing up to the door.

'I know,' Charlotte replied softly.

The creature flexed and unflexed, probing with its thin, sticky legs. It shifted suddenly towards them. 'I'm so hungry,' it hissed. It seemed to be preparing itself to spring at them. At that moment Peter threw the candlestick at it. The metal club connected with its face and knocked it off balance.

Bernice took that as a cue to evacuate. She ran through the door, followed by Peter and Charlotte. Bernice slammed it shut. 'This won't hold it,' she gasped, pressing the door closed with her body. 'We need a weapon.'

Peter and Charlotte tried to look about. The corridor was pitch black, no windows to illuminate the situation. Bernice had to have time to think. They had to do something or they were all dead. There was a loud movement from inside the room and the creature smashed into the door. Bernice shook with the blow but the wood held fast. She could see it would not last long.

She looked about in the gloom. Charlotte and Peter were looking at her, clearly waiting for instructions.

A limb smashed through the door to the left of her head. It was covered with evil-looking barbs. Bernice ducked from the splinters as the spiky member thrashed about, feeling for purchase. It whipped her across the face, drawing blood, but she continued to press against the door with determination. 'Help me then!' she screamed.

Charlotte ducked under Bernice's arm and pushed her shoulder to the wood. Another charge shook the door. Bernice dug her feet into the carpet to prevent losing purchase.

Peter found another candlestick on a chest of drawers and proceeded to hammer away with it at the clutching limb. With amazing strength it cracked into him and sent him flying back against the far wall, some vases crashing to the ground with him. With lightning speed the limb whipped back and raked across Bernice's chest. She coughed and fell away from the door. Once more, the creature launched itself at the wood. 'I can't hold it!' shouted Charlotte.

Bernice rolled, ignoring the line of pain across her chest. 'Leave it!' she barked at Charlotte. 'Run!'

Picking up the skirts of her night-dress, the woman turned and sprang away from the door. The creature screeched and smashed at it again. The hinges rattled with the blow.

Pulling Peter up, Bernice headed off back to her room. 'Come on!' she shouted, dragging the groggy boy along. She saw that Charlotte was right on her heels. Behind them, something large and angry shattered the bedroom door to pieces.

They headed for the stairs but Bernice realized they weren't going to make it. 'In here!' she ordered and dived into her bedroom. Charlotte and Peter followed. Bernice heard the sound of the thing scrabbling up the corridor and she bolted the door at panic speed. This second barrier bulged under the impact of a tremendous force.

'Now what?' Bernice asked the others. 'We're trapped.'

'Get some furniture in front of the door,' suggested Charlotte. Bernice nodded and together they began to pull a large table across the room.

'Peter, find some light,' Bernice said, straining with effort. The boy looked about. 'What can I use?' he asked.

The table thumped against the door. The wood buckled as the creature blasted into it.

Sweating, Bernice pulled her denim jacket off and scanned the room. There was a small table by the bed with a vase full of flowers resting on it. She threw the vase off and upturned the table. Peter and Charlotte looked at her in apparent confusion. Another blow smashed a panel out of the door. The creature began to force its way through the opening. Glowing eyes pierced the dark. The air was heavy with the stench of its breath.

Bernice kicked a leg off the table and wrapped her jacket around one end. 'It works in the vids,' she gasped. 'Give us a light, Peter.'

Stunned still for a moment, Peter began searching the pockets of his uniform. At last he pulled out a taper.

'It's getting in!' screamed Charlotte. A limb began ripping away the door. Bernice grabbed the taper and struck it on the side of the table leg. Flame sparked up and she moved it under the jacket. 'Here we go!' she cried with delight.

The material began to smoulder gently.

'Marvellous,' sighed Bernice. 'I knew it wouldn't work.'

The remains of the door smashed apart. The huge creature squeezed itself into the gap over the table. It smiled and stared at its three victims. 'Ahhh . . .' it sneered.

Looking about desperately, Bernice spotted her bedspread. She threw the taper onto it. Immediately, the thin fabric began to burn.

The table shifted and toppled as the creature's immense strength shoved it over. Charlotte backed away. The room began to fill with smoke.

'Peter!' Bernice yelled, 'grab the end.' She threw her useless makeshift torch to Charlotte.

The boy went to the end of the bed and tentatively picked up a corner of the burning cover. Together they lifted the bedspread.

With a shriek of triumph the creature burst into the room. Charlotte screamed and attacked it with the table leg. Immediately, she was smothered by its rope-like arms. It opened its mouth.

110

'Now!' cried Bernice, and they threw the burning bedspread over the creature's head.

To Bernice's amazement, the thing burst into flames. It thrashed about violently and knocked her and Peter over. Screaming in pain, it released its grip on Charlotte. It twisted its head fiercely in a vain attempt to avoid the flames.

Smoke choked Bernice's lungs as she tried to dodge the shuddering, burning creature. It writhed and rolled around, smashing furniture as it went. A flying piece of porcelain scythed into Peter and he slumped to the ground with a groan.

The creature, perhaps in a last-ditch attempt to save itself, launched itself at the window and smashed its way out. With a cry it plummeted two storeys and Bernice heard it land with a sickening, dead thump.

She ran to the shattered pane with Charlotte. Looking down, she saw a burning heap feebly trying to move itself. It crawled and mewled but at last became still.

Bernice looked at Charlotte and Peter's soot-stained faces. Smoke rose and wreathed their bodies. The creature had taken the burning bedspread down with it. There was nothing in the room but smoke and a cold wind. 'Round Two to us I think,' she quipped, feeling slightly hysterical. She fell back, giggling.

Charlotte, not laughing, stared out at the dark. The first threads of dawn were beginning to appear on the horizon.

Through the kitchen window the Doctor watched the sun rise on a beautiful, crisp autumn morning. High up in the hills, the dead fires sent up pillars of half-hearted smoke. The bare trees sat in a carpet of gold, the leaves they had shed overnight.

A chilly breeze wafted lazily around the room, catching the smell of the Doctor's cooking. He cracked some eggs into a large pan, added some milk, salt and pepper and began stirring enthusiastically. He sniffed, to test its freshness. 'Hmm,' he sighed. 'Not bad.'

The door rattled open and in walked three dishevelled, exhausted figures.

'Here you are,' said Bernice. 'You wouldn't believe what happened to us last night.'

Peter and Charlotte dropped simultaneously into chairs.

'Use the sink to clean yourselves up,' said the Doctor casually, mixing the eggs. 'It's time for breakfast.'

Over the welcome food, Bernice recounted the events of the night to the Doctor. He ate and listened, occasionally commenting. 'You're sure it was Victoria?' he asked.

Charlotte nodded, 'It was and it wasn't. It was like something had got into her.'

'Or out of her.'

Bernice looked out at a mound of freshly dug earth in the kitchen garden. 'What's that?' she asked.

For a moment a cloud crossed the Doctor's brow. He sagged and looked like an old man in braces. To Bernice he seemed alien again, as he had on the previous night. After a pause he replied, 'That's the cook. I believe she too had a visit from Victoria.'

Peter stood up, visibly shocked. 'Mrs Chamberlain?'

Changing the subject, the Doctor sipped at his tea and said, 'I want you to do something for me today, Bernice. And you, Charlotte.'

Bernice looked up, very tired. 'What do you mean?'

'I want you to go to the lake and find that man in the black suit you talked about.'

Bernice went to the sink and began to wash her hands. She was cold without her jacket. Even though it hadn't caught fire it was still ruined. 'I thought no one believed me about that.'

The Doctor looked affronted. 'Of course I believed you Benny. I always do.'

'And I thought you told me I couldn't go outside.'

'The situation has changed. I don't like it but there's no choice.'

112

Charlotte interrupted. 'Doctor,' she said, 'there is no one here of that description.'

The Doctor nodded. 'Exactly. So if this person is another stranger, like Bernice and myself, and wherever Ace has got to, then perhaps he or she has some information about what is going on here.' He stared at Charlotte once more. 'You know, I am certain we have met before. Not as you look now but . . .' He stopped, apparently put off by Charlotte's confused expression.

Bernice dried her hands. She was curious but knew the Doctor would not give away any clues unless he was sure. After the wash she felt a little more alive. 'All right. We'll go straight away so we've got plenty of light. I have no desire to meet anything big and nasty in the dark again, unless it's Ace. Come on Charlotte, finish your eggs.'

Peter sat in his dishevelled uniform, looking a little left out. 'What about me, Doctor?' he asked plaintively. 'Can't I help?'

The Doctor beamed a grin. 'Pleased to meet you, Peter. Don't worry, we've got work to do, believe me.'

It was nice to be in the open air again, thought Bernice, especially on such a beautiful day. As she and Charlotte walked across the fresh, dew-wet lawn she took a deep breath of autumn air. She exhaled, producing a white fog.

'What is it?' asked Charlotte. She wore a long brown coat over her dress, with black riding boots on her feet, all that now fitted her from her wardrobe.

'Nothing,' Bernice sighed. 'It's just very pleasant, after the thick air that was out here before.'

'I've stopped trying to understand all this,' Charlotte mused. 'I'm just going to take everything as it comes.'

Bernice nodded blankly. 'I'm sorry,' she said. 'I have absolutely no advice to give to someone who has aged five years in half an hour.'

Charlotte tried to examine herself. 'Have I changed again?' she asked despondently.

Bernice looked. Charlotte's face had weathered a little

more, now having the appearance of mid-thirties. The signs of youth had been totally obliterated. 'A little,' she replied cautiously. 'Don't worry, we'll find out what's going on.'

The two women skirted the House. It was still magnificent to Bernice, despite the changes that had taken place in and around it.

In a flower bed by one of the walls, they found the remains of a burnt bedspread. It was surrounded by a wreath of broken glass.

'No body,' said Bernice. Charlotte made no reply. 'Either it burned to nothing,' Bernice hypothesized, 'or it got up and ran off. Or something else we don't know about.'

Charlotte pulled her away. 'Come on,' she said practically. 'No point in wondering. We must go to the lake, like the Doctor said.'

Bernice grinned and clapped her hands to warm them. She felt cold out in the grounds, much colder than inside. 'I wish I'd brought some gloves.'

They strolled off to the lake which lay somewhere in the misty distance.

Peter struggled to keep up with the Doctor as he hurried along through the ground floor of the House.

'Everyone must be found,' the Time Lord spoke hurriedly. Peter found his accent strange and funny. 'Peter, you know where the staff are. I want you to find them and bring them to the dining-room.'

Peter nodded keenly and began to run up a flight of stairs. Whatever was happening in the House he did not want to neglect his duty. He stopped and turned as he heard the Doctor mutter, 'Whoever's left.'

There was a noise from the corridor. The Doctor whirled round, as if expecting trouble.

Garvey stood there, bent iron poker hanging lazily in his grip. His normally impeccable butler's uniform was ripped and torn. Blood had congealed in a cut above his left eye.

'Are you all right Mr Garvey?' asked the Doctor worriedly. Garvey nodded and brushed past him growling. 'Must have a wash and clean myself up. Duties to perform.'

Peter was shocked. He had never seen Mr Garvey like this before. Or anyone else for that matter. He felt afraid.

The Doctor grabbed Garvey's arm. The butler spun round, gazing in exhaustion and fear. For a second Peter thought he was going to hit the Doctor. 'What happened?' asked the little man.

Garvey stumbled and the Doctor led him to a chair. Pulling a handkerchief from his jacket pocket he started to clean the wound above the eye. Spittle hung from Garvey's lip. 'Ted,' he said quietly. Peter strained to listen. 'It was Ted, in the wine cellar. He was my friend.'

'It's all right,' said the Doctor.

'I left him down there. He'd . . . changed. He won't be coming back any more.' Garvey sagged like a puppet cut from its strings.

Peter rushed down the stairs, surprised and worried. 'Mr Garvey?' he stuttered.

The Doctor stood up and put his arm round Peter's shoulders, discreetly edging him away from the shocked butler. The boy looked up at him in dismay. 'What happened to Mr Garvey?'

'I gave you a job to do.'

'I know, I . . .'

'I suggest you go and do it.'

Peter nodded vigorously, his pill-box hat dropping over his eyes. He straightened it. The Doctor grasped his shoulders firmly. 'Peter!' he snapped. 'You must not panic. You are important to me. Please, go about your business. Leave Mr Garvey to me.'

Peter felt guilty. He had never felt it before but he knew what it was. 'Yes sir,' he said dejectedly. 'I . . . I'm sorry.'

The Doctor shook his head impatiently. 'All right. Never mind that now. Find everyone. When you've done that, get them into the dining-room. Then find hammers, nails, wood and anything else.'

Peter screwed his face up, not understanding. 'Why?'

The Doctor sighed. Slowly, he replied. 'We're going to barricade ourselves into the dining-room.'

They had crossed the grounds and almost reached the lake. From this angle, looking up the wooded hills, Bernice thought that the scenery was astonishing. It seemed almost deliberate, like a sculpture.

'You know,' she said, 'I know it's a cliché but I can't help feeling that we're being watched.'

'Watched?'

'I'm really going to have to show you those vids, Charlotte.'

The hills framed the valley so neatly, so precisely, that it was almost a perfect circle. A ring or a barrier. No road led up any of them and there was no way of seeing beyond the hills in any direction. It was as if nothing existed beyond what the eye could see. Fires smouldered in the distance. They were on every hill, surrounding the valley with vertical lines of smoke.

Strangely, Bernice could not shake off a feeling of enclosure, even out in the countryside. She looked at Charlotte trudging elegantly along beside her. 'I wish the Doctor would tell me why the sight of you disturbs him so much.' Charlotte either didn't hear or ignored her.

They were nearly at the lake, outside the small ring of trees that surrounded the water. The trees were bare, leaves lying dead at their feet. Despite the lack of foliage, Bernice could not see through them to get a clear view of the lake.

'Can you hear something?' Charlotte asked and stopped.

'What is it?' Bernice frowned and listened. She heard

nothing but the lapping of water and branches creaking in the wind.

Charlotte took a tentative step forward, her marble cheeks flushed with cold. Her intense eyes seemed to scan the wood ahead.

Then Bernice heard it. Music. A recording. Something very old, with a scratch and hiss to it.

' "Strange Fruit",' she whispered. Charlotte turned to her, as if not having heard properly. Bernice explained what she knew: 'It's an old twentieth-century Earth song.'

This version was slow, very slow. Bernice only had a sketchy memory of the words, the last lines:

'For the tree to drop,
Here is a strange and fatal crop.'

She wondered where the music was coming from.

'This way,' shouted Charlotte as she bounded off into the trees.

'Wait!' cried Bernice. 'It might be dangerous.'

She was amazed to see Charlotte turn and look almost angry, ankle-deep in leaves. 'We have to find out. We've got to get everything sorted out.'

'All right, all right,' Bernice said to the excited woman. 'But let's not be stupid. We go quietly until we know what's waiting for us.'

Bernice noted what appeared to be a new facet in Charlotte's emotional register: impatience. For some reason it made her smile.

She followed Charlotte around the shore to the far side of the lake. On the side of the hill, previously hidden by the trees, Bernice saw a field of wheat. It rose up as a backdrop to the water by their side.

'There,' pointed Charlotte.

Bernice saw a thicker clump of trees ahead, almost a copse. Through them she spied what she could only describe as an old, wooden gypsy caravan. It was like some of the ones she'd seen on Heaven. It was covered in bright red and yellow paint. Pots and pans hung from the sides. Two large bars rested on the ground at its front,

117

as if waiting for a horse. Three wooden steps led to a tiny, carved door at the back. This door was open and the music emerged from the gap.

She wondered if it was the music, evocative and unsettling as it was, that made her suspicious.

Charlotte ventured forward, seemingly entranced by the song. Bernice followed cautiously.

Standing at the shore of the lake was a man. He had his back to the two women and was lazily throwing stones into the water. He was dressed in a black top hat, black tailcoat, black trousers and shiny black shoes. He was tall and very thin. To Bernice he looked like a shabby funeral director.

The air was still and quiet, crisp with cold. The peace was disturbed only by the music and the sound of the stones plopping into the water. Charlotte looked at Bernice in surprise, obviously wondering what to do.

Bernice decided to introduce herself. 'Excuse me,' she announced.

The man whirled around, as if startled. His face was pale and thin. He wore little round glasses and wisps of straggly beard hung from his chin. His eyes were sunken and black as coal. He smiled a warm grin. 'Hello sweet ladies,' he laughed in a fruity, humorous voice. 'At last. I seem to have lost my way, could you perhaps help me?'

Charlotte walked forward, seemingly drawn by the stranger's infectious enthusiasm. 'I'm Charlotte, lady of the House, and this is my friend Professor Bernice Summerfield.'

Bernice decided not to get too friendly straight away. 'Who are you?' she asked suspiciously.

The man laughed and pointed to the caravan. Painted on the side of it, in black stencil against the reds and golds of the decoration, were the words: 'PATENT MEDICINES AND CURE-ALLS'.

He lifted his hat and bowed gracefully, sending a slick of black hair over his forehead. 'Allow me to introduce myself,' he said. 'I am the Quack.'

Chapter 5

Doctor Patrick Rix would not have described himself as a pleasant man. He had no interest in definitions of this kind. He eyed the three strangers suspiciously as his men tied them into kitchen chairs. 'I trust you will excuse the behaviour of my employees. Having been brought up in the manner of rough peasants they have none of society's fineries.'

The young woman glared at him. He made a mental note to keep an eye on her. Enjoying himself, he continued with his little speech: 'If they had lived in a city they would have made excellent rampsmen. As it is, they have grown into louts with nothing better to do than thrash the occasional beggar that comes mooching round the village. That is, until I introduced them to more worthwhile endeavours. Isn't that right, Thos?'

The larger brother looked up briefly from his work. 'Whatever you say, Doctor Rix.'

'For myself,' Rix continued, 'I have known the dubious pleasures of society. As you may have noticed from my accent I hail from Scotland. Edinburgh, to be precise. Also, if you were very observant you may also have divined that I am a doctor. Were you?'

He walked to each of the three in turn, the sickly-looking man, the frightened gentleman and the fiery young woman. His men backed off to the walls of the kitchen. Archie was puffing heartily on a clay pipe. 'Well?' Rix asked.

'What?' said the grumpy woman, moodily. 'I wasn't listening.'

'Were you observant enough?'

She shook her head wearily. Rix wondered if her name really was Ace, as Archie had claimed. 'Yes, I am a doctor. Or was. I performed what I thought was God's work, healing the sick, trying to find cures to some of our more virulent plagues.'

The gentleman, Aickland, seemed to be about to say something. Rix slapped him hard across the face. 'Don't speak unless I ask you to.' He composed himself and continued with his speech: 'For many years I practised medicine, sometimes successfully, sometimes not. I was happy. Then something happened to me. My dear wife, now sadly departed from us, delivered me a child. He was not ... whole. And I realized, I realized that I had not been performing God's work at all. Disease, illness, pain, these are all God's gifts to mankind and he did not want mankind to eliminate them. So he punished me. He visited a curse upon me. He gave me a son who was beyond all hope of cure.'

Rix sighed. He scanned his audience. The men, of course, were listening attentively, as they always did. They were good, they realized that he needed to speak his thoughts, that his words were important. As for the girl, she seemed to be watching him with contempt. She would learn. He grinned at the thought of the pleasures he was going to inflict upon her.

'So I altered my profession. I renounced God and his cruelty. I left Edinburgh under something of a cloud. I had been experimenting, you see. Experimenting with pain. I hoped to conquer it, to deny God His pleasure. You see, He wants us to suffer and I have vowed to stop him. I used some back-street rabble to identify the source of pain. There were some deaths, not important. I was discovered and disgraced. So I came to Wychborn, where I have lived these five years constantly working on my experiments. I'm afraid I am somewhat suspicious of

120

strangers, I worry that my old colleagues might try and find me. But I will not be defied!'

He paused again, aware that he had been exciting himself. 'I hope you understand. You will help me.'

At last he managed to force a reaction from Ace. She sat up angrily and hissed, 'Help you? You're joking.'

Rix laughed. 'Whether you volunteer or not, you will help me. It is for the common good. Anyway, that is enough of my life. I would like to hear about yours. Archie has been telling me a fairy-story about glowing men and women that come back from the dead.'

'I know you don't believe me, Doctor Rix, but it's true!' bleated Archie, sweating and clearly afraid.

'Oh shut up,' snapped Rix and turned to the three strangers sitting, firmly tied, in their chairs. His men began to look uncomfortable. 'Is this ... story true?' he asked them all. He tried to sound reasonable, kind.

'No,' said Aickland.

'Yes,' said Ace.

'Oh dear,' Rix remarked, 'this means that one of you is lying.' He shook his balding head in a gesture of sadness. 'Now I shall have to use violence on both of you in order to discover the truth.'

Ace struggled round to catch Aickland's eye. 'There's no point in lying,' she insisted. 'Tell him the truth. What harm can it do?'

Rix knelt down by Ace. 'So you're the one that felled two grown men in the inn, are you? You look strong. I could use you.'

Ace sneered at him. 'Go to hell.'

Rix straightened up again. He placed a pair of round glasses onto his nose. 'Lovely. The strong ones always last the longest. What about him?' He indicated Arthur, lying slumped in his chair. He addressed his question to Archie who gabbled, 'You want to stay away sir. 'E's dangerous. 'E's the one what glowed.'

'Did he say anything?'

'Nothing I recall sir. Except that he was hurtin'.'

Rix scratched his chin and walked around behind Ace. Through the kitchen window the dawn light had given way to another murky, drizzly day. The others watched him in anticipation. He inspected the back of her head and then placed his hands round her neck.

'Don't touch me,' she growled, 'I'll break you in half.'

Rix looked up at Archie, interested in the girl. 'This is the one that came back from the dead you say?' Throat dry, Archie nodded. Rix probed the neck with his fingers. It was incredible, the bone structure was perfect, not even a blemish on it. At last he came to a decision, keeping his hands on Ace. 'I doubt, Archibald, that you have the wit to lie so no matter how far-fetched your story seems, it must be true.'

Archie relaxed. Rix was pleased to see that his men were so in fear of him. It was a comforting advantage. He continued to stroke Ace's neck. Her skin felt warm and soft, despite the muscles lying beneath the surface.

'I'm warning you.' She twisted about, expressing a physical revulsion at his touch. He was used to that. It did not matter. She would learn.

Aickland shouted out from his chair in the corner of the room, 'Take your hands off her!' To Rix he sounded uncertain, frightened. He could be a weak link. Aickland continued, 'What you are doing is quite illegal.' A stunning blow from Thos silenced him.

Rix waved the thug away. 'Let him speak. I am interested.'

Aickland raised his head. Unlike Ace, his face and neck were a mass of blood and bruises. He seemed to be trying to clear his senses. 'If it's money you want, I have plenty. You can have whatever you want. Just let us go before you get into trouble.' He nodded towards Arthur. 'This man is sick, possibly dying. He needs help. He needs a doctor.'

Rix scrutinized him with old eyes. He turned to his men in feigned confusion. He enjoyed his theatricals. 'But I am the village doctor. If he is sick I will cure him. You're

122

in my safe hands now. As for money, I have plenty and I think you will find that these are the best-paid men in the area. But please, continue to beg if you so wish. I should like to study your behaviour.'

Aickland slumped, defeated by Rix's words. Ace struggled in her bonds. 'Ignore him Richard. You're wasting your time. He's mad.'

Rix reacted as if stung. He reeled round and slapped Ace across the face. He went bright red and shook as he spoke: 'Mad am I? You wait, young lady. I will show you madness. Madness and pain the like of which you have never dreamed.'

Ace laughed in his face. 'Save it mate. I've heard it all before. You're just the bog-standard loony who wants to take over the world. Only on a smaller, more pathetic scale.'

Furiously, having lost all restraint, Rix lashed out again. His men backed off, they had seen these moods before.

'Ace!' shouted Aickland sharply. 'Be quiet!'

Rix barely heard the shout, such was his fury. He dashed across to a drawer and dragged it open. He whirled round clutching a large, heavy pistol. Calmly he pulled back the catch and pressed it against Ace's face. 'Goodbye,' he whispered. Ace closed her eyes. Much to the doctor's chagrin she refused to show fear or weakness. Well, he would teach her.

He pulled the trigger. There was a hollow click.

Rix regained his composure and watched Ace open her eyes. He lifted the gun away. 'Next time you answer me back,' he said, 'I'll put a big hole in that pretty little forehead of yours.'

He placed the pistol back into the drawer. As if nothing had happened, he continued speaking: 'I am perfectly willing to let you go and help your sick friend. On one condition. I wish to see his "work" at first hand.'

He decided to believe Archie's story. If this drained-looking man had brought the girl back from the brink of death then . . . He breathed heavily, trying to conceal signs of hope and excitement. 'I told you of my son. A seven-year-old boy. He is crippled, his legs useless. God interfered with my life and I am going to interfere and change His. I will do this through scientific discovery. I live now in a world of cause and effect. Of rationality.' He smiled, a little too widely. 'Cause: This man cures my son. Effect: I let you all go.'

Ace seemed about to say something when Aickland interrupted her: 'How can we believe you?'

Rix fixed him a sincere stare. 'You have my word. Why should I lie?' He struggled to sound reasonable. 'I apologize for the manner in which I brought you here. I have many enemies.' He was sounding good, convincing. 'What have you to lose?'

Of course they would agree. What choice did they have? They were totally in his power and he could always shoot one of them to make the others co-operate. He would shoot the girl. He would like that.

Ace remained impassive. Aickland, clearly seeing she was not going to contribute, started negotiations. 'How is Arthur?' he asked, unable to turn his head to see the man.

Rix bent down to investigate. He ran his hands across the man's head. He listened to Arthur's breathing and checked his pulse. 'He's alive. Archibald, wake him up.'

Archie hurriedly brushed past Frankie, Billy and Gray to stand behind Arthur. He pulled the man's head back and slapped it. Arthur moaned his way into consciousness. Fawningly, as if Rix was some draconian headmaster, Archie mumbled to Billy, 'Fetch some water. A pan.' Billy obeyed instantly.

Clumsily, Archie threw the water into Arthur's face. The bound man coughed and spluttered. 'Wha's happenin'?' he asked, blinking water from his eyes. He looked lost.

Rix placed a fatherly arm around his shoulders. 'Arthur.' He glanced briefly at Archie to gain confirmation of the name. 'We want to help you. You're not well.' He liked

Not like Tillie, his friend. She was as energetic and enthusiastic as himself and he liked that. He had strange feelings about her in his mind. He was curious to find out what these feelings meant. He wanted to be with her, to talk to her, to touch her. He felt attracted to her short, curly hair and slim frame.

He had asked the Doctor why he felt like this. The little man had laughed and said cryptically, 'Perhaps you're both from the same design.'

The Doctor had used Peter and Tillie as what he described as 'sounding boards' for his ideas. The two servants had worked as he talked. 'It's becoming clear to me that there is a design to this world. It's like a fantastically advanced doll's house.'

Peter had smiled, not understanding, and tried to catch Tillie's eye. She had smiled back. Something in his heart had fluttered. He took off his jacket and worked in his white shirt, braces and uniform trousers. He wanted to appear more . . . manly for Tillie to watch. 'Sealed up nice and tight,' he said, nailing up the last of the boards.

'Good, good, Peter,' the Doctor replied. 'Just a precaution, you understand.'

Tillie carried the last of the planks of wood to the main double doors of the dining-room. Peter had offered to help but the chambermaid had warned him off, saying that she was just as capable as men in carrying heavy things. Peter had gone red and felt foolish. 'There,' she said, dropping the wood. 'Just in case.'

She had suggested that they keep the main table by the doors in case they had to block them in a hurry. The Doctor had agreed. He said he wanted the doors kept accessible in case Bernice and Miss Charlotte had to get in quickly. Also, Mr Garvey had not yet appeared. Peter was beginning to worry about him.

The grandfather clock in the hallway struck twelve noon. 'That's odd,' said the Doctor and fished out a pocket watch from his jacket.

'What is it?' asked Peter.

127

'It should only be half past nine in the morning. Is this normal?'

Tillie and Peter shook their heads. The Doctor went to the nearest window and looked out through a gap in the boards. 'I hope Benny and Charlotte have spotted this. If time continues at this rate, it'll be dark in half an hour. I don't want them outside when that happens.'

'Can we help?' asked Tillie.

Peter wanted to volunteer something as well, so Tillie would acknowledge him. 'What do you want us to do?' he enquired.

The Doctor turned and walked to the fire. He hoisted up a huge cauldron of cold water and fitted it over the roaring fire. It swung gently on its chain. Peter and the others stared at him, wondering what he was going to do. At last, he lifted his hat and smiled. 'Tea anyone?'

'It's so nice to have company,' said the man who called himself the Quack. He invited the two women into his caravan. 'For a cup of my own blend of very special tea.'

Bernice still found it difficult to believe that he could have such a name. 'Oh yes . . .' she said suspiciously.

'Most kind,' agreed Charlotte, following him through the trees to the caravan. Bernice vowed not to drink anything until she discovered the truth about him.

The Quack led the way up the small, rickety steps of the caravan and went in. Overcoming her doubts, Bernice followed Charlotte inside.

The interior was cramped but fascinating. It was full of bottles. They were lined up on shelves and dangling from the roof, tied with string. Handwritten labels gave a name to each substance. Liquids of all kinds were contained in the bottles, of all different colours and densities. Some of them steamed and bubbled. It reminded Bernice of an alchemist's laboratory. She made up her mind to definitely not try any of his tea.

There was a tiny table in the centre of the caravan and on it was a chunky wooden board covered in black and white squares. 'A chessboard,' uttered Bernice in surprise. 'Do you play?'

'A little,' the Quack replied cryptically. He placed his top hat in a little niche somewhere in the recesses of the room. His head was almost bald, crowned with a layer of fine, wispy hair.

Charlotte pointed at some moth-eaten, stuffed animal heads bolted to the walls. 'What are these?' she enquired.

'Tropies,' came the reply. Charlotte peered at the heads, staring out blindly with their glass eyes. 'They're wonderful. I've never seen anything like them.'

Bernice did not share Charlotte's enthusiasm. She had survived for too long by treating the unfamiliar with suspicion. She squeezed herself through the cramped space and sat down in a small, feeble-looking chair. 'Where exactly do you come from?' she asked.

For some reason, Charlotte shot Bernice a look of irritation. It surprised Bernice to find that the other woman had so easily accepted the Quack and his odd caravan. She found it difficult to think. The air was stuffy and the scratchy music seemed to be getting louder. After the stately decor of the House, this room seemed vulgar, tacky.

The Quack countered with a question of his own: 'Could you tell me where I am now? I seem to have got myself a little lost.'

Bernice refused to be side-stepped. 'I believe I asked first. Where did you say you were from?'

Scratching his scalp, the Quack replied, 'Well, I don't really remember, to tell you the truth. I just sort of found myself here, in my caravan.'

'But you're a seller of patent medicines?'

He placed an old, iron kettle on a minute stove and lit a flame. 'Tea. I forgot, I'll make it now. Well, Miss Bernice, I do many things. Selling the medicines keeps me going but what I really like is the showmanship. Hence the rather affected stage name.'

He seemed so sincere and earnest that Bernice found it difficult to sustain her suspicions. She had just presumed that he had to be bad, all her experience telling her so. She now found herself warming to him, he was like a lost little boy. And hadn't the Doctor been just as strange when she had first met him?

'I must say,' interrupted Charlotte, 'you really do have the most interesting items in here.' Bernice realized that the woman was jealous and was trying to draw the Quack's attention. He seemed oblivious, bending his reed-like body over the stove, producing three cups from somewhere.

'Thank you Miss Charlotte,' he said after a while. 'It has taken me a long time to build up this collection.'

A stopper on one of the bottles suddenly exploded upwards and the caravan became filled with a noxious brown fog. The Quack picked up the stopper and replaced it. 'Excuse me ladies,' he apologized, 'it can get a little fruity in here.'

He opened a tiny, smeared round window to release the fumes. As he went back to preparing the tea, Bernice pulled Charlotte's arm and whispered in her ear, 'What's the matter with you? Be more careful.'

'What do you mean?'

'Have you forgotten about last night? Why the Doctor sent us here? We mustn't trust him until we know more about him.'

Charlotte straightened up, clearly indignant. 'He seems perfectly friendly to me. He's another stranger, like you. Why trust you and not him? It doesn't make sense.'

Bernice sighed and just managed to speak before the Quack turned round: 'Be careful, that's all.'

Tea was served and, after watching the Quack drink some himself, Bernice took a sip. It was delicious, reminding her of the tea that the Doctor occasionally brewed in the TARDIS.

She wondered why, despite her harsh words to Charlotte, she was finding herself beginning to trust this odd, thin man. His assumed name should have made her more suspicious, was it some sort of pun on the Doctor's own name? She wondered what the Quack's motivations might be. Should she play the situation politely, or dive straight in?

'I have to warn you,' she said, choosing her words carefully, 'there is something very strange going on around here.'

The Quack grimaced as he swallowed his tea. 'Such as?'

Bernice paused; she had to say exactly the right thing if she was going to learn anything. It was only fair to warn him. Perhaps Charlotte was right, they had to give the Quack the benefit of the doubt. 'It is ... dangerous, in this valley.' She spoke cautiously. 'Some presence exists here. People have died. We're trying to find out why.'

The Quack put down his cup, leaned across to a tough-looking locker and pulled out a small wooden box. He opened the box and lifted up a fat, brown cigar. Snapping a match across his boot, he lit the cigar. The caravan was again filled with suffocating, evil-smelling smoke. 'I don't think I understand you rightly,' he said at last.

Bernice noticed that Charlotte appeared to be tired or sleepy. Her head was nodding as she stood by the door. What was wrong with the woman?

She tried to keep talking. 'Since we arrived here, that is my two companions and I, this valley has physically ... altered. Creatures have appeared, attacking and killing the occupants.'

Even to herself, she knew her words sounded false, unconvincing. He must think she was mad. 'What I am trying to say,' she coughed in the smoke, 'is that there is danger here. You'd be safer coming back to the House with us.'

The Quack smiled. 'Would I now?'

Bernice suddenly felt ill. She was sick, dizzy. The atmosphere was too oppressive, the air thick and unhealthy. The faces of Charlotte and the Quack seemed to loom in and out of focus.

The man was speaking, his voice insistent and irresistible, almost musical. Bernice wondered how she could

131

ever have found him menacing. 'Danger is an odd word,' he explained. 'I have found, in my experience, that danger only really exists in the minds of those who fear it. Without our suspicions perhaps danger would not exist at all.'

Despite lacking the concentration to closely follow the logic of his words, Bernice realized the Quack was right. He was speaking the truth. Very nearly anyway. She was feeling increasingly unwell.

He continued, still in that beautiful, sincere voice, 'Since arriving here, I have learned a great many things. Or dreamed them. Great things.'

Bernice looked over at Charlotte. Her head was lolling and she leaned heavily against a shelf. Idly, Bernice realized that she should have been more concerned than she was. 'Things? What things?' She wanted to know.

The Quack ignored her, following his own, elliptical line of conversation: 'I feel that I have become someone. Someone new. Out of nothing. I like it.'

Bernice struggled to comprehend. 'What do you mean?'

He frowned, as if unable to fully articulate his own thoughts. 'I feel like . . . like someone in a dream. Somebody else's dream. A doctor's dream.'

Somewhere in the back of Bernice's mind alarm bells were ringing but she found herself unable to react. She was attracted to his sense of wonder, his delight. A Doctor's dream. She liked his choice of words.

'The more the doctor dreams,' he said, 'the more real I become. He has not yet dreamed me fully but he will. You too . . .'

And then he said something else, something that Bernice did not catch. It might have been 'We all dream,' or 'I am a dream,' or even 'You are a dream.'

She struggled to clear her head. 'The tea . . . drugged,' she mumbled.

The Quack shook his head. He clasped Bernice's hands with his own. Charlotte was apparently oblivious, perhaps wrapped up in her own dream. Perhaps the Quack was speaking to her in different words.

'No,' he said, 'not drugged. Part of the change. The arrival of self-knowledge and enlightenment. Come on, I've just remembered something I want to show you.'

He stood up. Bernice did the same, unable to shake off his influence. She was both aware and not aware of herself. He was leading her and Charlotte out of the caravan, walking across leaves.

'Where are we going?' asked Charlotte.

'To the lake,' he replied.

Ace decided the best course of action was to try and ignore the cold metal digging into her face and back. There was nothing she could do. As firearms went they were extremely primitive but perfectly capable of providing her with a permanent headache. She was hustled up the stairs by the three goons. Two men bundled Arthur along in front of her. He didn't look any better and this situation wasn't helping him. Aickland was wrong to trust this doctor, he was dangerous.

There was no way she could dodge all three guns at once, unless she was extremely lucky. Two and she would have tried it but these bozos were so clumsy that they'd probably get her by mistake.

Rix stopped at the head of the stairs and turned back to Ace. He looked her up and down and pulled Arthur round. 'Talk to him,' he commanded.

Awkwardly, aware of her captors' nervousness, Ace clasped Arthur's hand. What to say? His head was casting about like he was blind or something. He jerked on every slight noise. Close up, she could see he was still glowing slightly. It was getting stronger. She was appalled at how little strength he seemed to possess. He was emaciated, deathly. 'How you doing mate?' she asked softly.

'Ace?' he replied and smiled. 'Nice to see you again.' His blue eyes finally focused on her. 'I'm weak.'

Rix breathed into Ace's ear. It was hot and unpleasant. Hatred coursed through her. She wouldn't do it, she wouldn't betray Arthur, she'd rather risk a shot . . .

'Do this and you can all leave,' Rix whispered.

The doctor's words permeated Ace's brain like a foul smell. Logic impelled her to comply, although it made her sick. Aickland was right; if there was a child, it had to be helped. Besides, as he'd said, it really made no difference. 'Where?' she asked Rix.

'Along this landing please,' he replied, victorious.

Gingerly, Ace led Arthur by the hand along a corridor. He stumbled but she kept him upright. Rix led them past walls lined with medical honours and watercolour prints.

They made their way to a door. Rix produced a key and worked on the lock. 'In here,' he said breathlessly, 'is my son, Stephen.'

The room was dark, thick curtains keeping the light out. Rix lit the gas lamp. In a bed a small boy lay asleep. He looked thin and pale. Poor sod, thought Ace, having this monster as your dad. The boy was young. A dash of brown hair fell across his face.

Rix pulled the bedclothes off the boy, waking him up. Stephen seemed understandably frightened by the strangers in his room. He stared with bright, moist eyes at Arthur, whose glow was more apparent in the gloom. 'Papa?' he whimpered in the same Scots burr as his father.

'Hush, wee one,' said Rix with a tenderness that surprised Ace. 'Time to be brave.'

Rix indicated the boy's tiny, withered legs. Ace gave up on cynicism. She realized that Aickland had been right. They had to help this boy if they could. If Arthur had brought her back from near death . . .

'Arthur,' she said firmly, 'you've got to help the kid. Make him better.'

Arthur turned slowly to her. 'I'm weak, Ace. I don't know if I can do it. I need time.'

Ace touched his arm. 'I know, but you saved my life and you're okay. How does it work? What did you do to me?'

Arthur struggled to remember. 'I – I touched you.'

'Then touch him. Get his legs working.'

Father and son held each other on the bed. 'Don't let him, Papa. I don't want him to,' cried the boy.

Rix put his finger to his son's lips. 'Everything will be all right.'

'Ace,' pleaded Arthur, 'I can't do it.'

'You must, there is no other way.'

'It's dangerous. I don't know why but it is.' There was a menace in his voice that unsettled Ace. For once, he seemed to know what he was talking about. She leaned back and felt the three guns pressed against her. 'Keep talking,' hissed Archie.

Rix let go of his son and stood up. He polished his spectacles. 'You must cure him Arthur,' he stated calmly. 'If you don't, I'll have my men kill the girl in front of you.'

Thanks a lot, thought Ace, I'm doing my best. Suddenly, the pressure on her right cheek disappeared. Billy stepped back, his young face red with emotion. 'Doctor Rix. You can't just shoot a lady like that.'

Rix walked straight up to him. 'You get that gun back on her, Billy, or I'll have Thos take care of you now.' To Ace his words did not sound like a threat, more a request.

Shaking, Billy obeyed. The gun pressed into Ace's cheek once more. 'Now Arthur,' continued Rix. 'When you are ready.'

Arthur stared about in panic. His glow was intensifying, as if he was willing it. He held out his hands. Thin veins of the light traced themselves across his palms. He clutched his chest, staring down at himself. 'It kills me,' he groaned. 'I'm changing.'

Ace clasped his hands and led him across the room to the child. The three gunmen struggled to simultaneously aim their weapons, avoid stumbling and keep up with her.

Steven cringed. 'Stop him,' he moaned, crying.

Ace positioned Arthur's hands over the trembling boy. The thin man was now looking blankly at the wall.

'Do it!' shouted Rix.

Ace stared at Arthur's fingers. The flesh was draining

135

of colour, melting away into the all-pervading light. As she watched, his features blurred and mixed like paint. His head became a ball of glowing energy.

Something worried Ace. His light did not seem to be as strong as she had expected. It fluctuated and pulsed at irregular intervals. She wondered whether he had been right, perhaps he had not been ready for the metamorphosis. There was a brief second when she thought she could stop the process and then it was too late. Arthur placed his hands onto the terrified boy's legs.

Ace observed with a mounting feeling of horror as worms of light fled from Arthur's fingertips and burrowed into Stephen's flesh. The child screeched. Again, the air stank of ozone and charring. 'Oh my God!' cried Ace. 'No!'

The legs began to lengthen and crack. They altered shape, becoming distorted and wrong. Tiny black hairs erupted from beneath the skin. The limbs began to move, jerkily at first and then into a flurry of buzzing action. They were the legs of an insect.

The boy's eyes widened and he screamed. The sound penetrated Ace's mind and filled her with an almost supernatural sense of revulsion and fear. Rix let go of Stephen as if hit by an electric shock. He stared, slack-jawed, and pointed. 'What have you done to my son?' he shouted, and then he began screaming too.

Arthur staggered across the room, howling in pain and anguish. Rix sagged in shock and then Ace saw his anger take over. 'Kill them!' he bellowed. 'Kill them all!'

Thos pulled his rifle around and fired a shot into Arthur's back. The glowing man flew into the bedroom window, breaking it. Wounded, he tried to turn but managed only to fall back against the glass. It shattered and he toppled out. A few spots of golden, glowing blood splashed onto the floor of the room.

Despite mounting panic, Ace was composed enough to realize that this was her only chance of escape. She ducked and simultaneously kicked out behind her. Archie's revolver fired once over her head and he fell back, clearly crippled by Ace's blow to his knee. Billy was too shocked to move, he stood and did nothing.

Thos whirled back to where he must have remembered Ace being. He fired his rifle instinctively into Billy's head. The boy spun backwards and crashed into the far wall. 'I'm shot,' he murmured through a ruined mouth and slid to the ground.

Ace was heading for the door when she got herself tangled up in Archie's legs as he thrashed about in pain. She slammed into the floor. Rolling over quickly, she found herself staring into the barrel of Thos's rifle. There were tears of rage in his eyes. 'You made me kill Billy!' he screamed and pulled the trigger. Ace did not even have time to close her eyes.

The hammer crashed down. Thos stared in disbelief at his gun. The rifle was empty.

Ace struggled to free herself but Archie managed to keep her pinned down. She watched helplessly as Frankie and Gray piled into the room. What they saw there clearly almost made them run right back out again.

'Wait!' commanded Rix from the bed. Ace turned to observe him. The doctor stood over his son who lay screaming and thrashing on the sheets. The room was filled with the stench of burning and cordite.

After some time, as Ace caught her breath, the boy fell silent and fainted. Rix pointed at her. 'Hold her down,' he ordered. Frankie and Gray jumped onto her. Ace watched helplessly as Rix bent over Billy's corpse and picked up a bloodied revolver.

Thos was hurriedly reloading his weapon, his fingers trembling as he clumsily forced the rounds in. 'You made me kill Billy,' he gabbled, 'you made me kill Billy . . .'

Rix knocked his rifle away. Thos turned on him, clearly angry enough to murder anybody who got in his way. Rix pointed the revolver into the large man's face. 'Leave it Thos,' he said calmly, 'or I'll put a hole in you too.'

Thos wept with frustration and anger. 'But Billy . . .'

'I said leave it!'

Thos stood trembling for a moment, then twisted his head round and spat on the floor. Rix looked at Archie. 'Is he dead? Really?'

Ace watched Archie glance distastefully at the dripping body slumped against the far wall. He nodded. 'He's dead. His head's half off.'

Thos made a move for his rifle. Rix lowered his revolver and dug it into the man's ribs. 'We need her, for now,' he said.

'What for?' Thos protested.

Rix pointed to the window. 'Take a look.' Puzzled, Thos moved to the broken frame and looked out. He shuddered and jumped back in. 'He's gone. But how . . .?'

'Never mind,' said Rix. 'He's alive and must be persuaded to come up and save my son. He might be easier to convince if he knows we've still got her.'

Thos shook his head. To Ace, he looked half mad. 'No,' he stated. 'I want her dead. And what about that bloke downstairs?'

Rix kept the gun very still on Thos's abdomen. 'Aickland?' he replied, as if just remembering the man they had left tied up in the kitchen. 'I think he got involved by accident. You can go and shoot him if you want. Outside, mind.'

'Right.' Thos gripped his rifle again. He was about to leave the room when he turned back to the pinioned Ace. 'Don't worry, I'll be back. You're next.'

Ace spat at him. He seemed about to attack her when he controlled his anger. He stood up and left the room.

'What about her?' moaned Archie, clearly uncomfortable. 'I want to get out of here.'

Ace struggled once more, only to find herself helplessly restrained by Archie, Frankie and Gray. 'She's mad,' hissed Gray. 'She'll kill us all given half a chance.'

'Damn right I will, you scum,' shouted Ace, thinking that keeping them frightened could be an advantage. She had to have some hope.

Rix looked at her and licked his lips. 'Frankie, hold her hands out.'

Ace was taken by surprise by this. 'What are you going to do?' she asked, trying to conceal her nervousness.

Rix smiled. His eyes were wet with tears but Ace detected something else, a madness in them. Calmly he explained: 'I'm going to break your fingers, so we can tie you up and you won't be able to escape.'

Peter and Tillie drank their tea whilst the Doctor attempted to talk to Mary and Jane. He had said he wanted to find out how much or how little they knew.

Peter stared at the hallway outside, diligently keeping watch whilst Tillie, on finishing her tea, began to tidy the room up.

The maids were answering the Doctor's questions politely but he seemed irritated by their perfunctory statements. Clearly they weren't saying what he wanted to hear. 'What do you do in the House?' he asked.

'We cook and clean, sir,' answered Mary.

'When did you begin working in the House?'

'We have always worked here.'

'What is your favourite food?'

'Whatever is given.'

'Do you like working here?'

'We cook and clean.'

The Doctor sighed and joined Peter on watch. The man seemed confused. 'They're like blanks,' he said. 'Half-formed automatons. And very dull company.'

The maids gave no reaction and continued to sit by the fire, clearly waiting for instructions.

Thinking aloud, the Doctor sat down in a comfortable padded chair. He stared up at the brass and crystal chandelier that dominated the ceiling. Wearily, he looked at Peter. 'Something has gone very wrong in this valley. I presume we should still be in high summer, the pattern of life as unchanged as ever. It's as if this place has become stained, tainted. Some outside influence has got inside it and is gnawing away at its heart.'

Peter felt that the Doctor was seeing right through him. Was he supposed to think of an answer?

'So who or what has interfered?' the Doctor continued. 'What is manipulating the design and running of this House? It's a bit of a complicated plan. Why doesn't whatever it is just invade and take over? Hmm. Because it can't, this is the easiest method for it.' He glanced up at the chandelier again. 'Why do I feel like a goldfish in a bowl?' he said suddenly. 'Who's watching me?'

The Doctor leapt up and ran to one of the boarded-up windows. He looked out into the dark night. Fumbling with his pocket watch, he muttered, 'Eight o'clock. Impossible. Why haven't I detected it? Funny how quickly the nights are drawing in.'

He turned abruptly and stared at the maids by the fire. Peter noticed that the air had become very still. 'What is it?' he asked.

'Did you say something?' replied the Doctor.

Peter shook his head. He wondered what had alarmed the little man. 'No. Why?'

The Doctor shook his head, as if to clear his thoughts. 'I heard a voice,' he said. 'Didn't you hear a voice?'

Peter glanced at Tillie who was listening intently. 'No. What was it?' she asked.

Frowning, the Doctor sat back down in his chair. 'It was one word,' he stated mysteriously. 'Leave.'

The Quack strolled through the copse and down to the shore. The air was cold and crisp but to Bernice it seemed as thick as in the caravan. Oddly, she noticed that the sky seemed to be getting dark already.

The lake was still there, vast and grey and quiet, like a sheet of rippled steel. A mist rose from the water.

'Over here,' the Quack beckoned, walking along the shoreline. Bernice followed, her feet registering the crunch of leaves beneath her shoes but not comprehending why she walked. Charlotte was right next to her.

The Quack stopped by three enormous wooden barrels. They were cylindrical, old and dotted with decay and rust. They sat upon a trailer and were bound by great iron strips. All three barrels were pouring thick purple liquid into the lake.

'What are you doing?' asked Charlotte sleepily.

Almost sadly, the Quack leaned against the nearest barrel. The water churned and bubbled as it mixed with the purple liquid. The sound echoed like a waterfall in Bernice's ears. 'Poisoning the lake,' he stated mournfully.

'I knew it,' Bernice moaned, tired and lazy. She wondered why she could not rouse herself to action.

'The dream grows,' the Quack said to the air. His tone was not pompous, just matter-of-fact. 'Many dreamers now. This is a symbol, you must interpret it. I am sorry, but I can only do what is dreamed of me.'

Bernice gritted her teeth to dredge up some will-power. 'I'll fight you,' she hissed.

The Quack pushed himself away from the barrel and approached her. 'Of course you will,' he said. 'You must.'

He opened his coat and pulled a large, sharp knife from an inside pocket. He placed it on the ground in front of Bernice. 'Kill me.'

Bernice felt the spell melt away. She looked at Charlotte and realized that they could both now move and think freely. The Quack knelt down and lowered his head. The knife was between them.

Bernice instinctively made a move for the blade and then stopped herself. 'Why?' she asked the Quack.

He looked up at her. 'The dream. It must continue.'

Charlotte grasped Bernice's shoulder. 'Listen,' she breathed.

From the wood came the sound of movement. The copse was enveloped in blue shadows as twilight closed in. Dark shapes were moving in the trees. Bernice heard an inhuman chattering from a multitude of voices. The

141

sounds made her feel sick, they reminded her of evil children, giggling.

Peering at the bare branches, she saw little, jumping shapes, the vague occasional outline of tiny creatures. They were hairless, like wizened babies but with long stringy arms and legs. They hopped about on the branches, glaring with hateful, shining eyes. There were hundreds of them. 'Oh great,' Bernice whispered.

Charlotte was backing away towards the lake, face filled with fear. Bernice turned back to where the Quack was kneeling. He was a black smudge against the darkening hills. His eyes glinted. 'I'm sorry,' he said. His voice dropped an octave to become an unnatural whisper. 'I tried to help. It's your fault, end the dream.'

Steam or smoke began to emerge from his clothes. Bernice heard a metallic tearing sound and the Quack's body began to change.

She decided she was not going to hang around to watch any transformations. She would rather risk the little nightmare creatures. 'Run!' she shouted and pulled Charlotte along with her into the copse.

Tied to his chair in the kitchen, Aickland was terrified. He had heard the sound of glass breaking and several shots from upstairs. He presumed, wryly, that Arthur had not managed to cure Rix's son.

His bruises were sore and his muscles ached through lack of use. He wondered what he could constructively do to get himself out of the situation. There had to be somebody in the village who could help them. Struggling with the ropes once more, he came to the inevitable conclusion that he wasn't going to escape. He looked at the clock. It was a quarter past ten.

Aickland's heart sank when he saw Thos come into the kitchen, carrying a rifle. He had a face like thunder and was clearly only just keeping himself under control. It did not take a genius to work out that something had gone seriously wrong. 'Where's Ace? Arthur?' he asked.

142

Thos ignored him, instead placing his rifle onto the kitchen table and pulling a large knife from his belt. Aickland moaned, praying he was not going to be stabbed to death.

Silently, like a man possessed, Thos cut free the ropes that held Aickland. He pulled him out of his chair.

Aickland's knees quivered, his legs protesting at the sudden call for movement. He was still afraid, if he was not to be stabbed then he wondered what was going to happen.

There came a cry from upstairs. Aickland recognized Ace's voice. So she was still alive.

'Come on, sir,' Thos sneered and, picking up his rifle, dragged Aickland to the back door.

'Where are we going?'

Thos unlatched the door and pulled Aickland outside into the cold morning. The drizzle was still falling and the back yard was ankle-deep in mud. Thos threw him into the slime. Aickland sighed inwardly, this seemed to be becoming a habit. He heard a click. A bolt being drawn back on a rifle. He rolled over to see Thos aiming the gun at him. 'Don't!' he cried, raising his arms in a futile gesture of protection.

Thos aimed the rifle at Aickland's stomach. 'Slower this way, sir,' he said. 'You'll be alive for the second bullet.' Aickland felt cold and his guts clenched, sending a sharp pain through him. He closed his eyes.

Thos squeezed the trigger.

The mud next to Aickland's body exploded, showering him with filth. He opened his eyes in surprise to see Thos scrabbling on the ground with somebody on top of him. Rolling over, Aickland leapt up. His cramps had gone, the need to survive overcoming them. He stared at the man fighting with Thos. He was old and portly, with silver hair. Aickland recognized Mr Robbins from the Wychborn Arms.

'Get out of here!' Bert shouted at him just before Thos grabbed his neck in a powerful grip.

Aickland very nearly broke and ran. He could feel his nerve slipping away. However, some sense of loyalty to the landlord kept him in the yard. Thos was strangling the life out of him.

Looking about for a weapon, Aickland saw that the rifle was lost somewhere in the mud beneath the struggling couple. Desperately, he scanned the yard. Leaning against the rear wall of the farm, like a prop from a play, was a rusty shovel. He decided that would have to do.

Picking it up, he found the tool heavier than he had expected. Aickland had never used a weapon in his life before, had never even considered using violence, but he felt enough fire and hate in him now to kill three men.

Thos was now on top of Bert and punching him into the mud. Hefty, clumsy blows rained down on the landlord who was unable to prevent them landing.

Aickland stared at the large, thuggish man who had done the same to him. He decided that this was going to be a pleasure. He ran at Thos and smacked the shovel against the side of his head. There was a metallic thud and Thos toppled over.

Aickland howled in triumph. He felt good, righteous. He danced in the mud as Bert pulled himself up, blood streaming from his head. The landlord stared at Aickland. 'Sir! Sir! Stop this!' he shouted.

Aickland suddenly came to his senses. He looked at Bert and was sickened to see that the landlord seemed to be frightened of him. The thought of his actions overwhelmed him. It had been necessary to strike Thos, but to dance and scream like a savage . . .

He grasped Bert's arm. 'I'm sorry,' he said. 'I had to hit him. You saved my life. Thank you. Thank you.'

Bert gingerly dabbed at his broken nose. 'Reckon I've lost a few teeth and I'll have a few bruises but I'll be all right.'

Aickland began to realize the extent of his good fortune. 'Where did you spring from, old man?'

Bert jerked a thumb back towards the village. 'Didn't

like what I saw in my inn, sir. Liberty it was. Them boys went too far. Time they realized they can't just bully everybody they want. Came to see what I could do for you. Saw that glowin' feller headin' up to the old house. What's wrong with him? Why does he glow like that?'

Aickland was astounded by the landlord's sense of justice and conscience. 'Mr Robbins,' he said seriously, 'I came here to learn about life. Meeting you, I feel uplifted. You are a good man. I have learned something.'

Bert looked embarrassed. 'Just doin' what any normal man would do . . .'

The rifle roared and something wet splashed over Aickland. He looked down to see blood all over him. Bert fell into his arms, a hole in his stomach spilling his life away. 'Run, sir,' the old man whispered and went limp. Aickland saw Thos, ten yards away, aiming the gun at him. He dropped Bert's body and dived to the ground as the shot blasted over his head.

Cursing, Thos seemed torn between reloading the gun and clubbing Aickland to death with it. Aickland used the indecision to make a break for the nearby fields. Panic struck, he scrabbled for safety, expecting any second to feel a shot hit him in the back.

Thos watched angrily as Aickland scrambled over the low stone wall of the farm and reached the first fallow field. He reloaded the rifle and aimed but the frightened man was too far away, already a dot in the dull morning light. He was going to get away again.

Frustrated, still unfulfilled, Thos stamped about in the yard, rubbing his injured forehead. He wondered what to do. Rix would kill him for this.

He saw a movement out of the corner of his eye. Bert was feebly trying to crawl through the mud. He left a wet, thick slick of red in his wake.

Calmly Thos walked up to Bert, put the gun to his head and pulled the trigger. At last, Thos thought, something had gone right for him.

145

In his tiny, spartan room, Garvey washed and changed. The events in the cellar had altered his life beyond recognition.

He noticed his old hands shaking as he knotted his tie. He looked into the mirror, something he normally only did to check the neatness of his suit. He inspected the new lines engraved on his face. He felt as if he was seeing a different person. He tried to repress the panic he felt in his mind.

There were still duties to perform. Miss Charlotte had to be protected. The House was finished forever. He accepted that statement as a fact. He did not know why. It was time to switch his allegiance from the building to the occupants.

Garvey became aware, as he stared at himself in the mirror, of a love of life. How it might be a pleasure to experience change, to not know what was to happen from one moment to the next, to influence the course of one's own life. He felt different, less sure but more alert. He was surprised to find himself relishing that feeling.

Shaking his head, Garvey checked his uniform once more, smoothing out its creases. He picked up the poker and glanced round his room. Bed, chair, wardrobe, lamp. They were the old, the familiar. It was time to leave them behind.

He turned, left the room and locked the door behind him.

Bernice ran for her life. She pulled Charlotte through the thin band of trees, casting worried glances up at the creatures in the branches above. They were leaping about agitatedly and chattering in the voices that she had heard up on the hills the night before. No move had been made so far to stop their escape.

'What are those things?' asked Charlotte breathlessly.

Bernice hurried her along. 'We can discuss their origins at a better time, back at the House.'

She noticed how dark it had become in a matter of

seconds. She wondered how it was possible for night to arrive so quickly. Only moments ago it had been morning.

Behind her, from the lake, came a sound like a steam engine. Pistons were thumping up and down, faster and faster. Bernice tried not think about what the Quack might be becoming.

At last, they cleared the trees and found themselves back on the lawn. Charlotte was puffing and grunting beside her. Her breath steamed out in clumps of fog. The House was in front of them, beautiful and imposing against the night sky. Bernice felt a moment of unease and then realized that there were no lights on in the building.

As she ran, she became aware of a deathly hush from the copse they had just run away from. The steam engine had stopped pounding, the creatures had ceased their jabbering. Bernice allowed herself a quick look back. Charlotte braked to a halt and watched with her. 'What is it?' she asked.

'It's gone quiet,' Bernice replied.

The dam burst. A huge metallic, boiling machine drove itself through the trees towards them. Fierce yellow eyes, like lamps, glared at them over a champing, snorting iron mouth filled with smoking teeth. It was like a massive artificial worm or insect and sizzled with heat. It was heading straight for them, throwing up earth and leaves in its wake.

'Oh my God . . .' mouthed Bernice.

Climbing all over it, apparently oblivious to the heat it was generating, were hundreds of the little hairless creatures. They were screeching and whooping with vicious joy. Even more leaped and bounced along behind it.

'Come on!' screamed Charlotte and began to sprint to the House. Bernice needed no further prompting. The creature bellowed and launched itself across the lawn, leaving a great fiery trail behind it. Smoke spurted from its joints and gears as its screeches echoed round the valley.

Looking at the House, Bernice desperately tried to judge distances. They had a chance, as long as they didn't slip up. A frost had formed on the grass but this could not be allowed to impede their run. All thoughts were pushed aside as she concentrated on keeping her feet and making it to the door.

'Can't . . . go on,' wheezed Charlotte, her Victorian coat flapping around her, weighing her down. Her black hair had come loose and whipped out in a trail from her head.

Bernice, without breaking stride, grabbed the coat and pulled. 'Keep going!' she cried. 'Just keep going!' A stitch burned away in her side.

The creature was gaining. Bernice felt scalding air on the back of her neck, as if the thing was snorting fire at them. The stench of scorched earth assailed her nostrils and made it even more difficult to snatch breaths from the air.

She could see the gravel path, the one that led to the main entrance. She prayed that the Doctor had left the doors unlocked. She tried not to wonder why she should think it would be any safer inside than out. Her stomach knotted in agony but she did not relent. The multitude of screeches in her ears kept her legs pumping.

At last they reached the gravel path and skidded across the tiny stones to the steps. Bernice leapt up them to the main doors. She crashed into the wood. 'Come on! Come on!' panted Charlotte, thumping into her back.

Bernice struggled with the vast iron ring embedded in the studded door. She almost begged it to be unlocked.

The noise was upon them. The beast held them in its searchlight eyes. It was going to punch them right through the door and out of the other side of the House.

Instinctively, Bernice twisted the ring and the door swung open. Without even waiting for the swing to end, the women were inside. They dived to the floor and dragged themselves behind a pillar.

Something smashed into the doors. There was a deafening explosion and a roar as the creature burst into the hall. The pillars of the room shook and split, sending debris down from the cracked ceiling. A thunderous echo reverberated round the House. Bernice and Charlotte covered their ears as the walls shook with pounding and crashing.

The creature was stuck in the doorway. It had wedged itself between the double doors but was unable to make enough space to proceed any further. Bernice stared at the face of the iron beast. It was a distorted, cobbled-together version of the Quack, constructed seemingly from girders. It knotted its metal eyebrows in anger and puzzlement, then twisted itself round to grind itself forward. Its roars were deafening. Sparks blossomed from its side as it gnashed and fought itself free. The smaller creatures burned on its casing, furious and in agony.

'Got to rest,' shouted Charlotte, her chest heaving in the darkness.

'No time,' replied Bernice hoarsely. She snatched a few breaths of air and tried to stand.

The creature thrashed and spasmed like a dying fish as it bashed away at the doorway. Clouds of dust fell from the ceiling. 'It'll be through in a minute,' Bernice warned. She sat down again, in too much agony to stand. Suddenly the creature stopped moving. It just sat and fumed.

'I hate to tempt fate,' Bernice laughed breathlessly, 'but I think we might have made it.'

Something buzzed at her out of the darkness. Bernice had no time to react as a thin, furry body leaped onto her face. She screamed as spikes bit into her flesh. It was one of the insects that had killed Victoria.

Bernice was vaguely aware that Charlotte was trying to pull the thing off her face but she kept her eyes shut to avoid its flapping wings. It forced its head between her teeth and she felt herself unable to bite down on it.

Charlotte shouted, 'Get off' and Bernice's head reeled as the woman caught her an accidental punch on the side of the head.

With a shock of fear, Bernice felt a sharp needle punch

into her vocal cords. She couldn't breathe, she felt sick. Strength flooded away from her body. The vile insect hoisted itself further into her throat. Its wings ceased their frenzied fluttering. Consciousness was slipping away.

Bernice opened her eyes one last time to see dust and concrete falling out of the darkness at her. She heard Charlotte scream, felt the insect stop her breath and then something hit her head and everything went black.

Ace was dragged downstairs. All she could feel was the intense pain in her hands. Rix had clinically broken both middle and index fingers and tied her up again. Unable to stop herself, she had been sick. She struggled to rise above the pain, ignore it, but it could not be avoided.

'Get her down here,' shouted Rix. Archie, pushing Ace, complied. Ace realized that the bullying hard man in this brother had gone, replaced by a numbed, shocked boy. He had clearly seen too much. Helped by Frankie and Gray, he bundled Ace into the kitchen.

Rix took ammunition from the drawer and checked his gun. His tubby face was a mask of shock and hate. 'We must find that . . . devil. Bring him back, get him to cure my son and then destroy him.'

The door opened and Thos walked back in. Ace had heard the shots from outside and presumed that Aickland was dead. Another reason to get her revenge on this scum.

'Well?' demanded Rix.

Thos reloaded his rifle, keeping his eyes on the job in hand. 'He got away. That bastard Bert Robbins jumped me. I dealt with him.'

Rix paused, then put his pistol onto the table. Suddenly he screamed, 'You bungling, incompetent oaf! He'll bring the authorities down on us all.'

Thos went white, then recovered himself. To Ace, he looked in as bad shape as his brother. He was shaking and sweating. He appeared to be speaking for his life. 'I know where he's gone. We'll get him. Up the House. I heard Bert say. That . . . other bloke's gone there too'

Rix gave an unexpectedly contented sigh. 'Good,' he mused, 'then we'll have them both yet.'

He turned to his men, fixing each with a terrible, insane stare. 'Listen. We find Aickland, we kill him. No more mistakes. The other must be taken alive. He must make amends for his transgression.'

A terrible cry erupted from upstairs. Ace closed her eyes, trying to block out the anguish it contained. It was a young boy's cry, hopeless and terrified. Rix slammed his fist down onto the table. Ace saw that the men were too terrified to say anything to the doctor.

Agonizing minutes passed as the scream continued. At last it stopped. Ace reasoned that the boy had probably fainted again.

'Boss?' ventured Archie. 'What shall we do about the boy?'

Rix remained impassive, as if he had not heard. Archie looked around for support, then continued. 'Doctor? We can't leave him up there, what with Billy and all . . .'

Rix picked the pistol up from the table. He looked out of the window at the road. 'Right,' he said, 'let's get moving. Archie, bring the woman.'

There was a moment's confusion amongst the men. Rix shouted, 'Come on then!'

Archie jerked the rope and Ace was pulled up. She felt consciousness slipping away, the pain was overcoming her again. She vowed to keep going. Her fingers felt like ingots of fire. 'Rix,' she groaned. 'That's your son up there. You can't just leave him.'

Rix bounded over to her and slapped her across the face. She realized he had totally lost his mind. 'Don't tell me what I can and can't do! I can do anything!' He regained his composure. He breathed deeply and slowly. 'Listen men. We're all very tired and have seen some terrible things today. Let's stay alert. Wychborn Manor is waiting.'

Ace watched them pull on heavy overcoats and hats. They remained silent. Rix opened the door and led them out into the yard. Ace was dragged to the road. The screaming from upstairs began again and followed her until she was so far up the road as to be out of earshot.

Peter, standing on watch at the doors of the dining room, heard the roaring and crashing sounds echoing round the House. He jumped as the Doctor placed a hand on his shoulder. 'Bernice and Charlotte, I shouldn't wonder,' he muttered supportively. However, when Peter looked at his face he saw only lines of worry.

The boy had been much relieved when, minutes before, Garvey had joined them. The butler appeared normal again, smart and clean. Only a new, alien look on his face hinted that everything was not as it should be.

Now, once more, Peter was worried. First the sudden darkness and then this unearthly noise. Something big had got into the House. He was discovering a new emotion. Fear. He lacked the imagination to visualize what might be responsible for this noise but it sent waves of terror through him.

'Careful now Peter,' said the Doctor, apparently possessed with great prescience concerning other people's emotions. 'Don't give in to your fear. Be aware of it but don't give in.'

Peter gave him an unconvincing smile and looked back at Tillie for reassurance. She was standing by the fire, frowning and listening. Mary and Jane were expressionless as usual, seemingly not even hearing the noises.

The Doctor took a step into the corridor. He seemed to be listening. 'There's somebody coming,' he said at last.

A few seconds passed and then Peter heard it too. Footsteps.

Garvey was suddenly by his side brandishing his iron poker. Peter wished that he had a weapon. The Doctor pushed the butler gently back into the room. 'I think they're friendly, Mr Garvey.'

Charlotte emerged from the gloom of the hallway. She was covered in dust, tears streaking down her beautiful face. The Doctor clasped his hand around her wrist and pulled her into the dining room. 'Block it up,' he ordered.

The roaring ceased. In its place came the sound of many voices, chattering and screeching: an animal sound that was getting louder. Garvey closed the doors and began to nail them to each other.

Peter started to drag the dining-table across the room. Garvey got himself out of the way and, with Tillie's help, they jammed the table up against the entrance. Tillie handed Peter a plank, and he held it for Garvey to nail to the doors.

The Doctor led Charlotte to a green velvet chair and sat her down. She was staring into space, brushing black hair from her forehead. Peter saw that the Doctor was watching her intently. Tillie rushed to make a cup of tea for their mistress.

'Charlotte, what happened to Bernice?' asked the Doctor. 'Where is she?'

Tillie placed the cup into her hand. It slipped from Charlotte's feeble grip and crashed to the floor. Tea soaked into the carpet. She looked up at the Doctor. 'I . . . I had to leave her. She was buried in the hall. The ceiling fell in. I couldn't reach her. I tried!' Fresh tears appeared in her eyes.

'I know, it's all right,' whispered the Doctor. He sighed.

Charlotte clutched his wrist. 'There is more.' She wiped her eyes, bolstering herself for her next words. The Doctor nodded for her to continue. 'One of those things. The insects. It got into her mouth. I . . .' She began to sob again.

Peter, unused to witnessing emotions of this nature, turned back to the main doors. He listened carefully. Immediately he whipped his head back, white with fear. Garvey tried to listen. 'What is it, lad?' he asked.

'More footsteps, softer ones, coming towards us.'

Garvey nodded and said calmly to the Doctor, 'Something coming!'

Doctor looked worried, and a little angry. 'I've got get out there and fetch Bernice.'

Abruptly, several large objects crashed into the doors. The handles were twisted fiercely. Scratches and moans could be heard, excited and heated.

'I don't think you're going anywhere,' said Garvey grimly. The Doctor gave no reply but Peter noticed that he was furiously biting his lip.

Not knowing what to do, Peter crept back. Tillie bumped into him, two candlesticks in her hands. 'One for you,' she said bravely and hugged him. He smiled at her. It dawned on him that he wanted to protect her, defend her against whatever was outside the doors. Despite the feelings of panic, he experienced an elation unlike anything he had ever experienced before.

Embarrassed, he looked at Charlotte. She was slowly coming to terms with her sobbing. 'I apologize, Doctor. I did not want to leave her.'

'Don't worry,' he replied. 'Now, I'm sorry but we don't have much time. You must tell me everything that happened to you both. Did you find the man at the lake? What did you do?'

Charlotte sighed and started to recount her story. Despite the noises at the door, Peter was curious and wanted to listen. He crept over to them.

When she had finished, Peter looked up at the Doctor. Once again, he was surprised to see an expression of anger on the man's normally impish and friendly face. 'I see,' he whispered. 'At last, I see.'

'What?' asked Peter. He was unable to contain his curiosity.

'I understand,' said the Doctor. 'This is all a terrible mistake. My dream. The man by the lake who calls himself the Quack. Neither of them are really dreams.'

He seemed to see Peter for the first time. He stared into the boy's face with those deep, deep eyes of his. 'Well, aren't you going to ask me?' he exclaimed.

'What?'

'If they're not dreams, what are they?'

Peter was puzzled and slightly afraid of the Doctor. 'All right, sir, what are they?'

The little man slapped his own forehead. 'Isn't it obvious? They're warnings!'

The noises and scrabblings at the door increased in volume and intensity.

Aickland had heard the thunderclap of a shot behind him and he knew that Bert Robbins was dead. Thos had killed him in cold blood.

Stumbling through the woodland at the side of the road, he started to realize that he was in shock. The reality of events was crashing into his mind. He would never have believed it but he found himself yearning for the comforts of Camberwell and his doting aunts. He missed civilized society. And Ace. He wondered briefly whether he should go back and find her. He shook his head. She was dead, she had to be. All he could do now was find Arthur and help him. He presumed that the strange man was going to Wychborn House. It was logical, even with Bert's clue. The place was a legendary centre of unnatural visions. It made sense that such a creature as Arthur would find sanctuary there.

Every now and then, Aickland saw gleaming patches of liquid, diluted by rain water but still emitting a feeble glow. He used them as a trail and followed the road up the hill.

He stopped and sat down on a wet, grassy bank. His hands were shaking and his teeth were chattering. He wasn't built for this sort of excitement. He didn't feel much like a ghost hunter any more.

Throughout the House, creatures were moving. The building was almost alive, so profuse was the activity inside it.

The hairless beasts bounded and leapt through room after room upturning furniture, ripping up decorations, destroying anything they could get their long, pale fingers on.

Outside the dining room, wherein the last of the original occupants cowered and waited, other bigger creatures prowled and probed. They were themselves waiting for a signal, for the time to enter and devour.

Where Bernice lay buried under rubble, the insect connecting her to a new world, sucking the life from her, a figure walked by. He had shrunk from his earlier form to one he preferred. He walked down the steps to the secret cellar. The nexus point.

There he would wait. Wait for his meeting with the Doctor. He knew he would not have to wait long.

Interlude:
AD 1868

The woman in white looked sadly at the ruin of Wychborn House. It was still burning in places, though not as spectacularly as on the night before.

It was all a very great shame. Lady Edith had showed her the utmost kindness and civility, as had the servants. She had been tempted to tell them about the fire but a lifetime of warnings about the dangers of interference remained too firmly instilled in her mind. It was part of the unfolding text of the universe and had to remain as such. An unhappy accident. At least she would be able to salvage something from the ruins.

The old woman felt tired as she stood amid the well-kept lawns. Death was a phenomenon she was acutely unfamiliar with and she was shocked by its proximity. It seemed odd that the sun still rose, that summer could be so beautiful, that the universe still carried on despite the parts lost from it. It brought home to her what a sheltered life she had lived.

Still, it was time to build. To produce something that was good from the ashes. A symbol.

The old woman walked ruefully towards the smoking house. It was going to be a hot, marvellous day, but she had work to do.

Chapter 6

Bernice was sitting in a chair in the middle of a vast expanse of whiteness. She could see no walls in any direction. She felt the same disorientation she had experienced in the Land of Fiction. A nowhere, a nothing.

'Professor Summerfield?' came a voice.

A human form materialized in front of Bernice. It was a young girl with fair hair. 'Victoria?' she asked.

The girl flickered, as if she was a picture on a television screen. She wore the same clothes that she had died in. It seemed a long time ago to Bernice that they had carried her down from the bluebells.

'That's better,' said Victoria as her image steadied itself and became real. 'Thank you for trying to save my life. You shouldn't have.'

'It was nothing,' Bernice replied uneasily. 'I wish we could have done better.'

'No matter.' The girl smiled.

There was an uncomfortable pause. At last Bernice broke the silence. 'Where am I now?' she asked. 'The last thing I remember is getting an insect in the throat . . .' Her voice tailed off. She wondered whether Victoria would be embarrassed by being reminded of her own death. She decided events must really be getting weird if she was worrying about things like that.

'You are still there,' said Victoria. 'You have become patched into the Matrix again. It happens to us all. Life was nice but all good things come to an end.'

'Matrix?' The word seemed familiar to Bernice but she was unable to trace its origin.

'The Matrix is everything. All is the Matrix. You are the Matrix.'

'I don't follow.'

Victoria smiled again. 'You will. The Assimilator will be here soon to bring you back inside. You will follow then.'

Bernice distinctly did not like the sound of that. 'Assimilator?' she asked warily.

'It might take a while. He is awfully busy at the moment and, to be honest, I don't think he quite knows what he's doing. We've never needed him before. It's all a bit confused. I'd like to talk to you to help pass the time.'

Bernice pondered for a minute. Perhaps it was time to try a new gambit. She might just find something out. 'I think there's been a mistake,' she said.

Victoria sat down in a second white chair that had appeared from nowhere. 'Really? What's that?' she asked.

'I don't want to be assimilated. I don't think I'm part of any matrix.'

Bernice looked about, worried. All she could see was the white void stretching away in all directions. If the Assimilator was around, he was well hidden. Then again, hadn't the girl come out of nowhere?

Victoria shrugged. 'I'll agree with you about the mistake. Instructions have become confused of late. With these new elements. You see, the Matrix can't find the bit of itself that created them. Until it does, things will be a little disrupted. Now you're here, we should be able to sort it all out in no time. Don't worry, of course you are part of the Matrix. Everything is. We just have the self-knowledge kept from us until we are assimilated. It's part of the plan.'

'What plan?'

'The plan. The why.'

Bernice shook her head. Apart from having some suspicions about what these 'new elements' were, she could not understand the logic of this non-place. 'Victoria,' she stated, 'you're not real are you.'

'I am Victoria. An anthropomorphism.'

'Anthropomorphism representing what?'

'Access.'

Bernice smiled, bewildered. She decided to find out some facts. 'All right then. Where are we in relation to the House?'

Victoria spread out her arms. 'We are in it,' she exclaimed. 'In Control. All will become clear.'

Bernice stood up, alarm bells sounding in her mind. Clearly, she had got herself mixed up in something that was programmed. Some machine with delusions of grandeur and devastating power. She had to get away but had no notion of how to do it. Frighteningly, what Victoria was telling her seemed unerringly similar to the orthodox view of an afterlife. Most galactic cultures had some sort of similar myth. The big plan, the creator, the coming of enlightenment. If that was true then the implications were . . . No, it had to be coincidence. She was not dead.

'Be patient,' reassured Victoria. 'All will become clear.'

Unable to think of anything else to do, Bernice sat down again.

At least Archie had allowed Ace to walk freely this time. She trudged through the mud, feeling better despite the fiery pain in her hands. Frankie and Gray were covering her suspiciously with their guns. She laughed ironically, wondering what they thought she could do to them with her black and swollen fingers.

The pain was beginning to dull and she knew that if she could keep shock at bay then she could remain functional. She had considered an escape attempt but two factors held her back. Firstly, in her present condition she could well get blown away by her captors. Secondly, they were looking for Arthur, which was exactly what she wanted to do anyway. It was when they found him that she would have to come up with a plan.

Ace looked around. Frankie and Gray were scared to death; given half a chance they would prove no trouble. They would run if things turned nasty for them.

Archie appeared to be on the verge of cracking, his swarthy little head nodding at the ground, hands drumming at the rope as he pulled her along. He would be dangerous but was not thinking clearly.

Thos and Rix were a different matter. They seemed almost confident as they led the way up the hill. Thos had apparently lost his earlier all-consuming rage. She had seen Bert's body in the yard. Some people took murder in their stride and Thos had clearly found his hobby. As for Rix, he was an icy psychotic and the most dangerous of them all.

They were led along the muddy road by Thos who was following the trail of glowing blood. Nobody spoke, which allowed Ace plenty of time to recover. She wondered whether Aickland was ahead of them.

At last, the road dipped into a small valley and Ace saw Wychborn House.

It was a gutted ruin. There were similarities to the other mansion she had briefly seen but this building was less ordered, less symmetrical. The roof had gone and several sections had been burnt to the ground. What remained had the melancholy atmosphere of a tomb. A large spiky tower grew at one end, still intact. The rest of the house hung open like an eviscerated corpse, broken brick and wood lying intertwined between gaping holes in the walls. Overgrown vines clung to the building, gripping parasitically to the stonework. Bushes and shrubs grew chaotically in and around the grounds. Ace found it difficult to believe that this could ever have been a place of habitation, let alone luxury. She assumed it had caught fire years ago and been abandoned.

She watched the group of men, overcoats flapping in the cold wind, stare down at the house. 'Boss,' said Archie, 'let's get out of here. We don't really want to go in there.'

'You know the stories,' Gray agreed. 'It's haunted.'

161

Rix swung round to Archie and pointed his pistol at him. He looked to Ace as if he was going to use it. 'Nobody backs out now,' he whispered. 'You move and I'll kill you.' His Scots burr had become even more pronounced.

Archie staggered back, clearly too frightened to even make a fight of it. Wildly, he turned to his brother, 'Thos,' he cried, 'tell him. He can't . . .'

Thos kept his gun pointing at the ground. He stared at his feet. 'Shut your mouth Archie,' he grunted, 'or I'll shoot you myself.'

Rix cocked his pistol. Archie let his gun drop to the floor, as well as Ace's rope. He was sweating and his breath emerged in short, foggy bursts. 'All right, all right!' he begged. 'Don't shoot. I'll come.'

For a few seconds, Rix kept the gun trained on him. At last, he moved, pointing it at the others in turn. They stepped back. Ace wondered whether she should try and make a break for it.

'Get the rope Archie,' he hissed, perhaps guessing Ace's intentions.

The frightened man obeyed. Rix continued speaking. 'We have a job to do. We have to save a boy's life. There will be no going back. No walking out. You're involved in this whether you like it or not. Anybody disobeys me again, they get punished. They get shot. I run this village and I'm telling you, you had better start proving yourselves. There is an evil here and we are about to purge it. Do I make myself clear?'

Ace tried to look into his eyes but all she could see was a grey light reflected off his spectacles. Rix lowered his gun. He coughed. 'We're wasting time here. Let's go.'

Suddenly Frankie pointed towards the house. 'Look,' he squealed fearfully. Ace turned to see.

Through one of the gaping window frames on the ground floor, she saw a light. A golden glow, faint but unmistakably Arthur's. It contrasted eerily with the depressing grey of the daylight. Rix smiled. 'He's there. We've got him.'

After a long time crying, Charlotte was beginning to feel better. To have lost Bernice had been a shattering realization. She had relied on the kind, resourceful woman to be her guide through the transformations that were sweeping through the House. Without her she felt isolated and useless.

Brushing the tears from her face, she looked around at the dining room. It was still a shock to see the familiar now so unfamiliar.

Garvey stood by the doors, poker in hand, lost in his own new thoughts. Peter and Tillie sat together, whispering by the fire. Mary and Jane were seated in identical chairs, staring at the walls. Charlotte realized that she had never once spoken to them. Even that had seemed normal until she thought about it.

'Feeling better?' asked the Doctor. Charlotte had not seen him there, sitting silently cross-legged next to her. There was a power in him. Her mind went back to yesterday's conversation about him with Bernice.

He did look like a man who could explain things, who would tell you things and you would believe them. He was like the Quack, full of mysterious knowledge. 'Tell me what is happening here,' she asked, without understanding why she thought he might be able to explain.

He laughed and a strange look appeared in his eyes. 'I wish I knew,' he replied. 'You have given me some clues. You did a very brave thing, confronting that Quack fellow. I wonder if you know how brave.'

'Who is he?'

'A warning, like my dream. Someone is trying to communicate, tell us what is happening here. But they are unable to address us directly. They are using symbols, dreams. I'm sure it's no accident he called himself "the Quack".'

'Dreams?' Charlotte asked. She could not follow his

words fully, but at least they were an attempt at explanation, at reassurance.

He smiled again. 'I had a dream. A very rare event for me. I now believe it was someone attempting to contact me telepathically. They couldn't make much of a connection, only influence my subconscious. The Story of the Rock.'

'What is that?'

The Doctor raised his eyebrows and took a deep breath. 'I wonder if you comprehend anything that I'm saying. The Story of the Rock is an old Gallifreyan fairy-tale. It's a warning about interference, about leaving things alone. Only the story was altered and I did interfere: I went to save my companion. So I concluded it was a warning. Whether it was a warning about interfering or not interfering I must confess I don't know. Similarly, when you confronted the Quack he was warning you but, of course, was maddeningly unspecific about what or why. Reminds me of myself.'

He leaned back in his chair, as if having completed a great task. 'I am not often this lucid, Charlotte,' he said, 'I don't like having to make my thoughts known, but . . .'

Charlotte caught that strange look in his eyes again. She was learning to become suspicious. 'There's something you're not telling me, isn't there?' she said.

She felt an odd thrill of victory as she saw the Doctor noticeably flinch. 'My goodness, Charlotte,' he replied. 'You have learned a lot in two days. What do you think is going on?'

Charlotte was pleased with herself again in that she realized that the Doctor had not answered her question. No doubt he had good reason. She thought hard. 'Doctor?' she asked cautiously.

'Hmm?' he muttered. He seemed distracted, lost.

'You say the warnings are unclear.'

'Yes?'

Charlotte paused, trying to articulate and focus new

thoughts. 'Well, perhaps whoever is sending this warning is unclear in their own mind. Perhaps they don't know.'

All of a sudden, the Doctor leaped out of his chair. Charlotte jumped, surprised. The others in the room turned to him, clearly equally surprised. 'Eureka!' he shouted. He grasped Charlotte's shoulders. He beamed a bright, happy smile. 'Charlotte, you're a genius! You're absolutely right. It doesn't know why it's warning us. It wants our help!'

There was a loud crash on the ceiling that sent shockwaves through the dining-room. Something incredibly heavy had just landed on the floor of the room above. Cracks appeared in the plaster over their heads.

The Doctor stared up at the ceiling. 'I hope that whatever it is realizes that we could do with a little help ourselves.'

'Doctor!' shouted Garvey from the door. 'I think they're trying to get in.'

Charlotte shivered as the scrabbling sounds at the doors increased. She remembered the tiny, wizened shadow creatures in the trees.

Peter was up and dashing towards Garvey. His young face was alive with fear and anticipation. He kept glancing back at Tillie, as if wanting support. The maid gave him a frightened smile.

'Don't worry Miss Charlotte,' said Garvey, his body looking frail and old. 'We will protect you.'

Suddenly, the boards blocking one of the windows cracked and split. 'I think something wants to come in,' remarked the Doctor.

Charlotte stood up and looked around for a weapon. She found a candlestick lying on the floor and snatched it up. 'I've had enough of running,' she whispered, wondering where this new determination was coming from.

The Doctor shook his head. 'I think running away is a very underrated pastime. You know the old Earth saying . . .'

'No,' replied Charlotte. 'How does it go?'

'I'll tell you later.'

The window burst inwards in a blast of wood and glass. Charlotte shrieked. Quicker than she would have believed possible, a huge black shape bounded into the dining room. It was like the creature Victoria had become, only bigger and faster. It was Mrs Irving.

Screaming, Tillie suddenly threw herself at the beast, swinging at it with a plank of wood. It seemed to elongate itself before scampering forward on long muscular legs. It dodged Tillie's blow with frightening ease and pounced on her.

'Tillie!' roared Peter and ran at the creature. She flailed helplessly in its grip. Lithely, it leapt at one of the walls and scuttled, spider-like, up to the ceiling. Tillie punched and fought but could not release herself.

'Get back!' yelled the Doctor. 'Keep away from it!'

Charlotte heard a terrible ripping and tearing sound from the darkened ceiling. Tillie's screams became gurgles, then an explosion of blood and bone showered the room. The creature, with Mrs Irving's voice, screeched in delight.

Peter screamed, clearly overcome with anger and horror. Charlotte clapped her hands over her ears to block out his wail of despair. The boy hefted his poker and hurled it up at the creature. It bounced uselessly off the convulsing black flesh and clattered to the floor again.

Charlotte heard another heavy thump behind her. A second creature, reminding her vaguely of Alleyn, scampered in through the window.

Garvey appeared by her side. He shouted hoarsely and swung out at the insect-like carapace. The monster caught the poker neatly in one of its dextrous limbs and threw the butler into a corner.

Charlotte raised her candlestick and threw it at the beast. It hit the creature in the head, halting its advance for a second. It glared at her with fierce yellow eyes, hissed with anticipation and advanced. Limbs clicked and flexed. Charlotte realized she was helpless.

There came a movement from behind her. As the creature sprang, the Doctor somehow interposed himself between it and her. He whacked at its head with a log from the burning fire.

Like Victoria on the previous night, the creature screeched and burst into flames. It tottered around unsteadily, setting light to tablecloths, napkins and anything else that would burn. The dining-room began to fill with smoke. 'Don't you just love being in control?' quipped the Doctor smugly.

Another creature appeared at the window. The Doctor threw the log out at it. 'I think it's time we made a hasty departure. Obviously my plan to barricade ourselves in has . . .'

He was silenced by a black thread of gum that spattered onto his back. Charlotte followed the trail of the gum back up to the ceiling, where the creature scuttled. It had fired some sort of line.

With a yelp, the Doctor was hauled up into the air. He hung on to his fedora with one hand, his legs flailing about as the creature reeled him in.

Charlotte attempted to grab his feet but fell back empty-handed. The Doctor was disappearing into the shadows above.

The burning creature suddenly pounced on her. She managed to dodge its clumsy charge, blinded and wounded as it was. It overbalanced in the eagerness of its spring and fell onto its back, in flames. Screeching and crisping, it thrashed about like an upturned beetle. Peter clasped Charlotte's hand and pulled her out of the way.

The Doctor was struggling with the sticky, web-like fluid that held him. The creature on the ceiling fired out another line and caught his right shoulder. He used the impact to give himself the momentum to start swinging. He was rising faster and faster.

Charlotte caught a glimpse of a cavernous mouth opening up and arms reaching out to ensnare the little man.

Just in time, the Doctor managed to gain enough momentum to give himself a powerful swing and he flew across the room, clasping his legs round the ornate decoration of the chandelier. He let out a cry as the creature savagely jerked its threads, almost pulling him in half. He was clearly struggling to keep his grip. The chandelier groaned as it was hauled off-centre by the creature.

The Doctor thrust forward and sent the chandelier swinging away from the creature. To Charlotte, the scene became almost comic. The Doctor and the creature played a bizarre game of see-saw, neither side gaining enough momentum to pull the other down.

Suddenly there was a grinding, tearing sound from the bolts that fastened the chandelier to the ceiling. They were being torn out by the violence of the swings. His face a mask of determination, the Doctor continued his pushes.

As if changing its mind, the creature launched itself across the ceiling. It scrabbled towards the Doctor, threads becoming slack. Finding himself swinging freely, he increased the action on the chandelier. The bolts in the ceiling squealed in protest at the strain.

With a cry, the creature sprang onto the metal framework. It landed next to the Doctor with a shattering thump. They stared at each other as if surprised. The bolts gave way. Everything, Doctor, creature and chandelier, plummeted to the ground.

For a second, Charlotte's vision was obscured by falling masonry and the need to get out of the way. The chandelier hit the floor with a deafening, heavy crash. The room went silent.

Charlotte and Peter slowly walked to the tangle of metal in the centre of the room.

The creature hissed and spat, broken and buried under the remains of the chandelier. A viscous green liquid oozed from its split body. It mewled and howled like a kitten. Of the Doctor, there was no sign.

'You know something,' came a voice behind them. Charlotte swivelled round to see the Doctor lying on a padded leather chaise longue. He stretched out and dusted himself down. 'I knew those trapeze lessons with the

168

Venusian State Circus would come in handy one day. Very difficult technique to master, they've got eight arms y'see.'

Charlotte laughed. She couldn't believe that he had survived.

The creature under the chandelier screeched again. Peter walked, stony faced, to the fire. Using two pokers, he carefully lifted out a burning log.

Charlotte could see an intelligence in the beast's eyes, glaring at the boy as he turned to it. For a second she felt compassion for the creature, sitting and waiting for extinction, but the look on Peter's face prevented any interference.

'I hope this hurts,' he said bitterly and dropped the burning brand onto its flesh. The creature flared up like a torch.

The Doctor turned Charlotte away from the fire and together they went to help Garvey who was lying in the broken remains of a bookcase. He had a trickle of blood on his scalp but was regaining consciousness. The Doctor gave him a quick examination and lifted him up. 'Come on Mr Garvey,' he said. 'We've still got a long night ahead of us.'

There came another screech from the window. Through the smoke from the two burning creatures, Charlotte could see dark shapes moving outside. 'Doctor,' she said, 'I think we should leave.'

With Peter's help, the Doctor pulled Garvey to his feet. 'Miss Charlotte?' he asked feebly.

'I am perfectly all right, Mr Garvey,' she replied. 'Come on, we've got to go.'

The small creatures, like curious, deformed babies, were poking their large, domed heads in through the gaping window. A cold, winter wind blew into the room. Time seemed oddly still to Charlotte. All of a sudden, despite the creatures, she felt safe. It was as if she knew the danger had passed. How could that be? The little creatures still spat and gibbered at the window. Larger ones, out of sight, hissed in anticipation.

'What about Mary and Jane?' asked Garvey, clearly recovering his wits. Charlotte looked across to the maids. They sat, still as statues, in their seats. It was as if they had not registered anything happening in the room. 'Mary? Jane?' she asked, going over to them.

The Doctor followed, giving himself a final dusting down. 'Ladies?' he asked. 'Care for a stroll?' He straightened his lapels out. Charlotte was beginning to realize that this man did not always say what he meant, that he used buffoonery as a way of diverting interest in his intentions. She was pleased with herself for detecting this. Perhaps she was becoming 'experienced' at last.

He gave each of the maids a hearty slap on the back. As one, they keeled over, dropping to the floor with a thud. They lay on the hearth rug, locked into their seated positions. The Doctor knelt down and touched Mary's neck. Hurriedly, he whipped his hand away. 'I knew they were cold in company,' he remarked, 'but this is ridiculous. Frozen solid. As a bird's eye.'

Charlotte frowned, confused. The Doctor stood up. 'Obviously they had outgrown their function. Either that or their batteries ran out. I think we'd better leave.'

Garvey, rubbing the obviously painful wound on his head, asked, 'Excuse me, Doctor, how are we going to get out? Those creatures are everywhere.'

The Doctor grinned. 'Oh I think we'll be all right. Think about it, Mr Garvey. They could have been all over us by now, all this time we've spent chatting. Someone called them off. I don't think they're too happy about it either.' He pointed to the impatient, hairless creatures at the window. 'No, I believe we shall be allowed to leave, within a certain limit.'

'I don't understand.' Garvey's hollow, lined face looked kind and puzzled. The fire highlighted his prominent cheek-bones and set his eyes in shadow. Charlotte found his presence comforting.

'Don't worry, Mr Garvey,' replied the Doctor chirpily, 'I think I'm beginning to work it out. Anyway, I must try and get to Bernice.' He walked briskly to the double doors and pulled away the table that blocked it. Charlotte watched in astonishment as he wrestled the planks of wood off from the panels. He turned the handles and, with a flourish, wrenched the doors open.

Lining the corridor, hanging from every available orna-ment, were hundreds of the little shadow creatures. They were crushed together on the floor, like a moving carpet. Their eyes stared excitedly at the four humans. Charlotte saw a malice in their eyes, aggression and hatred, and she felt a barely controllable terror. Their anger was like a physical force, their eager fingers and mouths barely restrained from attack. She realized some compulsion held them back, but how easily they could overwhelm her and the others.

'After you,' said the Doctor brightly. It was as if he was inviting them to take a stroll in the grounds. Nobody moved. 'Oh well,' he continued. 'Age before beauty.' With that, he stepped forward into the seething, malevolent corridor.

Charlotte looked around for advice and saw Peter star-ing back at the remains of Tillie scattered across the dining room. His expression was a mixture of despair and anger. She could sympathize with him. She felt sad and angry too.

Garvey swallowed and tentatively walked out after the Doctor, picking his way through the little creatures, obvi-ously trying not to tread on any. Charlotte and Peter, having no other option, stepped out after him.

Close up, the house looked even more frightening. Aick-land stared up at the dead walls and long-rotted wooden beams. He poked his head through one of the ruined doorways. The interior was worse than the exterior. Wrecked rooms were filled with decaying furniture and sodden carpets. Insects, moss, pools of water and vermin were everywhere and the stench of damp was overpower-ing. Aickland presumed that nothing had been moved in the six years since the fire. It was not quite what he had expected from 'Grissom's Almanack of Hauntings', the source of his knowledge about Wychborn House.

He went inside, feet splashing in the water. It was almost pitch black, the only light being the daylight streaming in through the gaps. 'Arthur?' Aickland whispered. He paused to listen but heard no sound except running water.

Standing there, in that room, the full truth of what he might have to do dawned on him. Rix and the others would be here soon. They had murdered once, perhaps twice, and were after him. He would have to take them on and kill them. All of them. He gasped in horror. He did not want to think about that.

Instead, he looked around for a weapon. His wounds were very painful and he wondered how long he would last before exhaustion and shock overcame him. Everything in the room was rotten. He wished Ace, or anyone, was here to tell him what to do.

He had to set a trap. If he could prepare himself for the enemy, sort out some form of defence, find Arthur.

Despairing, wet and cold, Aickland searched the dark room for inspiration.

Despite the threat of 'the Assimilator', whatever that was, Bernice found herself becoming a little bored. She had forgotten how long she had waited here in this white nothingness but it felt like days. Victoria, or her construct, had disappeared leaving her alone with just the two empty chairs for company.

She tried various methods to find out where she was. She wandered as far away from the chairs as she could without losing sight of them. She found nothing, just the whiteness stretching off to infinity.

She tried closing her eyes and denying the reality of the place, an idea she'd seen on an old sci-fi vid. That didn't work either. Finally, she gave up and sat down to think.

There was a pain in her throat where she presumed the insect had stung her. She wondered whether Victoria had been telling the truth. Perhaps she was still lying buried under a pile of rubble in the portico hall with a monster in her mouth. If that was the case then it made this place more preferable so she shouldn't worry too much about staying in it for a while.

Bernice yawned and sighed. She considered running as far as she could go but knew that it would be pointless. All she could do was wait and that made her feel restless and irritable. 'I suppose there are worse things in life,' she said and tried to make herself comfortable.

Charlotte, with Garvey and Peter, followed the Doctor through the ground floor of the wrecked House.

The creatures surrounding them had been busy. Not one item of furniture was intact, every flagstone in the hall had been pulled up and smashed and the portraits on the walls had been torn down and dismembered.

It was dark now and as cold as ice. Charlotte noticed that the newly discovered fog that came from her mouth was even thicker and wetter. She shivered.

The creatures were everywhere but scrabbled apart to allow access for the four survivors. The Doctor appeared to know where he was going so Charlotte followed him trustingly.

As they passed through the portico hall, Charlotte stifled a moan at seeing a large pile of rubble covering a body. 'Bernice!' she exclaimed. Her voice set up a disgruntled rustling amongst the creatures. The Doctor moved towards his companion's body but halted when they bounded together to block his path. They began hissing excitedly.

'Out of my way!' the Doctor commanded. 'I'm warning you.'

The monsters were excited now. They looked to Charlotte as if they were relishing the fact that the Doctor was going to try and move away from the prescribed path.

Tongues were licking grey lips. Claws were being flexed. The grotesque smiles filled her with disgust and horror. Still, if the Doctor was going to try to get to the body then it was her duty to help. Her guilt overcame her fear of the little creatures.

'You can't get to her, Doctor,' said Garvey calmly. 'They would tear you to pieces.'

The Doctor shook his head and kept his gaze firmly fixed on the supine body buried in the rubble. Gathering her courage, Charlotte did the same. The staring helped to focus her mind and ignore the fear.

'Doctor, Miss Charlotte, please,' said the butler. 'We must wait for another opportunity.'

The Doctor whirled round. His face broadened into a grin. 'Of course Mr Garvey. You're right. Forgive me, I do worry about my companions so. Perhaps wherever we are being led will provide an answer. Someone's got some explaining to do.'

Charlotte came to her senses again. She detected the bitter tone in the Doctor's speech. It frightened her almost as much as the creatures around them. Clearly, he did not take failure lightly. She felt foolish. Of course, there was no way to help Bernice. Yet. But she hoped that she never came between the Doctor and what he wanted to do.

He led them along a corridor towards the kitchen. At last he came to a blank wall and stopped. 'Here,' he said. He seemed to have regained his infectious good humour.

Charlotte looked blankly at the wall. 'What is it, Doctor?' she asked. Garvey and Peter seemed equally confused.

The Doctor frowned. 'Don't you see it?'

'What?' replied Garvey.

'The steps, leading down to a cellar. I nearly went down there last night but I changed my mind.'

Charlotte squinted but could see nothing but a wall. 'What do you mean, Doctor?'

Turning back to the wall, he said, 'Ah, I see. Even if you don't. Trust and follow me.' He lifted his fedora and

174

stepped through the wall. Charlotte was amazed. He just disappeared.

'Come on,' he shouted from nowhere. 'It's perfectly safe.'

Peter shrugged and walked forward. He bumped confidently into the wall and fell back surprised. 'Doctor?' he asked, rubbing his bruised nose.

'Oh dear,' came the disembodied voice. 'I think you're going to have to stay there.'

Charlotte felt a chill run down her spine. First Bernice had gone, and now the Doctor. They really were on their own. She remembered Tillie being ripped to pieces and stared nervously at the watching creatures.

Garvey hefted his iron poker. 'I think we'd better do what he says, for the moment,' he whispered. He did not seem particularly pleased with his own suggestion.

Moving as slowly as they did, with Ace walking clumsily and at a snail's pace, it took half an hour to reach Wychborn House. She felt surprisingly healthy, despite the injuries. The only trouble was that it was impossible for her to get out of the ropes. She realized that Rix had thought his sadism through well: no matter how well she controlled the pain, the physical fact that her fingers were broken stopped any hope of untying herself.

'Doctor Rix?' asked an extremely tentative Gray. He pulled at his ginger moustache and appeared to be very frightened. Ace thought something must have really scared him about the house, to have the guts to question the mad doctor.

'This had better be good, Gray,' warned Rix. Gray spat at the ground and found the words. 'What about the ghost?' he whimpered. 'The White Woman.'

Rix laughed. Ace cringed at the madness in it. 'Don't be a fool, there's no ghost. The only monster in there is that thing that . . . ruined my son.'

Gray looked unconvinced but clearly realized he was

175

lucky. Rix had not taken his question as a sign of coward-ice. 'Sorry, Doctor,' he mumbled.

Rix inclined his head towards the house. Archie pulled Ace forwards. From here the gaps in the walls looked to her like the gouged-out eyes of a corpse. She shuddered. It was not lost on her that Arthur had apparently headed straight here. A haunted house. She felt she was beginning to get some way towards finding out what was going on. Much good that it seemed to do her. 'I've got to get out of these bloody ropes,' she cursed silently.

'What's the plan then, Doctor?' asked Thos.

Rix looked up at the house again and said, 'It's my guess that Mr Aickland, if he has come here, is already in the house. He has probably found the creature and is attempting to hide it. I suggest we stay in one group and work through the house room by room. If we split up we're just setting ourselves up. Archie will stay here with the girl in case of emergency, but always in earshot.' Archie seemed delighted by this order, his swarthy head bobbed about excitedly. Rix walked up to him. 'I trust you will be safe with the girl. Even you should be capable of shooting a crippled, exhausted woman. If Aickland tries to do anything, kill him. If you even see him, kill him. Got that?'

Archie nodded, too vigorously. He spat out a mouthful of rain. 'Of course, Doctor Rix. You can trust me. I won't let you down.'

Rix smiled humourlessly. 'I hope so. If you disappoint me I promise you pain beyond imagining.'

Archie nodded again, looking sick.

Ace watched as the men shouldered their weapons and picked their way through rubble into the front entrance. They looked frightened and trigger-happy. She hoped Aickland had had more sense than to come to the house. The men disappeared into the gloom. She heard them stumbling and cursing as they began their search. She wondered if they had realized what a big mistake they had made, leaving her alone with Archie.

'Cold, innit,' she said, testing the water.

Archie snapped round to her, his eyes wide and bulging. 'What?' he demanded.

'I just said it was cold.'

'Shut up.'

'Charmed I'm sure.'

Ace inwardly grinned. This guy really was cracking up. She started again. 'My hands hurt.'

Archie grimaced. 'Good . . . I mean, shut up.'

'You know Rix is totally mental, don't you?'

He raised his arm and Ace thought she had gone too far. There was a noise from inside the hallway. Archie turned hurriedly and glared at the dark doorway. 'Doctor Rix? Thos?' he whispered.

'Could be the ghost,' offered Ace.

'I told you to shut up.'

The noise came again. Distracted, Archie peered into the gloom. Ace also risked a glance. She couldn't see any movement. Archie raised the gun and looked on the verge of firing it.

'Hold it,' ordered Ace. 'It might be a friendly noise . . . I know, shut up.'

Archie took a step inside, constantly glancing back to check on Ace. She figured it was a matter of minutes before he turned and ran. She just hoped he wasn't in a position to kill her on the way. Archie nervously coughed, a tic flicking away over his right eye. 'Who's there?' he demanded in a cracked, reedy voice.

'Why don't we go and look?' asked Ace. Archie tugged on the rope and, dragging her behind him, stepped nervously through the doorway. Ace heard sounds of men moving about somewhere inside the house. Muffled voices chatted away. Archie held his pistol out like a torch.

Ace looked about. Mangy, stuffed animal heads stared back at her, dripping with lice and water. Burnt, unrecognizable paintings hung from the walls like windows into strange dark worlds. The carpet sank like mud under their feet.

The noise came again. Archie swung round. 'Rix? Thos?' he asked. Ace heard nothing but water trickling down the stairs.

Suddenly something leapt out from beneath the stairwell. Archie screamed and fired. A bright orange glow lit up the hallway and the report thundered through the house. The carpet burst open and sprayed water over them. Archie looked at the shape on the floor.

'It's a rat, you stupid bugger,' breathed Ace. Even she had been caught up in the tension. Archie let out a coughing laugh of relief.

A cupboard on the landing burst open and Richard Aickland swung out on an old, rusty chandelier chain. Archie looked up to see two boots heading for his face. He dived to the floor and Aickland swung right over him. He twisted wildly and wound himself up in the dangling chain. Archie looked up and laughed as Aickland spun round, tying himself up. He raised his pistol.

Aickland stared back helplessly as he prepared to fire. Archie cocked the pistol. 'Goodbye, mister gentleman,' he sneered.

Ace kicked him in the back of the neck, breaking it instantly. He fell face-first onto the sodden carpet. He twitched once and became still.

Ace looked up to see Aickland staring at her in apparent horror. 'You . . . you've killed him,' he said, clearly aghast.

'Of course,' she replied. 'Help me get out of these ropes.'

'You're alive.'

'Very good. The ropes, if you don't mind.'

Aickland untwisted himself and dropped to the floor. 'I don't believe you just killed him.' He stared at the body. Ace gave Archie a cursory glance. 'Had to be done. It was him or you. I know which one I prefer. Now come on, they'll be here any second.'

Rix and his men had searched most of the ground floor, dismantling any furniture that was not already wrecked.

178

They had found nothing. Despite this, Rix was certain that the glowing man was close.

Frankie and Gray were proving useless, jumping at their own shadows, and Rix regretted leaving Archie behind to look after the girl. For all his signs of cracking up, at least he was a professional.

The creature had to be somewhere and he would find him even if he had to take the place apart with his bare hands. He was still shaken by the vision of his son's legs.

In his mind, Rix had decided that the glowing man was an avenging angel sent by God. He had been sent here to further punish a beaten man. Had not the birth of his son been enough? He felt like Job, to be tormented and stricken his whole life.

Well, unlike Job, Rix had no intention of obeying this vengeful, monstrous creator. He would capture the creature, use it and destroy it. He was a man who would not take it any more.

A shot rang out from the depths of the house. The men stopped and Rix turned around, pistol ready.

'What was that?' shrieked Frankie, clearly ready to break and run.

'Archie,' said Thos. 'Got to be. The girl's trying to get away.'

Rix made up his mind. They had to cover their retreat. They had to be sure. 'We're going back. She's probably got away from him, knowing the state he's in. I don't want her coming after us.'

He led the jog back to the hallway.

When they got there, all Rix could see was a chandelier chain swinging noisily from a bracket in the ceiling. Archie lay face-down on the mildewed carpet.

He checked the body. 'Broken neck,' he whispered. Thos snapped down on the breech of his rifle angrily. Frankie and Gray were looking around nervously, as if expecting an attack from any direction.

'Stupid fool,' Rix continued. 'I told him to watch out. It must have been that girl. This time no mistakes. We kill her straight away. She won't get far with her fingers like that.'

Thos grunted. 'Unless Aickland's helping her.'

Rix stood up, furious with himself for allowing events to have become so bungled. His face was red. 'Then we kill anything that moves.'

'Doctor,' begged Gray, 'let's get out of here before she gets us too.'

Smiling, Rix aimed the pistol at Gray and shot him through the head. Again, the house was filled with an echoing explosion. Smoke spiralled from the discharged weapon. 'Too late for you,' Rix hissed.

Gray sank to his knees, an expression of disbelief on his face, and toppled over. Rix turned to his two remaining employees. 'Anybody else want to leave?'

Thos and Frankie shook their heads vigorously.

Suddenly, Rix lost his temper. A white, burning rage overwhelmed him, and he began to kick away at the rubbish that filled the hallway. 'Why don't people do what they're told?' he screamed. 'It's not hard, it's easy! Just obey orders! Cause and effect!' He splashed through the hall, pulling the rotten paintings off the walls and smashing them apart. Spittle flew from his lips. He stopped and confronted Thos and Frankie, who were backing away from him. He stared at them with dim, mad eyes. 'It's easy. It's so easy.'

He took off his spectacles and, getting his breath back, cleaned them with a handkerchief. A minute of silence passed between the three men. At last, Rix replaced his glasses. 'Come on,' he said. 'We've got work to do.'

Wary, but assuming a confident air, the Doctor strode down the dusty steps into the cellar.

He saw a faint yellow light below him and deduced that this would be a very large room. He was not wrong. The cellar was cavernous and dark. A large stone table was placed in the centre.

What immediately took the Doctor's attention was the

astonishing array of clocks in the cellar. They stood on their own or sat on plinths, separate from each other as if set out for display. They were all types and shapes, from impassive, wooden grandfathers, through ornate Swiss-style cuckoos to small carriage clocks. He even spotted a familiar-looking ormolu. Their combined ticking filled the cellar with noise. 'Another symbol,' muttered the Doctor. 'I think I can guess the message.'

He took a second look at the range of timepieces before him. 'All pre-electrical mechanized clocks. Springs and cogs. Nothing digital, not even LED.'

The clocks all displayed different times on their faces, so he could gain no immediate clues from that. 'Unless that fact itself has some meaning,' he conjectured. He reached the floor of the cellar and shivered. It was extremely cold down here, even for the new winter the House had descended into.

'Welcome, Doctor,' came a pleasant voice and the Quack stepped out of the shadows to stand behind the tables.

'Nice decor,' commented the Doctor. 'It has a timeless quality.'

The Quack was just as Charlotte had described him: a skeletal frame, black mourning suit, glasses and top hat. He smiled. 'I thought it was high time we had a chat.'

The Doctor sniffed, concealing his caution. 'I suppose you're going to tell me what's going on here?'

'*Au contraire*, Doctor,' replied the thin man. 'I'm just as much in the dark as you.'

'Really? And here was I thinking I was confronting the baddie at last.'

'Oh no,' he said, 'quite wrong. There are no "baddies". Only those you have brought here with you. That much I do know.'

'Who are you?' The Doctor took the offensive.

'If I may use a quotation, Doctor: "I am you".'

'Me?'

181

The Quack appeared to reconsider. 'All right then. How about a dream? A man you once dreamed.'

The Doctor rubbed his hands, as if affected by the intense cold in the cellar. He noticed that the Quack seemed to suffer no ill effects from the temperature. 'I don't know what you mean,' he said. 'I didn't dream you.'

'You will.' Again the Quack gave him an enigmatic smile. 'Just continue Doctor . . . continue to dream. The more you dream me, the more I learn about you. Have you never wondered about yourself, Doctor?'

The Doctor nodded ruefully. 'Often of late, I have to admit.'

'About what you do? Righting wrongs. Travelling around putting the cosmos to rights. Does it define what you are, Doctor?'

'It's a living.'

'Is it? Have you never wondered that you might be making things worse? The more you interfere with the timelines, the more problems you set up further along the line. You sort those out only to create even more.'

The Doctor breathed heavily. 'It had crossed my mind. You know, I hadn't expected a moral debate. I thought we were going to have a fight.'

The Quack kept an unblinking gaze fixed on the Doctor. He walked round the table and sat down. 'What about poor Charlotte? Why don't you tell her?'

The Doctor reeled, as if caught unawares. 'I'm sure it would do no good to tell her that she looks just like Galah.'

'Who are you to say? Why does she look like her? A Gallifreyan, here?' The Quack seemed almost apologetic. 'You two were never very close, were you?'

The Doctor seemed to be picking his words carefully. 'We . . . we barely knew each other.'

The Quack kept his eyes on him. 'She knew you, Doctor. She was a great admirer, throughout your "career".'

'What about Charlotte, Garvey and Peter? Will they be safe?'

The Quack jumped up. 'They're fine. For now. They will be assimilated soon. There are limited resources here, you know. We have to reuse everything.'

'We?'

'You'll find out. We have your friend, by the way.'

'Ace?'

'The one you call Bernice. The one called Ace left some time ago. She got away from me somehow.'

The Doctor seemed both relieved and angry. 'If anything's happened to either of them . . .'

The Quack held out his hands in appeasement. 'Calm down. They'll be fine. Bernice will be assimilated soon, when I've finished with you. Then we can sort this mess out. Things have gone a little astray. Thankfully for me, as it happens, or I would never have existed.'

'And you want me to help?' asked the Doctor.

The Quack smiled and at last broke off his stare. 'Exactly. I am glad you've decided to co-operate. When we've assimilated you we can find out why the Matrix has become so disrupted.'

For a moment, the Doctor thought he had misheard. He stepped back with surprise. 'The Matrix? The Gallifreyan Matrix?'

'The everything. Come now Doctor. Please join us.'

Concealing any emotion he replied, 'For dinner I presume. Yours. Just hold on a minute before I put myself on the menu, what about the three upstairs?'

'They will be assimilated. The Elementals can do it.'

'No,' stated the Doctor firmly. 'You will call those creatures off. What harm can they do?'

The Quack seemed puzzled. He took off his spectacles and breathed onto them. 'But they will be assimilated anyway.'

'I don't care. Do it or I won't help.'

The Quack pondered for a minute. He replaced his

spectacles. 'All right. You wouldn't be trying to deceive me, Doctor?'

The Doctor gave him a 'what, me?' smile. 'What difference does it make? I won't help if you don't.'

'I suppose whatever part of the Matrix you are has its reasons.' The Quack made his decision. 'All right.'

Ace's fingers had stopped being a distraction. They still felt like a bunch of swollen bananas but at least the pain had dwindled to a numbness that could he ignored. Aickland was pulling away furiously at her ropes.

They had run off into the depths of the house, away from the men who would doubtless soon be after them. It was too dark for Ace to see what sort of room they had ended up in. It was somewhere in one of the far wings of the mansion, but its decor resembled the rest of the rooms they had passed: ruin and decay. Ace reckoned they had about five minutes if their pursuers were serious about finding them.

'Richard, you're going to have to do the work. I can't do anything manual,' she said. Aickland nodded, still working on the ropes. At last, after what had seemed like days, she was free. 'Bind up my fingers,' she ordered and indicated her grimy shirt. Aickland ripped away at it and pulled off a couple of strips. He grimaced. 'You know how much this shirt cost?'

He started to bandage her fingers. A shot rang out in the distance. Nervously, Aickland looked up.

'Don't worry,' Ace reassured him. 'If they're shooting each other they're solving the problem for us.' Unless they've found Arthur, she thought glumly. She noticed that Aickland was working too quickly. His face was green and he was losing the co-ordination needed to bandage properly. 'Hey, hey,' she whispered softly. 'Stay cool.'

Aickland looked up at her. He was clearly in a state of combat shock. 'Richard,' she said, touched by his sensitivity. 'Don't worry. We'll make it.'

He stood up and Ace thought she could detect a resentment in him. She did not understand. He tried to speak. 'Ace. I-I don't think I can continue with this. All the killing. I'm not strong enough.'

'Listen,' she said sharply, 'there's no choice. We didn't start this, they did. We've got to survive, to help Arthur. Don't start losing it now.'

Aickland breathed heavily. He seemed unable to look Ace in the eye. 'I have seen things,' he said. 'Disgusting, degrading things. In the 'Holy Land' rookery of St Giles. Filth, squalor. But this . . . this is hell.'

'Don't worry,' Ace reassured him. 'Do what I do, you'll be okay.'

Aickland suddenly turned on her, his eyes blazing in fury. 'You think I want to be like you? What you've become? You're enjoying this.'

Ace found it difficult to take Aickland seriously. Perhaps long ago she might have responded to his words. She would have wound herself up, beaten herself with guilt.

No more. The light of reality had been shone into her eyes years ago. There were people and the things that people did. Nothing was set, nothing was purely one thing or the other. There was nobody up there handing out house points for good deeds done well. If others couldn't understand that, then that was their problem. She knew that Aickland only talked like this because he hadn't yet seen enough hurt. It would happen. It would happen or he would end up dead. She liked him but naive views like his were unimportant. 'Let's go,' she said indifferently, pushing these thoughts out of her mind.

Aickland looked suspicious. Ace could see that he was frightened of her. 'Where?' he asked bitterly.

Ace pulled a sour grin. 'Where you always find supernatural glowing men. In the cellar.'

The hungry creatures glaring at Charlotte became silent. They jerked their heads round as if they had lost something. Charlotte could sense their disappointment. She wondered what was going on.

'They're leaving,' whispered Peter disbelievingly. Garvey looked about in apparent surprise, his old head nodding and sagging.

Indeed, as Charlotte watched, the beasts began leaping up and down and started to scramble out of the House. She heard waves of movement from every direction. They tumbled and screeched over each other in their haste to leave. The noise of their passing boomed through the House. Charlotte had never heard so much noise in her life. The upstairs, the hall, the kitchen, all were deserted in a matter of minutes. Charlotte realized that Garvey, Peter and herself were standing totally alone in the dark corridor.

'The Doctor must have done something,' said Garvey. Peter nodded in agreement.

Charlotte wondered what positive work they could do. She had learned enough not to assume that the danger to the House had simply gone away. She clutched Garvey's arm. 'Bernice,' she cried. 'We can't reach the Doctor but we can help Bernice. It is our ... duty, after all she has done for us.'

Peter looked over to the kitchen at the far end of the corridor. His face was red and flushed. 'I'm going after those things. Tillie was my friend.'

'No!' Garvey commanded. 'You will only "die" too.'

'He's right,' said Charlotte. 'Tillie has gone but we can still help Bernice.' It was a new revelation to look at the boy's face and know that she was right, that she had convinced him. It boosted her confidence. Perhaps this new, complicated life could be managed after all.

They moved carefully along the corridor to the hall. For a second, Peter hung back. Charlotte realized he was very angry, more angry than she had ever seen anyone before. She shared his emotion but there was work to be done. Anger had to be controlled. 'Peter!' she snapped.

The boy turned, shamefaced, and followed her.

'You say she has some insect in her throat?' asked Garvey, distracting Charlotte. She heard the butler's knees click as he walked. She nodded, wondering why he had asked.

He smiled. 'I think I know of something that might help.'

For a second time, Thos followed Rix through the ground floor of the house. Their search was more cursory this time, Rix reasoning that Ace would not be in a condition to locate an elaborate hiding place. In Thos's case, it was his anger that compelled him to rush.

His mind was empty of everything except death. He wanted his revenge on the bitch woman who had killed his brother. He poked his head round a doorway and into an old, abandoned study. He spotted a filthy strip of cloth on the floor. 'Over here,' he said. Rix and Frankie broke off their search to come over.

'It must be Aickland,' Rix stated. 'He's here with her.' Thos watched him walk into the study.

Frankie pulled at the large man's elbow. He was sweating with fear. 'Thos, I want to get out of here.' The older man's voice was tentative, hushed. 'You saw what he did to Gray.' Thos stared at Rix, who was examining the strips of cloth. Frankie continued: 'He's mad. If we both stood up to him . . .'

Thos twisted round and grasped Frankie's jaw. 'Shut up Frankie,' he said grimly. 'I want blood and I'm going to have it.' He pushed the man away.

'What's going on?' called Rix from the study.

'Nothing.'

Frankie stared up to the end of the corridor, perhaps looking for a quick and immediate exit. He gave a shriek and again pulled at Thos.

'I'm warning you, Frankie,' Thos whispered angrily.

'It's them,' Frankie wailed, long grey hair matted with moisture. Thos looked and then hissed at Rix, 'Boss! We've got them.'

Rix came to the door whilst Thos and Frankie tucked themselves into the shadows. Thos squinted down the corridor and saw a small wooden door. It was being pushed open slowly. He watched as Ace and Aickland poked their heads round the door. The room behind them glowed with a faint light.

'Get them!' screamed Rix and began to charge. He raised his pistol to fire. Thos followed immediately, swallowed up in rage and a lust for blood. Some part of his mind registered Frankie following him.

Ace snapped her head up and spotted them. Thos bellowed in triumph. They were trapped. Sitting ducks.

'Oh no,' hissed Ace.

There came a burst of blue flame, like lightning, and suddenly the ghost was in the corridor, between Thos and his victims. The Woman in White stared at him, pale and translucent. Her hair trailed like seaweed and her insubstantial face mouthed silent words at him.

In front of Thos, Rix slid to a halt and fell to his knees, screaming in fear. Thos piled into him and toppled over. The woman's black eyes bore down on them. Frankie let out a yell of total terror, his mind clearly gone. The ghost raised its arms and floated towards them, arms outstretched. The outline of a white robe flailed out behind her.

Aickland gazed in wonder at the ghost's back. Through her pale body he vaguely saw Rix and Thos on their knees, staring up at the apparition. It was true, he thought, it was all true. 'The Woman in White!' he exclaimed. 'She is real!'

Beside him, at the top of the cellar steps, Ace grunted. 'When you've seen one holographic projection you've seen 'em all.'

Aickland did not understand. He could not take his eyes off the spectre. 'But she's real. A real ghost. I don't believe it.'

'Don't believe it. Come on. Into the cellar.'

Aickland just continued to stare at the ghost. It had reached Rix and Thos and was looming over them, as if to strike them down. He felt Ace grab his collar and haul him down into the glowing darkness.

Looking around the cellar, Aickland saw Arthur lying stretched out on the stone floor. The glow came from his dying body. Around him was what Aickland could only describe as machinery. He felt a shock of fear as he confronted devices which were so removed from his knowledge and experience that they filled him with an almost religious dread. He felt sanity slipping from his mind.

'Hmm,' said Ace, moving amongst the machinery. 'Power converters, micro-optical networks and, yep, this is the holographic projector.' She pointed with a bandaged hand and Aickland saw something that glowed and twinkled with devilish lights. 'Pretty advanced model too. I wonder why it's projecting such a stupid image.'

Aickland looked away and turned his attention to Arthur. The man barely existed any more. He reminded Aickland of the ghost upstairs, now nothing more than a flickering light. 'Arthur,' he whispered.

The burning head turned to him. 'Richard,' came that voice in his head. 'Thank you for coming.'

Ace was by Aickland's side. He was surprised to see tears glistening on her cheeks and regretted his rash words to her earlier. She was funny; hard and soft at the same time. 'Arthur,' she cried. 'We tried to save you. I wanted to take you home.'

Aickland heard the voice again. It was Arthur but sounded more wise, more experienced. 'It would not have worked, Ace. Innocence, once lost, can never be regained.'

Aickland looked at Ace in confusion. The voice continued: 'You followed me. I wanted to show you the door. I know it now.'

The glowing ghost smiled and locked its spectral hands round Ace's fingers. 'A last gift.'

Ace gasped as the light collapsed and drained away into her fingers. 'Arthur, no!' she shouted. She smashed her hands onto the ground. As Aickland watched, she unwrapped the bandages. 'They're mended again,' he gasped in awe. Ace wiggled her normal, completely intact digits.

Aickland stared at the space where Arthur had been lying. There was nothing there at all, not even the glow. 'He's dead,' he whispered, suddenly overwhelmed. 'All that pain for nothing.'

Ace grabbed his shirt with her freshly healed hands. Her grip was harsh and savage. 'Not for nothing,' she spat. 'We found all this. He led us here.'

Frightened, Aickland replied, 'He said it was a door.'

Ace nodded. Her face jumped, flickering red and green in the light from the machines. He realized she was as alien as the machinery, and just as terrifying. Not for the first time he wished he was drinking a cup of tea in his aunts' house.

Suddenly, she jumped up and dashed to the machines, one after the other, clearly making some sort of connection. 'Of course,' she said. 'It is a door. And I know how it opens!'

She gestured at the equipment. 'I should know. All this stuff. It's all electronic junk from a TARDIS!'

The cellar door crashed open and three dishevelled, screaming men burst into the room. Aickland dived back into a corner as they scrambled down the stone steps. Obviously they had found the courage to ignore the ghost. Either that or they just didn't care.

Rix fired his pistol. The wild shot blew a chunk out of the cellar wall. Aickland desperately tried to think of a way out. It was no good. The space was too confined, their numbers too great.

'The control panel!' shouted Ace and leapt up. She ran to the strange machinery. Thos drew a bead on her with his rifle. She pulled back one of the levers. Aickland watched in horror as Thos squeezed the trigger. At this range the bullet would take Ace's head off.

The room lurched and the men overbalanced. Thos's shot exploded into the ceiling. A wheezing, groaning noise assailed Aickland's ears. 'What's happening?' he shouted.

'We're leaving!' she replied, almost laughing.

The cellar vanished.

The Quack looked up after a spell of deep concentration. 'Well, Doctor, the Elementals have been called away.'

'I thought you said you didn't control them.'

'I don't. They have left of their own accord. Now for you.' He grinned and the Doctor found himself backing away from his terrible face. Smoke began to emerge from beneath the Quack's black suit. 'It's time you helped me . . .'

Before the Doctor's eyes, the Quack began to melt and change. He was growing larger and his face altered, becoming less animate. His skin was stretching, growing more solid. Its colour shifted to a dull metallic grey. 'It's for your own good,' it said in a harsh, rattling, inhuman tone.

The Doctor turned to run but was halted by a feature in the creature's steam and iron face. It was an expression of his own face. The features twisted sharply and the creature bellowed. The face moulded itself into an oval, feminine shape: Ace. It changed again, becoming a champing, snarling Bernice. Finally, all three expressions melted into one: a composite, metal face of hate and anger. The body reared up like a gigantic steam-powered horse. It breathed scorching blasts of steam over the Doctor.

He covered his face and staggered back. The creature darted its head, feinting an attack. He fell and tried to dodge its weaving, segmented body. The clocks that were dotted around the cellar were knocked over and crushed as the iron beast doubled in size.

Suddenly a familiar noise made itself heard over the echoing roar of the creature. A wheezing, groaning noise. The Doctor could not believe his ears.

The changing Quack turned, distracted, to the source of the noise. Another clock was knocked from its plinth and shattered on the floor with a chorus of chiming bells. Its innards spilled out over the stone ground.

The table in the centre of the room began to rise and fall. Started to glow, illuminated by a light deep within itself. The Doctor blinked as the room shimmered and blurred. He felt like the unwilling passenger on a ship in the middle of a force ten gale.

All of a sudden Ace and some other strange men faded into view, crowded round the stone table. She looked bloody, filthy and exhausted. 'Hi Doctor!' she cracked, seeing him.

For one of the few times in his life, the Doctor was lost for words.

With a screech, the creature in the cellar attacked.

Chapter 7

Charlotte led Peter back to the portico hall. Not one of the creatures remained. The House seemed completely empty.

After all the noise, she found the silence both reassuring and worrying. Reassuring because they were safe from attack but worrying in that something else, something worse, might be waiting for them.

The hall was dark and cold. Faint beams of moonlight streamed in through the high windows. Particles of dust were held, floating, in the light. The statues stared out from their cornices, shadowed eyes blank and impassive. Charlotte found herself breathing more heavily and increased her pace. She felt exposed here, open to attack.

They reached the pile of rubble where Bernice lay half-buried, face whitened with dust. Her head was arched back, the insect throbbing in her mouth.

Charlotte began to clear away the stones that covered her. She noticed that Peter was muttering to himself, whirling his poker around. His eyes darted from place to place. He seemed to be expecting trouble from any corner. 'Peter,' Charlotte sighed gently, 'I think we're safe enough for the present. The things have all gone.'

Peter grunted and continued his nervous pacing. Charlotte stopped pulling at the masonry. She stood up. 'Peter! You must stay calm. I'm as . . . sorry about Tillie as you are but she has gone. I want you, all of us, to remain safe. You're not helping. What's wrong with you?'

At last, Peter relaxed. He covered his eyes with one

hand. Despite that, Charlotte could see he was crying. She was beginning to understand why people did that. 'I'm sorry,' she said.

He shook his head. 'No, I'm sorry. It's just . . . oh, let's just help the Professor.' He dropped the poker and ran to Charlotte's side. Together they uncovered the unconscious woman. Charlotte checked Bernice's breathing. 'She's still alive,' she said hopefully. 'How do we get this thing out of her throat?'

Except for an ugly-looking bruise on her forehead there seemed to be no major wounds. They pulled Bernice out of the rubble and laid her on a more even area of the ruined floor.

Echoing footsteps rang out behind them. Charlotte watched Peter whip his hand round and snatch up his weapon. Garvey appeared, walking carefully into the hall. In one hand he held his poker, in the other a tiny pair of brass and wooden bellows.

Charlotte realized that the butler walked as if still attempting to retain his bearing despite the threat of danger. Ridiculously, this made her want to giggle. 'Miss Charlotte,' he said gravely, 'I hope this may be of some service. It is the smallest pair of bellows I could find.'

'What are you going to do?' she asked, suppressing her illogical urge to laugh. This was neither the time nor the place.

Garvey knelt down by Bernice. He ignored Charlotte's agonized sobs, if he had detected them at all. 'I thought we might try to beat this creature at its own game. If you don't mind me asking, do you possess a pin?'

At last, the laughing fit went away. Charlotte was beginning to make sense of Garvey's plan. She felt something like glee at the prospect of inflicting pain on this little monster. Even Peter appeared much calmer now that the butler had turned up.

Somewhere in the mess of her hair Charlotte located a pin and handed it to Garvey. 'Could you hold the insect for me, Peter?' he asked. Eagerly the boy knelt over

194

Bernice's face and tentatively wrapped his fingers round her throat. The oily body of the creature shifted and pulsed.

'Mind the spines,' warned Charlotte. As if complaining, the creature shuddered.

With great concentration, Garvey stabbed it with the pin. Fluid oozed out over his hands. He picked a hole in its side and removed the needle. The liquid continued to flow over Bernice's pale cheeks. 'The bellows, please,' he asked calmly.

The hole in the insect's side was wide enough for Garvey to squeeze the head of the bellows in. Its fragile-looking skin stretched but was clearly tough enough not to tear. Charlotte watched as the butler gently eased the brass point of the bellows further into its body. 'Here goes,' he said and pulled the bellows open.

The noise in the cellar was unbearable. Doctor Rix was looking at a demon. It reared up in front of him, a great hellish worm belching fire and smoke. He was confused. Experiencing so many unholy visions, one after the other, had left him disorientated and terrified. He wondered whether God had finally consigned him to Hell. First the ghost, then the earth tremor and now this, the room of clocks and monsters.

Ace and Aickland lay by the stone table in the centre of the cellar but Rix was no longer worried about them. His concern now was for his immortal soul.

The monster, a machine beast of vast dimensions, was swinging round to face him. Thos, by his side, fired his rifle at it. Rix wanted to tell him that it would be a futile gesture, that the demon was indestructable, it could not be killed. However, if this stupid man wanted to distract it for him he might have a chance to escape. He no longer cared about anyone's welfare but his own. Others weren't important. It was him the beast wanted.

The bullet ricocheted off the iron hide of the demon and it whirled its head wildly as if to detect its assailant.

Frankie was screaming and joined in with a fusillade of shots from his pistol. Rix could see that the silver-haired man had completely lost his reason.

There came a voice from the far end of the cellar: 'Run, Ace. Run!' and Rix was faintly surprised to hear an accent similar to his own. He wondered whether this was part of the torment.

The demon darted forward and scooped Frankie into its plated, iron jaws. Its eyes burned red with anger. Frankie screeched as it hoisted him up. His body sizzled with heat as the beast gobbled him down. There came the smell of seared flesh and then the screeching stopped.

Rix saw Ace and Aickland leap up and run towards the sound of the voice. The demon was busy chewing on Frankie so he decided to act quickly. Forcing his panic away, he dashed past the beast after them.

He managed to spot a set of steps when the demon called out after him. 'Doctor!' it roared in a voice full of sparks, and Rix knew it really was after him.

He reached the steps and saw Ace and Aickland jumping through a door at the top. There was a noise from behind and he turned, expecting the demon to take him there and then. Instead, it was Thos, following him the way he had followed the others. 'Right behind you, Boss,' he said hoarsely, eyes wide with fright.

Rix ignored the big man and dashed up the steps. At the top he risked a backwards glance and watched the demon spit a half-chewed Frankie out from its mouth. The body, black and scorched, dropped to the floor. Frankie's dead eyes stared sightlessly up as the huge metal creature towered victoriously over him.

Rix could watch no more. He turned and fled through the cellar door.

Bernice heard a noise. She had been half asleep and only just realized that something was approaching. She snapped awake.

In the distance, somewhere out in the white wastes, she

spied a black smudge. It could have been a kilometre away, it could have been forty. As she watched she spotted a plume of black smoke rising from the smudge. 'Uh oh,' she whispered to herself, 'It's assimilation time.'

The smudge grew bigger and the smoke cloud became many clouds. Approaching her was something like a huge steam locomotive. It was doing its approaching very quickly. Unfortunately, she had a good idea who this Assimilator might turn out to be.

Desperately she looked around for some sort of defence. There was nothing except the chairs. She started to feel more than a little nervous.

The black smudge had become a shape. Bernice saw a giant head and a large segmented body. Smoke streamed high up into the whiteness.

She decided that all that was left to do was run. It wasn't much of an option but it was the only one she had. 'Not again,' she sighed and began to sprint as fast as she could away from the creature.

Ace was so glad to see the Doctor again that she nearly crushed him to death with a hug. He looked sheepish and embarrassed, as if unused to receiving such attention.

Thanks to Arthur's final dying charge of energy, and the fact that she had found the Doctor again, she felt her exhaustion dissipate completely. The Doctor was trying to hurry them along a corridor in some strange house, coping with Ace's attentions as best he could. 'It's good to see you again,' she said sincerely.

'Who's your friend?' he remarked dryly.

Ace remembered her companion and came out of the embrace. She felt childish, silly. She coughed heartily. 'Right, err, Doctor this is Richard Aickland. He's a ghost hunter, from Camberwell.'

Aickland, clearly shaken by his experiences, just stared wide-eyed as the Doctor held out his hand. Automatically, Aickland clasped it. 'P-pleased to meet you Doctor,' he said mechanically.

197

'And you, Mr Aickland,' answered the Time Lord. He was practically running along the corridor. 'Come along now, Ace. That creature in the cellar wants us for its tea. I've been extremely concerned about you.'

Ace realized she had not heard any bellowing sounds behind them, nor any sounds of pursuit. She wondered if this was significant. The Doctor was looking around, apparently puzzled. 'Where have Charlotte and the others got to? I distinctly told them to stay where they were. They should have been at the top of the stairs.'

Ace could not resist a jibe. 'People disobeying orders again, Professor? It's a pain, isn't it. Anyway, where's Benny?'

'Benny? Of course,' exclaimed the Doctor. 'The hall, that's where they'll be.'

The Doctor strode off down the corridor. Ace spotted that this house was in much the same nick as the one she had just left. Some serious vandalism had taken place.

She stopped as Aickland tapped her on the shoulder. Turning round, she could see that the man was clearly on the verge of exhaustion, both mental and physical. She remembered, with some guilt, the harsh words they had spoken to each other. 'What about Rix and the other two?' he asked.

'Oh, I think they've got their hands full. You okay?'

He nodded. Ace felt a rush of admiration for him. 'Hey Doctor,' she called, 'what was that worm thing?'

The Doctor seemed determined to get them along the corridor. He had nearly disappeared out of sight. He grunted but did not reply. Ace followed him into a large hall supported by great tree-trunk pillars. Again, the place was a mess, with piles of rubble everywhere. The floor was ripped up and the pillars were streaked with great cracks. 'Some party,' she remarked.

Kneeling down by one particularly large pile of rubble were three figures: a young boy, a woman and an old man. They were doing something strange with a pair of bellows. Ace took a closer look and realized that part of that pile of rubble was Benny. The old man seemed to be sticking the bellows into her mouth. 'What the hell are you doing?' she yelled and ran at them. They jumped and looked up in alarm.

'Ace, no!' shouted the Doctor. 'They're on our side!'

Ace halted in mid-attack. 'Sorry,' she apologized, as the group surrounding Benny began to scatter. They stopped and stared at her, clearly puzzled and frightened. 'Hi, I'm Ace.'

She grabbed the woman's hand. She was about forty and looked like Kate Bush after a particularly gruelling video. 'I am Charlotte,' she replied. 'You must be Bernice's friend.'

As Ace nodded, she noticed that the Doctor had knelt down next to the old man. He inspected Bernice. With a shock, Ace realized that her friend had one of those insects in her throat.

Aickland was hanging back, perhaps unsure of quite how he fitted in here. He leaned against a pillar and looked about to collapse. She had obviously underestimated his state of shock. He'd had a very long day.

'Ace,' said the Doctor, distracting her. 'This is Mr Garvey and this is Peter. Now then, what's going on?'

Charlotte went to Aickland and he collapsed into her arms. Gently, she lowered him to the floor. 'I'll see to him,' she called. Ace felt a tug of emotion. She had looked after Aickland for so long, it seemed odd for someone else to take over. She realized that she was jealous.

The Doctor took the bellows from Garvey and pulled them out of the insect. 'I think I've killed it,' said the butler triumphantly. 'I sucked out its innards.'

The end of the bellows dripped with a clear, sticky fluid. The Doctor beamed. 'Thank you, Mr Garvey. I believe this is what is known as poetic justice. You have saved my companion's life.'

Ace squinted into Bernice's mouth. Indeed, the insect seemed to be nothing more than a husk, shrivelled up like an empty sock. The Doctor wiggled his fingers. 'With a bit of luck I should be able to get it out without the spines causing any damage.'

He reached in and gingerly lifted the dried-up insect out from the mouth. Bernice lay still, no movement except for her gentle breathing. To Ace she looked very pale, as if some life energy had been drawn out from her. Blue veins protruded from her temple. 'Will she be all right?' asked Ace.

The Doctor nodded. 'I think so, once the blood is oxygenated properly. You're a tough old bird, aren't you Benny?'

Ace glanced up to see that the boy the Doctor had called Peter looked distinctly unwell. He was staring at the shrivelled insect, his face turning green. 'I think I'll go and take a look around,' he said and staggered away.

'Wimp,' Ace giggled to herself.

The Doctor was furiously scratching his head. 'Hmm. I think that problem is solved. However, I don't think we've got much time. Ace, tell me everything that has happened to you. I can presume by the state of you that violence was involved. Never mind. I need to know.'

Ace opened her mouth to protest but the Doctor silenced her. 'Just tell me everything.'

The creature was gaining on Bernice. And yes, she realized, it was the Quack, or the beast that he had become. He was the Assimilator. Twice in one day was too much.

She ran blindly onwards, no signs or markings anywhere to tell her how far she had gone. It was like running through foam, there was no sense of progress, of there being anywhere to go.

The roaring behind her had increased in volume. It was going to catch her this time and there was nothing she could do about it.

The inevitable happened and she stumbled in her exhaustion. She hit what felt like a marble floor and the breath was knocked from her body. She rolled over quickly and saw a great gnashing mouth opening up for her. The searchlight eyes transfixed her like a rabbit.

Bernice lay there, hyperventilating. She felt light-headed and dizzy. She had done her best.

About twenty metres from her, the giant creature reared up and launched itself into the air. The mouth stretched wider and wider and great jets of steam belched out at her. Her self-control went and she screamed. The creature headed down towards her.

Abruptly the vision disappeared, to be replaced with three faces: Garvey, the Doctor and . . . Ace.

Confused, Bernice continued to scream but felt firm hands on her, holding her down. She shivered and realized that cold sweat was leaking out all over her body. It was like coming out of a nightmare.

Ace cradled her head and wiped her brow. 'It's okay Benny,' she said soothingly, 'it's okay.'

Bernice willed her control back. When she felt able, she spoke. 'What the hell happened to me? The insect?'

The Doctor held up something that looked like a blue rag. 'Here, thanks to Mr Garvey,' he said.

'I don't understand.'

Garvey's old, bony face stretched out a grin. He seemed very pleased with himself. 'It was nothing, Professor Summerfield. Just doing my duty.'

Confused, Bernice lay back onto the hard floor. 'How did you get here, Ace?'

Ace stood up. 'I've just explained it in great detail to the Doctor and I'm not going to say it again.'

The Doctor held out a hand. Bernice took it and he hauled her up. She coughed. 'I don't believe it,' she remarked, 'I'm covered in dust again.'

She stared out through the ruined door at the night. She felt cold. Then she remembered her vision. 'Doctor, I've worked out where this place is.'

The Doctor appeared interested but had that glint in his eye, the one that said he was holding something back. 'Really?' he answered cryptically. 'And where is that?'

Bernice looked around and gestured at the walls. 'It's a machine. A construct. And the Quack is a part of the program.'

The Doctor seemed unsurprised, unperturbed by the news. Bernice shrugged. 'Don't tell me, you've known for ages.'

'No,' said Ace. 'I've only just given him the clue. I arrived here in a TARDIS, or a part of one anyway.'

Bernice started to get excited. Things were beginning to make sense. 'Of course, a TARDIS! It can construct any landscape it wants, can't it Doctor?'

He nodded warily. 'Careful, Benny. Don't presume you know everything yet.'

'Listen,' she insisted. 'I talked to Victoria when I was out wherever I was. She said she was called "Access". It must mean Access to the program. Someone's put this place together out of the Architectural Configuration program from a TARDIS. And that would mean that Charlotte, Garvey and the others are ... are constructs too. Part of the machine ...' her voice tailed off. She realized the full import of what she was saying.

'Yes,' stated the Doctor, 'it's tricky, isn't it? A TARDIS cannot create living beings. They're not robots, they're flesh and blood. They may have a limited emotional programming and, up until now, no concept or experience of ageing and death, but they are definitely people. Now, I don't know how a TARDIS could be made to do that, do you?'

Bernice shook her head. 'So I'm completely wrong then?'

'No. We just aren't in full possession of the facts at the moment. Let's wait until we are.'

Ace looked at the Doctor. 'Unless we get ourselves killed first. Also, what about all that stuff in the cellar?'

'Well,' replied the Doctor, 'that is clearly a link between this artificial universe and the real one. A power link perhaps. I don't know. What we are going to do is get to our TARDIS.'

It took a few seconds for the meaning of his last statement to come clear in Bernice's mind. She glanced across at Garvey who was looking at them in confusion. 'What about them?' she asked the Doctor. 'Why are we going to the TARDIS? Why don't you just tell us for once?'

The Doctor seemed reticent, almost unfriendly. 'I can't tell you, Benny, but go we must. Now. Before these creatures come back, which they will, soon.'

Bernice found it difficult to trust the Doctor. She sensed he was holding something back, something important. A man, unknown to Bernice, moaned as he lay slumped against the pillar. He was clearly unwell. No doubt he was another pawn in one of the Doctor's interminable chess games. She felt sorry for him, he looked too young and too feeble for this sort of adventuring. Charlotte was by his side, trying to look after him. 'Are you all right?' she asked.

'Who's that?' Bernice mouthed at Ace.

'A man,' she replied. 'Richard Aickland,' she added, a bit more helpfully.

Aickland? All of a sudden the name seemed familiar to Bernice. An old name, someone she had read about perhaps. Was he famous?

Ace walked over to Charlotte and Aickland. 'You all right, mate?'

He gave her a weak smile. 'Getting better. For a moment I thought I was going to end up like Arthur. I'm getting a bit sick of being the one that needs help all the time.'

'You're doing fine.'

'Ace,' he said seriously. Bernice noticed that Charlotte was listening intently. 'I'm sorry about Arthur. There was nothing you could have done. I'm also sorry I said those things about you.'

'No, you were right,' Ace replied. 'I've learned a lot from you.' She glanced at Charlotte and Bernice thought that she caught a surprising look of jealousy pass between them.

Charlotte inspected Aickland's wounds. She produced a handkerchief and cleaned his face. 'I hope this helps,' she said softly, apparently perplexed by Ace's expression. 'I've not had much experience with this sort of thing. With anything at all for that matter.'

Aickland raised an eyebrow. 'You? Miss . . .'

'Charlotte.'

'Charlotte. I am afraid that when it comes to experience, I am the world's most successful novice.'

Charlotte laughed and Bernice began to understand why Ace might have been jealous. She turned and walked away. Her face held an expression familiar to Bernice. 'Trouble?' she asked, knowing exactly what the trouble was. For all of Ace's maturity and her casual choice of male companions, deep down she needed comfort and tenderness like everyone else. 'Not your sort, surely?'

Ace tensed but managed a rueful smile. 'I'm okay. I don't know what it is. You're right, he isn't my type at all.'

'Perhaps that's why.'

Ace reasserted her hard exterior. 'We've got more important things to worry about.'

'That's right, Ace,' remarked the Doctor. Bernice realized he had been standing and watching neutrally, as if waiting for children to finish their play. 'We must get to the TARDIS immediately and Mr Aickland must come with us, along with anyone else who doesn't belong here.'

Suddenly, before Bernice could ask any questions, she heard the snap of a rifle being cocked. 'Very touching,' sneered a voice.

Bernice looked round. Two men emerged from the corridor. One was big, burly and aiming a rifle at them, the other a plump, balding man who held Peter in an armlock with a pistol to his head. They were both in the same dishevelled state as Ace and Aickland. The large man swung his rifle to cover everyone in the hall. 'Don't move,' said the older man, 'or I kill the boy.'

'Rix!' hissed Ace, attempting to back away behind a pillar.

'Ah, gentlemen,' said the Doctor, placing himself confidently between Rix and the others. 'I've been expecting you. You really are in very great danger here, you know.'

Bernice backed away. She had never warmed to people who liked to wave guns about. The large man looked like he would enjoy using his rifle on anybody that got in his way.

She saw Aickland quiver and suspected that he had come across these people before in less than pleasant circumstances. Charlotte placed an arm around his shoulders.

'Who are you?' Rix demanded of the Doctor.

The little man raised his fedora. 'I am the Doctor and unless I am very much mistaken, you are Doctor Rix. Listen, don't worry, I am going to get you all out of here and back home.'

The large man raised his rifle and aimed it squarely at the Doctor. He looked across at Rix. 'What's 'e on about? D'you want me to shoot him?'

Rix shook his head. Bernice detected something in the man's body language, a malign confidence in the way he moved. He was arrogant, perhaps psychotically so. 'I don't think you should play your games with this one, Doctor,' she warned.

The Doctor seemed absurdly pleased with himself. 'No, no, Benny. I'm sure Doctor Rix would like to get home along with the rest of us.'

Rix appeared uneasy. He tightened his grip around Peter. The frightened boy uttered a choke. 'I'm warning you,' said Rix, 'you'd better tell me what's going on. I think Thos would like to settle some old scores.' Thos grinned, looking at Aickland.

Suddenly Garvey shouted out from the back of the hall, 'Let the boy go. He can do you no harm.'

Peter looked up, tears in his eyes. 'Mr Garvey!'

Rix laughed. 'I don't think so. Doctor? Going to tell me where we are?'

The Doctor sighed. He seemed frustrated by Rix's attitude. 'Don't you see I'm trying to help you?'

Rix shot Peter through the head. The boy dropped lifelessly to the ground as the echo of the shot rebounded round the hall. 'I asked you a question, Doctor.'

'No!' screamed Ace and charged at Rix. Bernice realized that her friend had lost all control. She also saw Thos raise his rifle. Instinctively, she dived into Ace's path and brought her crashing down.

'Out of my way, Benny!' Ace shouted at her as they struggled on the ground.

'No, leave it!' Bernice replied, trying to avoid getting her neck broken and yet keep Ace pinned down. She looked about for help but the others seemed too shocked to know what was going on.

'You didn't need to do that,' said the Doctor icily. 'I said I wanted to help you.'

Now he was freed from holding Peter, Rix took the opportunity to swagger across to the Doctor, waving the pistol carelessly. 'Of course you did, Doctor. I was just guaranteeing your goodwill and co-operation.'

Bernice looked at Peter's body. It lay face-down on the floor, blood leaking into the cracks in the flagstones. She too wanted to take Rix apart but knew they would have to wait. An out-of-control Ace would only make things worse.

She noticed that Garvey had fallen to his knees, tears in his eyes as he stared at his dead companion. Charlotte and Aickland sat by the pillar, clearly numbed and shocked. Ace relaxed beneath her. 'It's okay, Benny,' she said. 'I'm all right now.'

'How do you propose to "help" us then, Doctor?' asked Rix.

The Doctor looked straight into his eyes. Bernice saw that his calm exterior belied a furious tension within. His body was as tense as a coiled spring. He said, 'I want you to come with me in my travelling machine. All this violence just makes the situation worse. It may already be too late. Come with me now and we can sort out our differences elsewhere.'

Rix appeared to ponder. He was obviously suspecting a trick of some kind. 'I don't trust you,' he said. 'You look a very cunning sort of fellow. What are you a doctor of anyway?'

The Doctor waved his hands in the air in frustration. 'Does it matter? I'm offering you a chance to get home. Why don't you take it?' He was clearly trying to keep himself under control. This seemed to make Rix even more happy.

'I think we have got one or two matters to finish off first, eh, Thos?'

Thos nodded, keeping his aim firmly on the Doctor. 'That we have, sir.'

'Don't trust him!' yelled Aickland. 'He's completely mad!'

Rix swung round and punched the Doctor. The Time Lord dropped to the floor, taken completely by surprise. Rix smiled. 'Mr Aickland. You have been a constant thorn in my side. I'd like to deal with you first. Then . . .' He looked at Ace with his cold eyes. 'Then you my dear.'

Bernice felt Ace tense up again but before anyone could react, the stained glass windows of the hall shattered apart. Bernice groaned. The little creatures were back.

'Oh God! Oh Jesus Christ!' cried Thos and fired into the huge hairless mass that began to thunder towards the smashed entrance of the House.

'Run!' shouted the Doctor. 'Back to the TARDIS.'

Bernice leapt up and began to follow the Doctor into a corridor. He was heading for the kitchen. Despite her horror and panic, she realized he was leading them the only way out of the House.

The creatures screeched in triumph and bounded into the hall behind her. The will to survive prevented Bernice from seeing what was happening to everyone else. She just kept running, right on the Doctor's footsteps.

They dashed along the corridor, the screeches echoing and pounding in her ears. The Doctor sprinted into the kitchen and without a pause headed straight for the back door. As he reached it, something landed on Bernice's back. Little hands clutched her hair and pulled. She screamed, spinning around in mid-run. She banged into the kitchen table.

Vaguely she saw the Doctor turn back and look at her. She felt strong, bony fingers scrabble over her face, searching for her eyes. The creature smelt of dirty fish. It screamed into her face. She caught a glimpse of a pale, malformed face and brown, glistening teeth.

Abruptly, the pressure was torn off her. Head reeling, she made out Ace holding the struggling creature. She dashed it against the wall. It burst open like an overripe fruit, sending transparent fluid splashing over the shelves.

Behind Ace, Garvey was hurrying up the corridor, pursued by more of the creatures. 'Well done Ace,' shouted the Doctor. 'Now come on!'

Bernice felt Ace grab her wrist and drag her out through the back door and into the cold kitchen garden. For a second Bernice had a vision of hundreds more of the little creatures waiting for her outside. However, when her sight cleared she realized that they were alone.

Garvey hurriedly slammed the door shut and produced a large iron key from his pocket. He proceeded to lock the door. His breath came out in anguished gasps.

'What do we do now, Doctor?' asked Ace, who seemed superbly calm. Bernice wondered whether she really did feel at her best under situations of conflict and peril.

'The TARDIS,' replied the Doctor, 'if we can make it.'

Bernice opened her mouth to protest when the Doctor interrupted her: 'I know Benny, but we have to leave the others. I promise you, it's our only hope.'

Garvey seemed confused. 'What is this TARDIS?' he asked. 'How can it help?'

The Doctor looked back through the kitchen window.

His eyes widened in alarm. 'No time to explain, Mr Garvey. Off we go!'

Bernice took a quick peek and saw a dozen of the creatures piling into the kitchen. She did not need a second warning to start running off into the night.

Aickland led Charlotte at a sprint up a wide, luxurious staircase. Its ochre carpet had been shredded in the previous invasion by the creatures and it looked as if even more damage was going to be inflicted on it this time.

'Where are we going?' asked Charlotte as he pulled her up, leaping two or three steps at a time. Below, a boiling mass of creatures streamed after them.

'I don't have a clue!' Aickland shouted. He was still shocked and confused after so much had happened but was learning that the secret to survival was just to keep going. He reached a landing and launched himself along it. He realized he had made another mistake. They should have followed Ace into the corridor instead of trapping themselves up here. He had conveniently forgotten that there had been no way they could have cut through the charging creatures to have even made it to the corridor.

Charlotte stumbled along behind him, trusting him for some reason. He had to think, find a place to hide. There had to be somewhere they could go. Already the first of the tiny creatures had reached the top of the stairs. Continuing to run, he shouted, 'Is this your house?'

Apparently puzzled, Charlotte shouted back, 'Yes. Why?'

'We need to find a safe place!'

Abruptly, Aickland found himself pulled off course and running behind Charlotte up a different corridor. She obviously had a direction in mind. Hearing the shouts and screams in their wake, he decided to keep up with her.

He followed Charlotte round another corner in this maze and up towards a second flight of stairs. 'We can't just keep going up!' he yelled. 'What happens when we get to the top?'

Without a word, Charlotte ran headlong up the stairs. Sighing, hoping she knew what she was doing, Aickland followed.

Thos chased Rix through the ground floor of this strange, terrible house. After his initial burst of firing, he had realized that there were far too many of the goblin things for him to deal with. Rix had taken off up one of the corridors and he had followed blindly. He had trusted Rix up to now and survived. He hoped this would continue. The doctor knew what he was doing. Perhaps he had a plan.

Glancing back, Thos saw the corridor behind him was almost chest high with the little beasts. He fought back his superstitious terror. He had always believed in goblins and ghosts, what country man didn't, but he had never expected to encounter so many at once.

Rix turned a corner up ahead and scurried off out of sight. Obediently, desperately, Thos went after him. The goblins were screaming at him in triumph. He fancied he could hear them calling his name. Another corner came up quickly and again he followed Rix.

Thos looked ahead and his heart froze. The corridor ended in a door. There was no way backwards or forwards. Rix ran to the door and pounded on it. It was locked.

'Sir,' shouted Thos, 'The key! It's in the lock!'

Rix dropped to his knees and his fingers clasped the key. His breath came out in hoarse sobs. 'Hold them off for a few seconds, Thos,' he ordered and began to fiddle with the lock.

How? Thos asked himself. He turned and fired into the wall of creatures. The shot ripped into a couple of them and they split apart. The rest kept coming. He fired again. He thanked God that he had remembered to load the gun properly this time. He still had two shots left.

The creatures pulled up to a halt, about two yards in front of him. Their naked, puzzled heads stared curiously at the firearm. For a second, he had a wild thought that they would turn and flee.

He heard a click from the door. He turned to see it closing and then the lock snapped shut. Rix had left him out here.

Thos ran, sweating, to the door and thumped on it with gun butt. 'Rix! Rix! Open this door!'

There was the sound of movement behind him. 'Rix, I'll kill you for this!' he shrieked.

The noises increased. Thos whirled back and fired into the crowd. One of the creatures blew apart. It was immediately replaced by the hungry, jubilant face of another.

Thos gritted his teeth. Sweat and tears mingled cold upon his face. 'Come on then,' he whispered. 'Come on.'

He just had time to fire his last round when the creatures fell in on him.

Eventually, Thos's dying screams faded away. Rix sat on the bottom step of the wine cellar stairs and listened. Gradually, he managed to get his breath back. He cursed. Thos had been a good man. The sacrifice, however necessary, had been unpleasant.

Looking around, Rix spied row upon row of wooden shelves containing hundreds of bottles of wine. He wondered who owned this house. How had they got here?

There came a scrabbling sound at the door. The little demons were trying to get in. He didn't know how long the door would hold.

Suddenly he saw something lying in one of the aisles. It was a larger demon, big and black. He breathed again. The creature was dead, battered and almost hacked to pieces. He leaned against one of the shelves, dazed and shocked. How could such things exist? Were they really sent by God to punish and torment him?

He snapped up straight. Of course they were. He laughed, he wasn't beaten yet. The fight still went on. So many dead. Good men, the best. Billy, Gray, Frankie,

Archie, Thos. All because He was a jealous God who couldn't stand somebody trying to change His work for the better.

Rix sat down again. He would go on, he had to. He would never give in, never surrender. The scratching at the door became a banging.

He thought of his boy. 'Stephen,' he whispered. 'My son.' It had all been for him. Every experiment, every atrocity. And none of it had worked.

He was going to die. Nothing now could alter that fact. The demons must have been throwing themselves at the door, so violent were their crashes. Already, he could see that the hinges were splintering.

He wondered whether he should try to find an escape route, another way out of the cellar. It was a big place, there might be another door. He decided not to bother. It was hopeless. The aisles stretched far into the darkness, he would never find anything in time. 'Thou art a jealous and vengeful God!' he shouted out at the shelves. A misquotation. How appropriate. The door was buckling, hundreds of eager voices were shouting out excitedly.

Rix came to a decision. He would be his own man to the last. No one would dictate his fate. He stared at his pistol with a new determination.

He barely heard the door smash open, so great was his concentration. The creatures, swarms of them, bounded down the steps towards him. 'Stephen,' he whispered, 'forgive me.'

Rix put the pistol into his mouth and pulled the trigger.

Charlotte led Aickland into a small room right at the top of the House. He wondered whether she really knew where she was going or whether she was just panicstricken. 'Close the door,' she ordered, 'and lock it.'

Aickland obeyed, hearing the creatures scampering up the last set of steps after them. He slammed the door shut and bolted it, then looked around. The room was completely bare, without even a carpet on the floor. Charlotte stood in the middle of it, her white cheeks puffing in and out as she forced her breath back. Despite the sounds of pursuit, Aickland thought she was the most beautiful woman he had ever seen. She must have been in her late thirties but she had a look about her that made her seem much younger. If he died, which by now felt long overdue, he was glad that she would be the last person he had seen. Forcing his emotions away, he managed to say, 'What now? Do we just sit and wait?'

She shook her head, still too out of breath to speak. She glanced up at the ceiling. Aickland followed her gaze and saw a small wooden panel. 'What's that?' he asked.

The creatures crashed into the door. Aickland heard them squealing outside. 'Lift me up,' said Charlotte. 'It leads to the roof and it's the only way up there.'

'Isn't there a ladder?'

'No. I've never been up there. I just know that's what it is.'

The crashing on the door increased in intensity. Aickland realized the wood wasn't going to last much longer. How typical that the two least experienced members of the group had ended up together. They would have to bodge their way through. He hoped that he would not let Charlotte down. Even if he did not make it out alive, he had to make sure she survived.

'Quickly, stop day-dreaming,' snapped Charlotte.

Aickland obeyed, feeling embarrassed both at being caught out and at having to hold her by the waist. She was very light and smelled of lavender. 'Higher,' she insisted.

'Give me a chance,' he complained, 'I'm not very strong.'

'Oh stop moaning.' She shifted in his grip.

Smiling, Aickland redoubled his efforts and lifted her up onto his shoulders. He thought he was going to suffocate in the thick layers of her dress. He supposed that this experience would be one of his less painful memories.

Behind him the door began to splinter. 'Come on!' he shouted.

'I am! I am!' came a muffled reply. Charlotte moved and Aickland heard the panel swing open. Suddenly, the weight was off him and Charlotte was scrambling up into the night air.

Deformed, domed heads and a flurry of limbs bashed a hole through the panelling of the door. Aickland realized he only had seconds left.

Charlotte reached down and he jumped up, grabbing her hands. She cried out and let go. He hit the floor and the door was broken apart.

A creature, teeth bared, leapt across the room at Aickland. He punched at it desperately and it toppled over. Without pausing, he jumped up again and this time used Charlotte's hands as a lever to help him up to the edge of the open panel. She shrieked and he realized that he had nearly tipped her over and back into the room. He threw his other hand over the lip of the panel opening and dragged himself up.

A heavy weight yanked at his legs and, looking down, he saw one of the things clutching him. He tried to shake it off but it dug its claws into him.

'Come up!' shouted Charlotte and tried to haul him up onto the roof. Aickland understood her plan and hoisted himself out of the room. The creature mewled and howled as it came out onto the roof with him.

Charlotte slammed the panel shut and moved to help him. Aickland kicked out at the creature's head with his free leg and it released him with a bellow of anger. Charlotte scooped it up in her arms and threw it out over the edge of the roof. It disappeared and Aickland heard an unpleasant splash as it hit an object of some kind.

'Your leg's bleeding,' said Charlotte.

'I'm all right,' he replied. 'It looks worse than it is.' He winced at the pain.

Looking around, Aickland realized that they were at the top of some sort of tower. They were sitting on a gravel floor about five yards wide, lined with tiny brick battlements. It was extremely cold and bitter wind cut at their faces. Overhead, in a clear sky, a full moon covered them with a ghostly sheen. 'You think they can get up here?' he asked, listening to the excited chatter in the room below. The panel in the floor remained still, so far nothing had hit it.

'I don't think they can jump that high,' said Charlotte. 'I think we're safe.'

Aickland grimaced. 'Really? Stuck on a roof in the middle of a freezing night. How safe is that?'

'Better than being ripped to pieces. Or shot in the head.'

He saw the grief on her face. 'I'm sorry,' was all he could think of to say. Why did he always get nervous and tongue-tied? Charlotte was terribly upset but he didn't know how to help.

'I can't believe it,' she cried. 'Everyone has gone. Everyone except me.'

'You don't know that, Charlotte,' he replied. 'I know Ace. She doesn't die.'

Charlotte managed a smile. 'Bernice and the Doctor are also notoriously difficult to kill. I'm sure they will come for us.'

'And all we can do is wait, unless those things decide to go away.' His leg really was in pain. He rolled up his trousers and stared at the open, bloody wound. He felt sick and dizzy. 'I hope we don't have to do any more running.'

Charlotte shivered. 'It's cold.'

Clumsily, Aickland put his arm around her. He was heartened by contact with her body. She leaned against him. 'Come on, Ace,' he whispered. 'We're in trouble.'

Garvey was struggling to keep up with the Doctor and his companions. He was having equal trouble trying to follow their conversation.

'What about Richard and Charlotte?' Bernice asked. The Doctor continued hurrying up the hill. The moonlight cast giant shadows across the grass. Garvey appreciated the quiet out here, after all the turmoil in the House.

However, he was uneasy and afraid and kept thinking that the creatures were waiting for him, just out of vision. They seemed to be heading for the dark, bare wood at the top of the meadow.

'We have to help them!' insisted Bernice.

'We are helping them,' replied the Doctor, turning back to talk to her. 'We're helping them in the only way possible.'

Ace joined the questioning. 'Why are we going to the TARDIS? Have you got some equipment or something?'

The Doctor remained silent. Garvey trailed behind the trio, aware that exhaustion was catching up with him. He was not going to be able to travel much further. 'Doctor,' he moaned, 'I must rest.'

Still, the Doctor did not falter in his stride. 'No time for that Mr Garvey.'

Ace turned back and grabbed Garvey's hand. 'Come on mate,' she said brightly, 'I'll carry you if I have to.' Feeling his knees click, the butler stumbled along.

Bernice was pulling at the Doctor's jacket. 'Listen, you know I trust you but you've got to tell us why you're doing this. I can't believe you're leaving them to die.'

At last, the Doctor stopped. He turned and Garvey saw a tiredness in his face. He realized that this little man was like him: old. 'Benny. Ace,' he said. 'You must trust me. Absolutely. It's the only way.'

'Doctor, I . . .' Bernice stuttered.

'You must!' he insisted. All of a sudden, Garvey found him frightening. He seemed cold, distant. He felt the Doctor's eyes on him. 'Mr Garvey. You cannot enter my TARDIS.'

'What?' shrieked Ace. 'He'll die if you leave him!'

'It's impossible.' The Doctor was calm, emotionless.

'What's got into you, Doctor?' asked Bernice.

'Wait,' said Garvey. He pulled away from Ace. He stood up straight and brushed himself down. 'I am not afraid, Doctor. I will stay here if that is what you want. I trust you. You have done all you can. I will help you to your . . .

TARDIS and then I will come back to find Miss Charlotte.'

The Doctor looked sheepish and shamefaced. 'Thank you Mr Garvey. I hope I deserve your trust.'

Garvey turned back to the House. He stared down at it. The mansion glowed bone-white in the moonlight. He realized how much he loved the building. He felt sad that he had never before stood in this meadow and looked down. He knew he would never leave the House. 'I would not go with you anyway, Doctor. I'm getting too old for that sort of thing.'

The Doctor laughed, but Garvey detected no humour in it. He walked down the slope and placed an arm round the butler's shoulder. Behind him, Garvey saw Bernice and Ace watching suspiciously. 'It was a beautiful dream, Mr Garvey,' he said wistfully.

Garvey nodded 'It was my home and now it has gone. Only people matter.'

As he watched, there came a large explosion from the rear of the House. Flames turned the white walls red and spread like fingers over the brickwork. 'Come on,' said the Doctor.

Sadly, Garvey turned and walked with the others out of the meadow and into the woods.

Charlotte sniffed. She could definitely smell burning. 'I think the House is on fire,' she remarked.

Aickland stood up and looked over the battlements. Charlotte watched him. She had odd feelings towards this young man. A closeness. He seemed very like her, experienced and inexperienced all at the same time. And when he touched her, she felt a warmth that she could not explain. She imagined that Peter had thought the same about Tillie before she did. Before they had both died.

'I can see smoke,' he said. 'Yes. I think we're on fire.' He peered down. 'Well, if we don't get eaten we're going to burn to death.'

Despite his words, Charlotte had an urge to grin. He seemed unperturbed by their desperate situation. She held out her hands. 'Richard. Hold me.'

Aickland gave a thin smile and sat down next to her. She found his embrace comforting. 'Do you really think the Doctor or this Ace will come back?' she asked, frightened.

'Of course,' replied Aickland without hesitation.

'I like you holding me,' she said. 'It makes me feel better.'

Aickland nodded. 'I've never held a woman before like this. I like it too.'

In the attic below them, the creatures screamed in frustration. The flames crept up higher and higher.

The program was changing. A thousand billion voices chattered and spoke, each giving their opinion.

The unit named the Assimilator worked hard, trying to interpret conflicting instructions. Should the new elements be assimilated? Should they be allowed to leave? Should the program close down completely?

The Assimilator was pleased. It liked its job and had done well. Many rogue units had been taken back. It was unfortunate that Control was unable to isolate the source of the new elements. They had to have been created somewhere. It would find out in time, once the confusion had passed.

However, if the Assimilator could have had more emotion it would have wanted one thing. It would have wanted very much to assimilate the unit known as the Doctor. Permanently.

Somewhere, locked in the Matrix, an old white-haired woman slept and died. She had done so for many years. As she slept and died, a new element entered and was reborn. It would change many things.

The trees, although bare, were shrouded in a strange shadow. It was like a wicked witch's wood in a fairy-tale.

Ace hardly recognized the place. She wondered what had happened to the summer holiday. 'Doctor?' she asked. 'I don't understand how I managed to run up this hill and end up in a field on the other side of the valley.'

The Doctor rushed through the wood and appeared displeased by the interruption. 'Oh Ace, it's simple,' he said. 'We're in a closed universe with finite and recursive spatial parameters within an inverse point of singularity. Have you never read Dalton's Third Law of Dimensional Preposity?'

'You know I haven't.'

'Of course not, I've just made it up. Now come on!' With that, the Doctor huffed and stomped off through the trees.

'Which translates as: "We haven't time right now",' remarked Bernice, catching up with her.

'He gets worse,' said Ace.

Garvey creaked along behind them, snatching his breath. The trees and bushes became thicker. 'I don't like this,' said Bernice.

Ace saw the lines of concern and worry on her bruised face. 'What is it?'

'What's the Doctor up to? He doesn't usually run off to the TARDIS in the middle of trouble.'

'I don't know,' Ace replied truthfully. It had been bothering her too. 'He must have his reasons.'

'You heard what he said to that madman with the gun. He said he would take us all home. What did that mean? He's going to run away? I tell you, I'm not leaving Garvey or anyone else.'

Ace shrugged. They began to jog, the Doctor having increased his pace. 'I guess we just have to trust him. Garvey does. Remember, my friend's back there too. I hope he's all right.'

Garvey tripped and fell. Ace stopped and helped pull him up. 'Come on, we still need you,' she tried to sound reassuring. He looked very old and his face appeared to

219

have shrunk a little. It was as if he had suddenly aged ten years.

'I can't . . . keep up,' he said. 'Leave me.'

'No way,' stated Ace and hoisted him up onto her shoulder. He was surprisingly light. 'I'm not losing anyone else.'

Bernice was up ahead, looking cold in just a pair of jeans, tee-shirt and a coat. Her nose was bright red. She waved Ace onwards. Come to that, Ace realized that she was bloody freezing herself, dressed as she was in the remains of Aickland's best suit. 'Come on,' Bernice shouted, 'or we'll lose him.'

The wind increased and sent a chilly blast of air across Ace's body. She tasted something wet in her mouth. Looking up, she saw the air was thick with white flakes. 'I don't believe it,' she muttered. 'Snow!'

Within minutes, as they trudged through the wood, the snow had settled. A blizzard was stirred up by the wind. The cold was so intense that Ace had to close her eyes to prevent them blurring. 'Christmas comes early round here,' she muttered.

Garvey was shivering intensely. He seemed unable to speak as he clung to Ace's side. The moonlight, and Ace realized that clouds should have been covering the sky, illuminated the wood, giving it the appearance of some cadaverous lunar landscape.

At last, she saw the clearing where the TARDIS rested. She adjusted the weight of the semi-conscious Garvey and slogged onwards.

'Ace! Look out!' shouted Bernice, who had turned back.

Confused, Ace tensed and scanned the immediate vicinity. She heard a branch above her creak but before she could look up something landed on her head. Thin, grey hands snatched at her hair. She felt the hot, sour breath of one of the creatures. Instinctively, she let go of Garvey and he pitched over onto the frozen ground.

Another creature dropped onto her and she struggled desperately with them both. She heard the screeches start up in the trees. It was an ambush. Somewhere Bernice was yelling.

The creature on Ace's head snapped its teeth and clawed at her face, trying to get to her eyes. The other clung on to her right arm, digging into her ripped clothes.

She pulled the first creature away from her face with her free arm and dashed it to the ground. She slipped and fell over. Using the fall to her advantage, she rolled over and crushed the second creature into the earth. It exploded, covering her in a sticky, reeking mess.

Looking up, Ace saw Bernice struggling with another tiny beast that had leapt onto her shoulder. She stood up to help when yet another scrabbled onto her back and dug its fingers into her neck. She cursed loudly and fell over again, face down.

Another creature landed on her back. Ace was unable to gain purchase, the pain in her neck was too intense, and she could only shake on the ground while the things clawed at her. She realized she was helpless.

Abruptly, the pressure was released and she could move again. She rolled over, ignoring the blood streaming down her back.

Garvey was fighting with the two creatures. They bit at his arms as he tried to hold them off. As she watched, two more dropped from the branches and knocked him to the ground. 'Run!' he shouted weakly as he struggled with them.

Looking up, Ace saw more of the creatures, dozens of them peering greedily down at her. 'No!' she yelled as more jumped down onto Garvey. He muttered feebly as they began to work on him. The snow beneath him turned red.

Ace made a move towards the butler but his hand emerged from the mêlée and feebly waved her away. 'Go!' he gurgled.

Something touched her shoulder and she whirled round, ready for a fight. The Doctor pulled her away. 'It's too late, Ace. Come on.'

221

Ace struggled in his grip. 'Let me go!' she cried, tears coursing down her face. 'Got to help him!'

'He's drawing them off us, that's why we're not being attacked.' The Doctor had a grip like a pair of steel manacles.

Ace realized he was telling the truth. The creatures were ignoring her and concentrating on Garvey. More and more bounded down onto him. It was as if they preferred easy pickings to a difficult fight. Garvey cried out once more and became still, buried beneath the writhing mass of bodies. Even Ace accepted that it was too late. Another life lost.

Dazedly, she allowed the Doctor to lead her back to the TARDIS. The creatures were dropping by the handful now and starting to head towards them.

They reached the doors and almost fell inside. Bernice pulled at the lever for the doors and they closed.

For a few seconds, the warmth of the console room and the quiet hum disorientated Ace. It was as if nothing had happened. She couldn't even hear the creatures' screams. It was uncomfortably warm in here, she felt ill. Falling into a chair, she brushed the tears from her eyes.

Bernice sat opposite her, looking in a similar state. Her clothes were ripped and torn. Blood oozed and dried on her face. A fresh bruise was beginning to appear on her temple. She sat for a moment, clearly getting her breath back.

Only the Doctor seemed unaffected by their ordeal. He was umming and ahing round the console, flicking switches and pressing buttons.

It took her a while but Ace gradually realized what he was doing. She hauled herself wearily out of her chair. 'Doctor? You can't dematerialize!'

The Doctor looked up briefly and continued with his work. Bernice stood up and staggered over to him. 'I knew it! What about Charlotte and the others?'

He flicked the final switch and the central column began

to rise and fall. Ace made a move to stop the process but the Doctor halted her with a command. 'Leave it!'

Ace could make no sense out of the situation. 'Get us back, Doctor,' she pleaded. 'Please. They need our help.'

He looked up, a very grave expression on his face. 'I am helping them. I told you, this is the only way.'

'All right,' said Bernice, 'you want us to trust you. Tell us what's going on.'

The Doctor sighed. He bowed his head and stared at the console for a minute. Ace understood that he was suffering just as much as the rest of them. 'Doctor?' she asked, uncomfortable.

'Ace, Benny,' he said. 'Think about what has happened. Events were accelerating wildly. Most of the occupants, if not all, are dead by now. Dead . . . or assimilated. What choice did we have? You must understand the wider consequences.'

Bernice seemed to be getting angry again. 'What about Charlotte and Ace's friend, Richard? They could still be alive.'

The Doctor walked round the console to stand in front of her. 'Benny, you're not listening. Have you understood nothing? Charlotte, Garvey, Peter and the others. They're not real. They're not people. They can't die.'

'And Richard Aickland?' asked Ace belligerently.

The Doctor nodded. 'Yes. Yes, he is a problem. As are Rix and that other fellow.'

'Then we go back for them.' Bernice clearly refused to be reassured. 'Doctor, I don't care whether you call them people or not. Charlotte is real, she has emotions, a mind. So did Garvey. He felt pain and suffering.'

Ace tried not to recall the scene outside the TARDIS. 'I can't believe you're prejudiced, Doctor. Against constructs.' It was almost a joke.

'I know, I know,' the Doctor continued. 'I'm as sorry about all this as you are but we absolutely had to leave. That place, it was a TARDIS. Somehow its Architectural

Configuration had been programmed to resemble the environment of an English Victorian country house.'

'So what went wrong?' asked Bernice.

'And why?' Ace added.

'I'll tell you in a minute. Firstly, you must understand something of its nature. The occupants of the House weren't brought there from anywhere else. They were part of the Architectural Configuration Program itself. Organic components. Now, I don't understand how that was possible but it happened.'

'But Charlotte and Garvey and the others, they were real people!' insisted Bernice. 'They felt things and bled and breathed and lived.'

'I know,' answered the Doctor. To Ace, he seemed desperate, as if he was talking for his life. 'But they were still constructs. Ace gave me the clue that proved it.'

'I did?' She was as surprised as Bernice.

'Your friend Arthur. When he left the program he was unable to exist. He was experiencing too much data that was outside his programming. Things like ugliness, greed, murder.'

'You mean he just couldn't handle . . . badness?' asked Bernice, clearly amazed.

'If you like. Anything his programming hadn't equipped him for. So he overloaded and . . . you could say that the goodness just leaked out of him, enabling him to perform apparently impossible tasks.'

Ace remembered the time in Rix's house: the way that Arthur had glowed. 'So he was an angel,' she whispered.

'There was nothing you could have done Ace,' said the Doctor gently. 'He could never have existed for long outside his program. It wasn't your fault.'

Bernice thumped the console. 'Doctor, explanations are all very well but they aren't helping Charlotte and Richard. Or those other two for that matter.'

'Benny,' said the Doctor calmly, 'bear with me. I kept asking myself, if the House has existed for so long without anything changing, why did it suddenly alter? Something must have happened to the major program. It was confused, not working properly. The Quack told me that himself. He was the physical representation of the troubleshooting subprogram. However, he kept receiving conflicting orders as to what to do about us. We were alien to the program, something it couldn't deal with.'

This was too much for Ace's overwrought brain. She tried to understand what he was saying. 'So we were like a virus that got into the program and all that bit with monsters was its way of trying to clean itself out?'

'Exactly. At last, you're beginning to understand. Now, being a program it was incapable of thinking outside its own parameters . . .'

Bernice interrupted: 'And so it thought we were a part of itself that had got lost and couldn't find its way back into the program. It's incredible, this is exactly what Victoria told me.'

The Doctor leaned against the console. 'It could not conceive of anything outside its own existence because it wasn't programmed to do so. That's why it didn't kill us straight away. It was confused, trying to piece its mind together. It used various tactics to try to "assimilate" us. Firstly, it rejected Ace back to its control centre in the real Victorian England. It didn't know where you went, of course, it just sent you outside itself. But that was no good because it didn't learn anything.'

Ace began to pace the room. She felt tired, completely knackered. Her neck needed medical attention, the blood wouldn't stop flowing. It seemed a very long time ago that she had had a rest, or food, or anything pleasant happen to her.

'Doctor,' Bernice asked. 'I presume that programs, even TARDIS ones, don't write themselves. Not the original idea.'

'Yes?'

'Well,' she continued, 'who's written this one?'

The Doctor squinted mysteriously at the console. He twiddled with some of the dials. 'I have some ideas but

225

I'm not ready to share them with you. Yet. Suffice it to say that I am trying to find out. I've calculated the temporal and spatial co-ordinates of the closed universe and also the real house that Ace visited. If I can work out a triangulation point then we might find out who really is behind all this. You see, I wasn't running away. I was doing the only thing that will save whoever's left. We've got to find the controller of this TARDIS and stop them.'

Ace was still confused. 'But why couldn't we just tool up, go back and rescue them? Why did we have to leave them right in it?'

The Doctor shook his head. 'Ace, you have to understand. I had no choice. There is no other way. We cannot go back into the closed universe. Ever.'

Ace looked at Bernice. Silence hung in the air. It was like a tangible force. 'Why not?' she asked.

The Doctor sighed again. 'Have you understood nothing of what I've said? We cannot go back. The House only changed when we arrived. The program linked into our minds and read them, it picked up our emotions and brain patterns and tried to assimilate them into the fabric of the House. However, it had no concept of change or experience or memory. It had never heard of anger or frustration or fear or even death. I don't know why.'

'I see,' said Bernice. 'So everything that happened was because of what we brought with us.'

The Doctor continued, 'And the longer we stay there trying to solve the problem, the more suspicious we get, the harder we fight and the worse we make the situation. It's a paradox. Catch 22. There never was any evil in the House for us to fight. It was us. We caused it. We did it all ourselves.'

Chapter 8

Unable to cope with company, Bernice decided to shower and change. Every drop of water reinforced her guilt. She nearly put her old, torn clothes back on as some sort of penance to those they had left behind.

She stared at herself in the mirror and saw the cuts and bruises on her face. She pressed at them with her fingers, wanting to feel pain, looking at the intense, short-haired woman in the mirror wincing with her.

When she returned to the control room, she saw that Ace was sitting grumpily in a chair, whilst the Doctor continued to work the console. She had the feeling that words had been spoken in her absence. The atmosphere seemed tense.

For herself, Bernice had come to the decision to trust the Doctor. She had to, in reality there was no choice. It didn't make her feel any better. 'Take a shower, Ace,' she said, trying to get her friend back in a more positive mood. Ace just grunted. She seemed to be staring at her wrist, where the computer had once been.

Bernice tried again. 'Doctor, how are we doing?'

He looked up, concerned. 'This isn't going to be easy. I've tried to add in the recognition data for another TARDIS but it could still take time. Ace, I suggest you get your wounds attended to.'

She glanced sharply up at him but he was back round the console, playing with the buttons. 'You're right,' she sighed. 'Just tell me when we get there.' She stumbled morosely from the room.

Bernice realized that abandoning their friends had hit her extremely hard. Ace knew more about guilt than anyone else she had met. 'Doctor . . .' Bernice began, wanting to tell him to show concern for Ace. Didn't he see she was feeling bad? She needed his reassurance.

She sighed. What was the point? She changed her question: 'Do you think that we can still save Aickland and Charlotte?'

He stopped jogging about, sighed and straightened up. Bernice saw some of the old life and energy come back into his face. She realized how tense he must have been. 'I'm hoping that with our departure,' he said, 'things might slow down a little in the closed universe.'

'Won't Aickland and Rix interfere with the program as much as we did?'

He nodded. 'Yes, but hopefully they will have had less in the way of experiences than us, so it won't be so bad.'

'They might be dead. Got themselves "assimilated".'

The Doctor looked grim. 'That's what I'm most afraid of. If a real human got themselves mixed up in the Matrix, they could do some real damage.'

Bernice shook her head. 'That's not what I meant, Doctor. It means more lives lost. Because of us. Anyway, if they are dead . . . as well as Charlotte, what is there left to do? Why don't we just forget about it?'

The Doctor stared at her. 'Are you willing to take that chance?'

'Of course not. It's just that I do wonder about your motives sometimes. It was a tough decision. I didn't like you for doing it but I understand and I'm sorry I gave you a hard time.' The words seemed to all come out at once. Bernice felt she had no control over what she was saying.

The Doctor smiled but that odd glint in his eye remained. 'Perhaps I just want to find the owner of the machine. Someone who likes to play God but doesn't want the responsibility of allowing their creations to live and learn. Reminds me of the old heresy: "If there is a God he's either mad, bad or indifferent." '

228

Something popped into Bernice's mind: a memory. She wondered whether it was important. The memory grew and became whole. 'Of course!' she exclaimed.

'What is it?'

'Richard Aickland. That name. I thought it sounded familiar.'

'You know him?'

Bernice vigorously shook her head. 'No, not him. The name. Earth literature. That's it, the neo-Gothic revival of the early twenty-first century.'

The Doctor seemed intrigued. 'What about it?'

Bernice was getting very excited. It all made sense. 'Richard Aickland. He was a writer back in the early twentieth century. Ghost stories, spooks, that kind of thing. I can even remember a couple of books: *Cold Eyes*, that was one, and *The Wine Press*. Good books, creepy.'

The Doctor put a finger to his lips. 'I suppose it's possible. If it is the same Richard Aickland.'

Bernice refused to be stopped now. If there was even the slightest chance . . . 'Don't you see? It means he can make it. In my history, my original time stream, he does. I would have no knowledge of him if he didn't, would I? There still might be a way of saving him.'

'Possibly,' warned the Doctor. 'Don't get too hopeful. Remember, Time never runs along one corridor.'

'I know that. I've lived it. But it's a chance. Come on, Doctor, have a bit of optimism.'

A beeping noise began sounding from the console. The Doctor darted to the computer and read the information from the screen. 'Found it!' He patted his faithful machine affectionately. 'Well done, old girl.'

Bernice took a look. 'An asteroid? In the Sol system?'

'Yes.' The Doctor was busy again. 'A small one. It makes sense. The temporal location fits: AD 1873. I see no reason to delay. You'd better fetch Ace. Tell her she can bring her weapons this time.'

Bernice nodded and headed out of the console room.

Ace lay on her bed, staring up at the darkened ceiling. The old, uncool teenager was breaking through again.

She hated the logic the Doctor had used to escape the valley. It was an adult's logic, one of compromises: an acceptance that you could not always get what you wanted, no matter how hard you tried. She had never given in. Willpower was the most important human trait. Never surrender. She had always believed the Doctor had shared that philosophy.

'Ace?' Bernice asked. Ace looked round. Her friend was standing at the door.

'Hi, Benny. Come to join the teenage angst club? I think it suits me, even if I'm not a teenager any more.'

Bernice flicked the light on. 'No time for that, we've got work to do. The Doctor's found the other TARDIS. He wants you to bring your weapons. And I think we're in with a slight chance of saving Richard Aickland.'

Ace was up in an instant. She pulled her locker open and stared at its contents. Sitting in it was a suit of body armour, as well as a number of other interesting items. 'Be right there,' she said confidently.

When Ace had changed and powered up, she ran to the control room. The Doctor and Bernice were hunched over the console, reading the signs on the computer.

'I don't believe it,' said Bernice. 'A breathable atmosphere.'

The Doctor grinned. 'I think we might be getting somewhere. It's been artificially sealed.' He looked up. 'Galah? I wonder.'

'What?' Ace asked.

'Nothing,' he replied evasively. 'Not until I'm sure.'

Not wanting to get caught up in another row, Ace stayed quiet. Instead she forced herself to get prepared for whatever might be outside. Unlike their last stop, she hoped this was going to be peaceful.

'No time like the present,' said the Doctor. 'Let's go.' He pulled the lever that opened the doors.

Whatever they had landed on was moving. Stars revolved in the sky and Ace saw twinkling boulders rush past them. In the distance, a large familiar planet turned slowly. A gaseous red spot drifted across its surface. 'Jupiter,' whispered Ace. 'We're in the Asteroid Belt.' She felt quite overcome by the unexpected astral scenery.

'Come along, come along,' insisted the Doctor and ushered her and Bernice out of the TARDIS. Ace checked her weapons and computer. She didn't want them conking out again.

The surface of the asteroid was nothing but bare rock. It was large and irregular in shape which, Ace presumed, accounted for its haphazard movement. 'It's beautiful,' whispered Bernice.

'Where's this TARDIS then?' Ace asked pragmatically.

The Doctor led the way through the dust. 'I think this must be it,' he said, pointing.

Ace saw an obsidian block standing in the centre of the dustbowl. It appeared to have been carved out of a single chunk of black, shiny rock. 'Not much of a camouflage,' remarked Ace. 'Very *2001*.'

'No Ace,' replied Bernice seriously. '1873.'

Ace sighed. 'Never mind.'

In a way, she found the journey relaxing. Standing out here, in open space, her troubles seemed very small and insignificant. Nothing freed the mind like feeling totally unimportant. She realized that they shouldn't be able to talk, breathe or even keep their feet on the ground. 'Serious discreet technology,' she said.

'So discreet it's not there,' Bernice replied.

Ace began to feel very uneasy. She liked being in control.

They reached the block. 'Let me see,' said the Doctor. He pressed his hands against the stone. 'Warm. Vibrations. I think we've done it.'

'Now all we need to do is find the door,' said Ace. As if on cue a section of the rock hummed and slid open. A

231

shaft of warm light illuminated her. 'What did I do?' she asked.

The Doctor rubbed his hands. 'Shall we?'

Bernice looked around. 'I feel very exposed. Like we're being watched. It's too easy.'

'I'm sure complications will arise,' said the Doctor. 'There's no need to anticipate them.' He began to climb through the panel in the rock.

Ace unholstered her blaster. 'I'm not being caught out again.'

'Wait,' warned Bernice. 'What if the same rules apply? If we start messing about with guns, won't we make it worse?'

The Doctor looked pensive. 'I don't think so, Benny. I think we're in the normal universe now.'

'Whatever "normal" means,' Ace quipped. 'Come on, we've got to go for it.'

The Doctor went into the rock. Ace followed, gripping her gun tightly.

It was indeed a TARDIS. Despite the dim lighting, the roundels and console appeared much the same as in the Doctor's ship. However, to Ace this one seemed to have been seriously burgled. Wires, cables and metal were strewn everywhere and the console appeared to have had an axe taken to it. She whistled. 'Someone went to town on this.'

Bernice stepped into the control room. 'Can't say much for the interior decoration.'

The Doctor inspected the damage. He darted around, picking up pieces of equipment. 'It's still all working. Everything's linked up. There's a plan to this.'

Bernice strolled round the control column. Her face suddenly lit up in surprise. 'Doctor!' she shouted, shocked.

Ace followed the Time Lord round the console. Someone was lying on the floor. 'It's Charlotte!' she exclaimed.

It was the same woman, but much older than Ace remembered her. She was lying on what looked like a black plastic mattress. Her head was a mass of tiny fibre-optic lights, winking and changing while she slept. The wires were attached to hundreds of metal clips and embedded in her skull. To Ace she appeared to be about a hundred years old. She was wearing a white gown that reminded her of the holographic ghost she had encountered in Wychborn House. Thin white hair spread out from her head and lay intertwined with the wires. She looked troubled, as if she was having a bad dream.

'Is it really Charlotte?' asked Bernice.

Ace looked at the Doctor and was surprised to see an expression of tenderness on his face. 'Galah,' he whispered. 'It is you.'

'You know her?'

He knelt down to the old woman. 'Of course. We were at the Academy together, a very long time ago.'

Bernice appeared unusually shaken. 'You mean she's another Time Lord?'

'Or Lady,' replied the Doctor wistfully. 'Whatever you want to call it.' He appeared reflective for a moment. 'We had many arguments but were never very close.'

Ace gave a sardonic laugh. 'I'm not surprised, you never get close to anyone for long.'

'What's she doing with her brain linked up to a TARDIS?' asked Bernice.

'What do you think?' said the Doctor sharply. 'I don't know how she's done it but I suggest she has linked herself telepathically to her TARDIS in order to directly influence the Architectural Configuration Program. That's how Charlotte and the others could exist. It's incredible. Somehow, Galah has managed to form living tissue from the program.'

There was a pause as Ace tried to comprehend the full meaning of the Doctor's words. She realized that the Doctor was very impressed.

Bernice spoke first. 'You understand what she's done?' Her voice was full of awe. 'She's found a way to literally play God.'

The Doctor thumped his fist on the console. 'Except

that it can't be done! You cannot create living matter from inorganic components.'

Ace thought for a moment. 'Here, Doctor,' she said cautiously, 'you remember that time when the TARDIS went funny after the business with the Timewyrm?'

'Yes?'

'Well, isn't there an organic component in the TARDIS? Perhaps it was formed out of that?'

She expected him to dismiss her question but instead the Doctor appeared to think deeply about it. 'You could be right, Ace. Hmm. Come on, help me with these wires.'

Feeling a bit smug, Ace held up a cluster of fibre-optics that were dangling from the eviscerated console. The Doctor took them and began to inspect the glowing lights.

'What are you doing?' asked Bernice.

He ignored her, engrossed in fussing over the equipment. 'Doctor!' Ace hissed.

'Oh Ace, Ace, Ace,' he said distractedly, 'I'm going to link my mind to the TARDIS as well. Talk to Galah.'

'What about those silver headphone things?' asked Bernice. 'You know, the ones I put on when I met Jared Khan.' Ace winced at the unpleasant memory.

The Doctor still concentrated on the job in hand. 'This is a much more complex connection, Benny.'

Ace looked down at the wizened, ancient woman lying on the floor. 'Hang on,' she warned, 'you don't want to end up like that.'

The Doctor rubbed his chin. 'I don't think that will happen. I believe that's natural ageing. She must have reached a regeneration trigger point.' He snapped his fingers, eyes lighting up. 'Of course! That really is incredible.'

Ace sighed and looked at Bernice. 'Care to share it with us, Doctor?'

He appeared quite amazed by his own conclusions. 'Don't you see? She must have linked herself up at the exact moment of regeneration. The extra energy produced by her body has been channelled into this TARDIS. In a sense, she has become the TARDIS. It's her new body.'

Bernice gave a low whistle. 'I don't understand it. And I don't believe it.'

Ace was more suspicious. 'Hang on, Doc.' She ignored the wince as she shortened his name. 'You're saying that she is part of the TARDIS and she's got bags of power and energy?'

'Yes.'

'Well, doesn't that make her ridiculously dangerous? Maybe she hasn't forgotten those arguments you used to have.'

'Oh Ace,' he replied, 'you don't understand. In the arguments, she was always the pacifist. Now, help me fit this.'

He held up what looked like an electronic crown. Its jewels were fibre-optic lights that swam and pulsed over a metal frame. He put them on his head.

'Doctor, be careful,' warned Bernice.

Ace began to check the connections. The Doctor flashed a smile. 'Don't worry Benny, I'm always – ' He fell unconscious to the floor.

Panicking, Ace bent down to pull the crown from his head. Bernice held her back. Ace turned and saw that her friend looked worried but calm. 'It's what he wanted to do.'

Ace stared down at the Doctor's motionless body. His face had drained of colour and his mouth was twisted in a rictus of agony. He did not seem to be having a very pleasant time.

The old woman on the floor spasmed and groaned. Her old eyes flicked open. She stared up, unseeing. Bernice began to speak when the woman's mouth opened and a burst of mad, male laughter erupted from it.

The eyes swivelled and focused on Ace. A chill went down her spine. A voice spoke. 'Your friend is with us now.' It became sad. 'He will not survive.'

It was a voice Ace recognized. It belonged to Doctor Rix.

Pain coursed through the Doctor's mind. Waves of searing light poured into his eyes and a deafening rush assaulted his ears. At last he dropped, as if falling from a great height. He hit the ground, of sorts.

He was in a room. A white room. Victorian, Earth. Huge stained-glass windows filled the walls and silhouettes of trees could be seen through them. A fire blazed in the hearth. Galah was sitting by the flames. She looked young again, like Charlotte.

'Old friend,' said the Doctor warmly.

Galah turned to him and tried to speak. Her words sounded blurred, as if filtered through static. 'Friend... Doctor... Help...'

'What's the matter?' asked the Doctor.

Galah's expression remained unchanged. She seemed artificial, a half-formed construct. 'Will not enough... Protyon units confused... want to obey... new data...'

The Doctor shook his head. 'You linked up with the Protyon Unit? No wonder you're confused. You should have known you couldn't control them. Billions of voices all speaking at once. Why?'

Galah attempted to rise from her chair but was clearly unable to co-ordinate her body. 'Wanted... to show... Doctor. House... symbolic...'

'Symbolic of what?'

'Was dying... no more regenerations... had to prove Doctor wrong... show an example...'

The Doctor seemed to be thinking furiously, perhaps trying to dredge up a memory. 'You were a Time Lady,' he said, as if trying to give himself clues. 'A sculptor. You loved Gallifrey.'

Galah smiled weakly. 'Sculptor... yes. Still am.'

'I don't understand.'

The woman shook her head. 'Not enough... unable to

control new elements. Now, new will is within. Evil from good . . .'

'Evil? What do you mean?' asked the Doctor.

A new voice entered the conversation. 'I think she is referring to me.'

The white floor in front of the Doctor warped and buckled. A man's head fashioned from white stone rose from the ground. The Doctor stepped back.

Gradually, a man emerged from the floor. The stone changed to flesh and clothing. As the shape gained definition it grew to eight feet in height. The face sharpened until the Doctor recognized its features. 'Rix,' he said sadly. 'So you were assimilated.'

The man smiled humourlessly. 'Yes Doctor, but not without considerable pain and effort of will.'

Galah did not, or could not, move from her chair. The Doctor struggled to face his new enemy. 'You're part of the Architectural Configuration Program?'

Rix nodded. 'And more. Much more. Galah here was encountering one or two difficulties with her control over the Protyon Units. These difficulties have now been overcome.'

At last, the Doctor seemed to understand. 'The Protyon core. Of course. Instead of allowing the units their own program she manipulated it through force of will.'

'Top of the class, Doctor. You have a remarkable intellect.' Rix seemed almost pleased. 'Perhaps you understand my transformation better than I. That makes you exceedingly dangerous.'

The Doctor, perhaps aware of his lack of power in this artificial universe, tried to keep Rix interested. 'Oh not really,' he said. 'I just want to help. Sort a few things out.'

Rix laughed. The sound boomed round the room. 'You? Help me? I should be very careful if I were you, Doctor. You realize that here I have unlimited power. I have achieved my ambition. I can rival God!'

'No!' The Doctor spoke harshly, perhaps more harshly than he had intended. 'I cannot allow that. Just because you have ended up in this pitiable state does not mean you are omnipotent. Anyway, it isn't possible, look what happened to Galah.' He pointed to the woman in the chair. Her head remained still, eyes wide and unseeing.

'Oh come now, Doctor,' replied Rix. 'Galah is helping me. She facilitates the more mundane elements of the machine. It's not an easy job: life support, construct sustenance, maintaining the Earth power link, that sort of thing. This leaves me free to work as I please on the more creative elements. I saved her. You know, when I first arrived here, the place was in a terrible mess. New data was flooding the system and the Protyons were trying to assimilate everything in sight. It was all collapsing.'

'Perhaps it should have been allowed to collapse,' said the Doctor quietly.

Rix lowered his giant head and stared at him. 'Oh no, Doctor, there is so much to be done.'

'Such as?'

'Once I have mastered the workings of the machine I will create more and more constructs to my own design. I will drain the Protyon Unit and use it to re-enter the real universe. I have witnessed the power of one weak individual construct in my own world: imagine what an army of such beings could achieve. I will be master of everything!'

The Doctor had clearly had enough. 'What's wrong with you, Rix? You're not an idiot. Why act like one?'

He had overreached himself. Rix was becoming angry, the face twisting and warping. 'Nice try, Doctor.' He considered for a second. 'Let us debate then. What sort of God will I make? Shall I be like the old God? Tell me, what sort of God punishes a man for being good? Gives him an heir that is a failure, for all the world to see? How could I be worse?'

The Doctor went on the offensive. 'Is that it?' he shouted. 'You didn't get your own way so you want to destroy everything. Don't you think others have suffered? I have seen worse misfortune than yours a million times over. People with less intelligence and ability who have overcome their bitterness. Grow up!'

Suddenly Rix threw a punch at the Doctor. As if he had been expecting a show of force, the little man dodged. He grabbed his hat as the blow passed over his head. 'You dare!' screamed the eight-foot man.

The Doctor found himself plucked from the floor and thrown into the solid wall by an invisible force. He slammed into it and slumped breathlessly to the ground. 'I have ultimate power!' Rix bellowed. 'Nothing can stop me!'

The Doctor shook his head clear. He seemed unwilling to abandon his attack. 'Rix,' he said, 'it's called life. We're all stuck with it. No one can change that. Whatever happens, no matter how tragic, we cope with it and learn. That's all we can do.'

'No! I have the power to change, to shape life!'

The Doctor awaited a final blow. Abruptly, Rix's voice lost its emotion. He seemed to be concentrating. At last, he looked at the Doctor again. He became calmer, more reasonable. 'Why do we argue Doctor? According to Galah's memory, you are no passive victim of life. You travel, you fight. As I will.'

'No, Rix,' replied the Doctor. 'I fight for life. You fight against it to make it yours.'

Rix advanced on him. He tried to stand but his back hurt too much. He gritted his teeth and hauled himself up the wall. The force hit him again and he slumped to the ground. 'Ouch,' he muttered. 'There's nothing virtual about this reality. It hurts.'

Rix spoke again, still reasonable and pleasant. 'Doctor, you are useful to me. We are the same.'

The Doctor struggled to force his words out. 'We are not the same!'

'You will be. The time has come for assimilation. With your knowledge, the universe will quickly become mine.'

The Doctor could only watch as Rix began to change form again. 'Galah!' he cried.

239

The woman remained seated, immobile. The Doctor looked back and saw that Rix had completed his transformation. He relaxed.

Bernice realized she was biting her fingernails. 'Damn,' she admonished herself. 'I thought I'd given that up.'

Ace was kneeling by the old woman at the console. 'I think we should pull the Doctor out,' she said.

'No,' stated Bernice, 'he knows what he's doing.'

There had been no repetition of the incident. The woman had uttered those words with Rix's voice and then become still again. The Doctor lay next to her, equally still. 'We can't just stand here and do nothing!' Ace exclaimed.

Bernice sympathized with her desire for action but could think of nothing useful to do. 'Ace, we may need to help the Doctor later on. Besides, what is there to do?'

'We could link ourselves up with the TARDIS,' Ace suggested.

Bernice sniffed. 'Listen, I've tried that before. I think I'm out of my depth this time.'

'And I've trudged round an inside-out TARDIS. Believe me, it was hard work, complicated and no fun at all. Doesn't make me want to give up.'

Bernice controlled her temper. Ace only wanted something to do. 'All right, how do we get in? I don't know what to do, do you?'

Ace shook her head, frustrated. 'I'm sick of hanging around.' She thumped the console.

A door, previously hidden, slid open at the rear of the control room. Ace stared at it in surprise. 'I don't believe this. Not again.' She raised her shades as if to take a better look.

Bernice could see only darkness through the open door. It looked cold and uninviting. 'Wait a minute, Ace.' She glanced back at the Doctor.

240

Ace was unstrapping her blaster. 'I'm going to take a peek,' she said quickly, as if to avoid arguments.

'I said wait,' insisted Bernice, knowing that Ace would go through whatever happened. 'Let's think about this. What could be in there?'

Ace flicked her wrist computer into life. 'Why not just look?'

Bernice gestured back at the woman on the floor. 'Assuming this woman has set everything up, that means the House and the valley and all that are part of a TARDIS, right?'

Ace nodded impatiently. Bernice continued: 'Well if that is all true then we're going to walk straight back out into it again, aren't we? It must be there, through that door.'

Ace was clearly unconvinced. 'Then why did the Doctor bother flying about in the TARDIS trying to find it?'

Bernice shrugged. 'I don't know. Maybe he didn't know where it was, maybe he needed the exact co-ordinates. Maybe he's playing one of his stupid games. I don't know. I'm just saying that this could be a gateway back into that universe.'

Ace walked to the door. 'So let's go find out. We could still get Richard and Charlotte out.'

Bernice gasped with frustration. 'Ace! Haven't you realized? You heard what the Doctor said. We can't go back in there. It'll speed up the decay and make things more dangerous for everyone. I want to help as much as you, but . . .'

'Not if we get in and out fast enough. Bye,' Ace said and stepped through the door. Bernice lunged forward to stop her but had no chance.

'Oh great,' she said to herself. 'Now what do I do?'

She thought quickly. Was it really the gateway into the other world? If so then the Doctor had been quite specific, she would have to wait in case she made things worse. She realized she was biting her nails again. 'Damn!' she shouted, spat out the bits and ran off through the door after Ace.

The Doctor was pinned helplessly to the ground. He could only watch as Rix, now an eight-foot pillar of burning energy, approached. 'There's no need for the theatricals!' he shouted desperately. 'I know what you're doing!'

The energy continued to approach. There was nothing he could do. Bracing himself, he closed his eyes.

A buzzing noise assailed his ears, the assimilation program lurching into action. This time there would be no symbols, no constructs, just a TARDIS computer swallowing his brain whole.

The pain hit and stars showered across his mind. He was unable to prevent himself yelling.

'Welcome aboard, Doctor,' said an echoing voice.

He resisted, physically and mentally, but the power surged through his body.

He had a vision of a place. Not a place he recognized but a vast, red plain laced with rivers of fire. People were with him: Garvey, Peter, Tillie, Mrs Irving, Victoria, others. They were no longer individuals, knowing themselves only as part of the great program, the Matrix. They were enticing him, welcoming him in. He would have liked to have joined them, they were content.

'No!' he shouted and opened his eyes. The visions still swam before him, nothing had changed. 'I will not submit!'

It would have been nice. It would have been easy. No mind, no awareness, just comfort. To belong, to become part of a whole. To become the whole. He was necessary to complete the program. It made good sense. To make something better than himself. A good idea.

His will began to fade away, replaced by a contentment, a bliss. After so many years of fighting, he felt at peace.

'I . . . will not . . . submit . . .' he said again, summoning up the last vestiges of defiance.

Looking down at his own body, the Doctor saw he was

242

glowing brightly. Then the red plain appeared again and he was lost.

It was a vision of hell: a huge expanse of red sand broken up by rivers of burning oil. Flames seared and smoke billowed and Bernice tasted sulphur on her tongue. The heat was so intense she felt starved of oxygen. Coughing, she steeled herself to go on. 'There is no hell but that we make ourselves,' she muttered. 'Ace!'

'Benny?' came the reply from somewhere ahead. Bernice spotted a dark smudge against the flames. It was Ace running back. She looked at the wasteland stretching away in front of her. Black, top-heavy wooden scaffolds were dotted around at irregular intervals. They towered into the boiling, purple sky. At their tips, wheels turned pointlessly like windmills.

Bernice became aware that a kind of dread had gripped her. She shook herself free of it. Ace reached her.

'This doesn't look like the valley to me,' she said. There was the rushing of a great wind in Bernice's ears yet the air was still. A ball of fire shot up from one of the streams.

'Is this another universe?' Bernice yelled at Ace. 'Or is this what we've done to it?'

'Come on,' said Ace grimly.

Bernice followed her over the wasted red sand. The purple sky was shot through with a multitude of rainbows, like sunlight reflected on a patch of oil.

Ace held her blaster out. 'Over there.'

Bernice saw a crowd of black shapes clinging to one of the improbable scaffolds. They were birds, bloated and filthy. 'A murder of crows,' Ace whispered morbidly.

'We should climb one of those wooden things,' suggested Bernice, trying to keep her mind on practical matters. 'Take a look back. There's no door any more. Might as well try and see what's up ahead.'

'Good idea.'

They made their way carefully across to one of the

scaffolds, one that was clear of crows. 'Easy enough climb,' said Ace, about to commence her ascent.

Something erupted out of the sand beneath Bernice's feet. It seemed to be a monk with a long pointed mask. It screamed with delight and grasped Bernice's legs with thin, wasted arms. Ace shot it with her blaster.

Bernice realized she had been frozen with fear. This place was a nightmare, like a painting by Bosch or the Martian S'Klyr. She remembered the planet Lucifer and the problems they'd had there.

Ace, black armour appearing blood-red in the harsh light, shouldered her weapon. 'Come on, get moving.' Nimbly, she began to scale the beams.

Bernice stared at the dead figure at her feet. It was human and, though there was no doubt that it had been hostile, it seemed very pitiful as it crumbled away into the ground.

'Benny!' Ace bellowed. Bernice clicked out of her daze. She wondered whether Ace ever got scared or shocked by violence and death.

She started to climb the scaffolding. The wood was not only black but burnt as hard as diamond. As she climbed, she realized how poisoned the air really was. Each breath was a struggle. It reminded her uncomfortably of the noxious fumes inside the Quack's caravan.

Gradually, the landscape became clearer. As Bernice reached Ace at the top of the scaffold she could see the wide expanse of the wasteland. The wheel creaked round at her side, propelled by an invisible force. 'Jesus Christ,' Ace whispered. Bernice felt ill, her worst fears confirmed.

This was the valley. The ring of hills still loomed high in the distance, encircling them. The geography was familiar, everything was in the same place.

However, the lake was now a burning cauldron of fire, blazing ceaselessly. The trees lining the hills were black and belched out fumes. The fresh-cut lawns were a desert, little zephyrs spinning around and throwing up dust. Even the House remained, to an extent. However, it was nothing but a gutted ruin. Nothing of its architecture was intact and it was little more than an imprint on the ground, filled with rubble.

The valley was full of life. Again, it reminded Bernice of a painting of hell. The inhabitants were humanoid but bent and clad in masks and monks' habits. Occasionally Bernice caught a glimpse of a figure without a mask, bearing the head of a dog or a pig. They danced and gibbered round the ruins. Everything seemed distorted, deformed like some forgotten leper colony.

Despair ate away at Bernice. 'To think we caused all this,' she moaned.

'Wait,' Ace ordered, producing a tiny pair of field binoculars from her backpack. Bernice watched her peer down at the ruins of the House. 'Loads of those ... people,' she reported. 'Some sort of procession. They're dragging a big wooden cart. Benny, you take a look.'

She handed the binoculars to Bernice who scanned the throng. The flames from the streams impeded vision but she caught enough to make sense of the view. There was a large pile of rubble, very high, in the centre of the ruins. A file of cloaked beings were marching and dancing towards it. Some of them were pulling on thick ropes, hauling a wooden cage on wheels. Others were dancing round the cart, waving torches of fire. Bernice·noticed two figures in the cage, lying on dirty straw. She squinted to get a better look. 'Ace!' she cried. 'It's Charlotte and Richard.'

Keeping them in clear sight for a second, she saw that they were filthy and exhausted, their clothing ripped and torn.

'Give me the binoculars,' said Ace, who took a look. She appeared very relieved.

Bernice was not so confident. She was wondering why they were still alive. They must have been easy pickings, so why spare them? This brought to mind the unpleasant thought that the door sliding open in the TARDIS had been a little too convenient. Was it possible that she and Ace were working to someone else's plan?

245

'Let's go get 'em,' said Ace, repacking her binoculars.

'Wait,' interrupted Bernice. 'I think it's a trap.'

Ace was already climbing down the scaffold. 'I don't care. I owe it to Richard. I got him into this and I'll do everything I can to get him out.'

'Very noble, but we're not going to rescue anyone by getting ourselves killed. We've got to think of another way.'

'Another way?' Ace was looking impatient again.

'Well,' said Bernice hurriedly, 'it looks to me like they don't know we're here or they would have nabbed us by now. Maybe they want us to go in with all guns blazing, so we can accelerate events even more.'

Ace paused in her climb, apparently thinking. 'All right Benny, so we use brains not brawn. How?'

Bernice sat for a moment. 'We use our only weapon: surprise. Assuming that one you shot was a one-off we can still make it. Listen, first we find a couple of those monk things . . .'

Consciousness came slowly to the part of the TARDIS known as Galah. As if waking up, she became aware of events occurring around her, inside her, in the Matrix.

Memories came first. Dying, ill, slow. Lying back, placing complex probes over her head, pushing and pulling data in and out of her mind.

Memories of a House, insects, people, the Quack (what a ridiculous name), a program running out of control. Death. This wasn't what she'd wanted, what she'd meant. What had she meant? She couldn't remember.

Galah looked around inside her enlarged world. Three things: her new body with its billion connections, a human grown wrong and powerful, and an old friend. A Doctor.

Galah watched.

She was aware that he was losing the battle. The vision of the artificial universe was growing stronger for him. Despite his resistance, he was becoming more and more involved in the events taking place within it. He could sense the constructs that Rix had created, the ruin, the heat.

'You are weakening, Doctor,' she heard Rix's voice in the Doctor's mind. 'You cannot fight for long. You are already part of the Matrix. It is irresistible.'

The Doctor, now part of the artificial universe too, was sensing Bernice and Ace within himself. 'No, you idiots,' he said aloud.

Galah felt him centre his energy. Rix was gloating, taking his time. The Doctor was desperately preparing himself for something. She detected intense calm and inscrutability in his mind.

When it took place, Galah, with her sluggish reactions, was taken by surprise. The Doctor disappeared.

As Bernice and Ace reached the ground it shook beneath their feet. 'Did the earth move for you?' asked Ace, wondering whether they had been discovered.

Bernice looked extremely grave. 'Perhaps this place is unstable. Perhaps too much has happened.'

Ace sighed. Nothing was ever allowed to be easy, was it? 'We'd better move fast then.'

In her mind, Ace had already given herself up for dead. She was regretting her rash nature. If all that was left to do was reach Richard Aickland then nothing would stop her. She would not give in.

She led the way to the ruins of the House. A line of flames blocked their route but also covered their approach. She decided to worry about the fire when she got to it. There were no monks on this side. Looking back, she saw Bernice tracing her footsteps. 'Come on, hurry up,' she cajoled.

They reached the fire stream. 'Now what?' asked Ace.

Bernice inspected the flames. 'Now, I think we get hot,' she replied. 'It doesn't look too wide.' With that, she launched herself into the fire stream.

After the shock, Ace saw Bernice roll around on the ground on the other side. She had jumped straight through. She felt a new admiration for the older woman, she was still nicely unpredictable.

Not to be outdone, Ace walked back a few paces and dived across the stream, covering her face. She felt a second of intense heat even through her armour and then she hit the ground and rolled. Standing up, smoke trailing from her body, she looked at Bernice. 'How's that?'

Bernice was even more smoke-blackened than her and it was obvious that without armour she had suffered a lot more. However, she clearly remained determined. 'Now for those two monks.'

Ace turned and saw a group of the inhabitants approaching. 'As if on cue,' she said brightly.

She found it impossible to make out individual features beneath the dark folds of the robes and the tall masks. There were four of them. 'Ready?' she asked. Bernice licked her lips and nodded.

They fought against a backdrop of fire. Ace disabled one immediately with a drop-kick as it went for her. The other three screeched to a halt as if stunned, giving Bernice the chance to fell a second with a blow to the face. She reeled back immediately as the next robed figure struck her in the side. Ace tore off its mask and stared at the lumpen, misshapen features beneath. 'Sod this,' she growled and whipped her blaster out. She blasted the remaining two attackers down. They fell soundlessly, smoke billowing from their robes.

'Thanks,' Bernice grimaced, clutching her side.

'Well, we only needed two.' She looked around to see if they'd been spotted. She was surprised when it was obvious that the fight had gone unnoticed by the hundreds of robed creatures still milling around in the distance. They were busy following the cart up to the mound of rubble about quarter of a mile away. 'This is too easy,' remarked Ace. 'They must be blind or something.'

The mound itself was a black silhouette against the raging purple sky. Lightning flashed across the landscape, illuminating Bernice and Ace as they dragged the bodies together. 'Let's get this over with,' Bernice said, disrobing one of the unconscious figures. 'Oh my God!'

Ace looked down at the naked creature and tried to instantly put its image out of her mind. She pulled on one of the reeking, pestilent habits. It was stuffy and boiling hot.

'It's like some sort of apocalyptic religious hallucination,' said Bernice.

'If you say so,' replied Ace. She looked up at the procession and realized that the older woman was right. It was like a scene out of the Spanish Inquisition. There was a sense of mad Catholicism at work. Two of the hooded figures they had dealt with wore crude wooden crucifixes. In the procession, many more figures held aloft banners and signs bearing abstract and colourful religious symbols. The smell of incense was thick in the air. It was all a mixture of the ornate and the decorative with the drab and the dirty.

Ace soon caught up with the stragglers in the procession. The other hooded creatures made no sound and had clearly not noticed her. She could not help but become more and more suspicious. She had expected detection on sight, as had happened before. She felt very uneasy.

Quickly, she moved up through the crowd, attempting to remain quiet and anonymous. She was unable to see if Bernice was following. Clutching her blaster, she risked a look ahead. Sweat poured down from her face.

The wagon, or cart, was nearly at the mound. The Hoods, as Ace decided to call them, shuffled around slowly at its base. Two groups, Hoods that Ace hadn't seen before, clambered up the pile of masonry, each carrying a large wooden tree trunk.

These trunks were carried to the top of the mound and plunged into the rubble. As Ace closed in, they were hoisted up with ropes until Ace could see that they were two crosses.

With a sickening feeling in her stomach, Ace realized

249

what was going on. They were going to crucify Charlotte and Richard.

With a new awareness, Galah sensed the Doctor locked somewhere inside her. He had retreated into the dim recesses of the TARDIS. It had taken her some time to find him again. Rix was still looking.

She sensed Ace and Bernice sneaking along through the procession. Their presence felt like having a piece of grit stuck in the eye, small but irritating and intensely painful. She had an urge to dispose of them, assimilate them immediately.

She remembered herself just in time.

She was observing the Doctor closely. He seemed able to wield some power in the Matrix. She admired him for that. He had already protected his friends once, when they leaped through the river of fire, and was now shielding them from detection. It was an extremely difficult process, requiring vast concentration. Galah felt Rix and the other parts of the TARDIS probing, attempting to discover what he was holding back.

The Doctor was buried deep, still a long way away. Rix was stronger and closer, his mind burning and angry, wanting everything. Frankie and Thos were in here as well but Rix kept them firmly under control. Neither had any power. The fight was going to be between the Doctor and him, and it would be fought in the Matrix.

In the meantime, he was trying to keep Ace and Bernice out of trouble and undetected. Galah did not think he was going to be able to continue this for very long. She sighed.

Bernice watched Ace move up to the side of the cart. At least, she hoped it was Ace. Once in the middle of a hundred identical hoods it became very difficult to tell. Her heavy cloak weighed her down and she felt like she was being baked in an oven. The roaring in her ears would not subside. She hoped she wasn't going to faint.

250

She had spotted the crosses being raised on the mound of rubble and quickly deduced what was going to happen. She could still see Aickland and Charlotte, lying helplessly in their cage.

Bernice had given up trying to interpret what was going on here, concentrating only on rescue, escape and survival. Even if they did free the prisoners, that was still a long way from getting away alive. She was surprised that they had not been caught already.

The cage stopped moving. Respectfully, the hooded creatures looked up at the mound. Bernice used the opportunity to make her way to the cage. She bumped past one of the creatures but it made no move to stop her. She had lost Ace altogether by now but presumed that she was around somewhere, hopefully clutching a blob of Nitro.

'Charlotte!' she hissed at one of the raggedy creatures in the cage. She kept her voice low to avoid attracting attention to herself. The woman in the cart did not move.

Bernice was wondering whether they were dead when Aickland moved. He fell against the wooden bars, apparently oblivious to her. His thin, pointed face seemed old in the light. It was bloody and smeared with dirt, and the number of bruises gave him a stupefied, punch-drunk look.

Bernice took a risk and raised her hood to let him see her face. Other hooded figures jostled her and continued their march to the mound. The cart began moving again, rattling and thumping as it was hauled through the broken masonry to the foot of the hill. 'Aickland!' she hissed, rather more loudly than she had anticipated.

He turned to her, clearly puzzled, and finally recognized her. He seemed to be having trouble collecting his thoughts. 'You?' he asked dazedly.

'Just get ready. Ace and I are going to get you out.' Aickland nodded and then caught sight of something behind Bernice. He gave her a warning glance and sat back down in the straw.

The cart trundled past and Bernice turned round. She was surrounded by three of the creatures. Wet eyes glared at her beneath filthy hoods. 'Evening,' she said cheerfully and tried to run.

Thorny hands grabbed her robe and swung her to the ground. She tried to crawl free but there were too many standing over her. Within seconds she was held down and unable to move at all. She wanted to call for Ace but kept enough of her wits not to blow her friend's cover too.

Her head was pulled up. She saw a grinning, toothless mouth in a black hood and then something hit her.

Charlotte began to emerge from the black haze in which she had been immersed for an eternity.

She remembered being on the roof and then everything had changed. She had the vague recollection of a red sky, of lying on smoking, blackened ground and of a gigantic face looking down at her, altering her. There was nothing more.

She realized she was moving. Strange wooden bars surrounded her and there was a heat and a noise the like of which she had never experienced.

'Charlotte, are you well?' asked a familiar voice. She was unable to place it. A man with a pointed nose and curly hair? 'It's me, Richard.' He had supplied the information. Charlotte remembered him and her feelings for him.

At last her senses cleared and she saw she was in a cage. They were moving over uneven ground. The sky was an angry purple, the landscape a desert. Hundreds of oddly dressed people with frightening masks walked along with them. 'Richard?' she asked. 'What's happening?'

'I don't know, everything's changed.' He looked tired and ill. 'I have a suspicion we are about to be crucified.'

Despite not knowing what he meant, she shared his fear. She looked forwards, past the grunting men pulling the cage, to the two crosses raised up on the mound. A lone robed figure stood between the crosses. The sight of him sent a chill through her body. His robes were white and spotless, contrasting with the rubble and dirt.

'Bernice and Ace are here somewhere,' said Aickland. 'Although Bernice is in trouble.' He pointed at a group of figures struggling some way behind.

Charlotte recognized Bernice as they carried her forwards. 'What will they do with her?' she asked.

Aickland shrugged. 'I don't know. However, I don't think we'll have to worry about it for long. I believe we are at journey's end.'

The cart pulled up to a halt at the foot of the mound and the door was swung open. Robed men dragged them out onto the rubble. Charlotte was thirsty and exhausted. Her clothes hung off her in rags and everything in her body ached. She allowed herself to be pulled up the slope.

The imposing figure by the crosses glared down at her with savage red eyes. His mask was decorated and swept up far above his head, ending in a point. For a second their eyes connected and she seemed to recognize him.

'Hi Charlotte,' came a weary voice from behind.

'Bernice!' Charlotte struggled round to see her blood-stained friend being dragged forwards.

Looking out, Charlotte realized that the mound was surrounded by what must have been the entire population of hooded beings. They swarmed and chattered, their high masks turning them into one identical insect-like race. They began to hum, a drone that intensified, until she forgot that they were many and became one, insane voice. It was a low hypnotic tune full of anticipation and emotion, uniting the congregation round the rubble.

'Professor Summerfield!' bellowed the tall man by the crosses. 'I am so glad you have joined the service. There is, I regret, no cross for you at present but be certain that my brothers will find a way to make you part of the occasion.'

Charlotte started at the sound of the voice. She recognized it immediately despite the drone. She felt lost, totally without hope, and sagged in her captors' arms. It was the Quack. Aickland stared at her, clearly worried by her reaction.

'Go to hell!' Bernice yelled, struggling with the creatures holding her.

The Quack threw back his head and laughed. 'No, my dear. We are already in hell. We have a new world and a new master.' He spread out his arms and addressed the multitude below him. 'Brother Elementals!'

The humming ceased. Charlotte heard no sound at all, not even the rushing wind. She blinked repeatedly. At last there was time to think.

'Brother Elementals!' The Quack shouted again. 'We are gathered here today in the presence of our new Creator! He came unto the Matrix and cleansed it. We are one again.' There was a murmur of assent from the congregation.

'Save the speeches,' hissed Bernice. 'just get it over with.'

The Quack did not alter pace. 'The Creator has set us a task. After all he has done, he needs proof that we are worthy. We must help others as he has helped us. All must be brought unto the glory of the Matrix. We act with love, brothers, as we return these three to the bosom of our lord. They will become us! They will become one with the Creator!'

A great cry of affirmation erupted up from the masses as they raised their arms to the sky. 'You see,' said the Quack, looking down at Charlotte and the others, 'you will soon be free.' Charlotte thought she could see tears welling up in the eyes behind the mask. 'God is Love,' he said softly.

There was a scuffling noise to Charlotte's right. Aickland, clearly very angry, was fighting the hooded things restraining him. 'You twisted idiot!' he shouted at the Quack. 'How dare you!'

The Quack walked gracefully down from the crosses to face the enraged man. 'You must understand,' he said gently, 'I share your anxiety. Do not worry, in a few hours you will not be troubled. Yes, you will feel physical pain on the cross. That is how it should be, to remind you of earthly suffering, but it will not last long. You are soon to achieve divine grace.' Charlotte almost believed him; he was so sincere, so convincing.

'I see Rix has introduced a new element in you,' spat Bernice. 'Sadism. Next you'll be saying it's for our own good.'

'You will be at peace soon, Professor.' He turned and walked smugly back to the crosses.

Charlotte watched as Aickland, with a surprising strength, threw off his guards. He rounded on the Quack. 'In two days,' he snapped, 'I have been shot at, frozen, burned, tied up, beaten and chased and now you want me to listen to you making a speech. Well, I have had enough!' He punched the Quack straight in the mask. The robed man fell back, crashing into the ground.

'Nice one!' shouted Bernice, who took the opportunity to give her surprised captors the slip. She intercepted the three robed creatures trying to grab Aickland as he chased the Quack down the slope. Charlotte could only watch as Bernice struck out at all of them at once.

Aickland had reached the Quack and Charlotte saw him hoist him up by his robes. The mask had been torn off and the Quack's sneering face glared up at his assailant. 'Your death will be a slow and particularly unpleasant one,' he hissed at Aickland.

'Really?' Aickland replied and punched the Quack so hard in the face that he disappeared into a cloud of dust. Aickland was left, clearly confused, holding an empty piece of cloth.

Suddenly, from behind Charlotte came a great blast of heat, sound and light. A wave of energy knocked her and her captors over. Stones and cloth rained down on her.

'Ace!' shouted Bernice. 'At last!' Another blast rocked the ground. Bodies and rock flew in all directions. This time Charlotte spotted one of the robed figures below

255

throw something up the slope. A third explosion ripped up the ground in front of her. 'Let's get this party started!' yelled the figure, throwing back its hood. It was indeed Ace.

Charlotte's captors were up and trying to grab her. Instinctively, she elbowed one in the face and ran up to Bernice who was still fighting. Charlotte kicked a robed figure down the slope, whilst Bernice, quick as lightning, tripped the other and then felled him with a straight arm jab.

Ace was running up the slope towards them. Aickland looked round, clearly realized his predicament and also scrambled up to join Bernice and Charlotte. The congregation, previously stunned and still, began to advance on them from all directions.

'Benny!' Ace shouted and threw something at her. Bernice caught the object neatly and pointed it at one of the advancing robed figures. There was a flash of light and the figure fell, smoke issuing from its body.

At last Ace reached them. She cast off the remains of her robes and stood there, imposing and deadly, in her black body armour. Charlotte was suitably impressed.

Aickland put his arm round Charlotte. 'Try and stay with me,' he said, clearly trying to be brave. 'I don't want to lose you.' Charlotte was amazingly touched by his words. She had never heard words spoken with such desperate sincerity before.

'Here, take these,' said Ace, passing out a handful of what looked like small white stones. 'Five-second delay when it leaves your hand.'

Charlotte stared down at the pebbles in her hand. 'What do I do?'

Ace threw one into the advancing crowd. There was an explosion and once again bodies and robes flew everywhere. 'I see,' Charlotte replied dryly.

'Ace, there are hundreds of them,' said Aickland, turning a full circle. 'We're surrounded.'

'Up to the top of the pile,' ordered Bernice. 'To the crosses.'

As they began to move, something burst out of the rubble and grasped Charlotte's leg. The Quack, back in his old clothes, burst out of the masonry, knocking her over. She looked up but saw that Ace, Bernice and Aickland were still climbing. The Quack's face was twisted with blood and hate. 'At last,' he hissed, 'you're mine.'

Charlotte glared down at him as he hauled himself up her body. More than anything, he represented the chaos and death that her life had been plunged into. 'You annoying little man,' she said calmly and dropped one of the pebbles onto him. It disappeared into his shirt front and he looked down, a surprised expression on his face. Charlotte kicked him in the head and he tumbled down the slope. 'Rest in pieces,' she quipped.

The Quack tumbled into the approaching crowd and exploded.

Charlotte picked herself up and threw a few more explosives down into the advancing army. She reached the crosses as the blasts rocked the ground behind her. 'The bombs are holding them off,' said Bernice breathlessly as she surveyed the landscape below them.

Charlotte turned and saw the approaching forces, silhouetted in the flames from the rivers of fire. They looked like an army of giant rats, scrabbling up through the rubble. She saw how many of them there were and fear gripped her. Just when she thought they were going to make it. A hot wind had sprung up and was burning into her throat. 'How many explosives have we got?' she asked Ace.

'Not enough,' came the grim reply.

'We're not going to get away, are we?' asked Aickland, perhaps of himself.

Ace threw another bomb down. 'Never give in, Richard, never surrender.'

'Thanks Ace,' said Bernice, 'you really know how to cheer a girl up.' She raised the weapon that Ace had given her and fired a few bursts into the mass that was now only a few metres away. They were silent and this unnerved Charlotte even more. She realized that within minutes, no matter how many bombs they had, they were going to be overwhelmed. This was going to be a very final battle.

The sentience that had once been Doctor Patrick Rix was pleased with itself. It was enjoying its new life.

He observed the battle on the mound with a sense of pride. He had caused all of this. It was his world. He felt as if he was stirring up little ants in their nest, watching their struggles. They could not comprehend the vast and all-powerful nature of their foe. He was beyond the capacity of the human mind to understand. He was God.

Only the Doctor still posed any real threat and he would be dealt with very soon. It was annoying that he could not find the Time Lord but he was still in the Matrix, somewhere.

Rix knew that his problem was not killing the Doctor but trying to keep him alive. He wanted the mind intact, to boost his already considerable power. What had to be removed were those annoying tendencies to resist. 'Doctor, there is no point in fighting.' Rix shouted out, knowing the Doctor was listening. 'If you struggle you will simply lose your sanity. I will still use your mind but there will be nothing of yourself in it. Give in and you can retain your identity.'

Rix sensed that the Doctor was trying a new tack. He kept looking. Then, before he had time to counter, the Time Lord, or his mental construct, rushed straight into him. There he was!

Rix gathered his mental energy to attack when . . . the Doctor had gone.

He had seemed to fly right at Rix and enter him. Rix roared in anger. He was lurking somewhere in the subroutines right in the core of the TARDIS. He was unable to locate the little man anywhere. 'This will do no good Doctor!' he bellowed with frustration and rage. 'I will find you.'

Moments passed. Silence. Rix wondered what to do next.

He diverted his attention to the other foreign elements in the artificial universe. He saw the plain, the rivers of fire, the heaps of broken masonry. Aickland, Ace and the other two were fighting a rearguard action against his own organic constructs. They had somehow managed to smash the Assimilation Program.

Despite really wanting them dead, Rix knew that their violent actions were fuelling him, adding more data to the Protyon Units. They had to be kept alive, just. He would allow the fight to continue a little longer; after all, he could reconstruct his forces at will. When he had drained every last drop of energy out of the enemy then he would destroy them. He looked forward to that time.

She had scrawled words on the wall in chalk: 'Help Doctor come home.' Galah hoped he would understand. He was close now, very close. She sensed his cleverness, caught a glimpse of a plan in his warren-like mind.

He was in a long, dark tunnel. She sensed his puzzlement as he stared at the words. Cobwebs lined the stone crevices of the walls. She had given him a clue. He was in the most ancient part of the Matrix, one that had been unused for a very long time. Would he help, would he understand? Somehow the Doctor's resistance was bringing her, Galah, back to mobility. It seemed like years since she had last been able to make decisions on her own.

The corridor darkened as the Doctor walked along it, entering territory obviously unknown to him. Galah showed him a door, a small one so that Rix wouldn't notice. She knew that the new god had not completely mastered his existence. Perhaps the Doctor could find a weakness somewhere in the most obscure and fundamental part of the machine.

He was standing by the door gathering his strength, preparing himself for what lay behind it. 'Come home,' she whispered in her tiny voice. How much could she dare?

He opened the door.

He was in the room of eyes. Billions of them that winked and winked, large and bright. The Doctor reeled back from such an intense gaze. They were everywhere, in all directions, including above and below. There was no floor beneath his feet, just more eyes.

Whispering voices chattered and the sound bounced round him, shooting off into the distance. It was out of her hands now, either he would make the connection or he wouldn't.

'Doctor ... Doctor ... Doctor ...' came the whisper. Not Galah but with her. Perhaps the eyes themselves were speaking.

She saw that he had noticed the pattern in the winks. There was a sequence, an order to their movements. Open-shut, open-shut, in a variety of complex series. 'Of course,' he said aloud, 'a binary sequence. I'm in the Protyon Core.'

'Yes ... yes ... yes ...' came the voices. Galah kept her excitement a secret, it might alert Rix.

'Single-celled binary activators. The soul of a TARDIS. So this is where Galah transferred her consciousness at the moment of dying.'

'Yes ... yes ... yes ...' came the voices, 'we try to obey ... energy not strong.' The winking of the eyes increased in frequency and determination. 'Help ... confusion ... give us ...'

The Doctor nodded. 'Confusion. I'm not surprised. Galah was extremely optimistic to think she could match the power of an entire TARDIS. Listen, it's very important. Galah? Are you still there? Can you hear me?'

Yes! she wanted to cry. Yes! Yes! Yes! But she couldn't.

Silence. The whispering ceased and many of the eyes closed. 'Galah!' repeated the Doctor.

A chill wind blew through the chamber of eyes. Galah sensed his isolation and loneliness. He was breaking with the strain of hiding from Rix. He was weakening himself. 'Galah!' he cried. 'You must hear me! You are a Time Lady! You must resist!'

A group of eyes, close to the Doctor's left, started to cluster together. They coalesced, like combining cells. A shape began to form.

The Doctor stepped back, clearly hopeful but wary. The eyes became translucent and elongated. They were becoming human limbs. 'Galah?' whispered the Doctor. The shape gained definition and slowly, like liquid turning solid, features and expression appeared. Galah sighed. It was not her.

It was Rix.

'Oh no,' whispered the Doctor and fell to his knees.

Rix smiled, his body shifting and floating. He seemed to be composed of thousands of tiny lights. 'Hello Doctor, and goodbye.' It leapt at him.

The Doctor struggled but the amorphous body flowed over him. Galah shared his pain. Lights digging into his mind, clutching and sucking. It felt like swimming in glue. He was becoming less and less able to move. Agonizing rods of fire burnt scars into his mind. 'I'm going to suck you dry!' Rix screeched in triumph.

Still he did not give in. Galah felt his resistance. He was lost but fought on. It could be done. She felt empowered, confident. The impossibility of winning needn't matter. Fight, fight, fight. Why not do it? Realization breathed over Galah like a gossamer sheet. Never give in. You only live once.

Whatever remained of the Doctor's will was fighting for a solution. None came. He struggled but was completely caught. There was no escape and the Doctor knew it.

Rix was laughing; she felt it permeate her new body. How dare he! How dare he! 'Goodbye Doctor!' he was shouting, just like an angry, nasty child. 'I'm going to have all of you! All of you!'

Renewed, reborn almost, Galah steamed in.

He was in Edinburgh again. He could feel the cold wind on his face, the scent of the sea in his nostrils. He was looking up, up at the castle, hunched over the city like some upturned, barnacled crab. The market traders around him were hawking and shouting.

Everything was fine. He was a father-to-be. His wife was having his baby, somewhere in the maze of houses beyond the castle. He was a doctor at the hospital, performing work that would eventually liberate mankind.

He turned round, a full circle. The Grassmarket was in full swing, stalls selling fruit and fish, side-shows and inns full to the brim. A procession was leading a small man in a white suit up to the gallows in the centre of the market. He had heard of this man. A charlatan, a fake claiming medical knowledge and practising when he shouldn't have been. Nothing but a quack. He didn't know much but there were rumours. Botched handiwork. People had died. Hanging was unpleasant but necessary in this case. It was important to root out the imposters. For the common good.

The rope snapped taut, the body jumped and died. There was a smattering of applause.

Something nagged away at his mind. A vision. Putting a gun in his mouth in a house full of monsters. A dream, no more. He looked up at the sky. Was God looking down on him, a face forming in the clouds? A little man with the face of an imp and a hat on his head. He had things to do. His first child was being born.

'Patrick! Patrick!' shouted a voice. He turned and saw Cameron bustling through the crowds towards him. His friend, followed by an old woman in a white dress.

'Thank you for coming, Cameron,' he said, pleased that he had someone with whom he could share the joy of the day.

The other, corpulent, doctor was flushed and sweating. He was grinning. 'How could I miss it, Patrick?' he said. 'Your first child.'

He slapped Cameron on the back. The woman in white had disappeared. He felt a twinge, like the oncoming of a headache, or a storm.

As the giant sun lowered itself behind the castle, they

262

made their way to Princes Street, towards his house in Rose Street. It was an important day in his life. He had to keep reminding himself of that. Not the cellar with its demon, the muddy little village in Devon, the powerful girl that killed people.

They reached his front door. Cameron was still grinning, mopping at his brow with a handkerchief. 'Up you go Patrick,' he insisted. 'Time to see what's really going on. They say that children are mirrors.'

'Mirrors?'

'Of ourselves.'

He was puzzled; what did Cameron mean? 'Who said that?' he asked.

The door opened before Cameron could answer. He walked in and heard the reply only as a mumble from outside.

The stairs were dimly lit and he was surprised that Kathy the maid was nowhere to be seen. It didn't matter. Doctor MacKendrick would be up with his wife in the bedroom. He wondered if the child had been born yet.

The Doctor was waiting for him at the top of the stairs.

'Where's MacKendrick?' he asked the funny little man in the white linen suit and the hat.

'Gone, a long time ago,' came the reply in a gentle Edinburgh lilt.

'Has it happened yet?' A feeling of unease. Where did he recognize the man from?

'I'm afraid so.'

'Is there a problem?' he asked, still worried.

'It's up to you.'

The bedroom door opened and an old woman, again dressed in white, emerged. 'You can go in now,' she said. This time the accent was English.

He was scared. What were they not telling him? 'What's going on here?'

The Doctor looked sad, as if performing an unpleasant duty. 'We are what we do, Doctor Rix. It's time you saw what you have become.'

'I'm sorry,' said the woman in white. 'We did what we could.'

He felt a cold fear grip him. These two, they seemed unreal, like figures from a dream. He felt sick, ill. What were they doing to him? From behind the door he saw a glowing green light.

'Come and look,' said the Doctor.

'No, I don't want to,' he insisted desperately.

'Come and look behind the door.'

'No!'

'Come and look at what's there.'

He was choking, suffocating. The woman in white was growing larger.

'Who are you?' he asked, sobbing now.

They looked at each other and smiled. 'You are a dream,' they answered in perfect unison.

'I refuse. I am my own man!'

The Doctor seemed sad again. 'I know, but sometimes that isn't enough.'

The woman in white lifted her arms, surrounding him in silk. 'Go!' she commanded, terrifying.

With a single glance back, knowing he was lost, thinking about putting the gun in his mouth and pulling the trigger, about his son, about killing people, Doctor Patrick Rix walked through the door and met what was waiting for him in the bedroom.

Gently, layer by layer, Galah and the Doctor erased Rix from the Protyon Core and the TARDIS.

At the end, Galah realized that Rix had become aware of what was happening to him. He was seeing himself. 'My God,' he said plaintively as the last of his essence dwindled to nothing. 'What have I become?'

He was gone.

Ace threw out her last handful of Nitro, blowing yet another line of Hoods to pieces. Despite the rate at which they were destroying them, their numbers never seemed to decrease.

Bernice was firing her blaster almost non-stop into the crowd but no sooner did one fall than it was replaced by three more.

Ace knew that Aickland had been right, they weren't going to make it. Already, he and Charlotte had run out of bombs and were resorting to clubbing down any Hoods that got through to them.

She would never give up. Yelling, she dived at the nearest group, ready to put them down with sheer energy if she had to.

She heard Bernice's blaster pack up as she reached the first Hood. A swift kick put him out of action but another leaped onto her back. She elbowed him off but a third clubbed her in the face. There were just too many of them. She caught a glimpse of Aickland falling to the ground but her own predicament soon took priority. Standing over her was a Hood with a large rock in his hand. Ace struggled on the ground but was held firm by others, making it impossible to move.

All at once, the force holding her disappeared. Rolling to one side, she dodged the rock as it dropped.

She lay still for half a minute, face down, staring at the dusty red soil. Nothing happened. She heard Charlotte say, 'What's going on?'

Ace rolled back over to see hundreds of empty robes and masks lying scattered across the plain.

One by one, Ace, Bernice, Aickland and Charlotte stood up and surveyed the desolate scene. The rivers still burned, the sky still boiled purple and the desert still stretched away ahead of them. However, except for the flames, there was no movement anywhere.

'You know, I think we've made it,' said Bernice. Blood trickled down from a multitude of cuts on her face. Ace coughed out a laugh and sat down, exhausted.

Chapter 9

Still locked in telepathic communication with the other TARDIS, the Doctor sipped from a cup of tea.

He appeared to be in the front parlour of an English country cottage. The style was Victorian as usual and the floor was cluttered with furniture and ornaments. Opposite the Doctor, also drinking tea, was Galah.

At present the Time Lady looked exactly like Charlotte, which clearly confused him somewhat, and he kept getting her name wrong. 'You do realize,' he said, 'that by attacking Doctor Rix you have relinquished control over the Protyon Core for good.'

Galah brushed black hair from her face. She may have looked middle-aged but when she spoke it was with the voice of an old woman. 'It doesn't matter,' she replied sadly. 'The work had failed. You have proven me wrong.'

'What do you mean?'

'Let me tell you first that your friends are safe. Professor Summerfield, Ace and Richard Aickland will soon be returned to the control room. The death of the TARDIS will not harm them.'

The Doctor nodded. 'So you did sustain the Protyons?'

Galah looked up at him. 'I was dying. My regenerative capabilities had malfunctioned. I didn't mind. I had lived a long and tedious life on Gallifrey. Even when my body changed I always looked the same. I used the real Victorian Earth as a power coupling, retaining an interface with the real universe. It helped prevent feedback and overload. It also kept the Imagery Enhancer Systems on their toes. You know, I was very jealous of you, despite our disagreements.'

'What did we argue about?' The Doctor tried to sound tactful but the fact that he had forgotten seemed rude.

Galah just lifted her gaze to the ceiling. 'The only important topic, Doctor. Life and death. Good and evil.'

'In what way?'

'We both believed in good and evil and for a start that set us apart from most of our brothers and sisters. However, I believed in a state of pure and absolute goodness in which no evil could exist.'

Finally the Doctor understood why Galah had gone to these extraordinary lengths to produce a world of her own, of innocence and beauty. He gave the same opinion he had given all those centuries ago: 'And I believe that good is an action, a struggle. A verb and not a noun. I have to confess that we still disagree.'

Galah smiled. 'I know. You have won your argument. I tried to fashion a work of art, an object of beauty I could set up in the heavens as an example to all things. The ultimate state of goodness.'

The Doctor was fascinated. 'A world where evil did not exist, had never existed. A paradise, until I turned up in my TARDIS. I do feel guilty you know, although it was an accident.'

'Don't worry, Doctor,' said Galah, 'it couldn't have worked. Good can't exist outside of Evil. It became a symbol only of folly. Something would have turned up to destroy it. Universal change cannot be stopped, not even by Time Lords.'

The Doctor stood up. He brushed cake from his trousers. 'Well Galah, in my opinion you nearly succeeded. You showed what can be achieved. Even if it is never found, paradise is never lost, not while people can still dream of it. What will you do now?'

Galah looked rueful. She remained very beautiful, fresh and alive. Clearly, she had had quite an experience. 'I will die,' she said. 'When this TARDIS perishes I will perish with it. About time too.'

The Doctor looked around the room. Through the windows he could see the illusion of a summer afternoon, just like the one he had seen when they had first entered Galah's work of art. 'Ashes to ashes . . .' he whispered, then excitedly clicked his fingers. 'Wait!'

Galah looked up, confused. The Doctor continued, 'It doesn't have to end with nothing. Charlotte!'

'Charlotte?' The Doctor was fidgeting, thoughtful. He paced the room. Galah grinned, perhaps catching some of his infectious enthusiasm. 'What do you mean?' she asked.

He grasped her arm. 'You have much of Charlotte in you. She looks like you, she acts like you, she even grew into you. However, she is now a person in her own right, has experienced a great many things.'

'Doctor,' warned Galah, 'she is still only a construct, built from the organic protein of the TARDIS. She could not exist in the real universe, she would be unable to assimilate the data and input she would receive.'

'I know all of that,' he replied, 'unless you used the last of your energy to alter her physiology. You could join with her and exist in a symbiotic relationship.'

Galah rubbed her chin. 'It wouldn't work. You can't turn a construct into a fully functioning Gallifreyan.'

'No, no. Just an ordinary human being.'

The Doctor could see that Galah was interested. She stared out, perhaps imagining the idea. 'To re-create a human being, physically and mentally, with memory and personality. It would require an incredible amount of energy.'

'You have a whole TARDIS, Galah. You're a sculptor. How about one final piece of work? A masterpiece!'

'I would cease to exist.'

The Doctor went down onto his knees and stared straight into her eyes. 'You would become her. At least something of you would live on.'

268

Galah seemed to ponder for a moment, perhaps at the scale and ambition of the proposal. The Doctor was so excited he kept his hand firmly pressed to his head, as if holding his fiery brain in.

At last, she answered. She stood up. To the Doctor she looked like a ghost or a statue, clad as she was in white robes. 'Very well, Doctor,' she said proudly. 'I will do it.'

Aickland couldn't say he was getting used to the unexpected and the shocking but he was beginning to resign himself to it.

Again, the world had changed around him and he found himself standing in a large white room covered in circles. There was a glowing mushroom-shaped table in the middle, with the Doctor and an old woman lying next to it.

He realized that Ace, Bernice and Charlotte were still standing by him. 'You look terrible, as usual,' he said to Ace who was covered in grime, blood and perspiration.

'You don't look so hot yourself, as usual,' she replied with a smile.

Bernice slapped Ace on the back. 'Well old girl, once again we save the artificial universe as we know it.' She wiped the blood from her own face.

Aickland was not so sure about her statement. 'I don't recall that we did anything at all. Those creatures just seemed to collapse.' He glanced at Charlotte, eager to confirm that she was all right. He was having thoughts about this beautiful raven-haired woman, thoughts that pulled at his whole body.

She was paler than normal and seemed to be having trouble standing up. Aickland wondered whether one of the hooded creatures had done something to her.

'You okay?' asked Bernice. 'Don't tell me it's not over yet.'

'I feel faint,' she replied, and fell to the floor.

Aickland rushed over to her side. She looked pale and insubstantial. She was fading away. 'What's happening to me?' she asked weakly, beginning to glow. Aickland fought back tears; it was like Arthur all over again, only much quicker. Too many people had died: this one had to live. He felt like praying.

'Look at the old woman,' said Bernice suddenly. Aickland glanced round briefly. The figure next to the Doctor was glowing too.

Ace ran to them. 'She's fading away, like Arthur,' she cried. 'We've got to do something.'

'Richard, don't leave me,' moaned Charlotte.

'I won't,' he replied, 'not ever.' She closed her eyes and stopped breathing.

'Look,' shouted Ace. She grabbed Aickland as he sobbed and twisted him round. He saw the old woman vanish, the metal crown clatter noisily to the floor.

'What the hell is this?' said Bernice.

Suddenly Charlotte released a great breath of air. She sat bolt upright as if charged with electricity. She almost head-butted Aickland with the movement. He jumped back in surprise. An enormous smile appeared on her face. 'Charlotte?' asked Aickland warily, unwilling to believe this miracle.

'Don't worry, Richard,' she said. 'I'm feeling fine.' He was not reassured by her weak smile.

There came a loud coughing from the centre of the room. The Doctor was rolling around on the floor, still connected to the table. Ace scrambled across to him and ripped the wires from his body. The Doctor moaned and fell back, his head hitting the floor.

Guiltily, Ace looked at Bernice, who shrugged. Abruptly the Doctor sat up. 'Someone's been telling lies about me!' he bellowed and opened his eyes. 'Ah! Ace. Benny. And Richard and Charlotte. How nice to see you all again.'

Ace was in high spirits. At last things had got back to normal. She looked out at the Houses of Parliament across the river as she avoided the thieves and beggars who infested the South Bank. She breathed in some very dodgy air and stepped over the filth in the street. She didn't like the stupid clothes that the Doctor had made her wear but at least he'd allowed her to wear trousers instead of the usual crinoline and lace stuff. She'd had enough of Victorians to last a lifetime.

'This is getting to be a habit, Doctor,' said Bernice sternly. Ace turned to see her friend strolling arm in arm with the Time Lord. 'Last time I was here for two months, in uncannily similar circumstances.'

The Doctor twirled his brolley. 'That was Edwardian, Benny,' he replied. 'A completely different class of period altogether.'

Ace smiled and looked out over the river again. She was thinking about Arthur.

'Ace!' came a shout from behind them. Ace recognized the voice as Aickland's and turned to greet him. He was walking with Charlotte and they were now both dressed in clean, new clothes. Ace hardly recognized them.

'Mr Aickland, Miss Charlotte,' remarked the Doctor. 'How are the wedding preparations?'

'Wonderful,' replied a gushing Charlotte. 'Although I could do his bloody aunts a mischief. Also, the air is more than a little unsavoury in London.'

'You wait another hundred years,' quipped Ace, 'you'll know what bad smells are then.'

Aickland seemed to be blushing. Ace noticed he was clasping Charlotte's hand very tightly. 'You all right?' she asked.

'Yes,' he nodded nervously. 'It's just that I'm shocked that I decided to ask Charlotte to marry me so quickly. I hardly know her.'

'Well, as you said Richard,' Charlotte replied, 'I have no "surname". I think it only right that you should give me one as soon as possible. Apparently, that is a cause of some concern here.'

Bernice grinned. 'Don't worry, I'm sure you'll pick up the strange rituals of this primitive planet in no time. No offence Richard.'

271

Charlotte turned to the Doctor. 'One thing still puzzles me,' she said.

'Hmm?' he replied guardedly, gazing into the distance. Ace knew how much he hated having to explain things.

'Just what is a "Protyon Unit"?'

The Doctor looked forlornly at Ace. 'Do I have to?'

In unison, she and Bernice replied, 'Yes!'

He sighed. 'All right. They are the organic components of a TARDIS. Thousands of years ago my race realized that in order to master dimensional stability in space and time they would need more than electronics and machinery. So they went back to basics. How does a computer, how does anything work, right down at the bottom level? Well, essentially it all comes down to binary patterns, bits. On or off, one or nought, or in the case of an eye, open and shut.' He winked, making them all jump.

'The key came when we – I mean they – decided that rather than use magnetic pulses, as in your machines, they would have bits that were organic. Single cells of protein that would either flex one way or the other.'

'So what?' asked Ace. 'What difference does that make? You have to feed them or something?'

The Doctor began to stroll along the river bank. 'That's the really clever bit. The difference is that the Protyon bit has powers of deliberation, obviously very limited ones, based on the information that it receives. It chooses which way it wants to flex, therefore removing lots of the difficult time-consuming jobs normally done somewhere else. And when you have huge quantities of them all stuck together you have a thinking, intelligent machine capable of making independent, complex decisions. No need for endless probability programming. Quick too.'

'I'm lost,' wailed Charlotte.

'And me,' said Ace. 'I think you're making this all up.'

Aickland removed his hat and began to scratch his head. 'I think I need to find a new hobby. This is far too much like hard work. I need something easy like . . . like studying inland waterways.'

Bernice tapped him on the shoulder. 'May I borrow him for a second, Charlotte?'

Charlotte turned to her and raised a puzzled eyebrow. 'Of course. Why?'

'I have a suggestion of my own. Won't be a sec.'

Ace stopped listening and watched the river as it travelled forward on its sluggish journey. She thought about many things as the teeming, complex real life of London passed her by.

Richard Aickland woke up screaming. Icy sweat drenched his nightgown as he threw himself up out of bed. He stared uncomprehendingly at the thick, patterned curtains. He scampered up and down on the cold floor, not knowing where he was. Gradually, reality soaked into his mind. It was dark, he was at home, this was his life. He realized he was shouting and stopped.

He stood, cold, in silence.

'Richard?' asked Charlotte, back in the bed.

How long was this going to last, he wondered to himself. Suffocation, heat, tied up and helpless, something rushing out of the blackness at him. He managed to get his breathing under control. 'I'm sorry darling,' he stammered.

'These dreams again?' she said, with the sympathy of someone trying to understand.

He turned round and saw her, silhouetted but still beautiful. Somewhere there was a faint light. He fell back onto the bed. He needed her so much, it sometimes frightened him. He felt her warm arms cradle his head. She was so good. So strong. She never dreamed.

'It's all alright,' she cooed. 'It's all right.' Her hair draped over him, comforting, like a shawl.

Aickland fought off the tears. 'How long? How much more?' He felt so weak.

'It's a dream, Richard,' she said calmly. 'A dream but I'm here. I'm with you, for the nights. You're with me for the days.'

At last, Aickland relaxed. He thought of Charlotte, lost

273

in the streets of London, surrounded by people, by sights and smells. She too took fright, often shutting herself in their new house. They were moving soon to the country.

He felt better, not because he gloated over Charlotte's timidity with the world but because they made a unique partnership, unlike anyone else's ever.

But he had to do something about the dreams. You couldn't move away from them. He lay back and felt Charlotte brush the moisture from his brow.

Aickland and the new Mrs Aickland did move, to Hampshire, where Charlotte felt easier and more able to cope. Aickland understandably disliked villages but they soon settled down and grew comfortable with each other and their surroundings.

The dreams did not cease.

Aickland found himself in his study one summer afternoon. He looked out at the lawn. Charlotte was off somewhere in the woods, 'exploring' as she called it. He picked up a pen and began to write. He was surprised to find that story-telling came easily to him. He wrote a lot more.

Eventually, after some years, he reached a standard that he was content with. He began to write long stories. The stories helped him. They made the dreams stop.

Sometimes.

'I'm glad he's going to start writing. You should trust me occasionally, Doctor,' said Bernice loftily. She was feeling very pleased with herself.

She noticed that the Time Lord was playing hard of hearing again as he fiddled with the controls of his TARDIS. He had removed it from the artificial universe some time before the gradual destruction of that tragic place. Bernice was glad they were on their way. This adventure had thrown up a lot of uncomfortable questions.

They had left Aickland and Charlotte in 1873, and Bernice was relieved that some good had come out of all the violence. Despite the outward appearance of an age gap between them, she could sense that they were very alike. They certainly seemed very happy with each other.

'I don't believe a TARDIS can build a real person,' said Ace belligerently from the other side of the control room. 'Not even with a Time Lord's mind running it. You did make it up, didn't you Doctor, about the Protyons. It's silly.'

The Doctor was obviously not going to be drawn. 'Possibly,' he murmured.

'What worries me,' said Bernice, 'are the philosophical implications of all this.' At last she had gained the Doctor's interest. He looked up, eyes shadowed beneath his fedora. 'Really?'

Bernice hoped she would receive an honest answer for once. 'Don't you think we should learn a bit of humility? Here we go, interfering when and wherever we like, arrogantly presuming we're always in the right.'

Ace looked confused. She was sat in a chair, cleaning her combat boots. Bernice wondered whether she was even interested. She liked Ace but she wasn't one for complicated answers, not since she had rejoined the TARDIS crew.

The Doctor gave his answer. 'Benny, I admit we caused one or two of the problems in the artificial universe.'

'You can say that again,' exclaimed Ace. Perhaps she was really interested after all.

The Doctor continued. 'It was one isolated incident. The odds against something similar occurring are astronomical. We did what we always do: see wrong and fight against it. I have always done so and will continue to do so.'

Bernice leaned her head on the console, realizing he was not going to admit he was wrong. 'That's no answer,' she said. 'Who are we to say what is good and what is bad and that we'll always be right? That in the long run we're not just making things worse?'

Bernice was surprised to see the Doctor look almost angry. He stood up and hurriedly adjusted his paisley tie.

Ace stopped cleaning her boots and stared up at him, perhaps wondering if the bad old days of arguments were going to happen again. Bernice felt guilty but she had to know what he thought. 'Well?' she insisted.

The anger dissipated. The Doctor pulled three juggling balls from his pockets and threw them into the air, performing a multitude of tricks. He winked at Bernice. 'I know,' he said. 'Believe me Benny, I always know.'

Already published:

TIMEWYRM: GENESYS
John Peel

The Doctor and Ace are drawn to Ancient Mesopotamia in search of an evil sentience that has tumbled from the stars – the dreaded Timewyrm of ancient Gallifreyan legend.

ISBN 0 426 20355 0

TIMEWYRM: EXODUS
Terrance Dicks

Pursuit of the Timewyrm brings the Doctor and Ace to the Festival of Britain. But the London they find is strangely subdued, and patrolling the streets are the uniformed thugs of the Britischer Freikorps.

ISBN 0 426 20357 7

TIMEWYRM: APOCALYPSE
Nigel Robinson

Kirith seems an ideal planet – a world of peace and plenty, ruled by the kindly hand of the Great Matriarch. But it's here that the end of the universe – of everything – will be precipitated. Only the Doctor can stop the tragedy.

ISBN 0 426 20359 3

TIMEWYRM: REVELATION
Paul Cornell

Ace has died of oxygen starvation on the moon, having thought the place to be Norfolk. 'I do believe that's unique,' says the afterlife's receptionist.

ISBN 0 426 20360 7

CAT'S CRADLE: TIME'S CRUCIBLE
Marc Platt

The TARDIS is invaded by an alien presence and is then destroyed. The Doctor disappears. Ace, lost and alone, finds herself in a bizarre city where nothing is to be trusted – even time itself.

ISBN 0 426 20365 8

CAT'S CRADLE: WARHEAD
Andrew Cartmel

The place is Earth. The time is the near future – all too near. As environmental destruction reaches the point of no return, multinational corporations scheme to buy immortality in a poisoned world. If Earth is to survive, somebody has to stop them.

ISBN 0 426 20367 4

CAT'S CRADLE: WITCH MARK
Andrew Hunt

A small village in Wales is visited by creatures of myth. Nearby, a coach crashes on the M40, killing all its passengers. Police can find no record of their existence. The Doctor and Ace arrive, searching for a cure for the TARDIS, and uncover a gateway to another world.

ISBN 0 426 20368 2

NIGHTSHADE
Mark Gatiss

When the Doctor brings Ace to the village of Crook Marsham in 1968, he seems unwilling to recognize that something sinister is going on. But the villagers are being killed, one by one, and everyone's past is coming back to haunt them – including the Doctor's.

ISBN 0 426 20376 3

LOVE AND WAR
Paul Cornell

Heaven: a planet rich in history where the Doctor comes to meet a new friend, and betray an old one; a place where people come to die, but where the dead don't always rest in peace. On Heaven, the Doctor finally loses Ace, but finds archaeologist Bernice Summerfield, a new companion whose destiny is inextricably linked with his.

ISBN 0 426 20385 2

TRANSIT
Ben Aaronovitch

It's the ultimate mass transit system, binding the planets of the solar system together. But something is living in the network, chewing its way to the very heart of the system and leaving a trail of death and mutation behind. Once again, the Doctor is all that stands between humanity and its own mistakes.

ISBN 0 426 20384 4

THE HIGHEST SCIENCE
Gareth Roberts

The Highest Science – a technology so dangerous it destroyed its creators. Many people have searched for it, but now Sheldukher, the most wanted criminal in the galaxy, believes he has found it. The Doctor and Bernice must battle to stop him on a planet where chance and coincidence have become far too powerful.

ISBN 0 426 20377 1

THE PIT
Neil Penswick

One of the Seven Planets is a nameless giant, quarantined against all intruders. But when the TARDIS materializes, it becomes clear that the planet is far from empty – and the Doctor begins to realize that the planet hides a terrible secret from the Time Lords' past.

ISBN 0 426 20378 X

DECEIT
Peter Darvill-Evans

Ace – three years older, wiser and tougher – is back. She is part of a group of Irregular Auxiliaries on an expedition to the planet Aracadia. They think they are hunting Daleks, but the Doctor knows better. He knows that the paradise planet hides a being far more powerful than the Daleks – and much more dangerous.

ISBN 0 426 20362 3

LUCIFER RISING
Jim Mortimore & Andy Lane

Reunited, the Doctor, Ace and Bernice travel to Lucifer, the site of a scientific expedition that they know will shortly cease to exist. Discovering why involves them in sabotage, murder and the resurrection of eons-old alien powers. Are there Angels on Lucifer? And what does it all have to do with Ace?

ISBN 0 426 20338 7

WHITE DARKNESS
David McIntee

The TARDIS crew, hoping for a rest, come to Haiti in 1915. But they find that the island is far from peaceful: revolution is brewing in the city; the dead are walking from the cemeteries; and, far underground, the ancient rulers of the galaxy are stirring in their sleep.

ISBN 0 426 20395 X

SHADOWMIND
Christopher Bulis

On the colony world of Arden, something dangerous is growing stronger. Something that steals minds and memories. Something that can reach out to another planet, Tairgire, where the newest exhibit in the sculpture park is a blue box surmounted by a flashing light.

ISBN 0 426 20394 1

ICEBERG
David Banks

In 2006, an ecological disaster threatens the Earth; only the FLIPback team, working in an Antarctic base, can avert the catastrophe. But hidden beneath the ice, sinister forces have gathered to sabotage humanity's last hope. The Cybermen have returned and the Doctor must face them alone.

ISBN 0 426 20392 5

BLOOD HEAT
Jim Mortimore

The TARDIS is attacked by an alien force; Bernice is flung into the Vortex; and the Doctor and Ace crash-land on Earth. There they find dinosaurs roaming the derelict London streets, and Brigadier Lethbridge-Stewart leading the remnants of UNIT in a desperate fight against the Silurians who have taken over and changed his world.

ISBN 0 426 20399 2

THE DIMENSION RIDERS
Daniel Blythe

A holiday in Oxford is cut short when the Doctor is summoned to Space Station Q4, where ghostly soldiers from the future watch from the shadows among the dead. Soon, the Doctor is trapped in the past, Ace is accused of treason and Bernice is uncovering deceit among the college cloisters.

ISBN 0 426 20397 6

THE LEFT-HANDED HUMMINGBIRD
Kate Orman

Someone has been playing with time. The Doctor Ace and Bernice must travel to the Aztec Empire in 1487, to London in the Swinging Sixties and to the sinking of the *Titanic* as they attempt to rectify the temporal faults – and survive the attacks of the living god Huitzilin.

ISBN 0 426 20404 2

CONUNDRUM
Steve Lyons

A killer is stalking the streets of the village of Arandale. The victims are found each day, drained of blood. Someone has interfered with the Doctor's past again, and he's landed in a place he knows he once destroyed, from which it seems there can be no escape.

ISBN 0 426 20408 5

NO FUTURE
Paul Cornell

At last the Doctor comes face-to-face with the enemy who has been threatening him, leading him on a chase that has brought the TARDIS to London in 1976. There he finds that reality has been subtly changed and the country he once knew is rapidly descending into anarchy as an alien invasion force prepares to land . . .

ISBN 0 426 20409 3

TRAGEDY DAY
Gareth Roberts

When the TARDIS crew arrive on Olleril, they soon realise that all is not well. Assassins arrive to carry out a killing that may endanger the entire universe. A being known as the Supreme One tests horrific weapons. And a secret order of monks observes the growing chaos.

ISBN 0 426 20410 7

LEGACY
Gary Russell

The Doctor returns to Peladon, on the trail of a master criminal. Ace pursues intergalactic mercenaries who have stolen the galaxy's most evil artifact while Bernice strikes up a dangerous friendship with a Martian Ice Lord. The players are making the final moves in a devious and lethal plan – but for once it isn't the Doctor's.

ISBN 0 426 20412 3

THEATRE OF WAR
Justin Richards

Menaxus is a barren world on the front line of an interstellar war, home to a ruined theatre which hides sinister secrets. When the TARDIS crew land on the planet, they find themselves trapped in a deadly reenactment of an ancient theatrical tragedy.
ISBN 0 426 20414 X

ALL-CONSUMING FIRE
Andy Lane

The secret library of St John the Beheaded has been robbed. The thief has taken forbidden books which tell of gateways to other worlds. Only one team can be trusted to solve the crime: Sherlock Holmes, Doctor Watson – and a mysterious stranger who claims he travels in time and space.
ISBN 0 426 20415 8

Also available in July 1994 is *Goth Opera* by Paul Cornell, the first in a new series of Missing Adventures.